THE HEIGHT OF
THE STORM

Requests for permission to make copies of any part of the work should be
submitted online at info@mascotbooks.com or mailed to Mascot Books,
620 Herndon Parkway #320, Herndon, VA 20170.

ISBN-13: 978-1-68401-782-9
CPSIA Code: PRBANG0719A
Library of Congress Control Number: 2019902619

Printed in the United States

www.TripleCrownDreams.com
www.mascotbooks.com

BOOK THREE
TRIPLE CROWN TRILOGY

THE HEIGHT OF THE STORM

KIMBERLY CAMPBELL

*In recognition of the heart and courage of my
first racehorse, Height of the Storm.*

 # Acknowledgments

The Height of the Storm is the final installment of the Triple Crown Trilogy, and what an exciting ride it has been. Since I started this adventure six years ago, I have learned so much about the Thoroughbred racing industry and much more than I could have imagined about the details surrounding each of the Triple Crown races.

Along the way, I started a Facebook page, TripleCrownDreams, and I am thankful for my followers who have been on this journey with me. I have also ventured into racehorse ownership, my own dream coming true. I've experienced the ups and downs as I followed the progress of Height of the Storm, my grey filly, who has overcome long odds to make it to the race track. We have certainly had our share of stormy weather, and we hope to see some sunny days at the races.

I have so much to be thankful for. I wouldn't be here without the support of my husband, Kelly, as well as my three kids, Connor, Carter, and Codie. A special shout-out to Codie for pushing me to continue to write when I couldn't find the motivation and for being my right-hand girl in reading drafts and providing corrections.

With this book, I was introduced to a new editor with Mascot Books, Lauren Kanne. She was new to my trilogy, but took the project on full force, indoctrinating herself into the racing world and spending countless hours fulfilling my expectations of where I wanted this story to go.

I appreciate Naren Aryal and Susan Roberts of Mascot Books, who have patiently waited for the writing to be done and worked with finding just the right cover.

And finally, thank you to my readers, who have encouraged me through comments on Facebook and reviews on Amazon. I hope I meet your expectations in these final chapters as we follow the adventures of Charlie and Doug, Lilly and Buck, and the rest of the Storm team. My goal has been to educate and bring enlightenment to an industry that includes dreamers and romantics, critics and cynics, the ultra-wealthy and those struggling to make ends meet.

If I have encouraged you to think for a moment about these beautiful horses, the athletes that sit on their backs, and the hard-working people that love and care for them, then I have done my job.

Thank you for joining me on this wonderful ride.

Some are born great,
some achieve greatness, and
some have greatness thrust upon them.
                        – William Shakespeare

Prologue

Just twenty miles outside the bright lights of New York City sits the Big Sandy—Belmont Park. Dating back to the early 1900s, the largest race track in North America is a monument to the love of horse racing.

The population of Elmont, New York, swells from approximately 33,000 to over 90,000 during the first part of June in anticipation of the Belmont Stakes. The race is held on the third Saturday following the Preakness Stakes, which could be the first or second weekend in June, depending on the calendar.

The Belmont Stakes. The third leg of horse racing's Triple Crown. The Test of the Champion.

The Belmont Stakes was well-established long before the concept of the Triple Crown was introduced by sportswriter Charles Hatton of *The New York Times* in 1930. It is the oldest of the three races, as its inaugural run was in 1867, predating the Preakness by six years and the Kentucky Derby by eight years. The first track to host the Belmont was Jerome Park Racetrack in the Bronx. After twenty-three years, the race was moved to Morris Park Racecourse, and in 1905, it was moved to the newly-opened Belmont Park.

Over its 146 runnings (the race was not run in 1911 and 1912 due to anti-gambling legislation), the winners of the Belmont have included two geldings and three fillies, as well as the only female jockey to win any of the Triple Crown races, Julie Krone on Colonial Affair in 1993.

Depending on the outcome of the Kentucky Derby and the Preakness, the first two races of the Triple Crown, the racing community either awaits Belmont in anticipation of crowning a Triple Crown winner, or it becomes just another race on a trainer's schedule.

If the same horse wins the Derby and the Preakness, then New York and all its glam and glitter await. The pressure builds with each day as the horse and the team around him are as carefully scrutinized as the challengers that will be coming to block him from claiming his throne. Twenty-three times in the history of the race, the anticipation of a Triple Crown winner has been wiped out, some by truly heartbreaking losses. The spoiler on that day does not necessarily win under a blanket of applause, as the crowd can be quite disappointed in the results.

But is the Belmont Stakes ever really just "another race"? Not by a long shot.

The race is the longest a horse will run in its entire life. It is one and a half miles, the entire circumference of Belmont Park, which means the starting gate sits at exactly the same point as the finish line.

The Belmont's stature as the Test of the Champion can be attributed to its place in the journey to win the Triple Crown, its never-raced-at mile and a half, or its ability to handle the high energy that surrounds anything that happens in the Big Apple of New York City. The Belmont is racing's Broadway, and it tests the best for their ability to stand in her spotlight.

PART ONE

Into the Fire

Doug's mind was on overdrive and his legs churned beneath him as he raced down the hill, his eyes taking in the reds and yellows of the fire that was beginning to engulf one end of his main barn.

He had already called 911 while he was throwing on his boots and racing out the door; now his fingers worked his cell phone without thinking. The texts were flying into the midnight sky, which was lit by the fire beginning to rage below him. To Charlie, Lilly, Molly, Steve, Ben, Cappie, and Buck (to ensure Lilly got the message), he sent a simple command: "FIRE, COME QUICK." That was all he had time for as he jammed the phone in his back pocket. He could feel the reply texts coming in quickly, but he had no answer for them.

He heard the sirens in the distance. Help was coming. But right now, he was the one who was here.

How many are in the barn? It was early June, a cool evening, so many of the horses were on night turnout, thank God. But he was fully aware of one horse who was certainly in that barn—Genuine Storm, the Kentucky Derby and Preakness winner.

Doug watched the flames crawl up the near side of the massive main barn. *Think*, he ordered his brain. *How many stalls are occupied?* The barn had twenty stalls in it, ten down each side. Most were empty, but how many weren't?

He raced towards the far-right end of the barn, knowing that was where Storm was kept. Thankfully, the fire had not passed the center line yet—there was an office, feed room, and restroom in the area currently engulfed by flames—but who knew how fast it would move?

Doug went through a mental checklist. Besides Storm, he knew that Twilight, Oscar, and Rocky were all in the barn. Twilight had been scheduled to ship to Laurel in the morning, and Oscar and Rocky were recovering from injuries and wouldn't have been turned out without supervision. *Who else? Did any of the grooms decide to keep someone inside that I'm not aware of? Had Ben made any last-minute decisions?*

Charlie hadn't been able to sleep. Her worry over her rejection of Doug's marriage proposal weighed heavily on her heart. It was a lot to add to the everyday anxiety over her kids, Ryan and Skylar, and how the last few months had impacted them. She wondered if she had made the right decision, claiming Storm that fateful day in September nearly one year ago.

Everything had changed so much since then. They'd had great times, but they'd also had sad times. She'd often wondered if she had taken the best path, but she also knew they were all stronger for it, and that they had made great friends over the last nine months. Now, they were two weeks away from racing Storm in the Belmont, and they even had the potential of capturing the Triple Crown—a feat that had last been accomplished thirty-seven years ago.

Since she hadn't been able to sleep, Charlie had sought solace in her four-stall barn. It was as empty tonight as it had been on the night that Peter had finally finished building it for her. Storm was at Doug's Shamrock Hill Farm, and Hershey was right there with him, keeping him calm, keeping him company. Sarge, well, he was gone.

She sighed as she closed her eyes and lay back against the cool stall floor.

Her weary body relaxed as she started to meditate—a skill she had incorporated into her daily regimen as life changes had made it increasingly obvious that it was necessary.

The anxiety and panic attacks that had overcome her in the weeks and months after Peter had passed away from cancer had returned after Sarge died. Charlie was working hard just trying to fend it all off. She forced herself to be strong and confident around everyone else, but when it was just her, she could feel the depression pressing in. The edges of her vision would begin to blur and her breath would quicken; she would feel her heartbeat tremor like a butterfly in her chest that wanted to be let out.

Deep breath in through the nose…hold for a few seconds…and long slow breath out the mouth. She focused on the feeling of her body against the floor, sinking deeply into the cool mats, clean of all shavings since no one was home. She continued for several minutes, emptying her mind of all thought and focusing on her breathing.

Charlie's phone vibrated in her pocket.

She lay still for a few moments, trying to ignore it, not wanting to let go of the peace that she had achieved. *Deep breath in, slow breath out.*

The phone vibrated again. Charlie opened her eyes and stared at the roof of the barn where the rafters intersected, going through the checklist in her head. Ryan was home; he had come in and said goodnight when he'd gotten back from the movies with friends. Charlie had tucked Skylar into bed several hours ago after they had read a few chapters of *The Black Stallion's Courage* together. It was Charlie's favorite book in the Walter Farley series about Alec and the Black Stallion, a horse he had saved from certain death on an island, who mesmerized the racing world with their wins in a wide variety of circumstances. Charlie had always loved the way Farley had written about the relationships between horses and people, and she was amazed by all the different books and storylines he had written. Skylar was still wrestling with the loss of Sarge, and Charlie had wanted to distract her with an uplifting story.

Honestly, I'd needed the distraction as well…

Charlie's phone vibrated again. She finally pulled it from her pocket; it lit up with the movement, alerting her again that she had an unchecked message. Holding it a few inches from her face in the dark barn, she stared at the text—then blinked her eyes and read it again. The blood ran cold in her veins as she jumped up and bolted from the stall.

Charlie raced from the barn, yelling to Ryan and Skylar to get up, tears already streaming down her face.

A fire at Shamrock! How is that possible? Everything is kept so clean and organized...no one would dare smoke or barbeque near the barn, they don't have the spiderwebs or extension cords characteristic of so many working stables, they have sprinklers...what happened!?!

Having no control over the situation was overwhelming, and the panic started to overtake her, as it had in the past. Charlie took a deep breath as she slammed the door to the house.

Letting my anxiety take over isn't going to help anyone.

"Ryan, Skylar. Get up! There is a fire at Shamrock—we have to go!"

She grabbed at her Dubarry boots, stuffing her feet into them.

Ryan came racing down the stairs, his hair tousled from being awakened suddenly from a deep sleep. Skylar was on his heels, blinking her eyes to adjust to the bright lights of the living room.

"FIRE?!? But what about Storm?...And HERSHEY!" Skylar's eyes started filling with tears.

Charlie grabbed both of Skylar's shoulders and leaned down to her level. "Tears will not help us now, young lady. Get your boots on and grab your jacket."

Skylar took in a wobbly breath and did what she was told.

Ryan picked up the keys to the SUV at the same time Charlie went to grab them off the hook.

"I got this, Mom. You are in no condition to drive. Your hands are shaking like leaves."

Charlie paused. *When did my little boy get so responsible?* she asked herself.

"You're right," she replied, letting her empty hand fall back to her side.

Before she could say anything else, Ryan was out the door and starting the truck. Skylar and Charlie followed him out, yanking the door to the house closed behind them.

———————————

Lilly sighed heavily as she traced a finger along Buck's bare back.

"Bored of me already?" he asked.

"Ha, not likely; just trying to see if anything has changed in the years we've been apart," she replied, with a smile playing on her lips.

Buck turned and pulled Lilly close. With a serious look upon his face, he said, "This time, well—until death do us part."

Lilly's eyes widened. "Buck, what are you saying?"

"To honor and cherish," he continued.

"In sickness and in health," Lilly whispered.

Both of their cell phones buzzed at the same time, but neither of them moved. They would not allow anything to ruin this moment.

Lilly shook with an involuntary shudder of happiness and tucked herself closer to him.

Buck smiled, his chin resting on Lilly's head, and listened as her breathing got slow and deep, heavy with sleep. He closed his eyes, thankful that they had overcome the past, thinking about their future. The last few weeks had been a blur, but reconnecting with Lilly had made all the past pain worth it. She'd had her reasons for hiding, but now everything was out in the open and they were going to take on the future together.

Both of their phones buzzed again with the text reminder.

"Don't get it," Lilly mumbled sleepily. "It is probably just another reporter."

As competing jockeys in the season's most popular horse races, Lilly and Buck had both been inundated with requests for interviews and TV appearances. Everyone was trying to get any morsel of information about what had transpired in the Derby and Preakness, and what tactics they might use or plans they had for the upcoming Belmont. It was exhausting, and Lilly needed a break.

"It may be a ride for me for tomorrow. I am waiting for Paul to get back to me on a Baffert horse," Buck replied as he reached towards his phone.

Their friend Paul was an agent, and he was keeping his feelers out for Buck, even though Buck hadn't changed agents. *I might have to start considering it*, Buck thought. It would keep him closer to Lilly if Paul was working the same track for both of them. He would need to make sure it was okay with both Lilly and Paul, but he was confident it was the best thing for them to continue to recapture lost time.

It hadn't crossed his mind that Lilly's phone had been buzzing in unison with his own. Picking it up, the words leapt off the screen and illuminated the dark room: "FIRE, COME QUICK."

Molly and Steve were sitting on the couch, each sipping a glass of wine. It was late, but they had just finished watching a couple episodes of *Game of Thrones* and their nerves were on edge. It happened every time they had a chance to catch up—between the fighting, intrigue, and complicated medieval details, they always found it hard to go to sleep afterwards. They'd enjoyed dissecting the episodes of the whos, whats, and whys, but now their conversation had shifted to their own family challenges.

"Oh, Steve, I just can't come up with the best way to tell Jenny," Molly said. "What if she hates us?"

Steve pulled Molly closer to him on the couch. "She will not hate us. When she finds out that Lilly is her biological mom, she will be angry and confused, yes, and possibly turn away from us, but she is a smart girl, and she will come around. We need to continue to communicate, no matter what happens. She has a strong support group around her who will help her through it. We just need to figure out the best time and way to tell her."

"I keep wondering if we should just tell her now. I know there's a lot going on, but with all of the attention on Shamrock and the Triple Crown, my biggest fear is that some reporter looking for a scoop will uncover this and publish it." Molly swallowed another long gulp of her wine. "I'm not just thinking about Jenny. Lilly has been through so much, and I want to make sure she comes through this as well."

"You can't solve everything, Molly. I know you like to try. Don't get me wrong, I think you are incredible. I've never met someone more capable of moving mountains, especially when you're helping and protecting the people you love. We have no control over so many of the details right now, and I don't think it's ideal to add more complications by springing this on everyone at such a busy time. We don't know how Jenny will react, and we're going to have to roll with the punches—so let's do it at a time when we have the capacity to do so."

"There just doesn't seem to be a perfect way to tell her. Trust me, I've looked. I've been googling so much, my fingers hurt," Molly laughed. "You wouldn't believe the stories I have found."

"I think you need to stop the googling and go with your gut. Text Lilly right now and find some time to talk it through. You can come up with a plan that works well for everybody, and we will go from there," Steve said.

"You're right, of course. And you know how much it pains me to admit that to you," Molly smiled as she got up to retrieve her phone from the kitchen counter.

Steve sat there, wishing he did have all the right answers; he knew they were in uncharted territory. He had just picked up his glass and brought it to his lips to take a sip when he heard Molly screaming from the other room.

"THERE'S A FIRE AT THE MAIN BARN!"

His wine glass tumbled to the hardwood floor, shattering into pieces.

———————————

Ben raised his beer to his lips and took a long drink, pondering his next move. Cappie sat across the table with a smirk playing at the corners of his mouth; he had just bested Ben with the "check" he'd voiced when he moved his queen in position to take Ben's king.

Ben stared at all his remaining chess pieces on the board—knight, rook, and three pawns. He and Cappie had been dancing around the board for over an hour, each trying to take down the other, but he couldn't find a way out of this one.

"Do you think he will do it?" Cappie's voice broke into his thoughts.

"Do what?" Ben said, fully absorbed in trying to figure out what move to make.

"Storm. Do you think he can win the big one?"

Ben looked up at Cappie, his hand dropping from his beer as he set it on the table and leaned back in his chair. "Of course he will win," he said with conviction.

Cappie raised his gray eyebrows at his confident protégée. "It will be his third race in just five weeks. That's a lot to ask for a Thoroughbred, especially in this day and age, when they are usually only asked to run once every five or six weeks, at most."

"The Belmont is the test of champions, and Storm is a champion," Ben replied defiantly.

"I don't disagree, but I am just saying, twenty-three horses before him have won the Derby and Preakness, only to face failure in the Belmont. No horse has won them all since Affirmed in 1978, and here we are, thirty-seven years later. The stars all need to align, and you have to admit, our star pattern since we started this journey has been shaped more like the Big Dipper," Cappie finished.

"All the more reason for Storm to be victorious. He's a horse who never fails to do the impossible, or, at least, the highly incredible. No one would have predicted a simple claimer from West Virginia—owned by a widow, ridden by a long-lost jockey, and trained under unconventional means— would be at the pinnacle of the sport," Ben declared triumphantly as his cell phone buzzed in his pocket.

Cappie smiled at Ben and reached for his own buzzing phone at the same time. Glancing at the screen, the smile quickly turned to a grimace.

"Oh shit!"

Cappie looked up again just in time to catch sight of Ben's back as he raced out the door.

The Escape

Storm's frantic whinny rose into the clear night.

The muggy early summer air grew even warmer as Doug got closer to the barn. It had only been a few minutes since he had come flying out of the house, but it felt like it took an eternity to reach the barn.

Doug raced toward the far barn doors. They had been left open to allow the cool air to flow through the center aisle and comfort the horses through the night, but now that air was fanning the flames up higher. He had to get the horses out, *now*.

The sound of the sirens grew ever closer, but he knew they wouldn't arrive in time. He could only hope that Ben and Cappie hadn't gone to bed early, and that Molly and Steve had been up late to see his text.

Quickly covering the last few yards to the barn door, Doug took a deep breath before he ran into the barn and down the aisle towards Storm's stall.

Steve grabbed the keys from the counter while Molly stood frozen, looking at her text and thinking aloud.

"Fire? What does he mean, fire?? We have a state-of-the-art fire-prevention system, sprinklers, and alarms. Why haven't we heard any alarms?"

As she finished her comment, she could begin to hear the sound of sirens through the open screened back door.

Molly's eyes grew wide as another panic hit her. *Where are Jenny and Sam?* It took her a minute to remember her daughter was safely up in her room and that Sam hadn't yet come home from his semester abroad.

"Jenny!" Steve yelled up the stairs, "There is a barn fire, your mom and I need to go help."

They could hear the crutches thumping along the hall above their heads, then Jenny yelled down, "Ryan just called. They're all coming."

She sat on the top step, her injured leg in its cast in front of her, and bumped herself down the stairs on her butt, the fastest way she knew how to get to the bottom. "You are not leaving without me. I know I can't do much, but I need to help."

Molly looked at her daughter's worried face and then to her leg. It was still in a cast from the fall she'd had at the track that had also resulted in Sarge's death just a week ago. "Okay, but you need to stay close to the truck to ensure you don't further damage your leg."

Steve wrapped his arm around his daughter's back as Molly held the door open, and they all went as quickly as they could out to the pickup truck parked behind the house. Jenny slid into the backseat as Molly yanked the front driver's side door open and slid across to the passenger seat. Steve climbed in behind her.

As he put the truck in drive, Steve looked over at Molly. "They will be fine, they all will be fine. Doug was already on his way, and we can hear the fire trucks."

Molly looked back at him, then looked at Jenny in the backseat, and did her best to hold back the tears.

Steve slammed on the accelerator and the truck jumped down the driveway that would take them to the main barn. Their house was on the back of the Shamrock property; although it was just two miles from the center of the farm, where the main barn stood, the straightest path there weaved around paddocks and through the safety gates. The gates, which were supposed to open automatically whenever a vehicle approached, were one of the precautionary measures taken to separate different areas of the farm. They kept certain areas contained, so that if any horses got out of a paddock, they didn't have the ability to run all over the farm. Now, these gates were slowing them down.

Molly slammed her fist against the dashboard, waiting for the gate to open. "Why isn't it registering the darn truck?" she said impatiently, her voice wobbling with the effort it took her not to cry in panic and frustration. Finally, she jumped out of the vehicle and manually disabled the gate, flinging it open herself.

Hopping back into the truck, she pulled out her phone and started texting furiously. "The system must be down," she offered in explanation. "I'm asking Hunter to go disable the gates from the main road to the barn, or the fire trucks won't be able to get through."

As the farm manager, Molly kept running through all the safety precautions they had put in place to ensure a barn fire couldn't happen. *The hay is kept in a separate building, we have the most advanced sprinkler system on the market, with heat sensors. If any of the sensors had been triggered, alarms would have sounded in the grooms' apartments, at Doug's house, and at my house, and the local fire department would have been immediately notified. Why had none of the alarms gone off? What is wrong with the gates?*

Steve cut off as many turns as he could on the drive, and they finally came into view of the big barn ablaze in front of them. The fire trucks were approaching at the same time from the other direction along the main drive.

Molly had the door open before Steve had a chance to park the truck.

"Molly, stop!" Steve called behind her.

Molly kept running at top speed towards a figure barely recognizable as her brother. Steve and Jenny watched as soot-covered, half-dressed Doug dragged one of their prized racehorses behind him out of the burning building, his t-shirt tied over the horse's head.

———————————

Ben turned the corner of the grooms' apartment complex, knocking on doors as he went. He rallied as much help as he could as he rushed towards the barn. As the grooms and other Shamrock staff members got out of bed and quickly pulled on their working clothes, Ben continued on. Finally in sight of the barn, he stopped short against the railing, shocked as he took in the blaze before him.

The fire had not yet reached the far end of the barn, where Storm's stall was, but Ben knew it wouldn't be long before it engulfed the entire building. He glanced up the hill towards Doug's house and saw his boss run the last few yards and disappear behind the barn.

Ben took off down the stairs to the left. He could hear the commotion behind him as Cappie yelled and continued to wrestle the rest of the staff to their senses to come help.

Ben reached the other end of the barn and ran through the door, through air that was becoming opaque with smoke. He raced, semi-blind, for Storm's stall, knowing it was four down on the left. He couldn't see Doug, but he knew getting Storm out would be a top priority.

As he approached the stall, he could see Doug trying to calm the big grey horse. Storm was kicking out at him and rearing up, wild with fear, but at that moment, he had all four hooves on the ground. His senses were on high alert and his fight-or-flight instinct was in overdrive. Storm was contained in his stall, unable to run away from the fire, so he was determined to fight, not realizing Doug was there to help him.

A racehorse lives twenty-three hours a day in his stall for much of his life; his stall is his place of comfort. Ben knew that if they didn't get the horses physically removed and secured away from the barn, they might very well run back into their stalls, regardless of the fire.

"Storm, buddy, we are here to help," Ben said calmly as he slid into the stall behind Doug.

Storm swung his head towards the voice he trusted most. Ben was there when Storm was born, and he had a long memory of his voice. As much as Doug had been around in the past year, Storm didn't share the same history with him that he did with Ben.

Ben moved in front of Doug, grabbing the lead rope from his hand as he passed. *I wish that Doug had also grabbed the horse's halter, not just a lead rope. No time to turn back now, though*, he thought, looking at the smoke starting to billow in their direction.

The two men looked worriedly at each other, but Doug knew he wasn't helping the situation; if anyone could get Storm out of the stall, it was Ben. There were other horses to save. He squeezed Ben's shoulder and walked backwards out of the stall.

"Come on, boy. This big old barn is going up in flames, and we need to get you out of here."

Ben's quiet ways calmed Storm a bit, and he stood twitching in the corner. His nose quivered as he smelled the smoke billowing in through his stall door, and his ears took in the crackling of the flames grabbing at the wooden beams above. He whinnied loudly, calling to his herdmates, and several called out in return, terrified of the monster approaching from the other end of the barn. He pawed at the thick straw on the floor of his stall, embers floating in the air above his head.

Ben looked up and knew he had to move quickly. The sprinklers had come on in the aisle, delaying the barn's complete engulfment, but the fire was still moving through the sides, from stall to stall, creeping in on them. With one quick motion, he moved up next to Storm's shoulder and threw the lead rope around his head and nose in a makeshift halter.

Storm trusted this man, but his body was shaking with fear. He reared up briefly on his hind legs before coming swiftly back down, but as his front hooves hit the floor, the right one landed heavily on Ben's boot.

Pain emanated up Ben's leg and shot through his entire body as his foot was crushed under the weight of a thousand pounds, but he choked back his scream so he did not scare Storm even further. Hanging onto both ends of the lead rope, he guided Storm towards the stall door and opened it, praying his temporary halter would hold.

As he got the door wide enough for them to pass through, the fire took over the empty stall next to them. A piece of wood exploded above their heads, and fire-hot embers sprayed down on the hindquarters of Storm's dappled grey coat and Ben's head and shoulders.

Storm leapt forward out of his stall. Ben held tight to the lead rope, dragged along by the horse in his desperate flight away from the fire. Storm saw Doug leading another horse out the open barn door ahead, and followed them through.

Ben held on as long as he could, but once he'd ensured Storm was safely outside the barn, his burned hands released the rope and his broken foot collapsed underneath his weight.

Storm tossed his head loose of the lead rope. He came to a full stop, shaking with uncertainty. Ever fiber in his body encouraged him to return to the safe haven of his stall, but he could smell the thick smoke and the fire burned bright in his eyes. Hesitating, Storm took a step back towards the burning barn.

Jenny jumped in front of him, waving her crutch.

"Get away from the burning barn, you stupid horse!" she screamed at him.

Storm reared up in front of her, pawing the air. The pulsating heat from the barn, the sharp sting from the falling embers, the people screaming, and the confusion pressed in all around him. All he understood at that moment, in that space, was his fear. He heard the stampede of his fellow horses running in the field behind him; taking the cue, he pivoted and took off at a full gallop.

Storm had already proven himself to be one of the fastest Thoroughbreds in horse racing; now this incredible athlete put every ounce of energy, heart, and speed he had into escaping the fear that enveloped his mind and body. Grooms tried to wave him down, but they were no match. The Shamrock Hill Farm staff stood by helplessly as Storm's hooves echoed off the asphalt, moving further away.

Fence lines came and went along both sides of the driveway so quickly that they blurred. On the other side to his right, the herd of horses raced frantically alongside him. As he approached a closed gate, Storm slowed. Relief surged through the hearts of those who could still see him, but it was dashed as, in one smooth motion, he gathered himself, rocked back on his hind legs, and launched himself over the gate, into the dark night and the woods beyond.

 # Forgotten Friend

Ryan slammed on the brakes as they pulled up to the barn—well, as close as they could get. The firefighters were busy at work, and several fire trucks blocked their path to get closer.

"Stay far away from the barn!" Charlie screamed at her two kids, as she jumped out of the truck and raced towards the burning building.

"Stop!" a firefighter yelled at her. "You can't go over there."

Charlie ignored him and kept running. She could make out the shapes of Doug, Molly, and Steve standing near the paddock fence as she came up on them.

"WHERE IS HE?" she yelled, over and over, even before she was close enough for them to hear her. She did not wait for a response, and continued flying past them.

Crazed with fear, she was about to run directly into the burning barn when a hand reached out and grabbed her roughly by the shoulder.

She spun around, yelling into the face of the firefighter holding her, "I need to save my horse!"

"Ma'am, you can't go in there. We are doing all we can. I believe all the horses have gotten out." He looked over towards Doug, who nodded affirmatively, his eyes solemn.

The firefighter and Doug calmly herded Charlie over to the group by the paddock fence, but she was filled with the same fearful energy Storm had displayed just a short time ago.

"Where is he, Doug!?" she screamed.

Doug took a step towards her at the same time that Charlie backed away and put her hands up.

"Please, please...please don't tell me I've lost him too."

Doug grabbed Charlie's shaking hands and pulled her close.

"He got out of the fire, Charlie. He did. But after Ben led him out of the barn, he got loose and ran off down the driveway. The grooms couldn't contain him, and he jumped the gate in his frenzy. Cappie and several others are out looking for him."

Charlie whipped around to where Ben leaned heavily on the fence next to Jenny.

"How could you?" she said, her voice heavy with crazed fear and anger. "How could you just let him go, how could you—"

"No, Charlie, it isn't like that!" Jenny exclaimed passionately. "Ben saved Storm's life! If anyone is to blame, it's me, I scared Storm away!" Jenny's shoulders were shaking from crying. "I know that I shouldn't have rushed in front of him, but he was heading back into the burning barn and I just… just…acted instinctively, waving my crutch in front of him."

"No," Doug said firmly, "neither of you are to blame. You both did everything in your power to save him and keep him safe."

Charlie noticed that Ben wasn't putting any weight on his one leg, and that his jacket was covered in tiny burn marks. She looked at Doug quizzically.

"Charlie, he was amazing. Storm wouldn't let me near, but Ben worked his magic, even after his foot was stomped on and broken, and got Storm out," Doug finished.

Ryan and Skylar had joined the group during the conversation, escorted by another firefighter, and they all turned to watch the barn as it continued to burn. The water spraying the roof was no longer part of an effort to save the barn, but to contain the fire as the structure began to crumble. The firefighters knew that, soon enough, the fire would run out of fuel. With the building isolated and under control, they began to relax; some of them started taking off their helmets and guzzling water to rehydrate.

Charlie turned back to Ben to tell him she was sorry, but the apology died on her lips as Skylar walked over to Doug and grabbed his hand.

"Mr. Doug?"

Doug looked down into her worried face.

"Where's Hershey?"

Doug's heart stopped.

Hershey.

Where was Hershey?

Had anyone gotten him out? He was so small, you couldn't see him over the stall door. He had been in the stall next to Storm, so that Storm would be aware of his presence. They would nicker to each other throughout the day.

Doug looked frantically towards Ben, and trying to keep the panic from his voice, asked, "Ben, did you see Hershey?"

Ben straightened up against Jenny and the fence, and his face betrayed all the panic Doug had tried to hide.

"No! I didn't see anyone bringing him out after I came out with Storm, and I have been here the whole time!"

Doug didn't stop to think. He let go of Charlie and took off towards the burning barn, shrugging off the hands that tried to stop him.

"Doug, no!" Molly and Charlie yelled in unison.

———————————

Doug couldn't see, the smoke was so thick. The flames were lapping at the wood above the stall doors throughout the entire building. He dropped to his hands and knees and crawled towards the stall next to Storm's, afraid of what he would see inside when he slid the door open. Behind him, he could hear the ceiling support beams start to collapse in, weakened by the fire that had been chipping away at them and the weight of the water that had been pumped on top in the vain efforts to stop it. He said a quick prayer that the roof would hold, but he never stopped crawling forward.

He grabbed at the metal latch and yanked his hand away. It was scorching hot. He didn't have his shirt anymore, having used it to blindfold one of the horses, so there was nothing he could use to protect his hand while he opened the latch. Bracing himself, he reached up again. Through the pain and the smell of his own burning flesh, he yanked open the latch and slid the door open.

Hershey was huddled in the corner, holding his head close to the ground to inhale the cleanest air. Doug crawled through the straw, dragging his burnt hand, and leaned into Hershey.

"Thank God, Hershey. Come on, we need to get you out of here."

Doug reached around the stall door and grabbed the halter and lead rope hanging outside. Although he could see the burnt hairs around Hershey's head, he needed to use the halter. It was difficult to tell how the pony was feeling under the soot that covered him nearly completely, but he was certainly acting more docile than the horses had. Still, Doug couldn't risk bringing him out of the barn and having him spooked and run back into the flames, or losing a grip of him as they made it to the entrance—not with Skylar standing right there. He gently lifted the halter over Hershey's ears, then hesitated for just a moment before tying the other end of the attached lead rope around his own waist. Doug knew that if the pony bolted, he could be seriously injured, but it was also the best way to ensure that Hershey would make it out alive.

Doug leaned over the pony's back and gave him a hug. "We're going to do this, guy."

He'd barely gotten the last word out when a ceiling beam, weakened by the fire, crashed down. It slammed into the ground in front of the stall door, blocking their only exit.

That was the least of Doug's worries, though. The beam had connected with the back of his head on its arc down. He hadn't even had time to crumple to the floor of the stall. He was out cold, stretched across Hershey's back as the fire closed in on them.

 # The Explosion

Charlie and Molly's screams had startled the firefighters nearby into action before Doug had even reached the entrance to the burning barn, but not even the fastest and nearest could have caught him before he'd raced in. Cursing, three of the men who were still completely suited up lagged behind him by less than a minute, but that minute was enough. They'd barely cleared the threshold when the collapsing beams drove them back out again.

"CHIEF!" one of them bellowed.

Fire Chief Travis Johnson had already saved Charlie from rushing into the barn when she'd arrived, so he'd recognized her screams from across the yard. He had taken off at a dead sprint as soon as he'd heard the frantic cries; only the fact that he'd been at the farthest point from the entrance of the burning barn had kept him from rushing in himself. Stopping short of the now-flaming entrance, he assessed the situation in a heartbeat, then turned abruptly and ran to Charlie and Molly. The women frantically explained that Doug had gone in to save Skylar's pony. Without saying a word to them, he turned to Skylar.

"Can you point out exactly where Hershey's stall is?"

Skylar swallowed her tears and nodded bravely.

"Then you need to come with me."

Skylar took Travis' outstretched hand as he whisked her as close to the barn as he safely could, shouting at his men to bring their axes over to the side of the building. They stood at the ready.

"Okay, you need to concentrate very hard," Travis said, squatting down next to the little girl. "We don't know where Doug is, but we know he was heading for Hershey's stall. If he and your pony are in there together, we might still be able to save them. When we tell the firefighters to go, they are going to hack a big hole as quickly as possible in the side of the building, but we only have one chance. All this air is going to get in and feed the fire, and there will be an explosion. We need to be able to reach in and pull out your pony and Doug before that happens. We have to tell these men exactly where to cut."

Skylar nodded bravely once again and squared her tiny shoulders. "Tell them to go to the left."

Travis stood back up and shouted the directions at his men.

The young girl made several adjustments before finally nodding affirmatively.

"That's it, that's exactly where Hershey's stall is."

Travis took a deep breath and shouted the order, "Okay, men, GO!"

The firefighters with axes began to hack away at the side of the barn furiously, while others kept their hoses trained on the disappearing wall. Skylar was amazed; the gaping hole just seemed to open in front of her. The men were scrambling in before she remembered to breathe.

The explosion that came next sounded like nothing she had ever heard outside of action movies.

Time slowed down for Charlie.

The explosion had been blinding, like staring directly at a firework, but the flames retreated just as quickly. As her eyes adjusted, she could see the firefighters all clustered around a dripping wet, dark, misshapen mound, which they hurriedly dragged away from the burning barn and started to disassemble.

They were so covered in ash and soot that Charlie didn't realize that mound had been constructed of Doug and Hershey until the firefighters had taken the two pieces apart.

Charlie rushed to Doug's side. He was unconscious—at least she thought, hoped, and prayed he was. He looked broken and inhuman. She could barely hear the EMTs over the buzzing in her head as they told her he was burned, injured, suffering greatly from smoke inhalation, and needed to go to the hospital immediately.

As they loaded him into the waiting ambulance, she realized she'd been holding her breath so long that she felt dizzy. She released the stale air in her lungs and forced herself to breathe normally as she looked around at the pandemonium.

What should I do? Charlie thought, as the waves of panic rose again. *Skylar and Hershey, Storm, Shamrock, the Belmont…*

No. She straightened herself up, and a calm steadiness took over. *I know what I need to do.*

Suddenly, she became aware that Molly and Ryan were in front of her. Both of them looked very worried, and she was stunned to realize that at least part of their concern was directed towards her.

"Molly, I need to go to the hospital."

Molly's facial expression shifted into something more resolute as she too tapped into her deep reservoirs of inner fortitude. As much as she wanted to be there for her brother, she knew she needed to stay for the good of the farm. She couldn't let this fire derail all that Doug had worked for. As Shamrock Hill's manager, she had to be the one to stay and lead the recovery efforts. Their resources would already be scattered between horses, facilities, and ongoing operations. She gave Charlie a reassuring hug and nodded.

"We'll handle things here. Go. Doug is going to need your strength."

Charlie searched Ryan's face. Finally, he nodded too.

"I'll help. Go ahead, Mom."

Her heart swelled with pride as she hurried towards the ambulance, hopping in just before it left. As the doors closed behind her, Charlie said a quick prayer for all of her family and friends.

Skylar skirted around the crowd near Hershey, crying out to her pony.

The equine doctor had arrived to begin triaging and treating all the horses some time ago, but Hershey was the most critical case by far. Under the doctor's direction, Cappie hurriedly did as much as he could to ease the pony's pain and examine his injuries.

Cappie saw Skylar and beckoned her closer, stepping aside so that she could be right at Hershey's head.

"Skylar, talk to Hershey and let him know everything is going to be fine. The doctor is going to sedate him, and we need him to thrash as little as possible."

Skylar looked into her pony's frightened, bloodshot eyes and spoke gently to him as the doctor injected the sedative into his neck, watching as his head dropped and eyes dimmed.

Before she could ask any questions, Cappie said, "They're going to get the trailer now, and we have to load him in. I am going to take him up to an equine hospital in Pennsylvania called the New Bolton Center. You've heard of it, haven't you?"

"I think so," Skylar replied hesitantly, her silent tears dropping onto Hershey's scorched mane. She itched to rub her pony's face, but she was afraid of aggravating the spots where he had sustained the most serious burns.

"Well, they have the best vets in the country, and they have everything to give Hershey the treatments he needs to get better."

Skylar set her jaw. "I'm going with you."

Cappie opened his mouth to protest, but before he could say anything, he took a closer look at her. The little girl's face was sooty, tired, and tear-streaked, but, shining through all of that, he could see her determination. He nodded silently, and they stood together next to the sedated pony and watched the trailer pull up next to them.

As the adults loaded Hershey in as gently as they could, Skylar ran her hand over his burned and blackened tail.

Oh, Hershey, Skylar thought, *your beautiful tail is gone.*

She choked on a sob as she ran to get into the truck. She needed to be strong for her pony. She would not cry.

"Hurry, Cappie, please," she said to her companion as she slammed the truck's door.

Buck turned left onto the main road that would take them to Shamrock. Lilly knew the way by heart and she followed each of the turns in her head with her eyes closed. Her hands were tightly clasped around Buck's right hand as she prayed silently.

Please, God, please don't let anyone get hurt, human or horse. Why did we decide to ride at Penn National this week?? We should have been closer. The drive from Pennsylvania is taking forever.

She finally opened her eyes when she knew they would be turning into the entrance to Shamrock Hill Farm. She craned her head, searching out the main barn over the hills ahead. She could make out the billowing smoke rising high above it by the way it reflected the fire engines' blinking lights.

At least the fire trucks are here, Lilly thought to herself.

Seconds later, an ambulance screamed past them, followed by a Shamrock horse trailer. Lilly looked closely at the driver's seat and made out Cappie's shape. *Oh no, who is in the trailer?*

Buck knew Lilly well enough to leave her alone with her thoughts. During the most stressful of times, she was the type of person who turned inward to gain her strength. He followed the oak-lined driveway, knowing they would be able to see the big barn after they crested the hill. He took in a deep breath, held it, and hoped for the best. While not a praying man, he squeezed Lilly's hand tightly as the barn came into view.

Or what was left of it.

PART TWO

Sneaking Suspicions

In the beginning, Amanda Ault had just lucked into writing about Genuine Storm. She hadn't known the first thing about horses (and she still didn't know much, if she was being honest with herself). Her editor originally sent her out to Shamrock for another fluff piece; she had been tasked with just getting the basic details and finding some human-interest angle—maybe the owner's fashion sense, maybe something sweet about second chances. The sportswriter had been tasked with getting the backstory, but he'd complained enough to their editor that those duties had ended up on Amanda's shoulders instead. The seasoned reporter didn't have much love for the sport, or for any story that didn't offer him easy recognition and an instant readership. He figured that the public's interest in horse racing was dying (if it was not already completely dead), and with a salary tied to pageview quotas, he didn't like to waste his time. Whenever he couldn't avoid doing a story on horses, he focused on the heroes from other sports who got into racing partnerships, like Bode Miller, the Olympic gold skier who'd opened a high-tech horse training facility, or hockey great Eddie Olczyk, who'd turned his love of horse racing into being a guest commentator and handicapper for major races.

No one had foreseen Storm's meteoric rise through the racing world and the huge public following he would attract. Of course, after the horse won the Kentucky Derby, the sportswriter had tried to steal the beat away from Amanda, but she'd stubbornly resisted. He'd complained long and hard to their editor, but hearing him refer to her as "just a fashion writer" had certainly helped strengthen her resolve. She'd been lucky to be there on the ground floor, and now she was determined to turn this into her lucky break. She was green, but she knew she could become a good reporter—a great one, even. She just needed to be persistent, and to learn a lot about horses, fast.

Amanda had done her homework on the journalists who wrote about the racing industry, though it seemed like it was easier to dig up information on the history than it was to find pathways into the career now. Every newspaper in the country used to have a turf writer on staff, but it seemed like the less popular that racing had gotten, the more positions had fallen by the wayside. Back in the golden age of racing, the results of races at local tracks had been listed in the papers, and frequently the stories of the horses and their connections had gotten front page coverage. Amanda had learned that the profession had lost many iconic writers as people had become more interested in the results of football, baseball, and hockey. The fan base had dwindled so drastically that now you only read about horse racing during the Kentucky Derby, when papers would pick up a syndicated column. Frequently, these articles weren't even front page. The results of the other two Triple Crown races, the Preakness and Belmont, would be buried in the back of the sports section if they were given any print space at all.

The more she learned of the difficulties the profession faced, the more determined she was to make her mark. Genuine Storm was a once-in-a-generation horse, and she knew he deserved once-in-a-lifetime coverage. She could tell he was special, that something incredible was happening here, even if she didn't have the full education yet to be able to express why. Far from disqualifying her from covering this story, though, she figured it made her exactly the reporter for the job. The public, generally, was as ignorant about horses and horse racing as she was, and they were just as entranced by Storm. She had already conceptualized a series in which she not only taught herself more, but brought the readers along with her. She was excited.

Amanda's editor, trying to keep the peace in his newsroom, had first attempted to sweet talk her into passing off her claim to Storm. When he realized that she wasn't giving it up without a fight, he'd changed tactics. Now he was trying to bury her in other fluffy assignments until she begged for mercy.

Today, she'd been sent all the way into DC to cover one of the many festivals on the Mall. Heavy rain had battered the city all day, and the event was a bust. The crowds did not materialize, which had put the soggy vendors into increasingly horrible moods as the day dragged on, so interviewing them had been a challenge. To add insult to injury, she'd gotten a flat tire on her way out of the city, and it had taken hours for AAA to come change it.

What a waste of a day.

It was almost midnight as she pulled back into town, and she was looking forward to getting out of her still-damp clothes and crawling into bed. Just to keep herself alert, she flipped on the police and emergency scanner she'd gotten installed in her car.

It worked, and fast. She nearly jumped out of her skin, listening as the responders volleyed back and forth about the fire at Shamrock. She changed course immediately and raced to the farm, listening intently to the scanner and trying to ascertain whether anyone had been injured, for any clues about how it had started or whether it was now under control. She prayed that all of the other reporters had slept through it—this story was *hers*.

By the time she arrived, the fire had already been put out, but there was still a lot of activity around the charred wooden skeleton of the burnt-out barn. She pulled her small car off the driveway and behind one of the big oak trees, hoping it wouldn't be noticed among all the other vehicles scattered about.

The firefighters were still combing the scene, making sure that nothing was smoldering that could start the blaze anew, while farm hands were comforting, calming, and checking out each of the horses. Everyone was absorbed in their tasks, and no one noticed her as she skated around the outskirts. She eased over to a group of people and eavesdropped on their hushed conversation; they were concerned about Doug (who, she gathered, had been rushed to the hospital), as well as a few horses who had been seriously injured. They were also deciding who should take charge and organize the official search efforts, as the initial search had yielded nothing.

So...who are they searching for?

She scanned the faces, paddocks, and makeshift medical zones, trying to figure out who was missing.

Charlie? Her daughter? That silent one...I want to say...Chappy, maybe?

No absence loomed larger in her mind than Storm's, though. She frantically double checked, searching for the horse she'd been centering her career on.

Talk about having all your eggs in one basket—or horses in one barn, she grimaced at the analogy as she stood looking at the blackened barn in front of her.

She shook her head. Every plan she had relied on Storm, and she'd already peeved her editor, the sportswriter, and probably a bunch of the other seasoned reporters by staking her claim. If the horse was dead, she'd be investigating new Chapstick flavors and writing op-ed pieces on rising booth costs at farmer's markets for years to come.

She searched around for someone who didn't seem completely occupied, ducking when she saw Travis Johnson, the interim fire chief. If he saw her, she knew he'd kick her out. They'd had several run-ins as she worked on articles before, and he'd made it clear that he thought she was a pest and a nuisance.

To be fair, strictly speaking, I'm pretty sure I'm not supposed to be here in the first place.

A shockingly bright yellow shirt caught her attention, followed shortly thereafter by the good looks of the man wearing it. She'd noticed him on previous visits to Shamrock, though they'd never been introduced. He'd always had a magnetism about him, carrying himself with almost boisterous confidence around the farm. She was surprised to note the change in him now—he seemed dazed and frightened as he wandered near the wreckage. She hurried over to catch him.

"Excuse me?"

He blinked several times, seeming to stare right through her. Then, his green eyes focused, and immediately, his entire demeanor changed. He gave her a grin that made her entire face flush.

"Well, don't you look like an angel," he drawled, looking her up and down.

Amanda realized she was still in the white sundress she'd chosen to wear to the festival assignment—an outfit that had not served her well during her rainy day at the Mall, and certainly did not transition seamlessly into investigating a fire.

"Although," he continued, "you're going to have to pick up some boots one of these days, if you're so committed to hanging around."

He gestured towards her pointed stilettos, which were sinking into the muddy earth beneath her. The huge amount of water used to put out the fire had turned the grounds around the barn into a soggy bog that now sucked at her heels.

"You're never going to make friends around here with those on, as pretty as they are," he finished.

Amanda couldn't help herself. As she grinned back at him, she realized he was the first person to smile at her all day.

"Valuable advice—I'll have to hit you up for more tips, because God knows I need a friend at Shamrock. For now, though, would you please point me towards Storm?"

The man's facial expression shifted again, going nervous and somber—sad, even—and Amanda's heart dropped to the very bottom of her stomach as he shook his head.

"Wish I could, but he's gone missing. Broke free as they evacuated him from the barn. There's a search and rescue party out looking for him now..."

Before he could say anything else, they both caught sight of Molly across the driveway, waving her arm to catch his attention.

"Sorry, darlin', I need to go help out, and you need to scoot on out before you ruin those pretty shoes for good. I'd love to see them someday in a more appropriate setting."

Amanda grinned as she watched him walk away. He was graceful and slick—somehow, he managed to look like he was sauntering, though he made his way over to Molly quickly. She briefly considered running after him to give him her phone number.

Looking at her shoes, the burn site, and over at Chief Travis, though, she realized the man's advice had been solid. It would be better to get out before she got thrown out. No one was going to have the time to give her anything more in-depth. If she hurried home, she could write up a quick blurb about the fire and send it off to her editor before anyone else was even awake to beat her to it.

She skirted the wreckage and made her way back to her car, thinking about how to best spin this new chapter in her Storm saga. She felt a little guilty as she excitedly realized how huge it was for her that Storm was missing—it would bring her a lot of readers, a lot of views on the online edition.

The horse just a hair's breadth away from the Triple Crown has run off into the night...Is it wrong to hope that it might take them a day or two to find him?

She was so caught up in her thoughts that she nearly ran straight into Chief Travis. Her luck held, since his back was towards her, but as she crept past, she overheard some of his conversation with the firefighter next to him.

"They've done a search for anything overtly suspicious in the immediate area—nothing to report."

"All the confusion with the horses has made this scene almost impossible to read, but this all seems suspicious. I won't feel comfortable ruling out arson before the inspector does a full investigation."

Chief Travis had lowered his husky voice, but that word cut through the loud night and smoky air like a knife: *Arson!*

There's no way I am letting one of those old men in the newsroom take this out from under me, she thought. *I need a computer and an internet connection, STAT. I'm not leaving until I've gotten the whole story—this could be my big break into investigative journalism!*

She hurried back to her car and pulled her laptop out from the backseat. She needed to get up higher to get better reception; thinking quickly, she spotted a driveway that would take her up the big hill towards the big house. Creeping up the drive with her headlights off, she nestled her car into the meadow that overlooked the barn, opened her laptop, and scanned for her WiFi hotspot.

Typing furiously, she was soon ready to hit submit, shooting her small piece about the fire off to her editor. Even though it contained more cliffhangers and questions than information, she knew she would be first. Her finger hesitated over the enter key on her computer, and then...

Connection lost.

Right on the verge of throwing the laptop out the window, Amanda noticed the problem—the Shamrock WiFi had started fighting with hers. She'd forgotten that she'd saved the password on her last visit, and the signal had gotten stronger than her hotspot just as she'd tried to send the email. She reconnected, filed her story, and sat back, relieved.

She closed her eyes. Her contacts felt gritty from the smoke of the fire, but she was happier now than she'd been all day. Her brain filled with scenarios about what had happened—the fire, the horses, the possibility of arson...

Her eyelids fluttered as she sank into her dreams.

At first, she just watched the flames consume the barn, appreciating her detachment from them, appreciating their beauty out of the context of the devastation they were wreaking. She didn't consider running to safety as they drew closer; the warmth had been pleasant, comforting. It was not until they'd completely surrounded her, until the warmth had started registering as heat, true heat, bearing down on her that she started to get concerned. She looked down at her left arm and realized that one of those curling tendrils of flame was crawling up it.

Move your arm, she commanded herself silently.

The whole world stayed silent, and the arm, detached now from her mind, did not move.

Just lift your arm!

She watched the dead arm helplessly as the warm sensation turned the corner into pain.

From somewhere outside the circle of flames, she heard a soft cough. Out of the fringe of her unconscious mind, the cough sounded again, louder. It was just enough to break the spell; she concentrated all of her energy, and...

Amanda, just LIFT YOUR ARM!

She jolted awake as her arm flew towards her face, but she still barely missing slapping herself.

She glared at the offending extremity, feeling the pins and needles as the blood flow re-established itself, then focused her groggy anger at the driver's side door. She reached across herself with her more obedient right hand and traced the visible inch-wide lip of the open window. Reaching back out, she touched the side of her small black Miata; the mid-morning sun had heated the metal considerably. Ten, twenty more minutes, and she might have actually had a nice burn on her arm where she'd been resting it against the car.

Well, she thought, *imagine what the boys in the newsroom would have thought of that—injured on the job, getting the scoop. Injured while investigating a fire.*

She smiled, relieved to escape the embarrassment, then focused her attention out the windshield as she got her bearings.

She'd been to Shamrock before, when she had shown up unannounced to interview Charlie before the Preakness. She'd been concentrating so hard to avoid embarrassing herself that day that she hadn't had a moment alone to really look at the whole farm and appreciate it. From her vantage point now, though, in this field next to the big house on the hill, it was nearly unavoidable. Spread out below her, the farm was beautiful, verdant and green and lush, with tidy white fences and paddocks laid out in loose grids.

Beautiful, that is, except for the smoldering black scar that ripped through the center of her view, where the barn had stood only hours before.

She made a mental note to get the newspaper's photographer to this very spot; with a picture like this and the country's interest in Storm, Amanda knew she didn't even need a great story to make the front page. Luckily for her, she did have a great story—and one that seemed like it could get even better. Her heart and mind both raced with the possibilities, the dominos she needed to line up next to exploit this opportunity to its fullest. Storm had, once again, proven to be her lucky charm.

She shook her head slightly. Here she was, trespassing, and no one in the world knew her location—there was even maybe an arsonist on the loose, someone dangerous—and she'd fallen fast asleep, unprotected, in a field.

"If I'm going to be an investigative journalist, I'm going to need to drop some of these naïve habits," Amanda muttered to herself as she checked her wandering mascara in her rearview mirror. "Otherwise, I might not last long…"

She gasped and her reprimand went unfinished as she heard the cough from her dreams again and she realized she was not alone.

Storm Chasing

Skylar also woke up in a vehicle.

The trip up to New Bolton was grueling. She cried often and worried constantly about Hershey. Cappie had pulled over the first few times that Skylar asked him to, allowing her to check on her pony, but after the third time, he put his foot down firmly.

"I know you're worried about Hershey, Skylar. I am too. It's important for us to get him to the hospital before the sedation wears off, though. We don't know how much pain he will be in when he wakes up, or how urgently he needs to be treated. They'll know exactly what to do up there. But if we keep pulling over to check on him, he might wake up before we arrive."

Skylar nodded. She understood—nothing was more important to her than making sure Hershey was as comfortable and safe as possible. Those were the most words she'd ever heard Cappie string together at once, so she knew it was important for her to understand. Not checking on Hershey hadn't made the rest of the drive any less nerve-wracking for her, though.

The trip to the equine hospital took a little over two hours, which was more than expected, given the time of night, but traffic had slowed due to construction on the bridge near Havre de Grace over the Susquehanna River. The hospital staff was ready and waiting for their arrival, and they took Hershey gently out of the trailer. Cappie volunteered details about the fire and Hershey to them, like how long the pony had been subjected to the smoke, how he was moving before he'd been sedated, and other information that Skylar tuned out. She did pick up on the warnings the staff gave him: that horses, with their sensitive lungs, could suffer just as badly as humans from airway constriction, and that the full extent of smoke inhalation damage wouldn't typically show up until four or five days after exposure. Although they would treat him for the mild second degree burns and for corneal damage in both eyes, no one would truly know how badly he'd been hurt for close to another week.

"Is he going to have to stay in here?" Skylar blurted out. "He likes to be near horses, he's always had a horse friend nearby to take care of…"

Cappie and the nurse paused, and the nurse nodded and marked that on Hershey's chart.

"Thank you," the nurse said, smiling at Skylar. "It's important for us to know what makes him more comfortable, so he can focus on resting and getting better. We will make sure we find several friends for him to be close to. We will give Hershey an exam, and depending on what we see, we can offer him radiology services, MRIs, ultrasounds, and scintigraphy. We will be able to examine his soft tissues for tears and his bones for fractures without ever exposing him to additional pain. If he does need surgery, we have a full, horse-sized operating theater and recovery room and a specialized anesthesia service."

Skylar listened to all the information, wide-eyed. There was so much she had never even considered about horse medicine, but the night had been so overwhelming that she couldn't even formulate all the questions she had. After several fits and starts of jumbled words, the nurse jumped in again.

"I'll tell you what—why don't you go home and write down all your questions, and send them to me in an email. I'll make sure we answer each one of them and give you updates on Hershey."

Exhausted and grateful, Skylar nodded, and Cappie gently told her it was time to say goodbye.

The little girl promised Hershey that he would be back home with her and with Storm soon, hoping that both parts were true.

Back in the car, she was so silent that Cappie thought she'd gone to sleep several times. Each time, though, the still air in the cab of the truck was punctured by another soft sniffle.

"You should try to get some rest," he finally said.

"I can't," Skylar wailed, breaking into the sobs she'd been stifling.

Cappie looked over at her, amazed that such a small child could cry so hard. He scanned the road signs ahead, and they passed one, two, three more exits before he nodded decisively and took the fourth.

Skylar's sobs slowed as they pulled into the brightly lit rest stop.

Cappie stepped down on the parking brake, unfastened his seatbelt, slid out of the cab, and firmly shut the door behind him. Skylar watched, trying to calm herself down, as he made his way over to her side, but as he opened her door, she started wailing again.

"Don't leave me here, Cappie! I'm sorry, I will be quiet, I just…I just…I just…" Skylar sobbed so hard that she couldn't catch a breath to finish her thought.

Cappie looked bewildered. "What? Oh, no! Skylar, I wouldn't leave you here. I'm so sorry. Um, gummy worms."

Skylar looked at Cappie with total confusion—a confusion so complete that it stopped the sobbing in its tracks, like when her dad used to scare her hiccups away. Cappie took off his signature cap and scratched the thin hair underneath, taking a big breath.

"Let me start again. I, um. Well, I'm just not always the best with words. I wish I had the right ones that would help, but I don't, and I know I'm not going to find them. So, I thought we'd stop and pick up some gummy worms. Or a different candy. Whatever you want. I just like gummy worms."

Skylar stared back at poor Cappie, who was so much better with horses than with humans. With no horses around, he looked like a fish out of water. Finally, she gave him a wobbly smile.

"Sure, Cappie. Thank you. I do like gummy worms."

He nodded, visibly relieved, and led her into the rest stop. They'd silently picked out more candy than she'd ever seen at one time, even on Halloween, nodding affirmatively at each other's choices.

Back in the truck and on the road, they'd unwrapped piece after piece in silence, stuffing their mouths. As her sugar high kicked in, Skylar talked to Cappie, moving from one topic to another rapidly, not waiting for him to reply. Within a short period of time, the sugar ran its course, the conversation waned, and Skylar drifted into a deep sleep.

Skylar awoke with a start as they turned back onto the road that led up to Shamrock. She was still sleepy and sad, and now, kicking the loose mountain of wrappers at her feet, she had a bit of a tummy ache.

After the long night, the rising sun brought in a crisp, clear late May day. Cappie pulled up in front of the paddocks, where Ryan and Jenny and Molly were standing, and let Skylar out of the truck with a silent nod before continuing up the road to park the trailer.

Molly was on the phone; it sounded like serious business, as she rattled off facts and figures and policy numbers authoritatively. She seamlessly pulled Skylar into her arms and gave her a hug, never missing a beat with the person on the other line. She smiled at the little girl as she pulled away and headed quickly in the direction of the office.

Skylar slowly shuffled over to Jenny and Ryan. Jenny looked sad and mad, and Ryan stared intently at his phone. Of the two, Jenny noticed Skylar first. She balanced one of her crutches against the fence beside her to give Skylar a hug, but Skylar ignored her offer.

"Hey kiddo, how are you holding up? How's Hershey?" Jenny asked, genuinely anxious over the fate of her favorite pony.

Skylar shrugged, trying not to cry again. "Fine. Where's Mom?" she asked, looking at Ryan.

"Hospital," he replied, still distracted by his phone. "Look at this!" he exploded, waving the screen in Jenny's direction. "The barn fire is all over the internet, and the Belmont forums are already filled with conjectures about Storm being hurt. Thank God they don't know we haven't found him yet!"

Skylar's face crumpled. "Is she hurt?"

"Who? What are you talking about, Skylar?" Ryan barked.

"Mom! Is she hurt?"

"What? No, where…oh, hospital. She's at the hospital with Doug."

"Is Mr. Doug going to be okay? And Storm is still gone? We have to go find him! I promised…" Skylar stammered.

Jenny gave Ryan a warning look and said, "Skylar, everything is going to be okay. Everyone is out looking, and your mom will call us the moment she has news about Uncle Doug."

"No! Everyone needs to stop telling me everything is going to be alright! You don't even know that. Things aren't alright unless we go and make them all alright. We have to go out looking too! I promised Hershey he would come home soon and that Storm would be here and I told him that Storm needed his help to win the Belmont and…"

Jenny leaned down and wiped away the tears running from Skylar's eyes. Skylar flinched away.

"Sky, what you need right now is sleep. You can't join one of the search parties; you're exhausted, and you'd just end up being in the way. The most helpful thing you can do is stay here. Let's take a nap, and when we wake up, Storm will probably already be back, and we can plan something nice to do to show Hershey how much we love him."

Skylar gawked at Jenny in disbelief, and her sadness transformed to anger. "Me, in the way? You're the one in the way!" She pointed at Jenny accusatorially and continued, "If you hadn't been waving around your big dumb crutches, Storm never would have run away! And you want to say that you love Hershey? You were at the fire the whole time, and you didn't even remember him. None of you remembered him!"

"Skylar!" Ryan finally looked up from his phone, startled by his sister's outburst. He'd never heard such a stream of anger from her, and he couldn't come up with a proper response. Finally, he just stuttered out, "Apologize, now!"

It was too late. Jenny's face had already crumpled, and her first tears had started falling as she grabbed her crutches and made her way to the other side of the paddock as quickly as she could.

"YOU'RE IN TIME OUT, SKYLAR. GO TO THE OFFICE AND TAKE A NAP ON THE COUCH!" Ryan roared as he spun around to follow Jenny.

"Time out?" Skylar shouted at his retreating back, "I'm not a baby, Ryan!"

Skylar spun and marched away from the two teenagers, trying to figure out what to do next. With nowhere else to go, she dejectedly walked towards the building that housed the office for Shamrock Hill.

As she pulled the screen door open, a handsome German Short-haired Pointer got up from the foot of the desk to greet her.

"Bart!"

The aristocratic dog sat and lifted his paw, willing her to shake. Doug and Jenny had worked a lot with Sir Barton, who was named after the first Triple Crown winner. He knew how to greet everyone like a proper gentleman, even when he was so excited to see them that he could hardly stand it.

Skylar shook his paw and looked into his chocolate brown eyes. She scratched the top of his head, and his brown and white spotted body wiggled appreciatively.

"Oh, Bart, what should we do?"

Bart cocked his head. He seemed to be considering the question. Then he stood up and walked towards the door, looking off into the distance, listening to something only he could hear. Skylar stood next to him, flipping his ears with her fingers.

"Hm. Good point, Sir. After all, you do have a good nose for horses… and how mad can they really be if we find Storm ourselves?"

Skylar thought for a moment before tearing off her backpack. Shuffling through, she found one of Storm's brushes.

"I brought this along to the hospital to leave with Hershey 'cause I thought he'd feel safer if he thought Storm was nearby, and so the vets could brush what's left of his beautiful tail, but in all the confusion, I forgot to leave it with him. This is Storm's smell, Bart." She thrust the brush under his nose. "Let's go find him!"

Bart let out a bark.

"Shhh. We need to be quiet so the others don't notice us."

Skylar looked both ways as she slowly opened the screen door. Ryan and Jenny must have walked off even further, because they were nowhere in sight. Skylar could make out several grooms moving horses around into different paddocks and barns to accommodate for the loss of the main barn. All in all, the coast was clear; no one was on the lookout.

"Now, you stay with me until we get down to the woods," Skylar said quietly to the dog.

Bart danced, anxiously waiting to be set free after being held captive in the office all morning long. It was unusual for him to be cooped up; he usually had the run of the farm, moving from barn to barn with either Doug or Molly. Someone had put him away in the office to keep him from being underfoot during the fire and the cleanup, but Bart had been able to smell the fire and heard the commotion, and he couldn't wait to get outside and start exploring all the new developments.

No one seemed to notice as the young girl and her dog sidled down the road between two paddocks and headed to the far side of the farm.

They quickly disappeared into the woods, alternating between walking and running, and they took turns leading—sometimes Bart seemed to make a beeline in one direction, and then when he ran out of inspiration, Skylar would make an executive decision about their path.

They'd been making their way along for at least an hour when Skylar looked around and realized she had no idea where they were. She really hadn't spent much time at Shamrock—she certainly wasn't very familiar with these woods.

"Sir Barton, I certainly hope that you and Storm know the way home."

Bart stood still and lifted his front paw in his point stance, his short, docked tail straight out behind him. He wouldn't budge, even after she'd started moving forward again.

"What do you see, Bart? Do you hear something?" she asked, trying to follow his gaze. She listened intently, and was surprised to hear a man's voice in the distance calling her name over and over, closer each time. She could hear the sound of him crashing through the underbrush before he came into her line of sight, and Bart raced out to see him.

"OVER HERE!" Skylar shouted. "Oh, hi Buck!"

Buck had spent all night helping Lilly soothe the horses back at Shamrock, but as the night turned into morning, he'd had to admit that he'd been running out of steam. All of the horses had been tended to medically, and no one had been seriously injured besides Hershey. Most of them were just skittish and scared, and Lilly was the real talent there, the one with the knack for working with the horses emotionally. She'd still been operating in the zone as his energies waned, so she'd given him a quick kiss and told him to go catch a nap up in the office.

Buck had just turned the corner around the yearling barn when he'd noticed movement in the distance and spotted Skylar and Bart running into the woods. He'd caught a glimpse of Jenny and Ryan sitting in the timer's shed at the training track, and realized that Skylar was without supervision. Buck had quickly changed course, putting his nap on hold to run after them, but they'd had quite a lead. It had taken him a while to catch up.

"Skylar, you shouldn't be alone out here. We're already missing Storm, you can't go missing too! What if you got hurt? Does anyone even know you're out here?" Buck challenged her as he came closer.

Skylar's welcoming expression changed.

"Everyone else is busy. Storm is my horse too, and he's out here alone—what if he's hurt? No one knows where he is, and he doesn't even have Hershey with him to calm him down and make him feel safe…" She started to sniffle.

Buck knew that the chances of finding Storm in this direction were slim—the horse would have had to circle nearly the entire farm from the direction he'd taken off in when he'd broken away. Seeing Skylar's face, though, Buck realized she was trying to be brave so that she didn't cry.

This poor kid has so much to be worried about, he thought. *What does it really cost me to help her while she tries to help?*

His heart swelled up, and he briefly wondered what it would have been like to be a father to Jenny when she was this age.

"Hey, you know what, you're right. None of us thought to go in this direction, and another search party could only help. Sorry I was short—it was a long, scary night for all of us, and I let myself get grumpy. It's not a great idea to be out here alone, but now you're not—I'm officially joining your expedition. Give the orders, captain—which way should we search next?"

"That's okay. I got grumpy earlier too." Skylar shrugged and rubbed at her eyes, trying to drive the tears back in. "Well, I've mostly been asking Bart for directions. I gave him something with Storm's scent on it because in one of my favorite books, there's a girl detective, and her dog helps sniff things out, so I thought maybe Bart could smell him out, dog noses are a lot more powerful than ours, and…"

Skylar's words trailed off as Bart, who'd been happily running around and sniffing things in the area, stopped short and stuck his nose up in the air. He struck his pointer pose, paw cocked and tail straight. Suddenly, he let out several barks and took off, sprinting. It was all Skylar and Buck could do to try to keep up and follow the stream of barking in front of them.

New Friends, New Foes

"Sorry, Angel, wasn't trying to scare ya," the man called over, chewing on a piece of straw.

Amanda laughed. "It's my own fault, falling asleep out here. I didn't recognize you without that bright yellow shirt."

Smiling, she opened her car door and stepped out. The man pointed down at her bare feet.

"Well, at least you ditched the heels, although I still recommend you get yourself a pair of boots. Give me your size, I'll get 'em for ya."

"You seem awfully concerned about my footwear. And presents? Already? You don't even know my name yet!" Amanda pretended to be shocked.

The man grinned. "Well, of course I'll need your name. I'm going all out on these—the most colorfully painted boots you've ever seen. I've got a guy..." he paused, pretending to contemplate the possibilities. "Of course, I don't know your name. I could have him paint 'Angel' up the sides, or maybe just a big 'A' with some wings around it..."

"Amanda," she said, holding out her hand, "starts with the same letter."

"Hunter." He shook her hand, but immediately winced. "Sorry, didn't realize how sore I was. We all got so bumped around last night; I shouldn't complain. Turns out that pulling horses out of a fire is even more dangerous than it looks. I'm lucky to have gotten away with so little damage."

Amanda immediately shifted into reporter mode. "Was everyone so lucky? Any word about how it started? Is Storm still missing? Is he still going to the Belmont?"

"Whoa!" Hunter said, throwing up his hands in the air. "I believe you've got a few questions to answer, Amanda—like, what in the world are you doing, hiding up here?" He squinted his eyes at her, and playfully feigned suspicion as he asked, "You police?"

Amanda laughed. "Hardly. I came by last night when I heard about the fire, but you were the only one around who was kind enough to talk to me over all the action. I heard Chief Travis talking about the possibility of arson, but I knew that if he saw me, he'd kick me out in a heartbeat. We've already had our share of run-ins…"

Hunter held up a hand to stop her. "Sorry, did you say *arson?*"

As if on cue, the fire chief's marked car pulled into sight, headed right towards them.

Buck and Skylar broke through a line of trees into a clearing just in time to see Bart bolting around a barn that was set in the middle, next to a small house.

"Bart stopped barking. Do you think he found something?" Skylar asked, grabbing Buck's hand as they crossed the property.

As though he'd heard her, Bart's head peered around the corner. Satisfied that his companions had followed him, he disappeared again.

As Buck and Skylar turned the corner of the barn, a small pasture came into view; the big grey horse standing in the middle quickly spooked to the other side.

"Storm!" Skylar screamed, scrambling over the fence.

Buck jumped down next to her, but held her back from running across to Storm. Noting the horse's quivering body and how he could see the whites of his eyes, Buck realized he was in a high state of panic, in unfamiliar surroundings.

"He's afraid," came a voice from behind them.

In the excitement of finding their horse, Buck and Skylar had not noticed the boy sitting on an overturned bucket under the overhang of what amounted to a run-in shed. A big bloodhound lay at his feet; Bart started nudging at the big old dog, trying to taunt him into getting up and playing. The bloodhound didn't react; he had no intention of leaving his boy to play with this new intruder.

"Found him tangled in the underbrush out back a few hours ago," the boy said, not taking his eyes off the horse pacing in the paddock. "Actually, Buster here found him. We were out looking for rabbit with my bow and arrow before dawn, but when the sun rose, we saw this horse just standing in one spot, not moving a muscle, in a thicket of prickly bushes. They were all stuck in his tail and scraping up his legs. He had gotten himself tied up in some vines to the point that he was too exhausted to move."

Buck looked at the dark spots on Storm's legs, where the blood had dried.

"How did you get him out? How did you get him here?" Skylar asked the boy as she walked closer to grab Bart.

Sir Barton had, uncharacteristically, made a pest of himself. Skylar pushed his butt to the ground and sat down next to him, looping an arm around his shoulders to make him stay put. The bloodhound glanced down his long nose at them, seemingly appalled at the rambunctious short-haired pointer.

"He was real tired from fighting the underbrush, so he didn't give me much of a fight. I think he was just pretty happy to be saved from the vines. I made a halter from the rope I had with me, cut him out of the brush with my army knife, and me and Buster brought him back here. I walked him into the field and tried to put him in the barn over there," the boy said, pointing to the two stalls down the shed-row, "but he started freaking out and broke the halter. Luckily, I had already shut the gate, and this is all enclosed. I've been trying to get him to come over for some water and hay ever since.

Been a couple hours now."

"We appreciate you finding and helping our horse," Buck said to the boy. "I am Buck Wheeler, and this here is Skylar."

"And this is Bart," Skylar added, patting the dog on the head. "If it weren't for him, we wouldn't have found you all."

"I'm Drew, and this is Buster."

Buster looked up at the boy at the mention of his name and wagged his tail slowly. The boy looked down at him appreciatively and patted his flank.

"Has a nose that can't be beat, which is why he's a good huntin' dog," the boy said proudly.

"Are your parents home?" Buck asked.

"Nope. Dad's working on a big case, not sure when he will be back," Drew replied.

He stood up from the bucket, avoiding any more talk of his parents, and gestured towards the gate. "I guess you want to be taking him back."

"Well, Drew," Buck started, "this horse is pretty important to our families. We have to take him home and treat him for any injuries and get him in some familiar surroundings."

"Yeah, I know who he is. Who doesn't?" Drew said wistfully. "Genuine Storm. I'm one of his original Storm Troopers."

"Well, since you know these woods, do you think you can help us find our way back to Shamrock?" Skylar asked as she scrambled up from the ground and brushed herself off.

She was all ready to get back to taking care of business. She couldn't wait to see the looks on everyone's faces when she and Storm marched out of the woods.

That'll show Ryan and Jenny, she thought. *I'm not in the way—I saved the day!*

"I am going to call for the trailer, Skylar," Buck interjected. "We don't know the extent of Storm's injuries, and we have come quite a way through the woods."

"But I know a shortcut. It will only take about fifteen minutes," Drew said quickly. "Buster and I can lead the way. It will take a trailer over an hour to get here on the back roads."

Buck hesitated, but looking down at Skylar and Drew's excited faces, he thought about how miserable and anxious Lilly's had looked when he'd last seen her.

Torturing her for another hour or two doesn't make much sense, he thought.

"Alright, let me check out the cuts on Storm's legs and make sure he still has all four shoes. We do need to get him back as soon as we can."

Buck took the halter that Drew held out for him.

"Haven't needed to use one of these since the horses left," Drew said quietly, distracted by a memory.

Buck raised his eyebrows, but didn't press the boy for more information. He walked towards Storm.

"Hey, big fella, time to take you home."

Storm drew away and trotted to the other side of the small pasture.

"Skylar, he's got to be hungry. Drew, do you have any grain in that tack room? Skylar, grab a flake of hay. Approach him from the other side."

Skylar and Drew worked as a team on one side with Buck on the other. Storm trotted between them as they slowly closed the gap. After about fifteen minutes of trying to avoid capture, Storm stood with his sides heaving and sweat dripping off his neck and flanks, exhausted. He dropped his head and let Buck slide the halter over his ears. Buck ran the chain over his nose just to be safe, but he didn't think Storm had much fight left.

"Alright, big guy, let's take a look at these feet," Buck said calmly.

"Oh, his hooves are muddy, but I've seen all four shoes—he hasn't lost one," Drew said helpfully.

"Thanks," Buck said, smiling gratefully at the young boy and appreciating the care and attention he'd shown for the horse. "That's good news; means it's much less likely that Storm's cracked or torn a hoof. It's still a good idea for us to clean his hooves and check if any of his shoes have come loose or gotten bent before we try to walk him back. Do you have a hoof pick around here, by any chance?"

"Yup, pretty sure we do," Drew replied, ducking into a tack room at the end of the small barn.

After a few minutes of banging around, he emerged with an old, simple metal pick and handed it to Buck.

Moving closer to Storm, Buck said, "In the barns, you'll always hear the old-timer grooms say 'No foot, no horse.' These powerful creatures rely so much on their hooves, which are incredibly sensitive and delicate."

Buck kept up a calm stream of conversation with the two children to ease the tension and reassure Storm. Skylar and Drew listened and watched, alert for any sign that Storm was about to kick or lash out.

Standing close to Storm and facing his tail, Buck ran his hand down the horse's leg and gently squeezed the soft skin surrounding his cannon bone, pressing his weight against him.

He was pleased when Storm lifted his foot without incident, but kept his calm patter going so that he didn't spook the horse with a change in energy.

"See, I'm just going to hold the leg right here, supporting his hoof," Buck said. "We're going to use the pick to clean out everything from around the frog—that's this fleshy part right in the middle—and then we'll just trace it around the inside of the shoe, to make sure there are no pebbles between the shoe and the hoof."

Buck finished the first leg without incident. Guiding the hoof back down to the ground, he moved further back to check the hind leg.

"You've got to guide their feet back down gently, so they don't drop them and hurt themselves—or step on yours. Look at how I keep my feet together and turned away from Storm, because if he accidentally steps down on my toes right now, I'll be in bad shape for the Belmont."

Moving on to the next foot, Buck said, "Skylar, I know you know all this—Drew, how about you? Have you spent much time near horses?"

Drew hesitated before responding, "No, not much. My mom had a couple of horses, but..." he trailed off, still watching Buck and Storm intently.

Buck took the hint and changed the subject as he started cleaning the next foot.

"While we're down here, I'm also making sure the temperature of each hoof is okay and checking the strength of his pulse. If one of his feet feels warmer or has a stronger pulse, there's a good chance that the foot is injured."

Buck moved on to the last leg, the left fore. "Well, luckily, it looks like all the hooves are still in good condition, but he's sprung this shoe. By some great luck, it is still in place, and all the nails are in their original positions. We should take care of this before we set out back to Shamrock, though. If it slips, it can bruise the frog and the other soft tissues in the hoof, and the nails and clips can puncture and cut him up."

"Even if it doesn't injure him, it can make him really uncomfortable," Skylar volunteered. "Mom told me that some people think that Big Brown would have won the Triple Crown a few years ago if he hadn't been running on a loose shoe at the Belmont. It didn't injure him—nobody even noticed it until they looked at photos after the race—but he went from winning the Kentucky Derby and the Preakness to finishing last at the Belmont for no other apparent reason."

"So…are we going to take his shoe off ourselves? My dad also has nails in his workshop, if you just wanna hammer it back in," Drew offered.

"Oh no, I'm not trained to do that," Buck explained. "That's a complicated job. The only person who should shoe a horse is a professional farrier—and they have to apprentice for four years before they can even register." He wiggled the shoe again and said, "I don't think the shoe is loose enough that I should remove it, and I would need a farrier's rasp and puller to do that without damaging the hoof. Skylar, any ideas?"

"Ooh! Duct tape!" she said, excited to have the answer.

"Really?" Drew asked skeptically.

"Yup—short strips over the sole, just so long as we don't get it stuck on the coronary band or pastern," Buck said. "I am sure you have heard there is nothing that duct tape can't be used for. It is a staple in the barn."

Drew went to grab the tape from his father's stash, and Buck made quick work of wrapping the hoof.

"We should bring this with us, in case we need more," Buck said. "Drew, would you mind putting this in your pack?"

"Sure," Drew said, proud to be of help and obviously enjoying being part of the rescue team.

Buck pulled out his cell phone and typed in the words, "Found Storm. Meet us at the far end of the farm beyond the broodmare barn with trailer." He hit send, notifying the team that the champ had been found.

Chief Johnson stopped his car only feet away from Hunter and Amanda and jumped out.

He looks worse than tired, Amanda thought. *Maybe this is what the phrase "bone tired" means.*

To her relief, the chief stared right past her.

"You're Hunter?"

"Yessir, what can I do ya for?" Hunter said, with an easy tone that made Amanda suspect he cared little for the firefighter.

"Molly and I are preparing for the arson inspection, and we would appreciate it if you were available to interview when the marshal arrives."

Hunter raised an eyebrow. "I don't know what help I can be, Chief. I wasn't exactly the first one on the scene."

"No, Doug and Ben were the first on the scene...and they're both being treated at the hospital now. We need someone who can walk with us through the site and give us the layout of the barn, answer questions about possible accelerants we find and whether they would have been out of place in daily operations, tell us about the cleaning schedules."

"You know, I'm usually down at the Florida stables..."

Travis gave him a cold look. "Listen, guy, you seem to be the least busy person at Shamrock this morning. Finish your crucial business with..."

Amanda shivered as the chief's icy blue eyes met hers for the first time. She gave him a small wave as his sentence trailed off in a sigh.

"You know, I could have sworn I saw you last night, but then I thought no, there's no way that woman would have the audacity to trespass *again* and get in the way of my team while they're trying to do their jobs and save some lives, *AGAIN…*" Travis whipped his phone out, muttering loudly to himself. "Who is authorized to act on Doug's behalf while he's off the property? Molly, I bet. I'll be happy to witness if she'd like to press trespassing charges. I'm sure I can help the police come up with a number of other laws you've broken in the past twelve hours."

Hunter chuckled at the visibly infuriated fire chief. "You've got it all wrong, buddy. This lady here is a friend of mine. I'd invited her over last night to impress her with my cooking skills. When we heard the sirens, we both came running."

Travis looked at him incredulously, then over at Amanda. Hunter winked at her, and she grinned smugly at Travis.

"That's right. I'm an invited guest. Just pure dumb luck I happened to be here during the biggest fire—and the biggest news story—in the history of this tiny town."

The chief narrowed his eyes at her. Hunter's phone beeped loudly with an incoming text, interrupting Travis as he was about to open his mouth to reprimand Amanda again.

"Alright, *guy,* I was going to let you wear yourself out, but as I said, this lady has been a guest of mine the whole time, and frankly, I don't appreciate the way you're talkin' to her," Hunter drawled. "Storm is on his way back, so I'm needed elsewhere. Don't you have a job to get back to, Chief?"

Travis glared at them both, then jumped back into his cruiser and took off.

Hunter stared thoughtfully at the dust kicking up behind the cruiser.

"You know, there's just something about that guy that makes me wish there was a locker nearby I could shove him into."

"Thanks for the alibi," Amanda said, smiling at Hunter. "I owe you one."

Hunter grinned at her. "Sure thing. Not lyin' about Storm, though, so I'm out of time to collect. How about you just take my phone number, and if you think of a way to repay me for my truly heroic, super useful measures here this morning, you can ring me up?"

Amanda whipped out her phone and plugged in the digits as he rattled them off, then watched as he vanished even more quickly than Travis had.

Without the excitement of handsome Hunter around, Amanda was suddenly very aware of how much her contacts itched, how dirty her dress was, and how achy her feet were. Sighing to herself, she started up her car and took off towards a warm shower, her head filled with ideas for her next submission to the paper.

Safe Not Sound

Lilly watched as Sir Barton and a bloodhound emerged from the woods, followed by a very animated Skylar and a boy who looked about her age. The jockey held her breath for the big reveal, and finally, Buck and Storm came into sight. She studied the big grey horse closely as he clipped down the driveway, searching for anything amiss.

Was he limping? No, thank God, she thought.

She had already summoned the vet, Dr. Rollins, from another barn on the property. He had been there throughout the night, examining and treating the other horses who had been in the barn or in the nearby field during the fire. The chaos of the night had led to more than a few minor abrasions and kick marks, but he'd been pleased to report that, with the exception of Hershey, he'd seen very few other signs of serious trauma. Lilly knew the doctor would need to go over every square inch of Storm; she just hoped the luck would hold.

"Where do you want me to take him?" Buck called out.

"Let's go to the yearling barn. It is quiet in there. They are all turned out into the paddocks," Lilly replied.

"He was at a farm through the woods, Lilly. Bart found him," Skylar said excitedly, running ahead to fill Lilly in on the whole saga.

Lilly walked swiftly in front of Skylar, as she ran to catch up.

"This is Drew, and he was there taking care of him, and this is Buster, and…"

"That's great, Sky," Lilly said absentmindedly, cutting her off.

"Are you even listening to me?" Skylar asked, bewildered.

"Listen, Skylar, I can't right now. I am worried about Storm, and Doug, and your mom, and oh, just everything. Can you please just be quiet for a few minutes while we assess Storm?" Lilly said curtly.

Lilly did not realize how deeply her words had wounded Skylar. The young girl stopped short and dropped her head, allowing Lilly to keep walking, but once Buck and Storm had passed by, Skylar spun around in the other direction and ran, hot tears stinging her face and blinding her way.

Lilly and the vet stood in the open doorway of the yearling barn, evaluating Storm as he approached. Storm started getting antsy as he drew closer to the structure. He flared his nostrils, holding his head high. Buck stopped, running a hand along his neck.

"It's okay, buddy, I know it's not your old barn, but this one will do for now."

Buck pulled the lead shank, and Storm moved forward another few steps before he stopped again, turning quickly around Buck this time.

Good thing I put the chain over his nose, Buck thought. *I wouldn't have been able to control the horse through that sudden and unexpected maneuver.*

Storm stood stock still, his front legs locked at the knees. Buck couldn't do anything to make him move any closer to the barn.

"He's afraid of the barn," Lilly said to Dr. Rollins.

"Well, to be expected, given his experience last night. His home and safe haven went up in flames around him," the doctor replied.

Lilly walked out to Buck, holding out her hand for the lead shank.

"Come up, Storm, we need to make sure you are alright." Lilly glanced down at the hoof encased in duct tape. "Buck, can you please text the farrier to get up here, ASAP? I think he is working on the two-year-olds."

Lilly handed him her phone so he could send the text, then walked Storm away a bit from the barn and into a small adjacent medical paddock. She unhooked his lead shank and let him loose, settling herself against the fence to watch him.

The paddock was too small for Storm to get running around, but he started to pace nonetheless. Lilly had picked this barn as it wasn't in sight of the other horses on the farm, hoping Storm would be less distracted, but he kept turning his head to stare at the charred remains of the barn just beyond. He let out a loud whinny, and a few return whinnies could be heard from a far-off field.

Cappie came up behind her. "He scared of the barn now?"

"Yep, I think so. Or just overall traumatized," Lilly replied. "Can't blame him."

"Well, if anyone can get him over it, you can," Cappie said, putting a comforting hand on her shoulder.

"Not so sure this time, Cappie," Lilly said, more to herself than to him.

———————————

Drew rounded the corner of the big pickup truck with the two dogs flanking him, but Skylar was nowhere to be seen.

"Bart, I thought I told you to find Skylar. You're falling down on the job."

"No, he got it right," a hidden voice said.

Bart thumped his tail and wiggled under the truck to get close to Skylar.

"Whatcha doin' under there?" Drew asked, crouching down to see her face. She was stretched out like a starfish underneath the vehicle, lying on her stomach, and picking blades of grass. "It doesn't seem like a really safe idea. What happens if the owner comes out and tries to move it and they don't see you?"

"Nah. This is my mom's truck. She's at the hospital with Doug. This is a safe hiding spot."

"What are you hiding from?" Drew asked.

"I knew that everyone else would show up once they heard the news Storm had been found, and I didn't want to be near anybody," Skylar sniffled. "They won't care. Probably won't even notice I'm gone."

"Do you want us to leave you alone?" Drew asked, gesturing to include Buster and Bart.

Skylar smiled at the two dogs—Bart, who now had his nose pressed in the small of her back, and Buster, who sat patiently next to Drew's kneeling figure. Bart, who had been trying very hard to hold himself back, took her smile as an invitation to fix the problem, and army-crawled up to clean the tears off her face with his tongue. Skylar dissolved into a fit of giggles, and Drew laughed along as the noble-looking Buster joined in, letting out a baying, bloodhound howl.

"Nah, you guys don't count as anybodies," Skylar said, as she got control of Bart and crawled out into a patch of sunlight next to the truck. "It's just been a really crummy day already. My pony, Hershey, almost died in the fire, and I had to take him to the hospital, and my mom's friend, Mr. Doug, got hurt, so she's with him, and my brother is being a jerk, and everyone else is busy, and I just don't have anything important to do now that Storm is back. I was so happy that I got to be the one to find Storm, and then it didn't even seem like anyone cared."

"I know Storm cared," Drew said, taking a seat beside Skylar.

"Yeah, you know, you're right!" Skylar replied, brightening up considerably.

"I can't believe you own such a famous horse," Drew said enviously. "It must be like sharin' a home with a celebrity. Feedin' carrots to a hero! I don't know too much about horses, but I've been following his Facebook page since he won the Derby. I even have a signed picture of him; sent in my five dollars when you guys set up his crowdfunding page."

"You live so close; why didn't you ever just walk through the woods to come meet him?" Skylar asked.

"I thought about it a couple times when Buster and I were out huntin' or explorin'. I guess I didn't want to get caught trespassin' or for someone to call my dad. Dad thought I was nuts for throwing my money away on Storm. He doesn't really like horses."

"Then why do you have a whole little stable setup in your backyard?" Skylar asked, curious.

"Oh, my mom was the one who liked horses. When she left, she took her horses with her." Drew looked wistful, recalling old memories. "I used to help her brush them, and I'd sit on a bucket and watch her ride."

"Where did she go?"

Skylar felt bad for asking the question when she saw Drew's mouth draw into a shaky frown, so she changed the topic quickly without waiting for an answer. "Well, we have lots of horses here that you can help me brush, and maybe you can learn to ride one of the side ponies. Those are the horses that keep all the high strung racehorses in line."

Drew's eyes got huge. "Oh man, I can't wait to call my mom and tell her I'm going to learn to ride and hang out with the Triple Crown winner!"

"He hasn't won yet," Skylar warned.

"Oh, he will," Drew replied confidently.

Suddenly, both of the kids heard Drew's name being called from somewhere pretty close by. They scrambled up and peered over the hood of the truck, watching a man wandering through the nearby paddock as he called for Drew again.

"Oh, that's my—"

Drew didn't have the opportunity to finish his thought. Skylar dashed away towards the man, and Drew took off close behind her, curious about what was happening. He watched as Skylar barreled into the man and wrapped him in a ferocious hug.

"Uh, well, hi…"

"Drew! This man saved my pony—and he's, like, king of the firefighters!" Skylar said, releasing Chief Johnson.

Drew and Travis both laughed out loud. Skylar was confused, but she was too happy to be really bothered.

"What's so funny?"

Drew caught his breath and said, "Skylar, this is my dad."

"But I'll take the promotion to king," Travis mused.

Skylar took a step back and looked at Drew and Travis together.

"Woooowww! So…you saved Hershey," she said, pointing at Travis, "and you saved Storm," she continued, pointing at Drew. "You guys are THE BEST!"

 # Difficult Decisions

Buck and Lilly spent a restless night in one of the staff cottages. Sleep was hard to come by; Lilly tossed and turned, keeping Buck awake. She just wanted to be back out, helping Storm. Early in the morning, before the grooms even began the breakfast feeding ritual, she slipped on her jeans and crept out to the medical paddock, leaving Buck to the sleep he had only recently fallen into.

"Thanks for keeping Storm company, Cappie," Lilly said.

"Can't sleep with the boss in the hospital, so figured I would make myself useful. He's been resting a bit, actually laid down about two this morning for an hour, but he jerks to attention at most any little sound," Cappie informed her.

Lilly walked quietly up to Storm and reattached the lead shank, running the chain this time under his upper lip, as both a calming mechanism and to gain a bit more control if Storm tried to bolt.

She opened the gate, spoke to him softly, and walked him towards the wide open barn doors. Storm stopped. Lilly turned him in a circle and tried again, with the same result. Storm's skin began to quiver with fear. Nothing she could do would convince him that this barn was safer than the one he had escaped from two nights before.

Ben would be an asset right now, Lilly thought as she turned Storm around again, away from the barn.

Ben had gone off to the doctor to get his foot evaluated and hadn't been cleared to return yet. He'd been having a hard time walking on it after Storm stepped on it, but he had refused to leave Shamrock before Storm was home safe. Once the horse had been found and returned, Molly had been able to convince Ben to get his own injuries looked at. His exposure to the smoke had been bad enough that they ended up keeping him overnight for observation.

Well, it certainly won't do to have a horse that won't go into a barn, Lilly thought. *We're scheduled to leave for Belmont next week, so I need to come up with a solution quick.*

She backed Storm up a few steps, but she was no match for 1200 pounds of racehorse. Storm wouldn't budge, forward or backward.

Storm broke out into a sweat. He nodded his head repeatedly, blowing deeply out of his nose. Lilly rubbed it gently, pondering her next move. She looked again for signs of physical injury, but outside of a few scrapes from the underbrush he had been tangled in, Storm's body was in great shape. His eyes were the only windows into the terror and trauma churning underneath.

I can't have Storm out here, working himself into a mess, physically or mentally.

She looked over at Cappie, who was still leaning on the paddock fence. "Any suggestions?"

"Well, I do have one. A guy I know. He specializes in troubled horses. Might be worth a shot," Cappie said.

"We don't have a lot of time, Cappie," Lilly said.

"I know," he replied, pulling out his phone.

Feeling lost and hoping for clarity, or at least coffee, Lilly walked slowly over to the makeshift staff lounge that had been set up in one of the smaller barns.

"Hey Lilly," Molly said, giving the jockey a smile that cut through her fog the moment she walked through the door. "I whipped up a quick batch of egg salad sandwiches. I figured it was the closest we were going to get to a real breakfast, no matter how much I wish you had time to eat and I had time to cook."

"You're a lifesaver, Molly," Lilly replied, grabbing one of the plastic-wrapped bundles and sitting down, "and the only cook in the world I trust with egg salad."

"How does Storm seem this morning? I saw you working with him on my walk over, but I didn't want to interrupt."

Lilly shrugged, taking the first bite and savoring the taste of the saffron and curry that made Molly's recipe her favorite.

"I'm not sure what the right thing to do for him is at this moment," Lilly replied. "It's painful to watch. It's like he's regressed to the first day Charlie brought him home—he only anticipates fear and pain. He behaves like a caged animal, even in a completely open field. There's no way anyone could safely run or ride him. I think he's beyond my ability to help right now."

Molly laid a comforting hand on Lilly's shoulder. Lilly took a moment to appreciate the love and warmth that radiated from her.

She's always so strong, Lilly thought. *She makes me feel like we can work through anything. I can't imagine a better mom, and I hope Jenny knows how lucky she is.*

"I know you're incredibly talented at helping troubled horses, Lilly. I know Storm loves and trusts you, and that you've helped him so much already. I think it's brave of you to recognize your fears and limitations. Do you know anyone whose advice you'd like to seek out? It might be good for Storm to get away from Shamrock for a few days while there's so much chaos, and it would be good for you to have someone with the strength and expertise to at least bounce ideas off."

"Cappie actually just mentioned a horseman he trusts, kind of like a *real* horse whisperer." Lilly smirked, silently acknowledging that she had also been called a horse whisperer on occasion. "He was going to call and see if he's available and willing to work with us. Of course, Charlie will ultimately decide what route we take, but I need to be certain before I advise her one way or another."

"I think we should continue to work with Storm here, he'll be fine in a few days," Hunter piped in.

Lilly was startled. She hadn't realized anyone else was in the room, but there he was, sitting at a card table off to a corner, partially obstructed by Molly. Lilly had been collegial to Hunter since his arrival, but there was something in his southern drawl and the way he looked at Charlie, even when Doug was present, that she just didn't like.

"It'll be even more traumatizing to load him into a horse trailer for a long ride, then abandon him with strangers to poke and prod at him," Hunter continued.

"Don't you have Doug's racehorses to worry about? Shouldn't you be at Laurel, overseeing their training?" Lilly asked, taking another bite of her sandwich.

"Been there, done that. The early bird gets the worm, and I finished up all the gallops prior to sunrise. We don't have any racing until the weekend. I figured I was needed here to help with the cleanup and with Storm," Hunter said between bites of his own sandwich.

Lilly bristled at his implication that he was important in Storm's care. She grimaced at Molly, and Molly gave her a sympathetic smile in return.

"I need to get back to the office and battle it out with more insurance reps," Molly said. "If you need to talk through anything, come find me."

"Thanks, Molly."

Lilly and Hunter both watched in silence as she left the barn.

"Heard anything more about the cause of the fire?" Hunter asked.

"Not my focus, right now I need to figure out Storm. Molly's got the fire covered," Lilly responded. She pushed her chair back. "Well, can't sit here chatting, got work to do. Gotta run."

"But, with Doug and Charlie not here, we need to work together to figure out what to do about Storm's training," Hunter called at her retreating back.

"We will be fine. You stick with your horses and I'll take care of mine," Lilly said brusquely over her shoulder as she left the lounge and escaped into the tack room next door.

She grabbed an exercise saddle, thinking, *Maybe walking around the track with a side pony will calm Storm's nerves. If not...well, hopefully getting in the tack will calm mine and give me the clarity I need before I call Charlie.*

The Coma

Charlie hung up the phone.

From the moment Doug had proposed, she'd felt as though she'd been thrown underwater. She'd reacted to everything—the fire, Storm's disappearance, the panic about Hershey, watching Doug run into the fire and then watching his prone body being dragged out and into the screaming ambulance—as though they were events occurring some distance away from herself. She'd experienced everything in the range of panic, but still felt oddly removed. She hadn't been able to come up for air yet.

Pull yourself together, she softly chastised herself once again.

Even the voice inside her head couldn't work up the energy to shout. She was lost in her own thoughts, but there were so many of them that she wasn't able to concentrate on a single one.

Who had just called? Right, Lilly. What had Lilly asked? Something about Storm. Oh! Storm had been found!

Charlie found herself smiling. *At least that was one good thing.* Lilly had asked her something else too, but Charlie hadn't been able to fully process it over the roar inside her own mind. *What was it?* Charlie shook her head to try and organize her thoughts.

Oh well. Lilly will take care of it.

What am I doing here? Charlie looked ahead at the well-lit snacks without comprehension. *Vending machine, right. I need to eat something.*

Unable to choose between the selections, she stared vacantly into the machine. She quickly got lost again in her own thoughts.

After being rushed to the hospital from the fire, Doug had been placed in a medically induced coma. The doctors were working to ascertain the full extent of the damage to his lungs from the smoke and to relieve the swelling in his brain from the concussion he'd sustained. Charlie waited, shuffling between rooms as he went in and out of MRIs and surgery and critical care. Sometimes those rooms were empty but for her; sometimes she was surrounded by strangers; and sometimes they held Doug's body, hooked up to machines and breathing tubes and IV bags. She felt an unbearable panic when he was not in the room, but a deep sense of dread when he was.

All those tubes…Peter had been hooked up to all those same tubes… watching the men I love in those webs of tubes is too much…

"Excuse me, Ms. Jenkins?"

The warm, gentle voice cut through all of the other noise in Charlie's head and broke her reverie. She turned around to face the person who had interrupted the never-ending dialogue in her head. It was one of the nurses she had seen frequently over the past two days. Charlie returned her smile with a small one of her own.

"There's an update on Mr. Walker I'd like to speak with you about, and you look like you should have a better meal than anything you'll get out of that machine. I'm finishing up my shift; how do you feel about joining me in the cafeteria?"

Charlie nodded appreciatively. "Yes, thank you. I…" she paused, then promptly lost the next half of her sentence.

The nurse patted her gently on the arm. "Just follow me."

Charlie trailed after the nurse silently, through the busy hallways, into a packed elevator, through the cafeteria line, and to a secluded table.

Once they'd gotten seated and settled, the nurse gave Charlie the update on Doug. "The swelling in his brain has gone down quite a bit, and the doctors are going to start bringing him out of the induced coma…"

Charlie shot out of her seat, her fork clattering to the table. "I need to be there when he wakes up!"

The nurse grabbed Charlie's hand kindly but firmly. "Please, Ms. Jenkins, let's finish our conversation and our meal first. Mr. Walker will still spend the next few days mostly unconscious; even after they bring him out of the coma, he will be on very heavy sedation."

Charlie sat back down and picked up her fork. "Please, call him Doug. 'Mr. Walker' or 'the patient' seem so formal and removed from the man I know. And call me Charlie."

The nurse smiled. "I can do that."

Charlie stared down at the fork in her hands, distracted again by her own thoughts. The nurse recognized the far-away expression on her face, and began an effort to focus Charlie's attention on something other than the negatives of Doug's situation.

"I recognized you from the articles in the paper about Genuine Storm, although I didn't put two and two together until I heard about the barn fire. You've got a lot of people praying and pulling for you." The nurse's expression turned serious as she continued, "Charlie, Doug is really going to need your help over the next few days. The human brain hates not knowing what's happening, and when people are put into medically induced comas, their brains spend all that time trying to figure it out and filling in the blanks as best they can. Between the trauma and the inability to understand, patients like Doug usually have very vivid nightmares and hallucinations."

The nurse went on, giving as much detail about the injuries as she was able, and answering all of Charlie's questions.

Charlie faltered over her last question, starting and stopping several times before she could get it out. "Will Doug…remember…me?"

The nurse clasped her hand. "Charlie, I know this is hard to hear, but none of us have any idea what Doug's memories or thought processes will be like yet. It's completely uncertain how much he'll remember about any part of his life, especially the night of the fire. What I can tell you is that, even if he doesn't remember it, the support you have given him in the hospital has been so, so important."

Charlie held her head with her hands, staring silently at the table. Finally, she looked back up at the nurse. Her expression had changed; she'd made up her mind and was beginning to gather her resolve.

"Okay, what can I do now?"

"I suggest that you spend as much time as possible near Doug, offering your love and support and talking to him. One of the most helpful things you can do is to keep a diary for him to read when he regains consciousness, to help him recover and piece together the time he has lost. It will be a great tool to help him sort out for himself which parts of the dreams that he had were real, and which were false memories. I think writing could also be very therapeutic for you, and I know Genuine Storm's fans are worried and would like updates. I don't think you realize how many people you've never even met are rooting for you and Doug and your horse."

"I guess the world already knows about the fire and Storm?" Charlie asked.

"Word travels fast," the nurse replied. "I follow your Facebook page, and there are lots of concerned fans out there."

Charlie and the nurse finished their salads and their coffee and chatted a little longer about Storm and the Belmont. When they got up to go their separate ways, Charlie hugged her and thanked her.

As Charlie sat back down by Doug's bedside, she felt more like herself than she had in several days. Underneath the familiar web of tubes, Doug looked to her more like he was asleep than teetering on the edge.

I can fight for him, and I can fight alongside him, she thought as she picked up her phone and started texting. *He's not alone in here, and neither am I. I have the most amazing family and friends; it's time to reach out.*

"Skylar—thank you for finding Storm and making sure Hershey got to the hospital safely. I'm so grateful and proud of your bravery!"

"Lilly—trust your judgement. I support whatever decision you make re: horse whisperer."

"Kate—There are still fires to put out, and I need you! I'm deputizing you on all of Storm's social media accounts. Grab Ryan and put him to work."

Charlie's fingers flew over her screen, providing her some level of peace and a sense of control.

"We're going to make it, Doug," she said aloud.

She worked for hours, jumping between her phone and her laptop as she got new notifications and had different thoughts. Nurses were in and out of the room, checking on Doug and asking if she'd seen any signs of movement. He slept on, but Charlie talked to him all through the day, giving him the updates she knew he'd want if he was awake.

Squeezing the bridge of her nose and closing her eyes for a moment, Charlie realized how tired she was. It wasn't a mystery why, when she considered it—she hadn't slept since before the fire. She was somewhere between forty-eight and seventy-two hours into one of the more eventful periods of her life.

"I'm going to close my eyes for just a few minutes now, Doug," she said, reaching out and softly touching his unburnt left hand, "but if you wake up, please wake me up too."

———————————

Hours later, a new noise jostled Charlie from her sleep. She jumped up from her dozing position in the hospital chair by Doug's bedside, entirely discombobulated.

Is he awake? Did he say something?

Her heart sank a little as she wiped the sleep from her eyes and got a better look at Doug, still fast asleep under the sedation. Her phone chirruped again, sending her a reminder of the voicemail notification waiting for her.

Many texts, one voicemail. She flipped through her texts quickly but found nothing urgent. Charlie looked back over at Doug, uncertain about leaving to make calls and listen to the voicemail now. She was afraid to leave the room for even a moment.

What if he wakes up and I miss it? What if he wakes up and thinks I've abandoned him?

Charlie forced herself to breathe deeply and contemplate the vulnerability she felt. It was a very particular, painful, and familiar feeling, one that she had sworn she'd erase from her life forever shortly after Peter had died.

This might just be the price of being in love.

Checking her missed call log, she realized the voicemail was from a number she didn't have saved in her phone. An unknown number could be anything, sure, but that "anything" included anything regarding her children.

That decides that, she thought as she kissed Doug lightly on the forehead and scurried out into the hall.

No matter what personal hellfire she had to crawl through, she would always make sure her kids were safe and taken care of. It was a promise she'd made to herself the last time she'd felt this vulnerable, and it had been one of the strongest threads she'd had to follow back to a place of stability. Peter's death had shaken her to her core, but even on the worst days, she had done everything within her power to be a strong mother.

Her heartbeat was pounding in her ears as she hit the voicemail icon on her cell phone, terrified by the possibility that Ryan or Skylar might be hurt or in trouble. Her racing mind was quickly eased, though. The voicemail was from Cappie, relaying the update he had received from New Bolton about Hershey.

As everyone had suspected, Hershey had been deeply affected by the fire. He had just started displaying the unmistakable symptoms of smoke inhalation damage—a constant cough and runny nose. The doctors had started him on intravenous respiratory drugs, and they were monitoring him closely for bacterial infections. Even so, they were cautiously optimistic that Hershey could be out of intensive recovery in approximately two weeks.

Charlie smiled gently as she finished listening to the voicemail. She realized how much her heart ached for her family, children and equines alike.

Everyone needs this good news, she thought, wondering if Cappie had already informed Skylar. *Well, if she doesn't know, I can tell her—and if she does, we can celebrate together.*

Charlie selected her daughter's name to call. She grew concerned again as the number of rings drew out.

A very sleepy-sounding Skylar picked up on the last possible one. "Mommm?"

Charlie was confused until she looked at the clock hanging in the hallway. *Five o'clock in the morning.*

She decided to save the news for later, when Skylar could fully enjoy it.

"Hey sweetheart, just missed your voice. I love you; call me back whenever you wake up for the day."

"Love you, too, Mom," the voice said, already shrinking back into sleep.

Charlie, realizing she'd have better luck reaching people in a few hours, ducked back into Doug's room and put her phone away.

Carefully considering the three pieces of happy, hopeful news the last few hours had brought her—that Storm had been found, that Doug was coming out of his coma, and that Hershey could be home in as little as two weeks—she opened her laptop. She needed to keep her mind in the game; Doug wouldn't forgive her if he woke up and she didn't know anything about anything, and if Storm was going to run in the Belmont with the same supporting fans that had helped him through the Derby and Preakness, she needed to engage again with the Storm Troopers.

She pulled up the Facebook page and read several of the well-meaning posts in support of Storm, Lilly, and the rest of the team.

They truly helped Charlie gain a new perspective. In her mind, the fire had nearly destroyed the possibility of winning the Triple Crown. Most of Storm's fans, though, didn't seem to see it as a deal-breaker. From so many outsiders' perspectives, the fire seemed like just one of the challenges that any fairytale hero inevitably faces and triumphs against in the end. Genuine Storm had already beaten impossible odds, time and time again, and his fans had a lot of faith that he'd beat them now too. Impossible wasn't a problem for Storm—it was where he excelled.

Charlie knew she needed to wait and speak with Kate and Ryan about their social media plan before she addressed any of the news and rumors swirling around, but she still wanted to leave the Troopers with a few thoughts. It was a way to thank them for the strength they'd given her. She considered some of the stories of adversity Triple Crown winners had faced that she knew of, and she searched out a few more stories. After reading through a couple, she began to write:

The View Behind the Starting Gate

Of the eleven Triple Crown winners to date, eight were born and raised in the bluegrass state of Kentucky. Of the three outsiders, two wound up being a couple of the most famous winners: Secretariat, born in Virginia, and Affirmed, born in Florida. The third was not only an outsider, he was a true dark horse. Known as "the Club-footed Comet," the little wonder who won the Crown in 1946 took it home to Texas, where he was born and raised.

No one would have bet on Assault making it to the Spring Classics. Sure, his bloodlines were incredible (his sire, Bold Venture, had won the 1937 Derby and Preakness, and the blood of Man O' War ran through his dam's veins), but Assault was small—barely 15.2 hands high. More critically, he was injured. As a young horse, Assault had stepped on a surveyor's stake, driving it through his front right hoof.

Were it not for his pedigree, he would probably have been euthanized. Instead, his owner let the tough Mexican cowboys on his Texas ranch work their magic on the injured colt. They believed in him, trained him hard, and outfitted him with a special shoe to bind the hoof together. When they were done, Assault still walked and trotted with a limp, but when he was in full gallop, he never took a misstep.

He won the Kentucky Derby by a then-record eight lengths, held on by a neck to win the Preakness, and stormed by the leaders to win the Belmont and the 1946 Triple Crown.

As Assault taught us and Storm has learned, sometimes life doesn't take the turns we plan for, but having the right team around can make all the difference.

Here's hoping our Virginia-bred Storm can be the next outsider success story!

Charlie hit submit and closed her laptop. She lifted her eyes to look at Doug and felt a thrill of excitement run through her blood. She was so thankful for this man, and the rest of the team that surrounded her as they moved through this crazy life together.

PART THREE

Dark Clouds

By the time Lilly woke up on Saturday morning, the air had shifted. Ominous clouds hung low overhead, though it wasn't scheduled to rain for days. Lilly found herself studying the sky anxiously as she tried to prepare Storm and get her own things ready for the trip. With everything else going on, she wouldn't risk hauling Storm in a trailer for hours through bad weather. Though the idea of being rained out for a day was stressful, she wished fervently that it would hurry up and happen. If it just rained, it could be over and done with, and she could move on. The anticipation was worse.

Lilly didn't have any trouble loading Storm into the trailer. He seemed to relish getting away from the barns, including the burnt-out shell of the one he had lived in.

"Want me to go with you?" Buck asked as he wrapped Lilly in a big hug.

Lilly let a little of her anxiety flow into him as she relaxed in his embrace. "No, I've got this and you've got your own rides to think about. He needs to try and forget the last few days, or at least come to terms with them."

"He will be fine, and from what Cappie tells me, this guy…what's his name?"

"Doc. Doc Murphy," Lilly said, her voice muffled by her head pressed against his chest.

"Yes, this Doc. What kind of name is that anyway? Wonder what his real name is," Buck said as he held her close. "He must be something else if Cappie is recommending him. But he's got nothing over you. Don't forget that."

Lilly hugged him tighter and didn't say a word.

"Well, Cappie swears this Doc-or-whatever-his-name-is is quite the horse whisperer. He better be. I have seen you work wonders with some of the hardest horses alive, Lilly. Not sure what else this guy could possibly have up his sleeve," Buck said.

"We've got to try, and time is running out. Gotta go." She squeezed him once more and kissed him deeply, then extracted herself from Buck's arms and hopped into the truck.

"I will keep you posted. Love you!" she called out as she slammed the door.

Buck stood and watched the truck roll down the driveway, uncertain what the next two weeks would hold for any of them.

By mid-afternoon, Charlie's best friend Kate had arrived at Shamrock. As a well-respected, seasoned journalist who had worked the White House for many years before she'd left to pursue her love of horses by writing for *Blood-Horse,* she understood media relations and how to handle the press in a crisis.

Kate had been on assignment on the West Coast when she had gotten Charlie's initial text about Doug and the fire from the hospital. After calling Ryan for every known detail, she'd booked a ticket home and spent the whole flight formulating a plan. When the plane landed at BWI Airport, she drove straight to the farm. She'd set up a full social media basecamp at the kitchen table in Molly and Steve's house within moments of arriving.

"We're a few days behind, so it's going to be a little tough, but our job now is to stay ahead of the storm—no pun intended," Kate explained to Ryan. "To be effective, our first step is going to be a two-pronged approach. I'm going to be compiling what's out there, what people are saying, and what we need to address. Once we know where we are, we'll have a better idea of how we should respond and what we can expect over the next few days."

Jenny, standing at the countertop, smiled at Kate's intensity as she talked about Twitter like it was a warzone. She raised an eyebrow at Ryan, but he didn't see it. He looked just as serious and intense.

Oh boy, she thought, putting on a fresh pot of coffee. *I may have lost him to the internet.*

"Start compiling a list of the information we might want to disseminate on all the social media outlets, from Facebook to Twitter to Instagram, and the information we might want to downplay or keep under wraps. I need to know the full extent of the material we're working with so I can craft a coherent narrative that won't fall apart at the first critical glance. I want the full backstory and a constant stream of updates from Molly about what the fire chief, investigators, and insurance adjusters are saying, from Steve about the care of the horses and the details of how the search for Storm was conducted, from Cappie about Hershey, from Lilly about Storm and the horse whisperer, and from Charlie about Doug," Kate instructed Ryan.

All the cell phones in the room chirruped at the same time, but Jenny was the first to pick hers up.

"Looks like we have our first good update of the day," Jenny said excitedly, scrolling through the long text. "Uncle Doug is still heavily sedated, but he was just briefly conscious for the first time since the fire! He's still got the breathing tube in, but your mom said he tried to smile at her and that he gave her hand a squeeze before he fell back asleep."

"That's excellent," Ryan said, smiling up at her.

"Yeah, and just think…"

"Be sure to clear with Molly how reports of injuries and medical updates could complicate anything insurance related," Kate said to Ryan as she scrolled down her screen, inadvertently cutting Jenny off.

Jenny realized that Ryan was already back to staring at his screen too, totally caught up. She sighed and left them to it.

Ryan and Kate sat side-by-side with their laptops for hours, their fingers working feverishly, bantering back and forth about what they found on the internet. Every corner, from Storm's own official pages to racing forums and social media was humming—mostly with sympathy and prayers from the fans, but doused with a concerning amount of misinformation, half-truths, and blatant lies.

"I can't understand how the fire was reported on so fast," Ryan commented, taking a sip of his Coke.

Kate's eyes never left her screen. "With all the police scanners that people monitor, information has a way of being reported just by the innocent bystander. The problem is, they don't usually get all the details right. Take, for instance, this tweet...*Shamrock Hill Farm burned to the ground, all horses dead*...not true, or this one, *Greystone Stables goes up in flames...* wrong farm..." Kate hesitated as she squinted at her screen, her reading glasses perched on the tip of her nose.

"What?" Ryan asked, "What did you find?"

"An article by an Amanda Ault for *The Baltimore Herald—Shamrock Hill Farm Loses Main Barn—and Triple Crown Contender, Genuine Storm. Fire Chief Suspects Arson.* Seems a little too on the nose, and came out within hours of the fire. Here's another one from Thursday, *Storm Chasing,* all about the search for Storm, which was updated within an hour of Storm being found, according to your timeline," Kate said, tapping on the printed sheet Ryan had provided her.

"Oh, I've actually already seen that one. Jenny read it to me because she was upset about how she was portrayed for scaring Storm away from the barn. The reporter really did have a creepy amount of detail, now that I think about it," Ryan said thoughtfully.

"Here's one from yesterday, *Off the Radar,* in which she reports that Storm has been sent to a horse whisperer for behavioral issues," Kate said, still scanning the page. "Have you seen a reporter snooping around?"

Ryan shook his head. "No, but there has been a lot of activity since the fire, a lot of new faces in and out." He raised his eyebrow as something dawned on him. "So...the only thing she's been wrong about so far is when Storm left for Doc's? And that was because she managed to report it before it even happened?"

"Right. Well, technically right. All her facts are close to being accurate, but there's an undercurrent here I don't like at all. She's managed to make it look like Shamrock is full of people hiding things and lying."

"Well," Ryan grimaced, "we haven't exactly been forthcoming about a lot since Wednesday..."

"Sure, but there's a big difference between keeping private and lying. No one owes everyone every single detail of their lives. Like, here, in *Off the Radar,* she notes that Doug had no say in Storm's unorthodox treatment, which, while true, isn't the whole story. We don't owe people the detail that Doug's been in a coma, but it would definitely change the narrative. In fact, we owe it to Doug to keep his medical information private until he chooses what parts of that he would like to make public. We have to carefully tell people the story in the positive light we believe it should be portrayed in while respecting everyone's privacy and avoiding lying."

Ryan nodded. "I get it, but I see how it gets complicated quickly. I'm really glad Mom brought you in to lead."

"It gets more complicated when there's a reporter like Amanda around, trying to get the juiciest story, regardless of who it ends up hurting or how misleading it becomes. This is just strange, because she wrote a bunch of articles about Storm before the fire, but they're all pretty basic—some human-interest pieces and race reports, and it even looks like she may have cribbed the race reports from turf reporters and the official press releases." Kate paused and thought for a moment. "So, what happened the night of the fire that made her veer towards sensationalism?"

She scanned the reporter's page again, then clicked on the masthead. Her jaw dropped. "Oh my. I think I've got at least a few of the answers."

Ryan waited patiently while Kate quickly typed something into the comment field underneath Amanda's most recent article.

Kate looked up at him after she pressed submit. "Well, I imagine we'll know pretty soon, but..."

Her phone rang, cutting off her sentence. She looked at the screen and sighed.

"Looks like I have her editor on the line."

———————————

Amanda's phone just kept ringing. No matter how many pillows she held over her head, she couldn't block the noise. She reached her hand from under the covers and grabbed at the patch of floor until she found where her phone had dropped in the middle of the night. Seeing the newspaper office number on her screen, she panicked.

I've slept through my alarm, I'm late for work, I'm going to get fired— worse, I'm going to be taken off the Storm story and demoted to organizing the classifieds.

She answered the phone in the most clear, professional voice she could muster. "Good morning, Amanda Ault speaking."

"It's just barely morning," her boss growled. "Where in the world are you?"

Amanda hesitated and considered lying. *I could say I'm pulling permits at city council and get off the hook, no questions asked.*

She scowled at her reflection, knowing she wouldn't do it, then admitted the truth. "Just getting out of bed. I stayed up too long last night, researching barn fires and arson."

"Got anything?" her boss asked, curious and excited.

"Some questions I need to ask, for starters."

Her boss grunted. "Well, let me know what you come up with. I'll print anything short of wild conjecture."

"Because of journalistic integrity?"

Thankfully her boss didn't seem to hear her sarcastic reply. His voice was muffled and distracted. "Hey, I'm going to start a conference call. Stay on the line and don't say a word."

Amanda put her phone on speaker and muted it, laying it down on the kitchen counter so she could make coffee.

How much can I possibly miss if I turn on the grinder? she wondered.

Before she had a chance, a woman's voice answered.

"Hi Kevin, what do you need?"

Amanda smiled; this lady had clearly worked with her editor before.

"Hello, Kate," he replied. "Just calling to catch up. It's been too long. How's the husband? How're your kids?"

"Never married, no kids."

"Cool, cool. Now that we're all current, you don't happen to be anywhere close to Shamrock Hill Farm, right?"

"*Are* we all caught up, Kevin? I don't think I've made your Christmas card list in a while. Still at *The Washington Post?* You know, I heard the craziest story a few years back about some schmuck who managed to tank himself all the way back to the minor leagues..."

"Well, you'll have to fill me in on all the gory details after we go bowling or catch a movie. Unrelated, I happened to be perusing the comments on our article about the Shamrock arson. Your fingerprints are all over one of them, Kate."

Amanda poured herself a bowl of cereal and fired up her laptop to read the offending comment while they continued bickering. There were a number of comments underneath her article, but only one from Shamrock: "For full, factual coverage, please visit our social media accounts, website, and blog directly @..."

Cool, Amanda thought, admiring the move.

"Well, Kevin, I do need to go. I'm actually the liaison right now for a friend who has a very exclusive, very sought-after story, and I just have *so many* privately held details to sort through before I choose the news organizations we'll be granting interviews to. Hey, Gal Friday?"

Busted.

Amanda blushed, hesitated for a moment, then took herself off mute. "Yes?"

"Your boss hasn't changed his game much since I was his much-maligned cub reporter. Don't let him use your name to further his agenda," Kate said. "I know it's easy right now for him to convince you that the number of eyeballs on your work is the most important thing in the world, but the necks you step on are all attached to people with names and long memories. Now, you two have a great day. If the word 'Shamrock' comes out of your mouths in the next forty-eight hours, I'll press a lawsuit so frivolous and time-consuming that you won't have time to write even about the weather."

Kate hung up.

"Whoa. She's...awesome. And terrifying," Amanda said. "How did you know that comment was from her?"

Her boss scoffed. "Not the first time she's tried to cut me out of a great scoop. There was a minute or two, way back in the day, that I could count on some variation of that comment on every one of my articles. Like the form letter from hell."

"What's it like to be so universally adored?" Amanda asked, laughing.

"Get into the office, now," Kevin growled. "We need to figure out a game plan. We're going to install you as a permanent fixture at Shamrock."

Kevin hung up the phone without waiting for a response, as Amanda dumped her cereal into the sink.

A figure slunk around one of Shamrock's smaller barns, coming to a full stop in the darkest corner and looking around furtively. It was suspicious enough to put any observer on high alert, but everyone was far too busy taking care of all of the other issues facing the farm to notice.

The figure jumped at a shrill, sudden ring, then quickly withdrew the offending cell phone from a pocket and swatted it nervously to silence. Slumping against the dark wall, the figure gingerly placed that phone back into the pocket it had come from, and withdrew another from a different pocket. The new phone had only one number stored in it, but the figure still hesitated before choosing it, as though wishing for other options.

The man's voice on the other end of the line was oily and unpleasant as he answered, barking out, "Well?"

"The job is done. It got messy, but Storm won't race," the figure whispered.

"Well, I'm going to need more than your good word, now won't I?" the man sneered. "Is he dead?"

"He's not dead, but, between the smoke and the fear, no one could run that horse—not in two years, much less two weeks. Storm will never race again, I'd bet my life on it."

A snicker echoed through the speaker, and the figure put a hand over the phone to muffle the noise.

"Well, you already have bet your life on it, haven't you?" the man said nastily. "I already know how bad at gambling you are, though, and there's no reason for me to expect this is any different. Find a way to confirm it, and we'll settle your debts. If I find out you're lying to me…"

Hanging up the phone, the figure slumped back over against the barn, hoping fervently that Storm would truly not be able to race.

The Valley

The two-hour drive to Pine Grove, Pennsylvania, seemed to pass in a flash. Lilly was in a fog, processing the details of the last forty-eight hours— the fire, Doug in the hospital, and now Storm a mental mess.

How on earth is he going to be ready to race in fourteen days? Cappie says this Doc guy is a miracle worker, but from the mental state Storm seems to be in, it's going to take more than a miracle to get him through this.

Lilly gently pressed on the brakes as she took the ramp that would lead them to Doc Murphy's farm. She drove by small stand-alone diners, an occasional gas station, and farm after farm with barb wire fencing and trailer homes. The buildings became more sporadic and the farms larger; herds of cows grazed in the distance. She glanced at her phone, hoping she was still connected to the internet and her Google Maps app. The last thing she needed right now was to get lost.

After another five miles, she turned left onto Perry Lane. Her map told her that this road would dead end at the farm in another five miles. It was certainly narrow enough to function as a five-mile driveway. Lilly was more relieved than ever that Storm was a good traveler, and that the trailer behind the truck had been an easy pull for the whole ride. Horses that aren't good on the road can shake the trailer all over the place. It's never fun to look in the side mirror and see the top of the trailer swaying back and forth, but it would be even more nerve-wracking now. Perry Lane was not really wide enough to comfortably fit two cars abreast, and it had no center or side lines. Lilly took it slowly, in case another vehicle approached her from the other direction.

At two miles out, the road transitioned from asphalt to gravel and she noted a sign that read "End of State Maintenance."

Oh great, Lilly thought, as she tightened her grip on the steering wheel, *I am really in the boonies here.*

As she drove slowly around a curve, the trees on both sides of the road fell away and a massive farm came into view. Lilly slowed the trailer to a stop so she could take in the breathtaking view.

From this vantage point, she could tell she was at the top of a valley; she saw the road ahead weave down between fields where large herds of cows monitored their calves, ending at the doorstep of a modest, one-story ranch. There was no grand entrance, no large mansion or barn, and unless you were looking for it, you would have no idea it existed at all, as the forest encased it on all sides. The farm wasn't grandiose, but it was undeniably beautiful.

Lilly put the truck back into drive and slowly made her way down into the valley, taking in the more minute details of the things she'd admired from the panoramic view. She noticed as she got closer that the farmhouse was modest, but impeccably maintained. It was perfectly framed by several towering oak trees, and a tire swing hung from one of the branches. She hesitated as she reached a fork in the road that hadn't revealed itself from above, unsure whether she should go towards the house or continue on to what looked like the barn a little ways further.

The decision was made for her as the screen door of the house swung open. Two large black Labrador Retrievers came bounding out first, followed by a three-legged Chihuahua doing his best to keep up with his larger buddies. Behind the dogs was a man who Lilly could only describe as an authentic cowboy, hat, big belt buckle and all.

He tipped his black hat at her as he approached the open window of her truck. "Ma'am."

Lilly offered her hand out the window. "Lilly. Cappie said you would be expecting us."

"Yep, he called this morning," the cowboy replied, shaking her hand.

Lilly waited for more, but as the pause dragged on, she realized there was nothing else coming. She was at a bit of a loss for what to say next.

This is a man of few words.

"Ah, should I drive to the barn?" she asked.

"Nope. Let's see what we are dealing with here. Not sure I can help, so we shouldn't get anyone too comfortable," the cowboy said.

Lilly was surprised. "But Cappie said...I was under the impression that you work with problem horses, ah, Mr..."

"You can call me Doc," the cowboy said, watching Lilly closely. "And just because I can work with a horse doesn't mean he will want to work with me."

Lilly opened the door to the truck and got out, realizing too late that she should have stayed in the cab. Even standing on her tiptoes in her boots, she had lost the element of height. This cowboy stood at least six and a half feet tall, towering above her as much as the big oak trees that swayed behind him.

"Well, mister...Doc, we have nowhere else to go and this horse needs to be ready to run in the Belmont Stakes in two weeks."

"Needs? Or wants? And who needs or wants him to race?" Doc said, as he walked towards the back of the trailer.

Lilly followed him, but stopped short as she listened to him start to whistle softly. He walked around the vehicle once. Stopping by the side ramp of the gooseneck trailer, he leaned against it and continued whistling.

"Do you want me to get him out for you?" Lilly asked, quietly and curiously.

Doc ignored her and just kept whistling. Storm let out a long whinny and Lilly could hear his impatient pawing inside. Doc didn't move.

Lilly took a step towards the doors, starting to worry about Storm as he continued his pawing and calling inside the trailer. Doc shot her a look that stopped her in her tracks—not a mean one, somehow, just a clear one.

Storm soon stopped his pawing, and after a few minutes, Doc undid the latch and lowered the ramp, quickly and smoothly and without ever pausing his whistling. Storm poked his head out the door, taking in the sights and sounds of this new environment.

Well, he certainly knows he is not at the racetrack, Lilly thought to herself.

She watched as Doc went up the ramp and into the trailer, walking along the empty spot next to Storm and running his hands along Storm's back.

No, Lilly realized, looking closer. He wasn't actually touching Storm; his hands hovered above his back.

Great, Lilly thought, exasperated, *he's giving Storm a Reiki massage. Have I wasted everyone's time by bringing Storm here?*

Storm's attention alternated between the man next to him and Lilly, who was still standing outside the trailer. Lilly was surprised to notice Storm begin to relax. He blew out his nose, his head dropped a bit, and he shifted his weight to lean towards Doc and his whistling.

Doc slowly unsnapped the trailer ties from his halter and attached a rope that Lilly hadn't previously noticed he was carrying. He walked slowly to the front of Storm, encouraging him to follow along with his hands and whistle.

Storm readily walked out of the trailer stall and down the ramp, but upon reaching the firm ground, Storm broke out of his lulled trance and circled nervously around Doc. Doc allowed the rope to run through his hand until Storm reached the end of it, about thirty feet away. Storm would stop and stare into the far fields, and then take off into a gallop around Doc, bucking and kicking out. Upon seeing or smelling something new, he would stop again and raise himself into a half-rear before taking off again.

Lilly instinctively moved to help, but Doc waved her off with a shake of his head. He allowed Storm to continue to circle him, keeping his head focused and turned towards the horse. He moved the rope from one hand to the other, following Storm's movements in rhythm, and his whistling became a soft murmur. Lilly listened hard, but she couldn't make out what he was saying.

Storm finally came to a stop, sweat dripping from his chest and flanks, but every fiber of his body was still on high alert.

"Lilly, please open the gate to that small paddock behind me," Doc said, motioning with his head.

The horse whisperer walked slowly towards Storm, who was heaving with anxiety.

"That's enough for now, Big Grey. Let's get you some water and hay."

Without pulling on the lead rope, Storm readily followed Doc through the open gate. Doc unclipped the shank and closed the gate behind him. Storm stood, rigid and still, looking at Lilly and Doc for a few tense minutes. Once he seemed to decide that he wasn't going anywhere, he let out a big sigh through his nose and slowly walked towards the water trough.

An Odd Call

Lilly appreciated the light dinner, a white flaky fish that Doc had cooked over an open flame in the back of his house, along with a fresh salad that she suspected had been collected from the vegetable garden she had seen driving in.

She hadn't noticed the small building a bit removed from the barn and house, but it was certainly cozy. A twin bed, kitchenette, and bathroom was all it consisted of, but it was decorated with a female's touch. There were curtains on the windows, magazines on the table, and a vase with fake flowers on the counter.

She had laughed out loud when Doc had pointed to the phone attached to the wall, a long cord connecting the handset to the base.

"Down here in the valley, your fancy cell phone won't work," Doc had told her. Lilly had pulled the cell phone out of her back pocket; sure enough, no satellite bars registered.

"Crap," she said. "How am I to update Charlie?"

"Old school," Doc smirked, gesturing at the old phone. "You know how to punch in a phone number?"

Lilly looked at the faceplate of the base with twelve raised buttons, then swallowed her annoyance and let out a sigh very similar to the one she had witnessed Storm exhale earlier.

"Yes, thank you, I will be fine. And thank you for dinner. What time will you start working with Storm in the morning?"

"When he tells me he's ready," Doc replied. "Have a good night, Ms. Garrett."

He tilted his head, touched the brim of his hat, and walked out the door, closing it quietly behind him.

Lilly picked the receiver off the wall and started to punch in buttons. She hesitated, realizing she couldn't recall Buck's number off the top of her head. He was listed in her favorites on her cell phone and she always just hit his name. *Ugh,* she thought, pulling up her contacts and hitting the appropriate buttons on the ancient phone that was now her only mode of communication to the real world.

"Hello?" came the hesitant voice on the other end.

"Buck, it's me. Sorry you probably don't recognize the phone number, as I am using the land line here. No cell service or WiFi. It certainly has been an interesting day..." Lilly launched into sharing the details of her drive and observations from her first interaction with the horse whisperer.

"He didn't do much with Storm, except to let him run around him in circles for a bit. I hope tomorrow he works his magic a bit faster. Time is not on our side."

"Well, I'm sure—"

"He barely said two words at dinner," Lilly said, cutting off Buck without noticing as she wandered around, examining her room as far as the phone line tether allowed. "But, I will say, I have never had a better tasting piece of fish. There are definitely some female touches around that surprise me. Is he married? Can you ask Cappie?"

"I will see him in the morning at the track, so I will try and ask him," Buck replied, "But why don't you just text him?"

"No cell service, remember?" Lilly chided, balancing the ancient phone receiver against her ear. It was heavy, but not nearly as heavy as her eyelids, which had started to droop and close. "Okay, so I am feeling pretty exhausted from the long day and drive, I am going to head to bed. Talk to you tomorrow?"

"Ah, sure, I am glad you made it there safely, Lil," Buck said.

He waited a moment, but didn't hear a reply. "Lilly?"

"Yeah, I am here, but falling asleep. Talk tomorrow," Lilly's voice sounded far away.

"Sure, love you," Buck told her, but the line was dead. She had already hung up.

Buck looked at the dark screen of his phone, trying to push away the feeling he'd been neglected, to keep his mind off the fact that Lilly hadn't asked one question about how he was doing—or anyone else, for that matter.

The Tour

Amanda pulled up in front of Shamrock and gave the Sunday newspaper in the passenger seat a good last glare. Despite the fact that there'd been more interest shown for her article about the Shamrock fire than in anything else the paper had posted in the past week, it was the sportswriter's byline about the upcoming game between the Baltimore Orioles and the Washington Nationals that screamed across the front page.

"Get me more good details, I'll give you prime real estate," Kevin had said, shrugging off her indignation when she'd learned he'd rejected her latest piece.

Sure, it had been more rehashed conjecture, but she'd had nothing else to offer. Kate had been true to her word: Amanda hadn't gotten a peep from Shamrock since the veteran reporter had arrived.

If Kevin was relying on this headline to give me a spurt of motivation, Amanda thought, *he doesn't know me at all. I'm never lacking motivation.*

She'd gone to bed scheming for a way to get past Kate's defenses, and woken up still scheming. Devising and rejecting plot after plot through a very long shower, Amanda discovered the answer had been delivered directly to her doorstep.

Stepping out of her car, she admired her lower legs, now encased in the new tall leather cowboy boots she'd found waiting, and she grinned as she re-read the card that had been attached: "Angel, you're going to have to wait for that hand-painted pair, but these should save us both some embarrassment in the meantime. Why don't you c'mon by today and show them off? I'll give you a tour of the grounds."

The card hadn't been signed, but she'd had no doubts about who it was from.

"What took you so long?" she asked, as she stepped into the closest barn, where Hunter had said he'd be. She found him inspecting the walls in the long, narrow room, which were covered in various saddles and bits of leather and metal Amanda couldn't identify.

"Had to finish up my races for the weekend, darlin'," Hunter drawled, turning around to flash her his mega-watt grin. "Can't earn my keep giving out tours to the local troublemakers, no matter how cute they are."

"Speaking of making trouble, you sure this isn't going to make too much for you?" Amanda asked as they left the barn and set out to explore the rest of the property. "I believe Kate has made speaking with me a capital offense."

Hunter scoffed good-naturedly. "Don't you worry about Kate. We went to college together. I minored in how to handle Kate, given that she was attached at the hip to Charlie back in the day. This is an opportunity to educate the press. No way would Kate want me to turn this down."

Amanda raised her eyebrows and smirked, knowing this educational tour was nowhere near what Kate would allow.

She quickly discovered that Hunter was not only good company, he was a good tour guide, explaining the purpose and role of each person, building, and enclosure they passed. Amanda picked up more information about the business of raising racehorses during the afternoon with him than she had in a month of frantic Google searches, and had a lot of fun doing it.

As they passed a paddock with several horses lazily grazing on the rich green grass, Amanda expressed surprise that they'd bounced back so quickly after the fire: "I really thought, after seeing them the night of the fire, that they would be quivering messes for a while."

Hunter smiled. "Yeah, those guys are doing well. We got them out before they could sustain major smoke inhalation damage, and luckily no one got hurt or trampled in the confusion. Now we just need to monitor them and make sure they rest and relax for a few weeks. They're essentially on a horse spa retreat."

"You know, when I first was assigned to Storm, I thought for sure I could turn it into some whistleblower piece on how brutal this industry is…I'm pretty shocked how well the horses are being treated. I just assumed that a horse who couldn't be ridden or sold or anything would be discarded. Treating them like they're at a spa for a few weeks when they can't bring in any money just doesn't track with what I'd heard about the cutthroat world of competitive racing."

Hunter gave her a very serious, direct look. "Sorry we disappointed you by not being cutthroat killers?"

Amanda stopped suddenly and, wondering whether the day was about to be suddenly cut short, raised her hand. "Hey, no offense. I tend to blurt out what's on my mind at any given time."

Hunter's expression changed, and he grinned broadly at her. "No offense taken. I'm just messin' with ya. There are definitely some nasty parts to the trade, and when things get dirty, they're pretty scandalous. Horseracing is just like any other business, though—there are some unscrupulous people out here, but they shouldn't be the barometer the rest of us are judged by."

"How did you get involved?'

"Oh, gosh, I grew up on racetracks. Racing used to be a lot bigger—the sport of kings. The market has shrunk considerably, and also gotten much more competitive, so those of us still around tend to have been born into this world, one way or another."

"That makes sense. You'd certainly have a tactical advantage over someone like me, just learning the basics when I'm already an adult."

Hunter laughed. "That's very true. It's in my blood—I was definitely hanging out around race horses before I could walk or talk. I've broke them, rode them, and slept alongside 'em since I was a boy. My parents were in the horse trading business. The fancy word in today's market is pinhooking, but it boils down to buying and selling horses for profit."

Hunter shared more as they continued their walk. "I was determined not to stay in that stable all my life. Swore I didn't want a thing to do, professionally, with horses. I decided to major in finance when I got to college."

"Where you met Charlie and Peter and Kate?" Amanda asked, piecing together solid information and timelines from the many stories he'd told throughout the day.

"You got it. Turned out that I hated being away from horses on a daily basis, though. It took me two years to get horse-sick enough to drop out. My parents weren't too happy, but they were pleased when I offered to utilize what I had learned at college to help grow their business."

"Where were you located?"

"Oh, that was one of the nicest parts. I've always had a travel bug, and pinhooking was a good excuse. I convinced my parents to send me to auctions all over the country, from California to Kentucky to Florida and Maryland. I even went over to Europe to evaluate horses at the top auctions in the world. It was a high-risk business, and some of my moves were risky even by those standards, so I occasionally found myself in a bit of trouble, but rarely something I couldn't talk myself out of."

"What kind of trouble?" Amanda interjected, mesmerized by his story.

"Oh, nothing to worry yourself over," Hunter replied, taking her hand. "Just, every so often, I would lose too much or piss off the wrong person, and I'd have to try my hand at something else for a few weeks until the skies cleared up. But I will tell you, nothing competes with the thrill of seeing the bids for a horse that you own going up over hundreds of thousands of dollars. I had a pinhook that I bought for one of my clients for $7,500 and he sold eight months later for $150,000."

"How does that happen?" Amanda asked incredulously.

"Luck, some skill, and a good feel for it. I pride myself on seeing potential that others overlook," Hunter said. "This little colt was gangly, had a few confirmation issues, and had a thick winter coat on him in February, but by the fall he had grown into himself, shed out his baby coat and shined right up. He had a good head on his shoulders and showed really well to potential buyers. There was lot of competition for him, which drove up the price as well. No idea if he would turn out to be a runner, but my job was to just to get the best return possible for my owners."

"Is making that kind of money normal?" Amanda asked.

"Oh, it's a high-risk industry. You can win big, but you can also lose big. Horses have an uncanny ability to get hurt, even die, just when you need them most. You have to be able to stomach situations where you invest in a horse and it gets injured and doesn't make it to the sales ring. Or it doesn't blossom into what you thought it would be, so you have to decide if you should sell it at a loss just to get it off the books or race it yourself, hoping just to get back what you put in. Keep in mind, you are dealing with an animal with a mind of its own. It's not like car auctions, where you can make an antique lemon look pretty with a new paint job or replace an engine."

"So why get out?"

"My dad got sick and Mom needed help taking care of him. I was also getting tired of the travel and living out of hotels. We moved Dad to sunny Florida, which is where he wanted to spend the time he had left," Hunter said, getting more somber and subdued as he recounted that period. He paused for a moment before quietly saying, "The Big C, you know. Same hell of a disease that took Peter."

Amanda stayed respectfully silent, letting the man take a moment to remember his father and best friend. After a few seconds, he shook his head a little and met her eyes, forcing his mouth into a small, hurt, crooked smile.

"Anyways, after Dad passed, I didn't want to leave my mom, so I hooked up with a few folks I had met who worked out of Gulfstream Park, just north of Miami. That's where I met Doug. He was impressed enough with a few of the horses I had been training that he offered to send me a few of his own. The rest is history. Been working for Doug for two years now, and didn't know the Charlie he had mentioned to me was the Charlie I'd known in college until I came back up north a few weeks ago. Totally small world," he concluded.

Amanda smirked. "You're lucky. I've yet to find a friendly face around here; may as well have moved from the moon."

"Really? You're not from around here? Could have fooled me," Hunter laughed. In a stage whisper, he added, "Not many places and not much opportunity to wear some of those get-ups I've seen you in. You look a little fancy for these parts."

Amanda laughed appreciatively. "If you would have told me when I graduated from my journalism program that I'd wind up in a town with more fields than sidewalks, I would have laughed you out of the room."

"So how did you end up down here? Just a pit stop on your way to bigger and better things?"

"Not exactly. When I was a kid, I dreamt of being an investigative journalist—chasing stories, meeting with undisclosed sources, cracking mysteries wide open, the whole bit. Like racing, though, newspapers have seen better days. When I got out of school, I was supposed to beg to do a few years of unpaid internships, doing nothing but fact-checking and fluff pieces. I should have felt lucky when I landed an internship with a small fashion magazine, but I just felt impatient. The fashion world has plenty of scandals to uncover, but I wasn't anywhere close to those, and I realized it would be many, many years before I was."

"When *The Baltimore Herald* advertised their reporter position, someone forwarded it to my graduate listserv, bemoaning the good old days. It seemed like something out of a time capsule—a job that paid decently with flexibility across beats and real full-career potential. I guess I had stars in my eyes; where most of my colleagues just saw a sleepy newspaper and a dead-end gig, I loved the idea of being the biggest fish in a small pond. I applied on a whim, and I couldn't believe that I was interviewed and got the job offer. My editor seemed to like the idea of bringing in a fresh perspective and new energy, although I think he's second guessing himself now."

"Don't you miss the big city excitement? What about your family, your friends?"

Amanda shrugged, deflecting the more personal questions. "It seemed like I would have the freedom to chase the stories I wanted, even if there would be less to chase. Turns out, though, that when no one trusts you, no one wants to share the scoop. My only successful stories so far have been my pieces on Storm, which, given his meteoric rise, were bound to capture everyone's attention anyways."

"Don't knock being in the right place at the right time," cautioned Hunter. "From what I can tell, that accounts for much more success than most people realize."

"It might sound awful, but I was really hoping the drama with the fire and Storm was going to be bigger, that I'd be able to get a few more stories out of this. From the official Shamrock Twitter and website and the Storm Trooper message boards and Charlie's blog, it sounds like everything is going to be fine, that Storm hasn't skipped a single beat."

Hunter whistled and shook his head. "Are they really saying that?" He shook his head again. "Amazing what people think is true just 'cause they read it, right?"

Amanda's eyes got huge. "You can't just put that out there and not give me details! What do you mean?" She leaned in flirtatiously. "I mean, you could be that undisclosed source I've been dreaming of all these years."

Hunter laughed a little awkwardly and scratched his head. "Well, let me think about that. For now, all I'll say is that those horses in the paddock? They were in the exact same fire as Storm. They look good, but I wouldn't race one of them if my life depended on it—it could mess up, even kill, the poor horse. In Storm's case, though, I can see how tough it would be to bench him—he'll never have the chance to win the Triple Crown again, and he's so close."

The wheels in Amanda's head were visibly turning as she processed through that information. She was charmed by Hunter and flattered by how quickly he'd taken her into his confidence.

His phone chirped with an incoming text message before either of them could speak again. He read it silently, then looked back up at Amanda.

"I need to go help out with a few things. Thanks for coming out today, I've had a great time."

"Thank you, you have no idea how invaluable this has been to me. I'm going to have a lot of ideas to follow up on and toss by you. How about you let me take you to dinner later in the week?"

"Absolutely," he replied, grinning broadly at her as he turned to walk away.

He only got a few steps before he turned back.

"Hey, listen, you should probably just ignore anything I said about Storm. I'm sure I'm just worried for nothing…but since you are kind of at a dead end for information and I'd like to help you out, you should check out Doc Murphy up in Pennsylvania. Town called Pine Grove, I think. After all, you're Storm's best reporter."

Hunter walked off for real this time, thinking, *Lilly can handle herself if the reporter comes callin', and I just got credit for doing a good deed in Amanda's book.*

Amanda thought about what Hunter had said as she made her way back to her car. She walked past the little convertible and approached the paddock fence, watching the horses graze and enjoy themselves.

There were four kids and two dogs in the paddock now too. The two younger children were loping back and forth, chasing each other and the dogs, playing some game Amanda couldn't decipher. The two teenagers sat in the grass nearby, deep in conversation. Amanda noticed the cast on the girl's leg, and wondered whether the injury had been sustained in the fire.

Mmm, probably not—that's probably Jenny, Amanda thought, quickly thinking through the cast of characters. *There's Skylar and Ryan…but not sure who the younger boy is.*

The reporter pulled herself up and perched on the fence to enjoy the scene for just a bit longer, quickly getting lost in her own thoughts.

Imagine growing up like this, surrounded by this farm, these beautiful animals. It would feel like being in a fairytale. I could get used to this, Amanda thought.

She continued to watch from afar. *The kids are so comfortable with these huge animals that they're sitting where the horses could trample them, and running around where the horses could...catch them?* Amanda shook her head, watching the two younger kids play a very intricate version of tag with them, realizing how very little she still knew about the equine world.

Her phone rang and, as she shifted to fish it out of her back pocket, she lost her balance and fell backwards off the fence, hitting the ground hard.

I can't breathe, I can't breathe, I can't breathe, she thought in a panicked loop as she struggled to gasp. Her vision started to close in on the sides until there was nothing left but a small pinprick of light. *The ground is swallowing me.*

"Hey, miss, are you okay?"

Amanda heard the voice as though it was a million miles away. Then her face was being struck by wet lashes on both sides.

Can horses eat people?

The gasp she'd been waiting for finally came, and the light rushed back in so quickly that all she saw for a moment was a kaleidoscope of brown and black fur and two long pink whips.

"Ahhhhhrrrghhh!" she shouted.

She thrashed wildly, but the dogs were faster than her arms and legs. They bounced backwards, two different pitches of excited barking playing off each other.

"Miss, you seem to be okay. Just relax, you got the wind knocked out of you."

Amanda looked at the teenage boy and the two younger children flanking him, unable to form words quite yet. She watched in a daze as the fourth child, the teenage girl, made her way across the field and climbed over the fence—more gracefully than Amanda had, despite the cast on her leg.

"Are you okay?" the younger girl asked again.

Amanda moved her arms and legs, sitting up slowly and gathering her returning breath to answer, "Yes, I think so."

The kids looked back and forth at each other, trying to decide what they needed to do. Looking behind her, three of the faces looked suddenly relieved; only the little boy looked more anxious.

"I've got this, kids. I'll follow up with you all in sec," a somber baritone voice commanded, still some distance away.

Amanda watched as the two teenagers and younger girl turned and quickly marched off, with one of the dogs trailing behind them. The boy gave a small wave, like a salute, to the person Amanda knew would soon be standing behind her, then gestured to his dog and followed the others swiftly. They resumed their incomprehensible game before they'd even made it halfway back across the field.

Travis walked over in front of her and offered her a hand, which she begrudgingly accepted.

"I knew you sounded familiar," she said, sighing. She waited for the lecture she'd learned to expect already from the fire chief.

Travis looked away, gesturing with his chin at the two younger children playing their game of tag in the field beyond. "Looks like you understand dogs, horses, and children as well as you understand following the law and not being a pest."

Amanda rolled her eyes, attempting to hide how badly he'd stung her pride. "Oh sure, I bet you're just fantastic with kids. They must really respond to your natural warmth, your overwhelming friendliness." She tried to dust herself off, but just succeeded in spreading the mud on her jeans around a little more. "Like, if you were a dad, you'd have the house none of the other kids would want to play at, because they'd never know when you'd walk into the room and suck all the fun out of it."

Travis looked at her with unexpectedly sad eyes. She noticed an ever-so-slight drop in his firm stance. He shifted his gaze back to the kids in the field.

"So, you've already met my son, Drew. And my dog, Buster. I don't have a horse, but if you'd like to insult my mother or something, don't let me stop you. You're on a roll."

Amanda opened and closed her mouth several times, searching for words that would not form. She stopped and they both stared off at the children and their dogs for a moment in silence.

"You know what?" Amanda took a deep breath and faced Travis square on. "I was being a real jerk, for no reason, and I'm sorry. You don't owe me a do-over, but what I should have said was, 'Thanks so much for coming to check on me.' I scared myself silly, and I embarrassed myself in front of you, the kids, the dogs, and the horses, when all of you were really being kind and showing concern for me. I hope you'll strike anything I implied about your parenting off the record. I don't have kids, and I shouldn't have mouthed off about yours. From what I've seen, your son has better manners and is more generous than I've proven to be today."

Travis stood in silence and then slowly turned his head towards Amanda and gave her a lopsided grin.

"Man, that was a really good apology, and I know apologies—I have to make a lot of them. Might try to hire you on to write up my next one." He stuck out his hand. "Can't claim I was a completely innocent victim, though. We've been at each other's throats since our first meeting, and I imagine me trying...repeatedly...to get the police chief to arrest you at the scene may have had a little something to do with that. How about a truce?"

Amanda grinned back at him and shook his offered hand. "Truce," she said, before shifting back into reporter mode. "So, why are you here? Do you just drive around looking for damsels in distress and kittens in trees, or are there any updates on what happened here?"

"No updates. I came over to take another look at the burn site..." Travis hesitated, unwilling to express how the fire was still bothering him, and unable to figure out why. "Anyways, new mission is picking up the boy. Drew, as usual, must have forgotten to bring his phone along with him when he came to hang out with Skylar. Might stop in at the office to set up an appointment to discuss a Shamrock-specific emergency evacuation plan."

"To avoid a repeat of Wednesday night?" Amanda raised her eyebrow. "Everything that happened with Doug and Hershey?"

"Well, Wednesday certainly revealed some gaps in the emergency procedures here. Every facility is different, though, so evacuation plans should be designed specifically for each barn; now that they've lost their main stable, we'll need to design a new plan for their other buildings."

"Are Doug and Ben in any trouble for running into the burning barn?"

Travis shook his head. "No. When a barn fire starts, you can really only expect to have about five minutes to save your horses. People don't realize how fast barn fires move and how much smoke and carbon monoxide are produced. Horses can die well before the flames ever reach the stalls, but once a horse's stall catches fire, he will probably be dead within four minutes. Frankly, Doug should have never gone back into the barn to save Hershey, but if he hadn't been there from the beginning, I don't know if any of my firefighters could have completed the evacuation. When they arrived, they needed to focus immediately on containing the fire. Like we saw on Wednesday, a quick response is, by far, the best bet for saving the horses. Unless the fire department is already there and suited up, it is highly unlikely that we will be able to save the animals. Usually the ones who are rescued are saved by people already on the scene."

"Has Shamrock been difficult about developing better fire plans?" Amanda probed, wondering about an insurance fraud angle.

"Not at all. Haven't known her long, but every interaction I've had with Molly has been to my advantage. A lot of the farm owners and managers out here consider the building and fire codes suggestions, not rules. It was something my predecessor turned a blind eye to, but enforcing the mandatory safety features and annual inspections and promoting installment and maintenance of additional features have been my biggest focus since I took over the position. Quite a few of the farms have really dragged their feet and made this more difficult than it needs to be. Molly has been my point of contact at Shamrock, though, and she's built the model I'd love all the farms to aspire to."

Amanda nodded. "Having met and irritated quite a number of the locals so far, I can't imagine they're excited about a newcomer sweeping in with big changes, particularly when they cost money."

"It might surprise you to learn that I'm not uncomfortable being disliked." He smirked at her, but his face immediately sobered as he continued, "Fires, particularly fires that can grow as fast and get as big as barn fires, put first responders at great risk, oftentimes unnecessarily. My predecessor actually died on the job in a fire that consumed two barns, along with two of his men."

Amanda's raised her eyebrows as she listened to his story, realizing that much of the hostility he'd shown towards her during their previous encounters had been driven by his focus on the safety for the property owners and concern for the firefighters.

"Molly has gone above and beyond the letter of the fire code; we've actually been speaking about expanding the prevention program using Shamrock as a model, to build out fire drills and safety plans for the whole town. Which is one of the reasons I find it so odd that Shamrock was the one hit by this fire…"

"Oh?" Amanda started to play it dumb, and then caught herself. "Nope, going to be honest. I heard you talking with one of your men the night of the fire about the possibility of arson, and I've been wondering about it ever since."

Travis' face turned stormy, then cycled quickly through a range of emotions before settling on resigned. He shrugged. "Okay, Nancy Drew. If you promise to stop eavesdropping on my conversations, I'll let this one slide. Plus, it looks like I was wrong. I haven't gotten the final report back, but the investigator didn't seem to be interested in my arson suggestion when Molly and I took him around the site."

"Why do I get the feeling you still disagree?"

Travis gave her a suspicious look and vacillated for a moment, trying to decide whether or not to truly open up. That moment was all that was needed, though, as Molly and Kate stepped into view. The four children streaked across the field toward them, and Travis waved.

"Some other time, maybe," Travis said. "I should speak to Molly and drag my son home while I have the chance."

"Some other time," Amanda echoed, giving the horses one last curious look as she made her way towards her car.

"Is this Drew?" Molly asked excitedly. "I need to hug our new hero. I can't believe I didn't get a chance to meet you and thank you the other day, but Skylar told me every detail about how your kindness and quick thinking kept Storm safe. Thank you so much," she said, wrapping the young boy in a warm hug.

Drew lit up, clearly pleased and surprised at all the positive attention. "Oh, really, it was nothin'. I was just excited to tell the other Storm Troopers I got to spend a morning alone with the real live Genuine Storm."

The fire chief materialized right beside Molly, and she noted with silent interest that Drew looked like he'd gone from sunshine to shade in a heartbeat. Skylar had mentioned that Drew was Travis' son, but Molly hadn't yet considered what it would be like to have the quiet, intense firefighter as a father.

"What in the world are you doing here?" Travis demanded. "I've been trying to call your cell phone for hours. Where were you?"

Drew shrugged a little sulkily. "Went huntin', didn't take my phone. Scares the rabbits, even on vibrate. Stopped by to see how Storm was doin'. Skylar told me I could come ask about him whenever I wanted, and you were out all night on calls. Figured you wouldn't care."

Travis pinched the bridge of his own nose, trying to tamp down the headache that several long days and sleepless nights was causing and his son was exacerbating. "We will discuss this at home, Drew."

"But can Drew stay for dinner?" Skylar asked Molly and Travis. "We found a telescope up at Doug's house, and we were going to try it out as soon as it got dark."

Watching Drew's crestfallen face take on a glimmer of hope, Molly said, "Well, it's not going to be anything fancy, but I would love it if you two would join us for dinner. We're going to have a lot of hungry hands to feed pretty soon, so I was just going to send someone out for a big cook-out's worth of hot dogs and hamburgers we could throw on the grill."

"Thank you, but we need to get home," Travis said firmly, much to Drew's clear but silent disappointment.

"Well, it's going to be hectic around here for a while, but I'm going to have to throw a thank-you feast for you both at some point," Molly said in consolation.

Only half-listening to Skylar excitedly recount their adventures of the day, Molly watched the two Johnsons make their hasty retreat, wondering why they were unhappy, how she could help them, and when in the world she would have time.

Potential

Charlie peeked over the edge of her open laptop as Doug stirred in his sleep. *Not awake yet,* she thought. Relief washed over her, but that was chased out quickly by guilt.

Since they'd gotten to the hospital, Charlie had slept fitfully whenever she could manage, but last night was the first time she'd fallen asleep long enough to dream. In the back of her mind, she'd been dreading that for days. She'd assumed that her nightmares would transport her back, over and over, to the fire, to watching Doug disappear into the flames, to feeling like all the horses that had become part of her family would be gone forever.

In retrospect, she thought, *that would have been easier to handle.*

Instead, her dreams had transported her right back to another hospital, where she'd sat at a nearly identical bedside. Shamrock hadn't mattered, or maybe even existed. There had been no flames, no horses—and no Doug. She'd spent her entire dream waiting for Peter to wake up, and she'd woken up crying.

Please, she bargained, *just give me a few more minutes to compose myself.*

Her blog, *The View Behind the Starting Gate,* now had many functions. It was a historical exploration of the Triple Crown, a daily account for

Doug's recovery, and a forum to interact with Storm's eager fans all wrapped into one. Thankfully, Ryan and Kate were manning the Facebook page and other social media outlets, so she didn't need to keep updating those, but Charlie was surprised to find how much the blog was helping her sort through all the madness and uncertainty for herself. When she'd awoken with a gasp, she'd reached for her laptop right away, knowing that another post would not only be soothing, it would be helpful and productive. Reading Amanda Ault's latest piece, *The Fire/Storm's Aftermath* in the online edition of the local paper, only strengthened her resolve. The reporter was predicting that Storm's Triple Crown bid was already over; Charlie knew better than that, and she was anxious to respond.

After ascertaining that Doug was still asleep, she went back to work. The writing was smooth and easy until she was nearly done, when she suddenly got stuck and couldn't find the words to finish.

"Hey you," Doug interrupted her in a raspy whisper, testing out his voice. The doctors had removed his breathing tubes the night before, but he'd been too dazed and too raw to speak.

Charlie smiled at him and laid her laptop back under her chair, checking carefully to make sure the screen was closed. Doug had enough to deal with; he didn't need to know about the media firestorm. She scooched forward and gently took his hand.

"Hey yourself. How do you feel?" she said softly.

Doug raised an eyebrow and winced.

Even just that tiny motion hurt, she realized.

He whispered, "Can't complain," and gave her the biggest smile he could muster.

Charlie laughed, surprised. It had been five whole days since she'd heard his voice, and she realized how very much she'd missed it.

"I could feel you here with me. I went into the fire alone, but you've been with me ever since." Doug smiled faintly at himself. "Those aren't the words, but I'll find them."

Charlie returned his smile. "Don't worry about the words. You are drugged to the gills, and you shouldn't try to talk too much right now anyways. You just rest."

Doug's eyes were already fluttering back closed. "I love you, Charlie."

When she was sure he was under, Charlie quietly pulled her laptop back out and started reading over her post, editing and searching for a good way to end it.

The View Behind the Starting Gate
The Triple Crown Winners Who Never Were

Over the course of the last hundred years, there have been many close calls, several horses who could have (or should have) won the Triple Crown. Those horses that won two of the three races that make up the Triple Crown. That elusive Crown can slip through a horse's hooves at any point.

There are those whose dreams were dashed right in the middle, the eleven Derby winners who did not capture the Preakness, but who bravely rallied to win the Belmont. There are also the horses who lost their claims to the crown from the beginning, the ones who won the Preakness and the Belmont, but who either did not run or did not perform in the Kentucky Derby. The most celebrated of that elite group of eighteen is Man o'War. His owner, Samuel Riddle, chose not to run him in the Derby because he did not believe that it was healthy for a young horse to race the mile and a quarter distance so early in his career.

We tend to remember best those twenty-three horses who lost at the bitter end, the horses who won the Kentucky Derby and the Preakness only to dash our hopes and theirs at the Belmont—some, like Real Quiet, by just a nose.

"The greatest horse to ever look through a bridle," Spectacular Bid, is one of the most widely lamented Triple Crown winners-who-weren't. Including the Kentucky Derby and the Preakness,

The Bid had won 12 consecutive stakes races, and had raced 16 times over 12 different tracks prior to the Belmont.

But the gods were not on his side. The morning of the race, his trainer arrived to find that Spectacular Bid refused to put weight on one of his legs. Upon further examination, a safety pin was found sticking at least half an inch inside his hoof. Story has it that the groom had dropped the pin during morning feeding, and The Bid, in his fury to get to his breakfast, stomped so hard on it that it drove straight into his hoof.

After carefully removing the pin and soaking the hoof, The Bid seemed sound and back to his normal self. His trainer decided to keep the information to himself and the horse continued his quest for the Triple Crown. Sadly, the rigors of the one and half mile race, coupled with the pain in his hoof, resulted in Spectacular Bid finishing third.

The Kentucky Derby, Preakness, and Belmont have all existed since at least 1875. In the 140 years since, there have been 52 horses who attempted to win all three races, but only succeeded in winning two:

Derby/Preakness: 23 horses

Preakness/Belmont: 18 horses

Derby/Belmont: 11 horses

In the twelve year span from 1994 to 2005 alone, two of the three races were won by the same horse ten times. Amazingly, in the shorter time frames between 1997–1999 and then again from 2002–2004, the Triple Crown was contested three years in a row; each year, though, the horse who had won both the Kentucky Derby and Preakness was not able to win the Belmont.

The reasons that no horse has won all three races since Affirmed in 1978 are hotly contested. Many of the experts and members of the general population wonder if it can ever be done again.

However, in my line of thinking, there has been a potential Triple Crown winner 52 times over the span of 140 years—37% of the time. With the frequency that horses join the Two Win Club, I think it's silly to believe that we won't ever see another horse win the Crown.

Well, Genuine Storm is part of the Two Win Club, number 53, with the Derby and Preakness wins already under his belt. We will know soon enough, but I've got a good feeling, and I think the math is on our side. Here's hoping we can beat the odds as we head towards the ultimate goal—the first Triple Crown winner in 37 years.

Charlie smiled, and she finished off the final sentence with a flourish.

———————

"We will know soon enough, but I've got a good feeling, and I think the math is on our side," Skylar read aloud from her tablet. She looked up at Drew and Molly expectantly from her perch, sitting atop one of the desks in Molly's increasingly crowded office.

"Did you hear that? Over the span of the last 140 years, thirty-seven percent of the time—fifty-two times—there was a potential Triple Crown winner?" Skylar repeated, pulling the line from her mother's blog. "This year, though, Storm *has* to bring it home. That's so much pressure!"

"Pretty cool, I guess," Drew replied. "But if it doesn't happen this time, he can always try again next year, right?"

"No! These races are only for three-year-olds! You don't know a thing about the Triple Crown, do you?" Skylar asked incredulously.

Drew shrugged his shoulders. "My mom wasn't into the same type of horses your mom is. She spent her time at horse shows, jumping around a course of eight jumps. You know, looking pretty and all, getting blue ribbons."

Skylar watched a shadow cross Drew's face as he fought down his emotions of missing his mom. She decided it best she change the subject.

"Ms. Molly, did you hear that?"

Molly waved her hand to shush the two children, pointing to the phone pressed against her ear.

'Shorthanded' didn't even begin to describe the situation at Shamrock. Just the sheer amount of work, much less the complexity of it all, was staggering, and something seemed to go wrong at every turn. Molly was known in more than a few circles to be one of the most patient, competent, and clear-headed individuals, but even she was getting stressed and short-tempered. She was doing the work of eight in a crisis, and she was running herself ragged.

"And how many days after the report is filed can we expect to receive the payment?"

Molly ran her hands through her tangled hair, trying to wrestle it into the ponytail elastic on her wrist. Listening to the convoluted answer of the insurance representative on the line, she checked her reflection in the window to make sure she'd really gotten it all pulled back this time.

As poor a mirror as her office window made, it was enough to tell she was a mess, covered in a thick layer of dust and grime from working outside. Any other time, she wouldn't have allowed herself to come into the office this filthy, but right now, she just hoped she'd have the energy to take a shower before she got into bed at the end of the long day.

The representative said something different from what she'd been repeating for the last hour and it sent Molly back over to her mountains of insurance paperwork to verify.

Another loud noise startled her so badly that she nearly shoved over a stack of important papers, which would have led to a domino effect. She kept forgetting about the presence of Skylar and Drew, who were supposed to be quietly working on their homework on the far side of the office. One of the kids had knocked a textbook onto the ground, and it jarred her raw nerves. The dogs, taking the interruption as an invitation to start playing again, began wrestling each other. Molly snapped her fingers at Skylar and Drew, a signal to make the roughhousing stop so she could hear her call; she followed it up with a glare that made their eyes go wide.

With their mom watching over Doug at the hospital, Ryan and Skylar hadn't made it back home yet since the night of the fire. School had been put on the back burner; luckily, all the required standardized tests had already been given earlier in May. The teachers were just killing time and assigning busy work until school let out for summer, so Charlie had told Molly she wasn't too uptight about them missing a few days. Drew, who was following a homeschool curriculum with a neighbor, started showing up to meet Skylar each morning with his own assignments. They alternated between schoolwork and playing throughout the day and well into the evening, ostensibly under the care of Ryan and Jenny. The teenagers, however, were not always the easiest to track down or the most vigilant about making sure the kids stayed with them. Ryan was completely wrapped up in Kate's social media campaign, and Molly had no idea what was up with Jenny and her moodiness.

"Monday? Yes, of course I know it's Monday," Molly responded indignantly. She had actually lost track of what day of the week it was; since the fire, the time was always "now" and "overdue."

"You kept me on the phone for over an hour, knowing you couldn't even access the answer today? I…"

Molly firmly replaced the phone in its receiver as Buck walked into her office, also hanging up his phone with an irritated expression on his face.

"Have you spoken with Lilly today?" Buck asked.

Skylar, bubbling over with excitement, interrupted before Molly could respond. "Buck! Listen to this—"

"Excuse me, Skylar, that was rude, we were talking. I let you skip your homework last night and play, but you promised you'd sit quietly today and do it until it was finished," Molly bristled.

She immediately felt bad for snapping and had just opened her mouth to apologize when her office door swung open again. Jenny let it hit the wall before she clumped in dramatically.

She's looked mopey for days, Molly thought, *but today is just above and beyond.*

Jenny had been upset since the night of the fire. Molly suspected her daughter blamed herself for Storm's escape, but she was certain that Jenny felt awful about not being able to help out more, now that Shamrock was in crisis mode. The teen had been given one task and one task only, day in and out, which was to watch Skylar (and, by association, Drew). The moping was hindering her ability to follow through with her assignment, and she almost seemed to be avoiding Skylar.

Molly had never been an angry person and she still wasn't—but this was probably the closest to worried sick and completely overwhelmed she'd ever been. She knew that she was on the verge of becoming openly exasperated with Jenny, so she started to count backwards and subtly calm herself. The tension had been growing between them, and Molly did not want to lash out in frustration.

Like any close mother and daughter, Molly and Jenny's tempers could flare at each other on occasion, but Molly had always been careful to make sure they reconciled lovingly, respectfully, and quickly. With everything going on, there had been no time to spend talking through the issues with each other, and Molly knew there wouldn't be time today either.

"Hey sweetheart, would you please take Skylar and Drew up to Doug's house to finish up their homework? I've got 500 things to do and the space to do maybe three." Molly carefully moderated her tone and her expression to make sure she projected nothing but upbeat sunniness.

Jenny rolled her eyes. "Yeah, Mom, everyone knows that you're Wonder Woman and we are all in the way."

"Are you *kidding* me, Jenny? I've asked you to do just one thing for me over the past three days, and you really couldn't have gone any farther out of your way to not do it." Molly took a deep breath and turned away from her daughter to compose herself, only to hear Jenny head quickly back out the door—leaving Skylar and Drew behind.

Molly gaped at her self-centeredness, took a deep breath, and turned to Buck, who had watched all of this silently.

"I just have to remember that *being* a teenager was way, way worse than *parenting* one has been."

"Wish I could have been given the chance," Buck said absently, before remembering who was in the room.

Buck's comment was the last straw; before she could break down, Molly turned her emotions on the kids and roared for Drew and Skylar to get out of her office. As they scampered out with the dogs, she turned back to Buck, but he had quietly left through the back of the office. Molly sat back down at her desk, promptly knocking over a large stack of papers, and burst into tears.

The kids scrambled out of the office, running from Molly's wrath and their now-forgotten homework.

"Ouuhhh, Jenny's in trooooooouuuble," Drew said, laughing.

"Ha, that's nothing—you should see my mom and Ryan. They're almost always fighting," Skylar replied.

"Yelling at my dad would be like yelling at the principal. It would just never happen unless I went crazy or something," Drew said, his eyes widening at the thought.

Skylar shrugged. "I remember Mom and Ryan got into a big fight right after my dad died, and I got scared that we weren't going to love each other anymore or something—like our family had broken completely, and there was no way to put us back together. My mom told me then that 'Family was worth fighting for, so we're also worth fighting with.'"

"My dad usually says stuff like 'Everyone would be better off if they talked less and listened more.' He's a grump." Drew looked thoughtful for a moment, then said, "I wonder what Buck meant about wishing he'd been given the chance. It was a weird thing to say, and it really set Molly off."

Skylar fidgeted anxiously. "I'm pretty sure I know, but..."

"What? What is it?"

Skylar shook her head. "I swore on my life I wouldn't tell anyone, and if I do, Jenny might *actually* kill me."

"Now you have to tell me!" Drew said.

Skylar shook her head again and continued to fidget. It was obvious that she wanted to tell.

Drew tried a different approach. "It's okay. Everyone has secrets. I have a *big* one."

"Trust me, it can't be bigger than this one," Skylar said, looking worried.

"Wanna bet?"

"I'd bet a million dollars, and I'd win."

"Only one way to find out—we're gonna have to trade secrets." Drew leaned in closer and extended his hand. "I'll even go first, but you've got to promise not to tell anyone ever."

Skylar thought it over for a second, then linked pinkies with him. "I promise."

"Okay." Drew took a deep breath, and then his confession poured out like a stream. "When I was a little kid, my dad had a watch he really liked because his grandfather gave it to him, but he didn't wear it to work so it wouldn't get messed up, and sometimes I would take it and play with it. It's really cool, an old automatic that you can pop the back off of and watch the wheels turn inside. I always worried he'd get mad if he caught me playing with it, but he never found out. The night my mom moved out, I took it back to my bedroom, just to have something else to focus on, but then Dad came home unexpectedly. I had to hide it quick, so he wouldn't see it, so I just stuffed it inside this old toy train I keep on my bookshelf. I was going to put it back when he left again, but then he started going through his stuff. When he realized it was missing, he thought my mom stole it and he got so mad. I think it was the thing he was most mad about through the whole divorce. He kept bringing it up, trying to get it back from her, threatening to report it as a theft. I know it didn't cause their divorce or anything, but I'm pretty sure it made it much, much worse."

Skylar's eyes got wide. "Whoa. So...where is it now?"

"Still inside that toy train," Drew said. "I'm terrified to even touch it. If Dad ever finds it, he's gonna ship me off to military school or something."

Skylar tapped her chin thoughtfully. "You should hide it somewhere

where he could find it, like…under the sink or something. Then maybe he'll think he accidentally left it there and just forgot."

"He never forgets anything." Drew shook his head, looking miserable. Then, remembering the purpose of this exercise, he brightened up. "Hey! So, your turn—what's your big secret?"

"Well…that's the thing, it's not exactly mine…but…" Skylar hesitated.

Drew rolled his eyes and made the hand gesture to get on with it. "A deal is a deal. If you back out now, pretty sure you owe me a million dollars."

"Okay, okay…see, Molly isn't Jenny's mom—Lilly is," Skylar said hesitantly, "And, and…Buck is her dad."

Drew looked at her blankly.

"Dude! That's a big deal!" Skylar said.

"Jenny doesn't know she's adopted?"

"Uggh, this is where it gets worse. No, she knew that part," Skylar corrected him. "She's known her whole life that Molly and Steve adopted her when she was little, but she had no idea who her real parents were—"

"How did you find out?" Drew interrupted.

"I was sitting in Hershey's stall the other day, before the fire, eating my lunch and reading *The Black Stallion and the Girl* and just hanging out with him. I try and find time to spend alone with Hershey, so he knows he is just as important as Storm. Anyways, I'd been reading the book to him, but I took a big bite and I was still chewing. Then Lilly and Buck walked in, and they just started talking right away about how Jenny was their daughter and like, how they needed to tell her and stuff. By the time I'd finished chewing, I felt like I'd heard too much and I didn't know what to do, so I just hid."

"Okay, you're probably right. Jenny would freak out if she knew that her parents had been, like, right beside her this whole time. Imagine if you found out that your second-grade teacher or your soccer coach or someone like that was your real parent," Drew replied, considering the magnitude of the secret. "It'd be sooooo weird."

"So…" Skylar said hesitantly, "I kind of…told…her."

"What?!?"

"I was angry and scared about Hershey and the fire and Mr. Doug and my mom and just…you know, everything. I don't know, it's not an excuse, it's just… anyways, Jenny was lecturing me about something after we found Storm, and I just got so mad that I blurted it out." The young girl turned beet red with shame, remembering. She buried her face in her hands and started to cry.

Drew stayed quiet, shuffling his feet and looking around awkwardly, sad and embarrassed for his new friend.

"I don't think I've ever tried so hard to make someone feel bad on purpose, and when I saw how hurt she was, I knew right away that it was the worst thing I'd ever done. If I could take it all back, I would," Skylar finally said, wiping away her tears. "But Jenny made me swear not to tell anybody that I knew or that she knew. And now I've even messed that up."

"Don't worry, I won't tell anyone. Promise. If I do, you can tell my dad about the watch and totally ruin my life," Drew said gallantly.

Skylar smiled gratefully, then got quiet again. "Do you think I'm a bad person?"

"No way. We all say stuff we wish we could take back when we get that mad. Plus, if I was Jenny, I'd be really excited. Lilly is basically the most famous lady in sports at the moment, and Buck is so chill and the best rider in the world," Drew said, kicking dust up with the toe of his boot. "I know it's stupid, but it kind of makes me mad that Jenny has a bunch of parents when she's not even that nice to the ones she knows about."

"Jenny's nice. Everybody here is nice. You haven't got to really meet them for real due to this stupid fire," Skylar said, feeling defensive of her Shamrock family. "They're all usually much happier, but it's hard to be happy all the time when horses and ponies are hurt and people are hurt and everything is a mess."

"Okay," Drew said, holding up his hands in defense. "I didn't mean it. I'm just jealous of Jenny, is all. Imagine secretly being the daughter of Lilly and Buck…she's like, jockey royalty—a jockey princess…"

Stalled Investigation

"Well, I'd really like you to consider bringing in additional forensic experts to conduct a more thorough analysis of the fire," Travis repeated into the phone receiver in a measured tone.

"Johnson, weren't you one of the first responders?"

"Yes."

"Didn't I interview you? Have you thought of additional information or evidence you witnessed on the night of the fire that no longer exists?"

"No, but—"

"Son, listen. The International Association of Arson Investigators has a motto: 'We are truth seekers, not case makers.' You're asking me to build a case with you, and that's not what I do. There's no conclusive physical evidence. There's not even inconclusive physical evidence. As an investigator, I'm really only allowed to make limited inferences—where the fire started and how the fire started—and those I have to be able to articulate as expert opinions in court."

"I'm telling you, there's something—"

"What exactly are you hoping happens here? Even if I shared your conviction that this was suspicious—which I do not—and made the determination that this was an incidence of arson, there's no one to arrest. You want to know what you'd need to have to get an arson case to trial?"

Travis sighed. "Okay."

"Video proof, forensics, and a confession. You pretty much gotta want to get caught. Arson has one of the lowest clearance rates of any major crime, which means very few perpetrators are caught…you know that. We just don't end up catching the bad guys, not the ones starting fires. Unless you've got a name you'd like to put forward…"

Travis's heart leapt into his throat, but he continued to try and tamp down his fears. He slammed the phone down too late to get his frustration across; the disinterested messenger at the office of the fire marshal had already hung up.

No signs of arson, Travis thought to himself and snorted derisively. *They spent a few hours at the farm and didn't find any conclusive evidence, so they're perfectly content to close the book on this.*

He leaned back in his chair and sighed, slowly cooling himself down. He was frustrated, having spent the better part of the day trying to argue with unconvinced officials, but he understood; everyone was stretched thin at the moment, and there really weren't any obvious signs of arson on the ground that he could point to. Still, he couldn't shake his deep suspicion. He flipped through the file the fire station kept on Shamrock Hill Farm; they'd been up to date on their inspections and up to code.

Travis considered his options, finding them as limited as they'd been every other time he'd run through them that morning. There were no power plays or smart moves to make. He was only the interim fire chief, and worse, an interloper from out of town. He hadn't lived here long enough or made enough friends in high places to skirt around the system. Unless he was lucky enough to stumble across an arsonist wearing a t-shirt that proclaimed guilt, actively flicking lit matches against the side of another barn, he just had to suck it up and try to shrug this hunch off.

The phone on the desk started to ring again, but didn't make it through the first trill before Travis had answered.

"Hi, Travis, this is Molly. Any luck with the investigation? I have been on the phone all day with the insurance company and they are sending adjusters over tomorrow. I was hoping to be able to provide them more details as to what caused the fire."

Travis flipped through the file, only half listening. *There's got to be something...*

"I didn't realize that the arson investigation wasn't closed out yet; the inspector told me he was filing the report today, so that I could start haggling with the insurance company sooner rather than later. It...it was an accident, wasn't it?" Molly asked.

"Hmm? Oh, I... well, there may be a slight delay. A few more things to follow up on, do the job thoroughly," Travis responded.

"Alright, but can you tell me—"

Travis' other line chirruped.

"Molly, I need to take this. I'll get back to you with news when I have it."

I don't really have news yet, he thought. *The report isn't really filed until I sign off on it. Due diligence never hurt anybody.*

He quickly dispatched the person on the other line and went back to studying the file, pulling out photos and diagrams, heat readings and inspection reports. He'd just pulled up the weather reports from Wednesday night to check for any wind or storm anomalies when he was startled by a knock at his open door frame.

Amanda stormed in without permission, already talking a mile a minute and pouring over new files she'd brought with her.

"Okay, I've pulled all the permits and inspection reports filed with the city on that barn, and I need you to explain a few things to me."

"Hi?" the fire chief said, confused.

"Hi," Amanda said, flashing him a brilliant smile. "How do you feel about insurance fraud?"

"Personally, I'm against," Travis said, earning an appreciative smirk from Amanda. "But in all seriousness, that's a dangerous thing to accuse someone of."

"That's why I didn't print it...yet," Amanda replied. "My sole experience with the subject matter is made-for-TV movies. So I'd like for you to explain some things for me."

"Amanda, I don't really have time for this."

"What's wrong?" she questioned. "Afraid I'm going to find the evidence you need to make your arson case? I heard your last few phone calls—I know you're suspicious too."

Travis glared at her. "Didn't we already talk about your eavesdropping?"

She shrugged.

Sighing, Travis relented. "Well, just as long as you don't go fabricating evidence—if I'm wrong, I'm wrong. But okay, yeah, I could use another set of sharp eyes to help take a look, see if I'm missing something. I have to warn you, though, everything seems to have an answer."

"Okay...in no particular order," she said, shuffling through her research, "let's start with the smoke detectors."

"How about 'em?"

"They were disabled."

Travis looked through his own reports. "Right. The barn was older, and they had to make decisions about smoke and heat detectors that weren't ideal. Until they could raze the entire structure and rebuild, we suggested using heat detectors, which measure the rate of rising temperature, in place of smoke detectors. They did have smoke detectors, the 'dustproof' variety, in the barn, set up to alert their phones and the local fire department..."

Amanda flipped through her papers furiously. "I don't see anything about that in here."

"You didn't wait for the end of my sentence. Not dustproof enough. Smoke detectors use a beam to 'see' smoke, which is problematic in a high-dust environment like a horse barn; that dust looks exactly like smoke to the detectors. Even if we'd been able to set up truly dustproof detectors, with the ventilation necessary in a stable full of live animals, smoke can dissipate pretty quickly. By the time enough smoke concentrated to activate the detector, the fire would already be well-established. As it stood, though, they went off every time the horses kicked up some hay, and Shamrock ended up owing the fire department quite a bit of money for false alarms. When they had the new heat sensor system put in, we disabled the smoke detectors."

"You levy fines for false alarms?" Amanda asked skeptically.

"The majority of our fire department is volunteer, Amanda. False alarms are incredibly disruptive to their lives. Even a professional fire department can become a little less fast to respond when they are called to the same facility over and over when there is no fire."

"But…" Amanda checked her notes again, "Okay, right—I've had multiple people tell me that the alarms didn't sound until after the fire was significant, and that the sprinklers didn't come on until after the horses had been evacuated."

"Both of those issues have to do with the temperature ratings. The fire began in the open area, which got enough ventilation that the heat dissipated before it could reach the sensors, which are set to a very high temperature. If the fire had started in one of the closed spaces, like the tack room or staff lounge, they would have been more effective. By the time they were triggered in the open area stalls, the fire was out of control."

"What do you mean?"

"Well, let's talk sprinklers. Automatic fire sprinklers are designed to open in response to heat, ideally, obviously, from a fire. There's a metal element inside that melts at a specific temperature, usually either 135°F, 175°F, or 250°F. For their barn, we had to use 250°F. Unfortunately, that meant they didn't deploy until the fire was larger."

"Why not use one of the lower temperature options?"

"If a sprinkler with too low a temperature rating is used, it can activate when no fire has occurred. The high ceilings in those old barns keep the ground cooler for the horses, but the peaks get very hot. A sweltering summer day could make the roof hot enough to break those metal seals."

"Why didn't the sprinklers put out the fire?" Amanda dug out a diagram and pointed towards the sprinkler heads. "Here—why weren't they installed over the stalls? There's no way the water would be able to hit any-where but that center aisle."

"Sprinklers are designed to give people more time to escape, not to put out the fire. It doesn't matter if the water coming from the sprinkler head is actu-ally hitting the fire—it's just supposed to lower the air temperature and reduce the amount of oxygen feeding the fire." Travis shrugged again. "Smoke detec-tors, fire alarms, and sprinkler systems are notoriously difficult to employ properly in older barns, even with incredibly expensive retrofitting."

"Which Shamrock didn't do?" Amanda asked hopefully, looking up from her notes.

"No, Shamrock did. In hindsight, I would obviously make some changes, but I've poured over their plans again and again, and there's not much else I would have done differently."

"Aside from arson, what other things are commonly known to cause barn fires?" Amanda asked, changing tactics.

"Almost anything. Hay, which can spontaneously combust if it's over 22% moisture. Extension cords, which I've seen used in a whole lot of cre-ative ways, draped all around barn interiors. People use them for heating water buckets in the winter, and to run fans and electric clippers in the sum-mertime. Many cords I have seen are kinked or bent in places that causes the outer protective layer to become compromised. Not to mention all the phone chargers hanging around with their charging ends dangling mid-air, especially in a barn full of teenagers," Travis commented.

"How did the fire burn through the barn so quickly? Isn't that a sign of arson?" Amanda asked, sounding like she was clinging to one of her last straws.

Travis shook his head. "Actually, that was a pretty slow barn fire. Barns can burn very quickly and very hot because of the nature of the combus-tibles inside—hay, bedding, wood, rags, you name it. Basically, everything having to do with horses is flammable. It's a testament to how clean Sham-rock was and how seriously they take fire safety, overall, that the fire took as long as it did to build up to any sort of critical point."

"How is it that there were no cameras recording?"

Travis flipped through the statements he'd taken at the scene to check his response. "Seems like when the farm realized they'd be part of a Triple Crown effort, they were suddenly facing a whole different level of exposure and liability than previously, so they updated their security and insurance coverage. The insurance company required the installation of an anti-theft alarm and additional cameras just for that space. As best as the inspectors can currently tell, when the contractors were out hardwiring the new systems, they switched everything to WiFi for testing, and forgot to switch it back to WiFi and recording."

"And the WiFi was down," Amanda said bitterly, remembering her experience trying to file the scoop from the scene that night.

"Seems so," Travis said, closing his file. "Listen, I've got no evidence. The scene wasn't much help, between the damage due to the horses, the oxygen surge explosion when we cut through the barn wall, and how thoroughly the barn burned. When it comes down to it, though, there was no signs of an accelerant, the dogs didn't pick up on anything suspicious, and there was no obvious tampering. The fire didn't really start off very hot, which was a danger of its own, because it didn't trigger the sprinklers and alarms until it grew much larger. The fire inspector said that the most likely cause were cobwebs around an electrical socket—says that, because of how wet and warm the spring has been, he's seen a lot of spiders and spider damage, and a barn is likely to have even more spider issues than a home."

"So, if you have answers for all of this…what are you questioning?"

"I guess it's because I'm not supposed to have answers for all this, Amanda. It's supposed to be a little messy. It shouldn't be so textbook."

Travis watched Amanda process this. It felt good to talk through it with someone else, someone who really listened, considered the possibilities, and responded. That had certainly been in short supply as he'd run it up the hierarchy.

Amanda nodded, scribbled down some final notes, and shut her pad. "Well, thank you for your time," she said, poorly masking her disappointment.

Travis stood up from behind his desk and shook her hand. "Thanks for coming in, Amanda. I'm sorry it's not the front page news you were hoping for, and I'm sorry if I made you think there was something more."

Amanda gave him a tight smile, released herself from the handshake, and turned to leave. With her hand on the doorknob, she looked back over her shoulder.

"You still don't believe this was an accident, do you?"

Travis hesitated before he responded. "I guess it depends whether you believe with your head or your gut."

Amanda narrowed her eyes, thought for a moment, then nodded slowly. "Yeah, I know what you mean."

Jenny clumped around the barns, cutting the edges as tightly as she could on her crutches. She enjoyed watching the divots they made in the ground; there was something pleasantly unpleasant about the way the crutches pinched under her arms when she popped them back out of the holes, and the sweat plastering her shirt to her back from the effort. So much effort...for what?

Before the fire, she'd been enjoying spending time with Ryan. She really liked him, even if she would get irritated by the way he was so busy trying to do everything for her. Even if she'd wanted more alone time.

Now, it was 100% alone time, all the time. Ryan had his social media mission, her mother and father had the entire farm to try to juggle, and everyone else either needed to heal or needed to help heal someone. Jenny had Skylar to watch over, sure, but her mom hadn't even noticed that she and Skylar basically refused to talk to each other. Skylar ran away from her, actually. They hadn't made up since Hershey went to New Bolton. Jenny tried to congratulate Skylar after she found Storm, but that just managed to make everything—*everything*—so much more wrong.

Technically, she thought, *I'm supposed to be healing up too. I think I can handle the leg just fine, but what about...*

She didn't know how to label these lonely feelings, or how she could start fixing them.

"Ooof!" she grunted as she cut around the next corner and plowed straight into a solid person.

Buck staggered back, looking as startled as she felt. They both stared at each other just long enough for the moment to get awkward.

"I didn't recognize you without your bodyguard!" Buck joked weakly.

Jenny smiled at him. "It's all about striking that balance, right? That's what the women's magazines at the doctor's office tell me. We were spending about 90% of our time together there for a minute, and now we spend about 10%. If you average it out…"

"Ah, the honeymoon stage?" Buck nodded sagely. "I'm not sure I can give you much advice on that front."

Jenny smiled warmly.

Buck continued, "I'd love to tell you it gets easier when you get older, but I'm in the same boat. The difference between too much and too little can be tiny but feel massive, especially when times are stressful."

Jenny and Buck stood and chatted, talking about life and horses for a while. Jenny never spent much time with Buck, as she'd considered him just another one of Doug's jockeys. It wasn't until he reconnected with Lilly that he started coming around the farm a lot more. Jenny was surprised by how nice, funny, and just overall easy it was to talk with him.

The conversation didn't last more than ten minutes, and they didn't cover anything of consequence. They were just two lonely people being kind to each other.

Buck and Jenny were both genuinely happier as they excused themselves to continue on to their destinations. They probably would have both thought it was funny to know that they each crumpled against the side of the barn when the other was out of sight.

Like father, like daughter, right?

PART FOUR

Time's Up

Lilly leaned on the fence, watching Doc's movements closely. He hadn't made any drastic changes to the way he'd been handling Storm from their first afternoon at the farm. Still whistling. Still moving slowly. She had caught some subtle movements that most people, people without her extensive experience with difficult horses, wouldn't have even perceived—masterful light touches here and there that calmed certain horses, and some gestures even more subtle than those. It didn't seem to hurt—Storm certainly hadn't gotten more anxious since he'd started working with Doc—but it didn't seem to be helping much either. The horse had not dramatically improved.

In today's world, she thought, *most people move too fast and want things too quickly.* She took a deep breath and tried to release some of the tension still riding high in her shoulders. It was difficult to reconcile the need to work with Storm slowly and patiently with the time constraint they were under.

She'd been doing all she could to keep Storm in shape, but with the Belmont only ten days away, he needed to get back to the track soon if they were going to get his final conditioning runs in. Unfortunately, a lot of that work couldn't be done on just any track. Storm had never raced at Belmont; she needed to acclimate him to the mile and a half track, the sweeping turns, and all the bright lights, big city the environment had to offer.

If we had months, or even weeks...

Storm's workouts over the past few days had consisted of hill work, Lilly trotting him on a lead up and down the large trails that led off from the vast working farm. Doc usually rode out with them, both to keep Storm company and to provide an encouraging trail partner in case the horse didn't want to cross a stream or spooked at a deer.

Odd training regimen for a horse contending for the Triple Crown, Lilly thought, sighing heavily.

Doc and Storm finished their session, and Doc started to lead the horse back towards Lilly. The jockey braced herself for the inevitably awkward conversation she needed to start. For as much time as Lilly had spent over the past few days with Doc, she still didn't know a thing about him. He spoke easily and often, softly and hypnotically, in whistles, clicks, and half sentences to Storm and the small herd of rescue dogs she'd met on arrival, but he always seemed a little surprised and very stiff when he needed to respond to her. It took him a moment of hesitation, as though it had been so long since he'd routinely spoken with a person that he was no longer fully fluent in human conversation.

"Storm's gotten used to being out here in the country. Didn't blink an eye at the deer that jumped the fence," she said, struggling to start on a bright note. "What are you thinking, Doc? Do you think he's going to be ready to run in the Belmont?"

Doc looked at her thoughtfully and silently, then shrugged. "He'll be ready when he's ready."

"I appreciate that, I really do. But realistically, we only have four, five more days tops until he needs to be on that track—for his own safety. If that's not going to be feasible..."

Doc watched Lilly carefully as the realization that the Belmont might be out of reach hit her in a very real way for the first time. They both took a moment to look back at Storm, whose anxiety still showed, even while he was relaxing and grazing, through a series of sporadic twitches.

"He's not ready yet," Doc said. "That's all I can say for certain."

Lilly's heart was heavy. "Hypothetically, if he made as much incremental progress each day as he has for the first few—"

Doc gave her a sad smile. "No. No, he would not be ready."

Lilly nodded. "I need to call Charlie and let her know where we are."

She turned back towards her house, trudging slowly, trying to compose what she was going to say to Charlie. Right before she left earshot, she heard Doc calling her name, and she spun around.

"Remember, though, that's not how healing works. Everything happens on its own time table—sometimes slow, sometimes fast—and it can take you by surprise."

Lilly nodded, surprised by the emotion she heard choked up behind his words, and continued on her path.

———————

"What in the world is this?" Kevin barked, glaring at the reporter standing in front of his desk.

"An article on the Shamrock fire with more facts," Amanda responded. "I spent a good portion of the afternoon yesterday with the interim fire chief, I read the preliminary report from the arson investigator, and I had all my questions answered to the best of anyone's technical ability. These are what the facts look like, so that's how I wrote them up. It might not be the sensational story we would have liked, but I still think it's important. If nothing else, there's a lot in there about fire safety that could help other barns avoid the same…"

"I didn't hire you to write public service announcements, Amanda. If a lead you're following concludes with 'there is no story,' then you need to go back out and find another one, not write up the dead end." Kevin shook his head. "I can't print this. I won't. I'm pulling this copy."

Amanda's eyes flashed. "You promised me a spot on the front page until the Triple Crown was over."

"No, I didn't. I told you I would prioritize getting Storm front and center.

I still am. Get me better stuff, or I'll give the assignment to a reporter who will," her editor said, gesturing to the sportswriter on the opposite side of the small newsroom.

"Turns out I've got a little something written up that I think you'll like," the sportswriter called out.

"Bring it on over," Kevin said, ignoring Amanda as she marched out the door.

———————————

So, this is what the end of the line looks like, Charlie thought, sitting quietly in the passenger seat next to Cappie and watching Shamrock come into view through the windshield in front of them.

It was bittersweet, but Charlie was adjusting quickly. When Lilly had called and told her it was time to come to Pine Grove and pass the final judgment on Storm's Triple Crown bid, she'd expected to be devastated for a long time. She was sad, certainly, but as she'd hung up the phone and rejoined Doug in his hospital room, everything had flown into perspective.

Everything could have gone so much worse.

Returning Doug's smile, she'd checked the incoming text on her phone. It was from Cappie—good news. Hershey was healing up nicely, and they expected to be able to release him in less than two weeks.

Doug is going to be fine. Hershey is going to be fine. Even Storm is going to be fine in a few months. Trading a Triple Crown for three miracles seems like a bargain.

Charlie had returned the text and asked Cappie to come by and pick her up from the hospital. She'd shared an early lunch with Doug and they had discussed plans for the next day. Then they'd started to speak about the future. Even without the Triple Crown, even without Belmont, there was so much to be excited about.

Cappie pulled the truck up in front of the farm office and Charlie hopped out, eager to hug her kids. It felt like it had been years since she'd left.

The discussion in the office stopped as she walked in and beelined to

Ryan, giving him a huge hug and smiling broadly at Kate and Molly.

"We had no idea you were coming!" Molly exclaimed.

"Needed to see you all and pack a few things up," Charlie said.

She wanted to avoid telling them about her upcoming trip to see Storm; there was so much to celebrate, so much hard work to thank them all for, so much to just love about being near all of them again.

The room buzzed with happy chatter as Charlie gave them good news about Doug's recovery, and they filled her in on the trials and tribulations of the farm over the course of her absence.

Jenny hurried in excitedly just as Kate started filling Charlie in on how the social media push had been going.

"Well," Kate said, "I hope you know your son is a budding marketing and public relations wunderkind. Ryan has an instinct for this work and the tech skills to make it in this industry. He's got more going for him than I could have even imagined at his age."

"How's Uncle Doug?" Jenny asked.

Her question was drowned out by all the other questions and comments volleying at rapid speed around the room, and she stood quietly for several minutes while they continued.

"Oh! Jenny!" Molly said, realizing that her daughter had come in.

"Hi," Jenny replied. "Is there any news on Un—"

"Do you know where Skylar is?" Molly asked, cutting her off in her excitement. "I'm sure she'd love to see her mom!"

Jenny was taken aback by her mother's uncharacteristic rudeness. She was struggling to respond when Amanda Ault walked in the door, offering a cursory knock on the frame as she passed. The entire room went silent, and the entire tone changed.

"Hi," the reporter said brightly. "I haven't been able to reach anyone for comment for a few days, so I thought I'd stop by."

"That wasn't a mistake," Kate growled. "You're cut off. You're not going to get any comments…unless, of course, you manage to wrangle a few out Hunter. I've seen you snooping around."

"Jenny, do you not know where Skylar is again? Please, I really need you to keep a better eye on her," Molly said, taking the opportunity to speak privately to Jenny while Kate and Charlie were focused on Amanda.

"I…" Jenny sputtered, infuriated for so many reasons. Her emotions all welled up at once, and she turned to the room at large. Something in the energy of the office shifted, and suddenly, all eyes were on her.

"I HATE YOU ALL," she screamed, nearly incoherently, before she raced out of the room as quickly as her crutches would allow.

They were all quiet. Ryan looked like he was just about to run out after her, and Molly looked like she was about to cry in confusion. Charlie rested a comforting hand on each of their shoulders.

"Let her go," Charlie said. "She's told us, in her own way, that she needs a little space. Ryan, go find your sister, please."

Amanda tried to take advantage of the confusion to slink away as Ryan opened the door.

"No way," Kate barked, authoritatively pointing towards the empty chair in front of Molly's desk.

Amanda paused in her tracks, clearly considering her options. With a defeated shrug, she slumped into the chair and awaited her fate.

Containment

The meeting did not take long and did not go well. Charlie sat behind the desk, shaking her head with disbelief as Amanda walked briskly out the door of the office and hopped smoothly back into her waiting car. The reporter peeled out of the farm and headed back in the direction of the town.

"Can you believe the nerve? I swear, if she shows up and starts bothering Lilly, or Storm, or Doug…" Kate's thoughts trailed off as she tried to think up a consequence appropriately awful for the reporter if she got near Shamrock's most at-risk players.

Molly stood by the window silently, scanning the farm for a glimpse of her angry daughter, whose crutches wouldn't have allowed her to get too far. She had not said much since Jenny had left; it was obvious that she'd been hurt. Charlie, familiar with the sting, could tell Molly was just replaying the situation over and over in her head.

Charlie held her hands out comfortingly, beckoning Molly and Kate to take them. Both women were too caught up in the drama that had just swept through the room to even notice.

"I'm serious, though, I cannot believe her gall," Kate said, trying to relax the tension building in her clenched jaw. Lifting the pitch of her voice into a grating falsetto, she mimicked Amanda's final parting shot: "If you all are not interested in cooperating, I'll just follow up with Lilly and Doug directly. Care to provide the addresses for the horse whisperer and the hospital, or should I just look them up on my iPhone?"

Charlie shook her head and opened her mouth to respond, but Kate was on a roll.

"Did you see her face when I confronted her about how she's been cozying up to Hunter for info? Does she think we're blind? And suggesting that the fire was arson? I've looked over the reports and spoken with the investigator—both things she should have done before she dared to even mention such a thing! God, if nothing else, just think of what a mess it would make with the insurance companies if they caught a whiff of that! It would ruin all the work Molly has done over the past week, trying to get this place back in order."

Charlie had actually been quite impressed with the way the young reporter had stood up for herself. Her demeanor had been cool, but her eyes had been fiery when she'd said, "Listen, this is my job. I'm a reporter, and this is my beat—not a date, not a field trip, not anything. I'm on assignment, and I'm good at it, and you should respect that."

"Kate, please don't misunderstand me—I appreciate how protective you're being, and trust me, my hackles got raised too, just thinking about her bothering Doug and Lilly right now. But she's young and smart and ambitious, and she's chasing down her story. She actually reminds me a lot of you at that age."

Kate glared at Charlie. "How could you even—"

"I think we need to hire her," Molly said, spinning around to face the other two women and breaking her silence for the first time.

Kate shook her head in disbelief. "Have you both lost your minds? What did I miss that impressed you two so much? What about that entire exchange screamed 'job interview' to you?"

Molly stared at Kate and Charlie, calculating the risk of spreading the secret any further. After a moment, she nodded decisively.

"Here's the thing," she said, taking a deep breath. "As you both know, Steve and I adopted Jenny as a newborn. What is less well known—what, specifically, Jenny does not know—is that Lilly and Buck are her biological parents."

Charlie and Kate both listened in wide-eyed astonishment.

"When Jenny had her fall on Sarge at Pimlico, Lilly realized she couldn't keep it from Buck any longer. Harboring that information was what drove Lilly into seclusion in the first place, and it was killing her to be around Buck again at all these big races, still holding onto the secret. Lilly told Buck before the race and we were all going to sit down after the Preakness and discuss how to best tell Jenny, but then the fire happened, and everything spun out of control."

Kate started to nod slowly as the situation became clearer to her, but Charlie still looked confused. "Sorry, what in the world does that have to do with hiring Amanda?"

"I don't want Jenny to find out about this from a newspaper article, and I don't want her to be embarrassed by having the whole world know before she does," Molly explained.

"And you're right, Charlie. Amanda is smart, and she's driven," Kate said. "I don't love the comparison, but if I'd been desperate for leads and not getting much cooperation from sources, I'd be doing deep background checks."

"Okay, but it's not like any of us are going to say a word to her," Charlie said. "I'm glad Hunter doesn't know, but I'm sure even he would understand that this is private family business. No one is going to share anything." She turned to Kate. "Is there really a way for her to put this all together?"

"We're actually very lucky that no one has yet," Kate admitted. "Storm's rise has been so unexpected and meteoric that everyone has been focused on that. Lilly's return to the track has gotten some interest, but since the general public doesn't follow racing closely, no one has gone deep into exploring why she disappeared. Over at *BloodHorse,* there have been rumors for years, but they all have to do with her former mentor, Tom Malone. Thoroughbred racing and reporting are still highly insular, Charlie, and I don't think anyone wanted to do too much digging. If I was young and hungry and had no close ties to the community, though, I could see myself going deep and looking for records and asking questions about Lilly during that time."

Molly nodded, her fears confirmed. "The adoption was private, but Jenny's birth certificate lists Lilly as the mother. And anyone in the racing community at the time could have told you that Buck and Lilly were crazy about each other. Given that they're competitors now, it wouldn't take too much to connect those two dots for a very salacious story."

"Okay," Charlie said. "If this is what we need to do to protect Jenny—and Lilly and Buck—I am willing to have her join the Storm Trooper media team in whatever capacity you think you can handle, Kate."

Kate dropped her head into her hands and groaned at the thought of working closely with the reporter.

Well, I guess that's just another silver lining to Storm dropping out of the Belmont, Charlie thought, considering the looming probability that Storm's Triple Crown bid would end tomorrow when she went to visit him and Lilly. *Once we're out of the race, we should be out of the spotlight.*

 # Fleeing the Scene

Jenny had left the office and hobbled to one of the broodmare barns. As she sunk into the closest chair in the feed room, in another fit of defiance, she pulled her cell phone out and stabbed at the Uber app.

"Come on, be close," she wished through gritted teeth as she punched in a destination and the app searched for the nearest available driver.

"Yes!" Jenny whooped.

A car was less than fifteen minutes away, just long enough for her to drag herself to the end of the driveway. She didn't want her mom to see her leave the farm and start pestering her again.

The destination hadn't been important; she'd just needed to flee Shamrock.

Jenny waved down the black Toyota as it attempted to turn down the driveway, quickly hobbling over and flinging open the rear door.

"Robin?" she inquired, matching the middle-aged woman driving the car to the name that had been provided in the Uber app.

"That's me."

"Great. Thanks for picking me up," Jenny replied.

"Sure. Just confirming—we are heading to the Wawa over off of Main Street?"

"Yep, need to grab some sandwiches for the workers. My treat, and I want it to be a surprise," Jenny lied, not wanting to raise suspicion as to why she was out her by herself, on crutches. "Everyone has been so helpful taking on a lot of my duties since I got hurt, and I need to thank them."

"That is very kind and responsible of you, young lady," the driver said as she pulled away from the farm.

"Yeah, wish my mom thought so," Jenny muttered to herself.

Fifteen minutes later, the Uber dropped Jenny off in front of the Wawa.

"You need a ride back?" Robin asked her.

"No, my boyfriend is going to pick me up. Thanks, though,"

Oh great, another lie, Jenny thought.

Two of the gas station employees were out by the red picnic tables to the side of the building, finishing a smoke break. One of them gave her a little wave.

"Hey, Jenny, everything okay up there?" he said, gesturing up the road back towards the farm.

"What?" Jenny said, startled. "Oh! The fire. Yeah, everything is…"

Her words trailed off; she couldn't lie about everything being fine, or normal, or even necessarily getting better, but she masked it by hopping closer to the employees and acting as though the exertion of getting around on the crutches was to blame.

"Glad to hear it," the man said. "I better get inside and start making up your order. The usual?"

Jenny smiled, appreciating his kindness. She frequently stopped into the store on her way to the high school in the morning, as did many of the kids in the area. The store used high tech, self-service touchscreens, so she was surprised he remembered her usual order.

"Yes, please. I'll be in to grab it in a few minutes, gonna text a friend."

She sat down at the table and pulled out her phone as both employees went back inside the store. She was hoping to see a message from Ryan, and dreading seeing a message from Molly. It was anticlimactic to see that no one had tried to reach her yet.

She stood up to head inside and pick up her order when she realized she didn't have anything but her phone with her.

Oh great, how am I going to pay for my food? she thought, frustrated with her impulsivity. *What's wrong with me? I'm always so on top of things.*

I just can't handle all this pressure boiling up inside of me, she realized, *and I can't even talk to my own mom about it. Which* "Mom" *would I even talk to anyway?*

Jenny sat back down and put her head in her hands on the table and took a deep breath.

After a few moments, she lifted her head and sighed in desperation. She texted Ryan to see if he would bring her wallet over, then waited for a response. She tried to distract herself, flipping through the various social media feed notifications she'd missed from Snapchat, Facebook, and Instagram, absentmindedly spinning the lighter the employees had left behind. But inside her head, she was just playing out the scene to come, over and over, confronting her mother and father about Lilly and Buck. Each time was worse than the one before, and as she got more and more worked up, her eyes started to fill with tears again.

"Oooh, you smoke?" a voice beside her said brightly.

Jenny was startled; she hadn't heard anyone approach. The fact that it was the reporter she'd just left behind was an unpleasant realization. To cover her surprise and hide her sadness, she stared down at her phone, pretending to still be engrossed.

"What's it to you?" Jenny said sullenly. Realizing the employees had accidentally left not only the lighter but the pack of cigarettes behind, she grabbed it and took one out, immediately regretting it.

This is like playing a game of chicken, she thought, *and I'm losing. If I light this now, she's going to realize I've never smoked before.*

"May I?" Amanda asked, extending her hand.

Jenny handed her the pack of cigarettes.

Amanda rolled her eyes and deliberately dropped the pack on the ground, bringing her heel down on it like she was squishing a bug before taking the remaining one out of Jenny's hands and breaking it.

"Hey!" Jenny protested weakly. "You owe me, like..." Her voice trailed off again, as she realized she had no idea what the cost was.

Amanda smirked at her. "Oh, for sure, so sorry to ruin the awesome time you're having. You look like an idiot. Seriously. Your face is completely green, and it wasn't even lit."

Jenny, feeling every bit as nauseous as she looked, closed her eyes to stop the ground from spinning. "Leave me alone," she muttered. She flicked the lighter on and off, staring at the flame.

"Fine," Amanda said, sounding bored.

The reporter had just turned towards the convenience store when she smelled something awful. *Rotten eggs...salt marsh...gas leak...sulfur?*

Jenny shrieked, and Amanda spun right back around to see her clutch at a chunk of her hair.

"Nooonononono," the teenager wailed.

"Oh my God. Are you hurt?" Amanda asked, rushing over and pulling Jenny's hand away from her head. Realizing that the damage ran no deeper than the girl's now fried ends, she started to laugh. "Did you seriously just burn through a section of your hair?"

"I forgot I was holding...something...that was on fire," Jenny said, obviously miserable. "Like the genius I am. And now my mother is going to kill me."

Amanda sighed, equal parts amused, exasperated, and sympathetic. After a few moments' consideration, she said, "Oh, alright. Just get in my car."

"What? Why?"

"Well, it is obvious you need a friend right now," Amanda replied. "And a haircut. So, we're going to get your hair fixed."

"I don't have any money on me," Jenny said.

"It's on me."

Jenny, grateful for the distraction from her thoughts and the farm, stood up as quickly as her busted leg allowed. "Well, thanks. I'll pay you back. And for my sandwich that the guys are making me inside. I can't leave without paying them."

Amanda raised her eyebrows, surprised at the teenager's responsibility when most her age would probably just walk out on the tab. "Pay me back by promising me you never touch one of those things again," Amanda said, pointing to the squished remains of the pack on the ground.

After gathering Jenny's sandwich and a Diet Coke for Amanda, the two young women got into the car before Jenny asked, "Why do you even care that much? You know, about the smoking thing."

"My grandma, she smoked like a chimney. She was awesome and raised me after my folks split. Dad took off, and Mom had a drug problem. After my mom had racked up one too many trips to rehab and then to jail for dealing, Granny adopted me," Amanda said matter-of-factly. "Lung cancer from the smoking killed her by the time I was thirteen."

"Ugh, sorry," Jenny said. After a quiet moment, curiosity got the best of her. "So…what happened to you then?"

"Foster care system until I aged out. Not much fun."

"I'm adopted too," Jenny said, feeling the words bubble up in her mouth. It was the first time she'd ever said that to a stranger.

"I didn't know that," Amanda said, smiling at the younger girl.

"Yeah—you know, I'm not sure I've ever met anyone else who was adopted."

"You probably have," Amanda said. "About two percent of the US population is adopted, but it's not like we all wear nametags. A lot of people only think of things like international adoptions, but many of the situations are pretty complicated—like, stepparents adopting a child from a previous marriage, or, like in my case, being adopted by other family members."

"Oh, mine is complicated, for sure," Jenny said, settling back in the passenger seat. She saw her phone light up with a text, but she chose to ignore it. She sat quietly, pondering her next course of action, wrestling with her emotions, before she continued, "Have I ever got a story for you…"

Undated

Amanda had been a heavy sleeper all her life, and she could sleep any-where. They were useful talents that she'd relied on her entire life in NYC, from sharing a cramped one bedroom apartment with her grandma to sharing dorm rooms to sharing a studio with four other unpaid newspaper interns. She could sleep through parties and arguments and general mad-ness, but there was something about the way Hunter's cottage was amplify-ing the thunderstorm that had woken her and kept her up on high alert. The storm had moved in slowly, and the thunder had started rattling the bot-tles on Hunter's windowsill far before she had been able to hear its rumble or feel any vibrations. At first, the tiny tinkling noise was almost nice, but as the storm inched closer, the noise built up into louder crashes and exac-erbated the migraine blooming behind her eyes. Even if she wouldn't have been able to tell otherwise, the bottles kept her carefully informed as the storm reached its crescendo.

Wide awake, she navigated around mismatched furniture and clothing piles of dubious cleanliness to the bathroom.

What a weird day, Amanda thought, downing another glass of water and searching the strange medicine cabinet for aspirin.

Spending time with Jenny had actually been a lot of fun. It had also been very informative, but, regretfully, Amanda knew she wouldn't be able to use any of the information she'd gotten.

"We're going to have to work on not getting too close to your subjects," Amanda whispered sternly at her reflection.

They had both ignored multiple phone calls from Shamrock as they sat at the small salon in town. Jenny had gotten a sleek bob with short bangs, and Amanda had treated herself to a blowout in preparation for her evening plans. By the time she'd dropped Jenny back off at the farm, they were like old friends.

Driving back to her office, Amanda had finally checked her voicemail, and was surprised to hear Kate apologize for her attitude and ask her to come back to Shamrock in the morning for a follow-up discussion.

There had been no time to return the call. She'd only had a few minutes to check in with her editor and collect her things before her scheduled dinner with Hunter. At the time, she'd been vacillating about whether it was a date or not; by the end of the evening, though, she'd made up her mind for certain.

Hunter had obviously not had the same hesitation. She gave him high marks for his initiative; he'd avoided several of her pet peeves. He had called her with a specific plan—a certain restaurant that he had already made reservations at for a certain time—no shrugging off the details and expecting her to plan her own date. There had even been a flower waiting on her desk with a sweet note about how much he was looking forward to seeing her. She'd groaned as she looked around the newsroom and wondered what snide comments were headed her way, but it had actually made some of the older reporters a little nostalgic. They'd spent a few moments swapping stories about the girls they had really courted—some loves lost, some pursued all the way to the altar. It had seemed a little old-fashioned, but she'd liked it a lot.

She'd planned to drive over to the restaurant, but it had been a beautiful evening, so she had decided to walk. Now, looking out the window at the lightning spider-webbing across the sky, she had trouble believing it, but there hadn't been a cloud in sight.

She'd just approached the restaurant from the other side of the street when Hunter came around from the parking lot. She'd waited for a few cars to go by so she could jaywalk over, enjoying the clear view of his handsome face and the fact that he hadn't seemed to see her yet.

She'd watched him skirt around the café tables in the front, testing out her telepathy and trying to will him into asking for one of those, unable to imagine missing a moment of this incredible weather.

He'd seemed to be receptive to her mental magic, scoping out the tables, and she was just about to call out to him when she saw the expression on his face change completely. It became complicated and unpleasant in a way that she hadn't been able to decipher, which hit her in the gut hard. Hunter's openness had been a major draw for her, but he'd suddenly felt as much like a stranger as he, in fact, was.

She'd followed out his gaze, not sure what she was looking for—*Ex-wife? Current girlfriend? Ugh, current wife?*—but the patio hadn't been crowded. Unless he was or had been dating one portion of a couple in their seventies or a squat middle-aged man who seemed more into reading his phone than using his utensils properly, she didn't think she was about to walk into a lover's triangle.

In the next moment, he'd seen her, and the expression melted away so quickly she'd thought she might have imagined it. He'd flashed a dazzling smile and waved her over.

"Hiya, beautiful. I've been looking forward to seeing you all day. You would not believe the day I've had." Hunter had pulled a face that made Amanda laugh and launched into a humorous story.

He is an exceptional showman…quite the storyteller, Amanda had thought. She couldn't decide whether she should let the alarm bells in her head keep fading away, or if she should stubbornly keep them going. In her experience, liars were plentiful, and she'd been burned badly by a few.

"Feel free to say no, but I'd kick myself if I didn't ask—how do you feel about skipping out on the reservation and letting me make dinner for you back at my cottage?"

Hunter's smile had been blinding, but the alarm bells in her head were now deafening.

"Oh, is everything okay?" Her voice had sounded strange to her, but Hunter didn't seem to notice.

"It really couldn't be better. I can't tell you how excited I am to spend time with you. It's just that my day has been incredibly busy, with being at the track at the crack of dawn and then back at the farm. It would be great just to have a quiet night instead of dealing with waiters and menus."

Amanda had swallowed. *Maybe he isn't a liar,* she'd thought. *Maybe this is more of a brush off.*

"Oh, I mean, if you'd rather reschedule…"

"No!" Hunter had touched her arm gently, and his entire demeanor changed completely. "I'm sorry, I know this doesn't look great. Honestly, I wish Shamrock wasn't a mess right now, but it is, and I'm worried about Molly. I agreed right before I left to help her out with some extra work tomorrow. When I walked up and looked over the tables, it became so obvious to me that if I sit down here, between your company and their calamari and exotic cabernets, I'll never go home. Don't think that's not incredibly tempting, but I just can't let Molly—or Doug—down when we're this short-staffed."

Amanda had looked into his eyes as he'd spoken, and she'd seen how soft and affectionate they'd gotten when he'd said Molly and Doug's names.

Ugh, he's not a liar, Amanda, she'd chastised herself, *he's just a wonderful friend. And the crappy date might be…you. Like, give a dude a chance to even do something sketchy before you jump to thinking about him as a monster.*

Plus, I'd love to hear more about Doug. Amanda had perked up as soon as Hunter had mentioned him. The only updates she'd gotten were what Charlie posted in her blog or on the Facebook page. Everyone else at Shamrock seemed to have set a gag order on news of Doug and how he was doing in the hospital; even Jenny hadn't volunteered anything about his recovery. *Maybe Hunter will have some further details that he could let slip.*

Hunter had read her silence as waffling and raised the stakes. "Okay, how about a couple of steak filets, Caesar salad, and fresh buttered slices of the sourdough I made this morning, with those crazy gourmet cupcakes for dessert?"

"Bread you made this morning?" Amanda had retorted, suspicious.

"Yep, the best you have ever tasted," Hunter said, linking his fingers with hers and tugging her arm gently towards his truck in the back parking lot.

Amanda had resisted the urge to tell him she'd never ridden in a pickup truck before.

After a quick stop at the meat counter of the local grocery store, the two had made their way back to Hunter's cottage. It stood at one end of a row of six, all identical and charmingly simple. Amanda had seen it from the outside during the grand tour he'd taken her on. Though, he'd made sure she hadn't seen the inside before they'd split a bottle of wine while enjoying the sunset in the two Adirondack chairs on his front porch.

Looking at the mess strewn around her now, she thought, *Well, at least I know he wasn't fibbing about the spontaneity of our changed plans. He would have cleaned up at least a little if he'd thought I'd be here tonight.*

He'd grilled the steaks while she'd tossed the salad in Caesar dressing and sliced the bread he had indeed made himself, which she'd struggled to stay silently impressed by. He'd turned a speaker towards the open window and they'd eaten outside, laughing and listening to music as the world grew dark around them. The food and ambiance had been magical, and the conversation had been so great that she'd actually forgotten to play reporter and get the scoop on Doug.

Hunter had indeed grabbed several gourmet cupcakes from the bakery for dessert, and as they taste-tested each of them, Hunter talked about the horses running against Storm in the Belmont. Amanda had been intrigued with his extensive knowledge. Given his history in pinhooking and with horse auctions, he had been able to recite each horse's history from birth, from their breeder to which auction they had sold at to how often they had changed hands.

"That's a lot of information you keep in your head," Amanda had commented; her journalist mind, well-equipped for large data downloads, was reeling.

Hunter reached out and wiped a bit of frosting off Amanda's lip.

"Got to stay on top of your competition, from where they are from to how fast they go. Take for instance, Royal Duke: his speed figure in the Derby was 105, yet he had a 119 in the Santa Anita Derby, which is crazy good. I know he has the ability to run faster and more efficiently, and I want Doug to be aware that he may sneak up on Storm in the Belmont. We haven't seen the last of this rivalry," Hunter smiled.

"Speed figures?" Amanda asked. "What are those?"

Hunter raised his eyebrows. "You *are* a novice, aren't you?"

Amanda batted at his hand, which he'd rested lightly on her knee. "Unfair, you know I am just learning these ropes."

"Okay, okay." Hunter held up his hands. "Beyer Speed Figures are the numbers that rate a horse's performance in a race. They take into account the winning time, as well as the inherent speed of the track the race was run on, universalizing for the length of the race. The speed figures are used to compare horses, which is especially useful as they don't run against each other all the time. If one horse is competing on the East Coast and the other on the West Coast, how do you compare who might be better once they come up in a race against each other? The rating system was designed by Andrew Beyer, who is a horse racing columnist."

"A journalist." Amanda was impressed and envious that someone in her field would have a whole rating system named after him.

"The calculation is too complicated for me to go into, but basically, the theory is that the higher the rating, the better the horse. Stakes horses generally get speed figures in the 120s, good allowance horses run around 100, claimers eighty to ninety—you get the picture. Every performance of every horse in North America is assigned a Beyer number, and those appear exclusively in the *Daily Racing Form*. It's useful information, it truly is, but not to be considered in a vacuum. Keep in mind that each figure is a point in time in a horse's career and does not guarantee any future success. Reality is, a horse is an animal, and sometimes they just might not want to run the next time out." Hunter winked at Amanda.

They had bantered back and forth for a bit more. Eventually, Amanda had brought the conversation around to her favorite conspiracy theories about Shamrock, Storm, and the Triple Crown bid.

"I really haven't dug through all the insurance scam options," Amanda had said, referring to the fire.

Hunter had shaken his head. "All the other costs aside, do you know how much it costs to get a horse into a Triple Crown race? The Kentucky Derby itself has a $25,000 entry fee, and if your horse makes it to the gate, a $25,000 start fee. The Preakness and Belmont Stakes have $15,000 entry fees and $15,000 start fees. That doesn't even cover the cost of a Triple Crown nomination—you've got to announce that you're trying for it. If Charlie made the decision by the January deadline, she only paid $600—but if she missed that, she had until the middle of March to apply for a mere $6,000. If she waited any longer than that, it was a $200,000 fee. Storm isn't owned by some multinational corporation—she's invested a meaningful amount of money into him, same as Shamrock. Why would they have tanked his chances now?"

"Well, maybe they didn't want to take the risk of him losing—you said yourself, Duke is still a contender, as are the horses that are coming in fresh, having not endured competing in so many races so close together. From what I've read about stud fees, the possibility of owning a Triple Crown winner would more than pay for itself. It'd probably be more lucrative to own a horse that should have won than one who suffered a humiliating defeat."

"And what if Storm had gotten injured or killed in the fire?" Hunter had asked somberly. "Your arson theory sounds less like an investigation and more like you're getting into writing detective novels."

Amanda had started to get a little defensive. "Well, Travis disagrees. He senses something more is at play too, and he's certainly spent enough time around fires to get a feeling for when something isn't right. Maybe the issue isn't the idea of arson, but the motivations."

Hunter had started to clear their plates. "Hmm. Well, if we're going to start talking about the world's most boring fire fighter, I'm going to need another drink. Have you ever tried grappa?"

Amanda had shaken her head, and Hunter had given her one of his million-watt grins. "Well, then I have quite a treat for you!"

Disappearing inside the house, he'd come back out with two small glasses filled with a thick syrup so purple it was almost black.

Amanda had taken a small sip. "Oh no, I don't think so—too sweet, even for me!"

Hunter had pouted. "Well, I'll never make you drink it again, but you've got to at least finish the glass. I smuggled this bottle back from Italy with me on my last trip, and I cannot allow you to waste it."

Amanda had smiled. "Well, thank you for sharing your booty, even if it does taste like candied cough syrup." She took another sip and continued her thought. "Anyways, when Travis and I spoke about the investigator's report—"

Hunter had rolled his eyes. "Really, do we have to talk about him? Just thinking about that guy makes me sleepy. He's so boring, predictable, and stiff, too responsible and respectable for his own good."

Amanda had taken a longer sip of her grappa, suddenly aware of how sleepy she'd gotten. It was past time to tie up the evening. "Fine," she said amiably, "but—"

"But nothing," Hunter had said, putting his arms around her. "I'm not surprised that Travis is chasing ghosts to make his life seem more exciting, but you don't need to fall into that trap—I'll provide all the excitement you could ever need."

Hunter had swept her into a kiss, but Amanda was surprised to find that she hadn't immediately melted into it. She was attracted to Hunter's adventurous spirit, but Kate's insinuations from earlier in the day had preyed on her mind.

"Please," she'd said, gently pushing him away. "I find you absolutely charming, but it really wouldn't be professional for me to start something romantic until I'm finished the story."

"Oh," Hunter had said, pulling away. "I…feel like such a fool."

Amanda's heart had hurt for him as he'd looked around at the remains of their romantic meal. "No, no, I'm sorry—this was incredible, and I would love to have a real date after the Triple Crown wraps up." She'd been unable to stifle her yawn. "I really do enjoy your company."

Hunter shook his head. "Well, I still should have been much more considerate. I think that grappa may have been one drink too many for us both. I'd offer to drive you back to your place, but I'm in no shape. I can ask one of the folks from Shamrock, but I'm sure that wouldn't help your professional reputation. I can call you a cab…"

Amanda could feel the effects of the bottles of wine and after dinner drink as her head began to feel fuzzy. "If I could just lie down for a few minutes…"

"Of course," Hunter had said, gently helping her to her feet and leading her inside.

I must have been mostly asleep before I even hit the threshold, she thought.

She was relieved to find that, besides her shoes, all her other clothing was on and accounted for. The light of the bathroom illuminated part of the adjacent living room, and she could see Hunter asleep on the couch. His bare, muscular torso glowed in the dark with the exception of a narrow, jagged stripe burned down one side.

A wave of nausea ripped through her body in time with the storm raging outside. She grabbed at her shirt and held it against her mouth and ran back into the bathroom. Barely in time, her body deposited all that she had in her stomach into the toilet in front of her, but not before she could get her shirt out of the way.

Amazing—I drink too much, he gives me his bed, and this is how I repay him. So professional.

Head pounding and already embarrassed, she tore off the shirt and shoved it under the faucet, washing away as much of the bright purple stain as she could before her pounding head forced her to stop.

She grabbed the closest shirt she could from beside her on the bathroom floor and slipped it over her head before crawling back to Hunter's bed.

Height of the Storm

Across the farm a few acres, Jenny was also wide awake, but she couldn't blame it on the storm. She stared at her ceiling, so buried in her own thoughts that she didn't even process how brightly the lightning flashed around her room. The storm outside her window just couldn't compete with the one raging inside her mind.

It wasn't the first time she'd been unable to sleep since the fire; in fact, she'd been having insomnia problems ever since she'd broken her leg. It itched more at night; sometimes she'd just hobble around the farmhouse to keep the circulation going, enjoy some quiet time, and try to wear herself out.

Tonight, though, she wasn't getting out of bed. She couldn't risk meeting up with anyone. After she'd gotten back from her impromptu haircut, she'd texted Ryan to let everyone know she had gotten a ride home from the Wawa with a friend and had a headache, and subsequently holed up in her room all evening. Molly had crept in to check on her around dinner time, but Jenny had pretended to be fast asleep.

Jenny had teared up when she'd peeked out and seen the plate Molly had left behind on her nightstand. It was stacked with rolls of sweet Lebanon bologna filled with chunky peanut butter—a favorite food she and her mom shared, much to the disgust of the rest of the family. They were quick and easy, but Jenny knew they hadn't had the supplies in the house, which meant Molly must have taken at least an hour out of her impossibly long and hard day to go pick them up for her. She'd almost run down the stairs after her mom, but Jenny hadn't known whether she would cry or scream or just hug Molly if she caught her at that moment. Until she figured out exactly how she felt, she didn't want to risk talking to or seeing anyone.

Around midnight, she'd heard her mom and dad—that is Molly and Steve—come in from their long days just a few minutes apart. She'd expected them to come straight upstairs and go to bed, but there had been no foot-fall on the stairs.

She could hear the muffled sounds of them talking at first, and pictured her parents sitting together on the couch, sipping glasses of wine and unwinding from their long day. Her heart had hurt as she'd considered the fact that, even though they were dealing with the most stressful situation the farm had ever faced, they would still turn to each other for strength and comfort. This was the family she knew, the family she'd always known—loving, honest, strong. Some part of her had wanted to go join them, to curl up in between them like she was little again. Although she'd been sure they would have welcomed her, she could not bring herself to go downstairs. She'd been positive that they would be able to read her recently acquired knowledge written across her face.

Finally, the pain had gotten to be too much, and she'd decided to go and talk to them—to face everything head-on, the way they'd always taught her to deal with problems. She'd opened the door and quietly scooted along to the top of the steps when she'd realized she could make out parts of their conversation. It sounded like Molly was crying. She had rested her head against the cool wall at the top of the stairs to listen.

"Don't you realize what you've done?" she'd heard her mom say.

"Molly, I don't know what to say. I'm so sorry. I really thought I would be able to fix it before anyone got hurt. Please, please—" her father had pleaded. "It was never supposed to happen like this. The insurance...the fire...it all just spun out of control."

"'It' spun out of control?" Molly retorted in a venomous whisper. "*No, you threw any semblance of control out the window.* How could you do this to me...to our family...to my brother...to the whole farm? People could have died. Steve, we could lose *everything*. They could take Shamrock."

As she'd tried to puzzle out the meaning of their words, Jenny had started to wonder if this was some type of practical joke. She'd felt frozen to her spot at the top of the stairs, unable to move or make a sound, positive her heartbeat had to be reverberating throughout the entire house.

Did Dad set fire to the barn?

"What should we do?" Steve asked, his voice cracking.

There'd been a long moment of silence before Molly had replied, "The arson investigation should be closing shortly. I will continue to work with the insurance companies. You will touch no paperwork. You will say nothing. You will smile and be polite and show as little worry as possible."

The cold, calm calculation in Molly's voice had scared Jenny. It wasn't novel—Jenny had seen her mother take on everyone from playground bullies to racetrack adversaries with the same steely reserve. What chilled Jenny to the bone now was that Molly could apparently betray the rest of Shamrock to cover for Steve.

"What about the rest of the money?" Steve had asked.

"I don't know," Molly said sadly. "But you need to start praying now that Storm wins. If he loses, we're done. And if anything—I mean ANY-THING—happens to him, there will be so many people combing through the past—well, we'll be done. Life as we know it now rests on those broad, grey shoulders."

The blood had rushed to Jenny's face and pounded in her ears. She'd felt like she would collapse on the spot, so she practiced breathing in and out slowly, steadying herself. She crawled back to her room, unable to listen to anything more.

Watching as the lightning lit up the ceiling above her bed, she clenched and unclenched her fists, feeling betrayed and angry and guilty and afraid all at once. It wasn't raining inside, but the pillow on which Jenny's head rested was sopping wet from her tears.

———————

Across town, Charlie was wide awake. There were no windows in Doug's hospital room from which she could see the storm, but they were on the top floor and the roof was metal. The heavy rain pounded against it incessantly, and the rapid-fire thuds echoed down the long hallways and reverberated back. The sedatives that Charlie would have required to sleep through it would have rivaled the crazy cocktail Doug was on.

Over the past week, the nurses had snuck a second chair and a few extra pillows and blankets into the room for her, and Charlie had created a chair-bed-workstation. She looked down at the blog post she'd been working on—a thank you to Storm's supporters, announcing the sad news that he would not be able to run in the Belmont. As difficult as it was to write it now, she certainly didn't expect to be in the mood to do it after she saw Storm.

She looked over at Doug, fast asleep, and said a quick prayer that his dreams were good—or, if the nightmares continued, that he was fighting them and winning. It had been a rough day at Shamrock and a rough day back here at the hospital for Doug. As the nurse had warned, he was dealing with mild short-term memory loss, nasty flashbacks to the fire, and vivid nightmares from the induced coma.

Still, she thought warmly, *he has such grace and purpose. He is so committed to everything he does. He is very grateful for me, and we will only be stronger for having walked through this fire together.*

Charlie had continued working through her fears, and she'd also turned a corner. Helping Doug and being by his side, she'd started to become aware of inner-strength that she'd felt robbed of after Peter died.

I couldn't fix or help Peter, but I can help Doug.

In the early morning hours, after the storm had passed but before the sun rose, Charlie saved her farewell draft and slipped out the door to start the trip to Pine Grove. She left Doug with a tablet and a link to her blog, so he could catch up on everything that had been happening and what she had written about their situation and the history of the Triple Crown.

This storm didn't want to move off. The thunder and lightning were coming in quick succession, so Lilly knew it was sitting right on top of them. The rain had been pelting the roof for a good hour, and the electricity had gone out shortly after it started. A small candle flickered across the room on the kitchen counter. Lilly didn't like pitch blackness, as it tended to bring back old, horrible memories of her beating at the hands of Tom Malone. She had found the candle and matches in a cabinet.

Buck must be getting worried, Lilly thought, laying still in her bed. She knew through their limited conversations that he was back and forth between helping at Shamrock, riding races, and preparing Duke for the Belmont. However, her conversations with him had been short, as they couldn't seem to coordinate their schedules to have a long phone call.

I guess I'll have a lot more time on my hands once I get Storm back to Shamrock.

The decision to call Charlie up to the farm had weighed heavily on her all day, but in the end, she thought it had probably been the right call. Days were passing them by, and Doc didn't seem to be making progress with Storm; at a certain point, the most kind thing to do was to gracefully accept that the timelines for healing and the timelines for racing just were not going to match up for the Belmont. After placing the call to Charlie, Lilly had started making all of the arrangements to take Storm home in the morning. She'd gotten into bed early, but the lightning and thunder had woken her with a start.

The candle flickered and blew out from a blast of air that blew through the cabin as the height of the storm descended on the little valley.

"Shoot," Lilly said softly into the pitch blackness that now surrounded her. She swung her legs out of the bed and felt her way over to the counter. She could feel the sink in front of her.

A bolt of lightning lit up the cabin and the outside as Lilly lifted her eyes and looked out the window above the sink.

"What the...?" she said loudly, her fear of the darkness dissipating at she caught a glimpse of a man with a horse standing outside in the middle of the rain storm.

Lilly wiped at the window pane, trying to see through the pelting drops. She stood still.

Did I imagine it? She held her breath, waiting for the next bolt of lightning. The thunder roared outside. She counted one Mississippi, two Mississippi's, just like when she was a kid, counting off the seconds between the thunder and lightning.

The lightning came and lit up the whole valley.

And they were still there. Lilly felt the goosebumps rise on her arms.

Standing in the middle of the field was Doc, and at the end of his lead rope stood Storm. And then she couldn't see them.

"Oh crap, what is he doing?"

Lilly turned around to flip the light switch, not remembering the electric was out. She got on her hands and knees and crawled towards the front door of the cabin, feeling for her boots. Pulling them on, she realized she was pulling them over her jammy bottoms. Hesitating for a few seconds, she rationalized that she didn't have time to go crawl around for her clothes. She grabbed her windbreaker and threw it over her pajama top.

Lilly opened the door and pulled the hood up over her head and tightened the strings. The rain whipped at her face and the jammy bottoms were immediately soaked. Her body shook with the next round of thunder that broke above her head. Once again, Lilly waited for the lightning to help show her the way. She was rewarded a few seconds later as once again the sky lit up the valley and the fields around.

No horse or man to be seen.

"What? Where did they go?" Lilly asked herself aloud. "Did I imagine it?"

Where would he take him? Lilly stood at the door of her cabin, soaking wet, pondering her next move. As the storm continued to rage overhead, she reached behind her for the doorknob, forcing herself back into the cabin and convincing herself she had imagined the whole thing.

PART FIVE

 # A Busy Morning

Lilly awoke with a start, assuring herself that seeing Storm in the field last night had been a dream.

My nerves might be just as fried as Storm's, Lilly thought, shaking her head as she hooked the horse trailer to her truck. Today was going to be hard enough; once Charlie came and gave the final word, she wanted to be able to load Storm up and take him home with as little delay as possible. Everything would be ready and set.

Even if it did happen, what in the world does that change? Storm got wet? Doesn't make him any more ready to race than before.

She turned the corner of the barn to the open paddock area where she'd left Storm grazing the evening before, and her heart stopped.

Storm was gone.

Jumping the fence in one fluid motion, she took off running, looking in every direction for the missing horse. Her heart was in her throat, considering the possibilities—what if he'd been stolen? What if he'd jumped the fence during the night, scared of the thunder? How long had he been gone?

From the barn behind her, she heard a soft, friendly whinny.

Whirling around, she faced the open Dutch doors on the side of the barn Storm was, theoretically, staying in. The assignment had been more of a formality than an actual safety zone, as the horse had fearfully resisted entering the barn since they'd arrived. Now, though, he stood inside his stall, munching hay cheerfully and looking as relaxed as she'd ever seen him.

"Geez, Storm," Lilly said, her heartbeat slowly returning to a normal pace, "you shouldn't scare me like that."

The racehorse paused and gave her a look that almost seemed indignant.

"No, you're right," Lilly ceded, walking towards him. "I'm proud of you for going into the barn. I thought a lot about you out in the rain last night—I even dreamt about it. I'm glad you had the good sense to take yourself indoors. I guess that mean old storm convinced you the barn isn't all that bad."

Storm nuzzled her shoulder playfully as she stood next to him.

"You are in a much better place," Lilly said. "Do you know we're going home today? The heat is off."

"Not sure that it is," Doc said in his low, comfortably gruff growl as he approached silently from the other end of the barn.

"Oh, I didn't realize you were here," Lilly said. "I just came to see Storm, let him know that Charlie would be here shortly. I imagine things will go quickly once Charlie gets here, so just in case we don't have time later, I want to thank you now for everything you've done, Doc. Storm is certainly getting better, and just because he isn't in Belmont shape doesn't mean—"

Doc put out a hand, signaling Lilly to pause.

She waited for him to say something, but he remained silent so long, she figured that she had misread the signal, and continued, "Right, so, just because he isn't—"

Doc held out his hand again, accompanying it this time with an odd smile.

After another long moment of silence, Doc finally said, "Take a deep breath. Focus on what is right in front of you. Tell me what you see."

"A long drive and a longer bath," Lilly joked. "Time with my fiancé. More races, just further down the road. It's not like the Belmont Stakes is the end of the season. Maybe we'll make the Haskell Invitational at the end of July, or go out west in August for the Pacific Classic, or stay here and run the Travers at Saratoga…"

Lilly's voice petered out as Doc rested his heavy hand on her shoulder.

"Right in front of you," he repeated.

"Oh, right in front of me, right now? I see…" she paused, giving Storm a hard look. "Actually…I see a horse who looks better rested than anyone has any right to expect, all things considering."

"Stop getting ahead of yourself. You closed your heart off to hope, because you already decided it was hopeless. Be open to being wrong. Go get his saddle," Doc said.

Lilly considered protesting, but something is his nearly hypnotic voice tipped the scales.

Storm easily let Lilly tack him, showing none of the extreme anxiety he'd been displaying for the past week—showing not even some of his more standard high-strung behaviors. He let her lead him into the sunlight of the field next to the stables, and didn't balk when she hopped into the saddle.

As soon as she'd gotten her feet secured in the stirrups, though, he froze completely.

Time stood still as Lilly became suddenly aware of how exposed they were. Every muscle in his powerful body was tensed.

If he throws me right now—if he goes wild—if he hurts himself, if he hurts me—

Without warning, Storm gathered himself and took off, faster than Lilly had ever felt him start. Lilly braced herself and stayed with him; there was no jolt, no need for her to regain her sense of balance. He ran like water, more gracefully than she'd ever felt, on him or any horse.

This is what a horse running on pure joy feels like, she thought, feeling the elation spread from his body to hers. Storm didn't just love running, the way he had before the fire, he lived for it.

After a few minutes, Lilly took up the reins in earnest, slowing Storm down and steering him back towards Doc, who was waiting, watching, inscrutable.

"What…happened? What happened in the storm, Doc?" Lilly asked, bewildered. "I've worked with a lot of horses, I've ridden some of the best, and I've never felt anything like this."

Doc smiled at her in response and pointed at the road. "Keep looking in front of you, Lilly."

Lilly looked up and saw Charlie hanging out of her driver's side window, mouth agape.

It was going to be a very busy day.

———————————

Amanda was dreaming again, but it was a light early morning dream; part of her realized she was half aware. She'd incorporated the knocking into her dreams at first, but woke with a start when she realized it was real, and coming from the front door of Hunter's cottage.

She groaned inwardly at both the pounding in her head and at the fact that she had woken up in Hunter's bed, realizing once again that she'd never made it home last night.

She heard noises coming from the bathroom and realized that Hunter was in the shower. The knocking started again. She could hear someone saying something outside, but couldn't make out the words.

Amanda sleepily hobbled over to the door, running a hand through her hair as she opened it.

Her heart sank.

"Oh! You are…not Hunter," Kate said, clearly taken aback.

"Ummm…" Amanda wracked her wrecked brain for a clever response, but came up short. "What are you doing here?"

"My job," Kate smirked.

Amanda, realizing how this looked, went beet red. It felt like all the oxygen had been sucked out of the room. She opened her mouth to explain, but she'd only managed a lame "Me too," when the bathroom door opened. Hunter came out in a towel.

"Oh, hey Kate! Good morning, what can I do you for?" Hunter said jovially, walking up behind Amanda and draping his arm casually across her shoulders.

"Molly asked me to come grab you, you're not answering your phone," Kate said, pointing towards the small black phone resting conspicuously on the table. "Guess you were busy. Anyways, the storm last night felled some trees on the far side of the paddocks. With everyone moving in different directions, she was hoping you'd help Steve coordinate the workers to get everything cleared up."

"Sure thing, I'll be over there in a few."

"Thanks," Kate said to Hunter, turning back towards Shamrock's main office. "Sorry to interrupt your meeting," she smirked slightly, looking back at Amanda for the first time. "Please let me know if your busy professional schedule opens up for a few minutes today so we can talk."

Well, this is the most embarrassed I've ever been, thought Amanda.

"You should hop in the shower next, Amanda," Kate called over her shoulder as she walked away. "You smell like a moldy campfire."

No, never mind, this is the most embarrassed I've ever been, she corrected herself.

Shutting the door, she absentmindedly sniffed the t-shirt and realized Kate was right. Of all the shirts she could have chosen, this was the yellow one Hunter had been wearing the night of the fire, and it was pretty obvious he had not done laundry yet.

She became aware that Hunter was speaking to her, and she tuned back in. He was already in the kitchenette, leaning into the refrigerator, talking about what he could make for breakfast.

She was relieved that he hadn't seemed to notice that she hadn't been paying attention. She scurried over to the fridge to take a better look, so she wouldn't have to ask him to repeat any of the options. The fridge was a tangled mess of fresh ingredients she'd never seen before, and looking at them didn't help.

"Oh, I have no idea, surprise me," she said, leaning in to grab something she did recognize—orange juice.

Hunter straightened up at that same time that she pulled the juice container free, and she accidentally brushed into the ugly, dark wound that streaked his torso. He winced.

"Oh my goodness," she said. "I'm so sorry."

"Oh, don't worry about that," he said, giving her a smile.

"What happened there? It looks fresh."

"Just a souvenir from the fire," Hunter replied. "Looks uglier than it is. In all the excitement, I actually did not even notice how bad it was or how much it hurt until I came back home and got into the shower the next morning, right after I woke you up in the field."

"It's been a week," Amanda said, examining it closer, "and it's still so inflamed around the edges. You should really go see a doctor."

Hunter gave her a sheepish smile. "Well, yeah. It's a tough spot to heal, my shirt rubs against it all day. But I do appreciate your concern—and your interest in my torso—so I'll see what I can do about getting some proper medical attention."

They grinned at each other before Hunter dived back into the fridge, pulling out strange ingredients left and right for breakfast. While he was busy putting together something for them to eat, Amanda slipped back into the bedroom to retrieve her damp shirt and exchanged it with the smelly dirty yellow one.

"You may want to do a bit of laundry, given your clothes still smell like the fire," Amanda commented as she grabbed the sandwich Hunter held out for her.

"Yeah, been a bit busy. Care to come back and be not only my nurse maid, but my cleaning lady? Seems like your shirt could use a bit of cleaning as well," Hunter quipped at her with one of his lazy smiles as his eyes traveled to the faded purple stain on her own shirt.

"Not on your life," Amanda shot back with her own sly smile. "I may come back, but it will be with a great story…and I won't be partaking in that cough syrup you forced on me last night."

"Sounds like we've both got things to do—we can eat and run."

They both made their ways to the front door.

"Oh, wait!" Amanda said, running back to the table.

She picked up the phone and it lit up.

"You almost forgot your phone," she said, handing it over to him. "Don't want to miss another call from Molly."

"Thanks," he said, pocketing it smoothly while he shook his head. "Now, hurry up and finish your story, so I can take you on a real date before I get old and really senile."

They smiled at each other and left to start another hectic day.

 # Breaking News

Kate's eggs had been runny and perfect when she'd sat down in front of her laptop. She'd started the day early because she had plans—big plans. She'd slated the entire morning to relax and work on her own projects. It was the silver lining she'd sold herself on, the one bright spot for bringing Amanda into the Shamrock social media and PR fold. For the first time since she'd arrived, she was going to have the chance to make her way leisurely through her own research and notes, to prepare for covering the Belmont Stakes for *BloodHorse*.

Now her eggs were just a congealed mess on the plate, and her plans for the day looked similarly dismal.

I knew I'd regret bringing Amanda on to the team, Kate thought, scowling at the screen as she read the article for the hundredth time. *I had no idea how much, though, or how soon.*

Kate had to admit that Amanda had tried to warn them. The meeting had been awkward at first, at least for Kate; she had regretted being sarcastic when she'd caught Amanda in Hunter's cabin. Amanda, on the other hand, seemed cool as a cucumber as she was advised of the new role that Molly, Charlie, and Kate had envisioned.

"Frankly, we could use your help." Kate had held up her hand to lower Amanda's skeptical eyebrow. "I'm not asking you to sacrifice any of your… uh…journalistic integrity. Each and every one of us here at the farm is currently doing the work of five people, and our internal PR department, mostly me and Ryan, is no different. Ryan's been incredible, but we've got to get him back for the last few days of school before they send the truancy officers over state lines."

Amanda had given the smallest smirk possible in appreciation for Kate's humor. *Tough crowd.*

"I need to be able to take some time off, at least a few hours a day, from constantly combing the entire web for new rumors about Storm, Doug, Lilly, and the farm to dispel. I could use an ally, and as you are the person who has single handedly managed to create the most fires for me to put out, I want you on my team."

"Which means what?" the younger reporter had asked. "You're telling me I'm not supposed to sign away my integrity, but all I'm hearing is 'stop making messes.'"

"Is that an option? Will you just stop making messes? I think we'd actually pay money for that," Kate said, grinning wryly. "No. I know we've gotten off on the wrong foot, but you've got a talent. It's raw, but you've got good senses, a good gut for following details other people don't notice or dismiss as unimportant. I want you to keep following that—following that closer, in fact. You'll be given unprecedented access. And if there's a story, I'm not going to stop you from printing it, even if it doesn't paint us in the best light. The only catch is that, when you find something, you bring it to me first, before you write it up and submit it. Give me a minute to refute it if you're mistaken—and I'll get you proof. If it's true, it'll give me a moment to come up with a game plan to deal with it before it hits the news."

Amanda had finally given Kate a genuine smile. "I'm not sure if I like you, but you're a genius. You're right, that is a good deal…for both of us. Before I commit, though, I have to warn you, I've already submitted a piece for tomorrow's paper you're not going to love."

Kate sighed. "May I read it now, before the world does?"

Amanda had thought about it, then shook her head no. "Scout's honor, it's my last work as your nuisance reporter. But I went all out for it, and you're just going to have to make the deal knowing that you're going to wish you hadn't for at least a few hours tomorrow morning."

"So why can't I read it now?" Kate demanded again, frustrated.

"Two reasons," Amanda had said, ticking them off on her fingers as she collected her things to leave. "One, you've got a temper, and I don't know if you will still make this deal if you read it now. Two, payback. You were more interested in making a joke than checking your facts when you woke me up this morning."

Kate had held her breath and counted to ten silently, literally biting her tongue, as Amanda made her way to the door. Finally, she said, "So, we have a deal?"

Amanda had nodded. "We have a deal."

And with that, Kate thought, narrating her life inside her head in the humorous third-person manner she usually found helped calm her, *Kate made her life that much messier and infinitely more irritating.*

Kate reread the title of the article—"Something is Rotten at Shamrock Hill Farm." She took a huge, angry gulp of her coffee just as a knock started at the door. Realizing the mouthful of lukewarm coffee tasted more like dishwater than fuel for the day ahead, she let it dribble out of her mouth and back into the cup, stood up, and went to go meet her unexpected visitor.

Please don't let it be her, Kate prayed silently. *There's no reason why it would be, right? She should know better than to come around until we've all had time to cool down…*

"So, as I said, sure you're not thrilled with me, but the past is the past, and I've brought peacemaking cinnamon buns with me," Amanda said, charging past Kate without so much as a hello the moment the door was open.

Kate glared at the younger reporter silently.

Amanda noticed this, stopped talking, opened the box of cinnamon buns, and offered one to her.

Kate grabbed a bun. She took a large, angry bite out of it without ever breaking eye contact with Amanda or losing her scowl.

———————————

"Come on, you can't leave me in this type of suspense!"

Doug's voice was still hoarse and raspy, but Charlie could hear the smile in his voice, as warm and bright through hundreds of miles of telephone wire as it would have been if she was still only a foot from his hospital bed. She smiled back, hoping he could feel the same warmth returned.

"Oh, I don't know…" Charlie teased. "How could I possibly know so soon?"

"Twenty-four hours to figure out if a horse is a racer isn't 'so soon'—certainly not for the lady who first guessed at Genuine Storm's potential in three drunken minutes at a claiming race!"

Charlie laughed. "You're right, I know exactly what Storm and I are up to—but I'm not going to breathe a word of it to you until I see you in person."

"That good?" Doug's excitement was palpable. "You want to wait and tell me when you can see how happy I'm going to be?"

"I didn't say anything like that! Horse whisperers can do crazy things—maybe it's not real or going to transcend off this ranch…" Charlie hesitated as a worry wrinkle arose between her eyes. She shook her head and shrugged the negative thoughts away.

"Hey, hold on a second."

Charlie waited patiently as Doug went through the process of greeting a visitor. Her heart swelled as she realized how much effort Doug put into being kind and welcoming, even while he was obviously in pain.

"Okay, I'm back. Where were we? Oh, Storm's turnaround and your worry," Doug smiled into the phone. "You can't change the past, Charlie, but just keep living in the moment and looking forward to the future that is in front of all of us."

"You're so right, Doug. We've had enough craziness in the past year to fill a book. It will be nice to go back to a bit of peace and quiet after we're marr—ooh, um, I have to go! Or you have to go—we should go." Charlie blushed a thousand shades of red, realizing she'd just showed even more of her hand than she'd considered.

"You better be planning on running long distances, Charlie Jenkins," Doug said somberly.

"Hmm?" Charlie murmured, genuinely confused.

"'Marathoners,' right? 'After we're marathoners?' Or are we talking about the sea? Do you mean 'marine biologists,' crazy lady? Because if you were about to accept a marriage proposal now, with me laid up in a hospital and you in Nowhere, Pennsylvania…"

"Wouldn't dream of it. Psh," Charlie scoffed, still blushing very hard. "I'm serious, though, you should visit with your mystery guest. I do have to get going. The horse whisperer has some bonfire going and Lilly is doing a tribal dance."

Doug laughed, which turned quickly into a wheeze and a cough. "Well, don't let me keep you from using all his magical powers to bring Storm to New York. Hey, see you soon, okay? I can't live without you."

"You're pretty special yourself."

"No, I mean it. There's no way I'm going to be able to feed myself with these tubes and bandages everywhere."

"A hopeless romantic."

Doug hung up the phone and turned to his visitor. "Alright, buddy, make yourself comfortable. I need all the info on Shamrock that Molly and Charlie are too kind to tell me."

Hunter gave his boss a grin. "Well, jumping right into it, huh? That's fine, I can't stay long. I'm really just here to settle a bet. The boys down at the barn thought you'd be half bionic by now, but I knew you'd never settle for just half. In all seriousness, though, you look good, better than I would have expected for someone who tried to barbeque himself."

Doug groaned. "You have no idea. I don't know how to break it to every-one that I am banning any outdoor barbeques throughout the whole farm." Doug lifted his hand and moved his fingers slightly a bit above the bandages. "I won't be able to flip any burgers for a while with this mess of a hand. I am considering changing all the door hinges to rubber."

"Well, I should probably come up with a different theme for your welcome home party," Hunter said. "You sound like a man who wouldn't appreciate a good luau. And as for your hand, you said you always wanted a tattoo."

Doug looked at him appreciatively. *Hunter's a fun guy,* he thought. *I'd forgotten how easy and nice he was to talk to and banter with—why he was such a clear choice to hire in Florida. Seems like a million years ago that I thought he was out to steal Charlie.* Doug shook his head slightly, realizing how much had changed in such a short period of time.

Between the change of heart and the copious amounts of painkillers running through his system, Doug didn't even cringe at Hunter's next question.

"Was that our girl? Could only hear your half of the conversation, but it certainly sounds like there's excitement brewing."

"She certainly sounded happy and excited—I'm pretty sure Storm has taken a turn for the much, much better, but I guess I'll have to wait to hear in person," Doug agreed.

"Couldn't be happier to hear it, buddy," Hunter said jovially. "I was sick, thinking that magnificent horse might never race again. It's a shame to leave the Triple Crown on the table, but it's probably for the best. Who even knows how much of the frayed nerves were from the fire? Storm might just be a horse who needs a little more time between races. No harm in that, and by the end of the season—"

"Well, I don't want to get ahead of myself, but if I'm reading Charlie right, I'd say the Triple Crown bid is still very much a go," Doug said, thinking proudly of the passion and excitement in her voice.

Hunter looked surprised. "And…Lilly is going to be okay with that?"

"You know more than I do, remember?" Doug said, gesturing around the hospital room. "But if Charlie and Lilly say he's ready, I'll believe 'em. Sure, that experience would have broken many fine horses, but just goes to show, every horse is different."

Hunter whistled low, then got quiet and thoughtful for a moment.

"You here to give me some company, or are you just in it for the hospital food?" Doug asked playful. "What are you thinking so hard about?"

Hunter bit his thumbnail before answering, "A good trainer has to really know the horse—what he needs, what makes him strong, what keeps up his fighting spirit. If you're paying attention, a horse will tell you exactly what he needs—but you've got to be seeing the horse in front of you, not some idealized version."

"Are you questioning Lilly's ability to train horses? What are you saying?" Doug asked, confused and starting to get angry.

"No! No, absolutely not. I live in awe of the woman—she's got skills and instincts for the job better than anyone I've ever seen. The idea of seeing what she'd manage to do with even an unfit horse in a race like the Belmont is a hard one to give up. I guess what I am saying, though, is that I worry about Lilly and Charlie. They've gone through so much the past few months—hell, they've gone through so much in the past few weeks! It's not exactly provocative to recognize that trauma takes a toll on a person, affects the way they perceive the world. I question whether they're paying attention to what the real Storm—the one standing right in front of them—needs, or whether they're responding to the Storm they've built up in their heads— the magical horse who can make all this pain go away. And, well, we both know what, ah, Charlie goes through when she's stressed to the point of breaking." Hunter sighed and shoved his hands in his jean pockets.

Doug tried to access the part of his brain associated with deep concern, but he couldn't muster much through the painkiller haze. "What Charlie goes through?" he echoed.

Hunter looked increasingly uncomfortable. "Look, I'm not trying to start anything, and I'm not trying to tell tales out of school. I care about Charlie, and I know her stress reactions are…intense. She gets a little loopy, a little less able to connect the dots in the order we all usually would. From everything I've heard, taking care of Peter nearly killed the poor girl, so I can't imagine what she's going through right now. She must feel like a bad luck charm—and if she's doing something foolish to try and please you, I think you should know."

"I guess we've still never really talked about her anxiety, her panic attacks," Doug said quietly, more to himself than to Hunter.

Hunter shifted in the small hospital chair and changed topics. "Boss, you asked for the tough stuff out of Shamrock, and I'm here to deliver. I've 'wrassled with it a bit, but there's an article in today's Herald that's going to be a little rough for us. It's critical of parts of the farm, parts of racing, and I don't want it to be a shock to you while you're already on your heels."

Doug grinned again. "Ah, let 'em come for me. I'm on a monstrous load of painkillers, there's never been a better time for the reporters to take a swing. What is it, another think piece bemoaning the spoiled state of pampered ponies? Or drug usage? Or the unregulated use of whips? I will get on my own high horse about how the whip is a particularly useful steering mechanism for an animal racing at over 40 miles per hour…"

"I…think you should really read it for yourself, Doug."

Doug slowly nodded, but he knew he was losing steam. His voice was on its way out, and he was finding it tough to stay awake.

"Hunter, do me a favor? Make sure Molly gives it a read too. Despite all appearances," Doug smiled weakly, "I'm not actually in prime shape, physically or mentally."

"Of course, boss," Hunter said softly.

"Thanks again for dropping by."

Hunter shuffled out of the room, and soon Doug was slipping in and out of sleep. Awake or asleep, though, the bright warm smile he'd been wearing when he'd gotten Charlie's call was history.

An Informal Meeting

The bright orange backpack slammed down on the table in front of Amanda, but she didn't look up from her magazine.

"Hello, dear, how was work?"

"This year will never, ever end," Jenny said, flinging herself dramatically into an empty chair in the surprisingly bustling makeshift employee lounge. "It's been the beginning of June for at least six years already."

"Oh, don't wish these years away, darlin'. You will be old like me one day, trying to make your way in the world." Amanda looked up just in time to see Hunter enter the barn. She gave him a charming smile, which he returned with a flirtatious wink.

"Seems like you prefer them older," Jenny said, rolling her eyes towards Hunter, while grabbing the magazine Amanda had been reading. "*BloodHorse?*"

"He's cute," Amanda protested. "And he's not that old."

"He's literally the same age as Ryan's mom," Jenny said.

Amanda smiled at Jenny's perception of old. "Anyways, no dates until Storm's off my beat. And who knows, maybe this becomes my full-time gig. You know, since Kate seems to basically think of me like a daughter—"

Amanda paused to mimic Kate working at her computer, her glasses slid down her nose, looking over the tops of the lenses. Jenny laughed so hard that she started to snort a little, thinking back to the limited interactions she'd seen the two reporters have.

"Seems about right," Jenny replied.

"Ladies, do you think you are being unkind?" Buck's voice came from the other side of the aisle, where he had been finishing cleaning his gear from the morning exercise rides. With Jenny's leg broken and Lilly out of pocket, Buck had agreed to take on exercising Doug's horses that were training at the farm when he wasn't needed at the track. It also gave him the opportunity to keep tabs on Jenny and hear about Storm, as many of the updates were being funneled through Charlie. He and Lilly were having a hard time connecting, especially given her lack of cell service.

Before Jenny or Amanda could provide an answer to his question, Buck's cell phone rang. The women sat quietly, a bit ashamed over the tone of their conversation; they had not realized Buck was within earshot. They quickly buried those feelings, as they ended up eavesdropping the moment Buck started talking.

"Is there any truth to it, though?" Buck asked. "Is he alright? Is he going to be able to race? What type of additional security measures are being put in place?"

He paused to listen to the replies, and his lips tightened into a thin grimace. He said little else for the rest of the call, just listened intently to the voice on the other line.

Hanging up, he rubbed his temples and absentmindedly cracked the knuckles on his left hand, lost in thought. Jenny winced.

The silence broke Amanda's resolve first. "Everything okay?" she asked, curious and hopeful.

"There are rumors going around the internet that Duke was sponged. The threats—if you can even really call them that—were sloppy and vague, so everyone ignored them. This morning, though, someone mailed an envelope with a cut up sponge inside. They had Duke examined immediately.

He's fine, no signs of sabotage. The police and racing officials believe this is just frustrated talk from a losing gambler or sore competition, and that we shouldn't be too concerned about it. But with everything else going on, well, it is concerning."

"What's sponging?" Amanda asked.

"It's when someone inserts a small piece of sponge inside a horse's nostril. Makes it harder for them to breathe. It's very cruel to the horses, who can pass out or die if they don't get enough oxygen. It's especially cruel to racing horses, since running requires even more oxygen."

"How do they find the sponges?" Amanda asked.

"Usually an endoscopy," Buck replied.

"Why would anyone do such a thing?" Amanda asked, bewildered. "Even if they managed to get Duke dropped from the race, it's not like anyone else has a chance of beating Storm, right? How far are the other horses' people willing to go to ensure they lose less badly?"

"The suspicion, whether it has any basis in fact or not, is that this is more likely to be the work of a gambler trying to fix the race. Sabotaging Duke's breathing would allow a bettor to pick other horses in an exotic wager with higher pay outs. And with everything that's happened with Storm…" Buck paused, remembering Amanda's latest piece on the farm and not wanting to add fuel to the rumors.

"Is someone going around trying to kill all the competition?" Jenny asked in an odd, too-loud voice.

Amanda looked around to see what had set Jenny off, but everyone had left the barn except Steve and Hunter, who both seemed engaged in their respective coffee and phones.

"They don't really need to. With exotic wagering, the common wisdom is that if you can take out two of them in less than a twelve-horse field, then you can do it."

"Am I hearing right?" Hunter piped in. "Sponging seems a bit old fashioned to spook the horse set now. It's too rare—nearly unheard of at the Belmont level of racing. I remember dealing with a rash of it out on the West

Coast, years and years ago."

Jenny smirked at Amanda over the "years and years" reference, and Amanda rolled her eyes.

"It got pretty crazy," he continued. "Trainers swapping halters and nameplates with other horses to hide the more valuable identities. Of course, this was back before you could just look up a picture of any horse on your phone."

"Seabiscuit was the target of an attempted sponging in 1938," Steve chimed in. "I just finished a biography on him, and they went into some depth about—"

Jenny stood up abruptly and turned towards Amanda, pointedly avoiding looking at Steve. "I need to get out of here—would you mind giving me a ride over to the house?"

"Yeah, sure," Amanda said, hopping up and grabbing the orange backpack.

The two women left, and Hunter wandered over to the table to check out the magazine they'd left.

"*BloodHorse*," he said aloud to no one in particular.

"She does seem a lot more curious about horses than she was when she first got here," Cappie said, seemingly materializing from nowhere.

"Jeez, where were you just hiding? How long have you been standing there, waiting for them to leave?" Hunter asked.

"Over there," Cappie said, gesturing in the vague direction he'd just come through. "And long enough to make it work. Not about to get caught up in some exposé."

Steve shook his head. "You've got to admit, she's gutsy."

"Gutsy? Hanging us out to dry like that, then waltzing in to be friends?" Cappie asked.

"Oh, has my young protégé left, then?" Kate asked, walking in the door.

"Just missed her," Cappie confirmed.

"Well, what's the verdict?" Hunter asked. "What does the Great Kate have to say about our most recent starring role in the papers? It can't be too bad, since she's still here."

"Oh, we look awful. Shamrock seems like a bank that happens to use horses for currency. It heavily implied that Charlie and Doug are all but killing Genuine Storm if they race him in the Belmont." Kate shrugged.

"Subtlety is not her strength," Hunter said quietly, "but do you think she might have a point?"

Kate locked eyes with him and stared until he blinked before she replied, "No, I don't."

Steve cleared his throat and tried to dispel the growing tension. "Well, I certainly share some of her concerns. How can Charlie be so sure Storm is ready? Why don't any of us know what they did to heal him up there in Pine Grove? Even if there was something not quite right about it, it's possible that Charlie doesn't even know what's going on. There's been a lot happening, I don't think any of us have a perfect grasp on it all. I wish Storm was in top physical condition—and he may well be, I haven't seen him—but all of it is concerning."

Hunter shook his head. "I love Charlie dearly; she's one of my oldest friends. But there's nothing that absolves her from making the right choice here. Owners are usually excused, even when their trainers and veterinarians are charged with doping, abusing, and callously injuring—or even killing—racehorses. Apparently it's not that popular an opinion around here, but I think it's an owner's responsibility to know what's going on with her horse. I don't think she does—I don't think anyone really does. And I think Amanda might be right to say they might be playing with his life."

Cappie and Steve held their breaths and waited for Kate's response.

She never looked at Hunter again, never acknowledged that he'd spoken. "Anyways, the paper will create a small stir in the racing community. It's an opinion piece, it's out, I have over a week to deal with it. I won't need half that time. Everyone be nice, and when she's writing effusive praise for us next week, it'll seem like an even bigger coup than it is."

"Molly's told me we trust her now," Steve said, quickly agreeing with Kate and parroting his wife's words back to the group. "She's joined the team, she's ready to play ball, and she's going to really help us out. So, no matter how either of you feel about reporters, be hospitable to this one. She's Shamrock family now—maybe not closely related, but a distant cousin."

"Speaking of family," Cappie said, "Steve, are you getting the messages Ben's leaving you? He said you've yet to return several calls, and he needs some insurance information from you before he can move forward with some of the outpatient treatment for his foot."

"Sure, sure. I think this is the first time I've sat down during daylight hours since the fire. I'll give him a call later, though, thanks for the reminder," Steve replied breezily.

Hunter and Cappie watched in amazement as Steve continued to dawdle in the room. It was uncharacteristic for him to show so little concern for an employee, and both men found themselves wondering when Shamrock would start to feel like itself again.

 # Crossed Wires

"Hi, Chief Johnson, this is Molly over at Shamrock. I found a suspicious character lurking around here…"

Travis' heart leaped in his chest, though his somber deep monotone never revealed it. He'd stopped letting himself obsess over the Shamrock fire, but something inside hadn't let him sign off on the report and close the case yet either.

Maybe this is the break I needed, he thought.

"Molly, listen to me carefully," Travis' voice dropped low; he hoped the perpetrator wasn't in earshot. "I need you to figure out a way to stall him, some diversionary tactic."

"Um…"

"Did you get a confession? Is there any evidence? I need to call in the police chief, I'm not authorized to make the arrest, but…"

Molly's laughter stopped him short.

"Oh, my, I'm so sorry, Chief. That was the first laugh I've gotten in days. I don't have any suspects for you. I've just got Drew here again, and he told me he'd forgotten his phone. I know that bothers you—not that there's anything wrong with that, it would bother me too! But I wanted to let you know he was here, and I thought I'd check and see whether you both wanted to join us for dinner."

"Shoot, Molly, I can't believe you would make a joke at this time given all that's been going on," Travis growled, trying to disguise his disappointment as frustration at her.

The smile usually present in Molly's voice dropped away precipitously and there was a hesitation before she replied. "Well, so sorry for messing up your day. As I was saying, Chief Johnson..."

Drew stood up straight, holding his arms up in the air like a surgeon all scrubbed up and ready to operate. Unlike a surgeon, however, he was filthy. His hands and arms were clad in thick rubber dish gloves that Skylar had repurposed from Doug's house. They had been yellow when the kids had come down to the charred area where the barn had recently stood, but now they were black with soot and ashes.

"What have you found?" she asked, pointing at the blue water bucket they'd taken from one of the barns.

Drew tilted it towards her so she could see the contents, replying, "Not much."

The two kids had been told in no uncertain terms that they had to stay away from the site of the barn fire. The day before, though, a work crew had cleaned up the biggest pieces of debris. Once the workers had gone home and the area was mostly clear, without real supervision, Skylar and Drew had decided that the terms for their ban had changed and took to poking through the ashes.

Skylar's dramatic reenactment of Doug and Hershey's heroic escape hadn't taken long, but the charred area had turned out to be pretty good for more types of adventures. They had already explored an alien planet and survived a volcano and now they were sifting for gold (though they would not have turned their noses up at another form of treasure—dinosaur bones or mutated bugs that could give them superpowers would be fine substitutes).

"My dad would be so mad if he knew I was in here, and I think Molly might be too," Drew said.

"I mean, for the most part, everyone just ignores us. I could be on fire next and Ryan would just keep staring at his phone and Jenny," Skylar replied. "Molly is so forgetful now, and your dad—well, he doesn't live here. So, it's not that likely we will run into him."

Skylar had barely started trying to convince Drew that none of the adults would ever know they were there when Molly seemed to appear out of nowhere, flying out of thin air to shoo them away.

"What did I say, Skylar? It could still be dangerous in here—we have no idea what chemicals spilled or if there are nails poking up, nothing! Where in the world are Jenny and Ryan?" Molly asked.

The kids shrugged.

"Okay, get gone. Go…find the fishing rods and entertain yourselves at the pond."

"Um, what pond, Ms. Molly? You mean that puddle over there that *used* to be the pond?" Skylar said, pointing towards the muddy, shallow water in a nearby crater. "The firefighters used almost all the water."

"That's what the pond is for. Since stables don't have anything like access to a city fire hydrant, they have to build these big ponds and dry hydrants. There is a pipe that goes from the middle, the deepest part of their pond—the part that doesn't freeze, ever—to a hydrant next to the pond that the firefighters can hook a pumper to and draw water from," Drew said, proudly displaying some of the information he'd picked up at home through sheer osmosis. "It takes 500 gallons of water per minute to fight a hay fire of 250 bales."

"Whoa!" Skylar said, excited. "Molly, how many gallons does your pond hold?"

"Hmm?" Molly said. "Oh, right—about 20,000."

"Hey!" Drew said, brightening up. "If all the water from the pond has just soaked into the ground here, weren't we kinda already playing near the pond?"

"Refill pond, I'll add it to the list," Molly muttered to herself, rubbing her temples. "Fine, go brush the mini horses, they need some attention." Molly shook her head as she whipped out her cell phone and scanned her contacts. "Or do anything, really, that won't hurt you. You have a whole horse farm, guys, and you're insisting on playing in the one area that's off limits. Don't go too far, though, Drew, your dad will be by shortly."

Her eyes refocused on Skylar and Drew. "You two have to the count of three: one…"

"Stop the count," Travis said, jogging up to them.

"Hi, Dad," Drew said.

"Hi yourself. Let me borrow your phone for a second," Travis replied sternly, holding his hand out with the palm up.

"Must have left it behind," Drew muttered.

"We will discuss this at home," his father said. "Go get your things and say your goodbyes."

"Oh!" Molly said. The two adults watched the kids head to the office to retrieve Drew's backpack. "You're not staying for dinner?"

"He'd destroy any chair he sat on right now," Travis responded, looking after the filthy boy. "In the future, I would prefer that he not play in burn sites—much less active investigation crime scenes."

Molly shook her head. "Well, that cuts right to the heart of one of the matters I wanted to speak with you about tonight. Why hasn't there been any movement on the arson investigation? Why isn't it closed? How hard can it be to see that this is just one big accident, and help us move on?"

"Please, don't tell me how to do my job," Travis said curtly.

"Then please, do your job," Molly said, equally enraged.

Drew and Skylar walked back up quietly and stood beside their respective adults, watching them become increasingly rude to each other.

"Drew, we're leaving," Travis boomed, visibly upset. "Say goodbye to Skylar."

The awkward silences kept dragging out longer. Buck estimated that, at this rate, by the end of next week, his phone conversations with Lilly would be completely mute.

"Listen, Lil, I'm sorry. I'm stressed, you're stressed. I should have chosen my words more carefully."

"Why? You made yourself perfectly clear, Buck. I'm selfish because I don't ask enough about your days, I don't call you often enough, I don't… whatever." Lilly stared out the small window next to the phone, setting her jaw at a hard angle. "When it comes down to it, I'm never going to *need* you enough, am I?"

Buck felt as though he'd been slapped in the face. "It's not a matter of needing, Lilly. It's about wanting. I don't know if you want to be with me," he said quietly. "I've listened—because I want to listen—to every detail you've cared to share with me about Storm. I'm a jockey too, Lilly, and Duke is important to me. He was threatened, and I thought I could share my feelings about that with you—"

"Duke wasn't exactly threatened, though, was he? He was more…threatened with being threatened." Lilly sighed. "I'm sorry, Buck, that something sort of almost might have happened to your horse, but it just can't compare to what Storm and I have gone through recently—what we're still going through. I'm just being honest when I tell you Storm is my priority right now. Things will calm down again…soon."

Buck had picked up on Lilly's hesitation, and tried to dramatically lighten the mood. "Yeah, are things going that well up there? Tell me all about it, I haven't gotten an update in days." He winced as the words left his mouth; the statement felt like a deadweight of accusation. He crossed his fingers and hoped that Lilly wouldn't hear it that way.

Lilly narrowed her eyes and glared at the boxy phone receiver. "Now that you think things are going well, you're more curious, huh? When you didn't think we were competition for you and Duke, you didn't seem all that interested in updates anymore."

Buck jerked back as though he'd been slapped. "What are you saying?"

"I'm saying I'm not comfortable sharing any more information with a competitor. I'm saying I think you were happier when you were positive Storm wasn't racing, so you could finally win the Belmont, the one race you haven't been able to win."

"Okay, Lilly. Okay. There's always going to be a reason you don't want to share with me, and it seems like you're not interested in having me share with you. I love you, but I can't live like this. We're not kids anymore, and when we were, it was this type of secrecy and mistrust that killed us anyways. I'm sorry, Lilly. You're right, Storm should be your priority right now, and Duke should be mine. I made the mistake of prioritizing you and your life more than my own, and I should have known it would come back to bite me."

They both hung up without another word. Buck immediately began packing to head up to New York—for good, this time.

 # Crashing Down

Charlie was positively glowing as she got closer to Doug's hospital room. Right before she crossed the threshold, she had a thought so powerful that she actually stepped back for a moment to savor it.

I've been so excited to see him, to share the incredible news, to update him on where our amazing shared journey has brought us now, she thought. *But I didn't lose sleep—I slept better than I have in years. Knowing I have his support and knowing my support means the world to him makes me comfortable with excitement. This feels right—this is the future I want.*

Grinning, she stepped into the room, looked into the bed…and froze in place.

This was not the man she'd left. This was not the man she'd spoken with on the phone a few short hours before. This man looked like Doug, sure, superficially, but before he could even open his mouth, Charlie shivered. It was like looking into a black hole—without even speaking, his negative energy started sucking in all the positive thoughts that had kept her afloat.

Charlie shook herself. *No, this is in my head,* she thought. *This is some weird self-sabotage ploy.*

Still trying to shake the feeling, she pasted an unsteady smile to her face. "Guess what, handsome?"

Doug cocked his eyebrow, peering over the tablet screen silently.

"Genuine Storm is back—really and truly more magnificent and happier than I have ever seen him. Doug, you've never seen a horse so thrilled to run!" she said, hoping that the slight quiver in her voice hadn't been noticeable.

"Oh?" Doug slid the tablet in Charlie's direction.

Charlie stepped forward to take it off his tray and began reading the article pulled up on the screen:

Something is Rotten at Shamrock Hill Farm

Is the Triple Crown fairy tale about to turn into a Shakespearian tragedy? Genuine Storm's training home is plagued with interpersonal tension and family drama—and insiders worry for the horse's well-being.

Genuine Storm is the most famous and fortunate claiming race horse in history, and his training stable, Shamrock Hill Farm, has been widely lauded for its idyllic setting and cozy relationships. Now, with Storm posed to be the first horse crowned in the famous racing trifecta in nearly forty years, many believe that their barn is not the only thing going up in flames...

Charlie suppressed the urge to gasp several times, but some of the statements and innuendos cut her to the core. Along with exposing parts of their personal lives, the article painted a damning picture of Shamrock as a whole, and argued that racing Storm in the Belmont was a shortsighted, cruel decision motivated by greed and fueled with delusion. As she got to the end of the article, she let her arms drop by her sides. They'd progressively gotten heavier and heavier as she'd read, and by the time she'd finished, they felt like anvils.

"Why would she say such horrible things? How could she possibly think that I would run Storm if I wasn't positive he was 100%?" Charlie murmured, sinking onto the edge of the hospital bed.

"Is he?" Doug croaked.

"Is he…Doug, are you questioning whether I would put Storm at risk, all for some stupid prize?" Charlie asked, appalled.

"Charlie, I just know that you've had…problems…under stress…before," Doug's voice was getting fainter, already overexerted from the trauma.

He pursed his cracked and burned lips together in a way that made her eyes water empathetically, though the feeling was obviously not reciprocated. She stood, frozen and unable to speak. She was in a tight spot. She was positive that he was asking her if she was risking her horse's life for a race, but at the same time, she was equally positive he would never even consider her capable of that.

"Just—don't do anything on my behalf. I didn't rush into the barn for the Triple Crown; I'm not a martyr for an idea. Storm doesn't owe me anything, I would have saved him…and Hershey…no matter if they were the fastest horses in the world or part of a petting zoo. I love you, Charlie, no matter what the future holds, but I didn't even do it for you."

Charlie stared at him, mouth frozen around the words she'd just forgotten. She came to, quickly snapping her mouth shut. Her lips pulled into a tight, closed, thin smirk.

"Oh, get a grip."

"Excuse me?" Doug said, looking both angry and completely flabbergasted.

"You heard me. Get ahold of yourself. I know you're hurting, I know none of this was expected, but guess what? It happened. Sorry, Doug. You did a brave, incredible thing, and you're just going to have to deal with the fact that I think you're wonderful. When you stop feeling sorry for yourself, you come find me, and I'll tell you exactly how wonderful I think you are. Right now, though, I don't have that kind of time. You saved the day, which means I need to go get the rest of the days in order. Sit here and stew in the fake drama, for all I care, but you should really take a deep look and consider how you could love me if I was the type of person whose values could be that turned around by a race. I love Storm, and I've loved him before anyone thought he was worth anything, and he'd still mean the world to me if he couldn't even walk straight."

Charlie spun and marched out of the room before Doug could even hope to respond. He stared at the doorway for a long time after she'd left.

Even though she'd been back and forth to the farm over the past week and a half, driving up now, Charlie felt like she was seeing Shamrock for the first time since the fire. The black patch where the main barn had stood scarred the landscape and made the workers rushing around it look more harried, jerky, and off-kilter than they would have otherwise.

Charlie saw Lilly's truck ahead of her, parked right in front of the building that held the business office. She was momentarily relieved, as she'd been hoping to catch Lilly, Kate, and Molly first, to come up with a good plan before she had to wing it before everyone else.

As she pulled her SUV up next to the truck, though, she saw Ryan and Jenny approaching, and she waited for them.

"Hey, Jenny! Hey, you," she said, wrapping her son into a bear hug and marveling again at how tall he'd gotten. "Where's your sister?"

Both of the teens shrugged.

"I'll go ask my...mom," Jenny said awkwardly, hobbling on her crutches through the office door.

Charlie looked at her son more closely; his face had the closed off, difficult expression she'd come to associate with another parental battle. *Well, I guess I was a fool to believe those days were completely in the past.*

"What's going on, Ryan? How did keeping track of your sister end up on Molly's full plate?"

Ryan jutted his chin out defiantly. Charlie couldn't help but recognize how much he looked like Peter when he got upset—certainly a bittersweet association.

"Yes, Molly is busy. We're all busy. You have no idea what all has been happening here, Mom."

Charlie held up her hand, motioning him to stop. "Ryan, I'm not going to fight with you about this right now. You're right, I do need to get caught up, and I need to catch everyone else up too. You and I will speak later."

Ryan shook his head as she strode purposefully towards the office. He faltered for a moment, uncertain whether he should follow his mother and Jenny or go look for Skylar. Finally, jamming his hands into his pockets, he sauntered away towards the stables.

———————————

Jenny's blood boiled and froze as she walked through the door, knowing that both Molly and Lilly were inside and having no idea how she wanted to react.

"Charlie is outside looking for Skylar, have you seen her?" Jenny asked loudly, interrupting the ongoing discussion. She stared at the floor and kept her voice a careful monotone so she did not betray any emotion.

Molly looked at her, incredulous. "Jenny, I am taking care of something right now. How many more times do I have to stress that *you are the one who needs to know where Skylar is?* You're supposed to be watching her, and frankly, you should feel ashamed to need to keep asking. Irresponsibility seems to be contagious around here…"

As she finished her thought, Molly glared at Amanda, who was leaning against the wall with her arms crossed. Jenny had missed seeing her when she'd walked in, but now, angered by Molly's words, she failed to take in the significance.

"Molly, I fail to see how this is—" Kate started.

"Sorry, I'm the irresponsible one? Why? Because, unlike you, I don't feel the need to pretend to be someone else's mom?" Jenny sputtered, shooting venomous looks at Molly and Lilly both.

"Excuse me?" Molly said, knocked completely on her heels.

"Nothing. Never mind. I need to go find Skylar, obviously, and you all need to get back to what's important to you," Jenny said, wimping out of the confrontation at the last minute and letting her sails deflate.

"No, Jenny, what are you talking about?" Molly asked.

"Which part?" Jenny asked, feeling her anger rise again. "What's important to you? That's pretty clear, it's the farm—always the farm, all the time. Or...do you mean finding out who my real mom is?"

Molly and Lilly both looked shocked as they followed Jenny's accusatory finger pointed towards Lilly. The spell was only broken when Charlie opened the door. Jenny pushed past her and bolted from the room as quickly as she could.

"What in the world just happened?" Charlie said, thoroughly confused.

Molly and Lilly both looked like they were frozen in place, staring at the door Jenny had just left through.

"Oh no. How did she find out?" Molly whispered as she grabbed for her desk chair before her legs gave out.

It was Amanda who finally explained. "Jenny...knows who her biological parents are."

Charlie too stood in shocked silence, watching her two friends closely.

"Okay," Charlie took a deep breath, collected herself, the conversation with Doug pushed to the back of her mind. She kneeled down next to Molly and pulled Lilly next to her. "Now, I know this is not the way you wanted Jenny to find out, but it is what it is. How she found out is not the issue; you knew this day would come and now Jenny is guiding the next steps. You both need to go talk to her and get through this together."

Molly turned her tear-stained face to Lilly, knowing their common secret was now hurting their common bond. Jenny was in pain, and she had to help her through it, to help her understand why they did what they did those many years ago.

Lilly stood up and pulled Molly out of the chair, wrapping her in a big hug. "We did what was best, Molly. We maybe should have told her a lot sooner, but we all have reasons for the path we took and the choices we made. She is old enough to know the whole truth."

Molly nodded, acknowledging that the next several hours would be the hardest her relationship with her daughter might ever endure. Grabbing several tissues from the box on her desk, she looked over at Amanda and wondered aloud how Amanda already seemed to know what was happening.

The reporter gave her a sympathetic smile. "It's a long story, but I was adopted too. Go talk to her. She is a great girl, she will come around."

"I hope so." Molly gave Charlie a hug and took Lilly's hand as the two women left the office in search of their daughter.

———————————

Once they'd left the office, they hadn't needed to go far. Jenny had made it as far as the first tree on the drive before she'd flopped down in the grass, and she was treating herself to one of the cries she'd been bottling up for days.

Molly and Lilly quietly sat down on either side of her and waited silently for her to say what she needed to say.

Jenny glared at Lilly through her tear-soaked lashes. "How could you have kept this from me? How could you just give me away like that? Didn't you ever get jealous, watching someone else raise me? What's so wrong with me that you didn't want to be my mom? Didn't you love me enough?"

Jenny switched positions, curling up and hunching her shoulders around her one good knee with her cast stuck out at a strange angle from her body. Molly's heart broke over and over and over as she looked at her daughter, wishing she could take all the hurt away.

Lilly sighed and looked upwards, taking a moment to consider her next words. She put a hand on Jenny's hunched shoulders. Jenny shrugged it off, so Lilly changed her position and sat cross-legged facing her, her hands laid open on her lap.

"Jenny, I love you. I've always loved you, and I've loved being part of your life as you've grown up. You're so incredible, and I'm so lucky." Lilly took a deep breath. "I don't know what the right things to say are, so I'm just going to speak with you honestly. I don't think of myself as your mother—as a mother at all. I didn't feel like I would be a good mom to you, and now that I can look back on the past fifteen years, I'm more certain than I've ever been that I wasn't meant to be yours. I'm meant to be…well, your Lilly. I got to teach you how to ride and how to groom horses and how to look into their eyes and let them tell you how they feel. I was able to give you the best parts of me, while giving you a real mom—the best mom I've ever seen. I'll always be here to be your Lilly, and I would give you anything and everything I've ever had. I haven't been holding out on you—I just don't have that particular type of love to give."

"And what about my real dad, you know, Buck? Don't you think I should have known about him too?" Jenny spat out.

Lilly hesitated before she continued, "Jenny, I want you to know the truth and all the details when you are ready, but I was a scared teenager. I love Buck. I love him now, and I loved him then. He did not find out about you until just a few weeks ago, so don't hang him out to dry. He is in the same boat as you with regards to not knowing." Lilly sighed, her memories flooding back. She knew all the pain she had caused, but she also remembered all the pain she'd been in so many years ago. "I know this is so very hard for you and I am so very sorry." Lilly could feel her voice beginning to crack and just couldn't go on with revisiting all the details of those dark days.

Jenny didn't look up or respond, and after a tense moment, Lilly got up and backed away, wiping the tears that had started to fall. She awkwardly shrugged at Molly, feeling at a loss to provide Jenny any more of the history she knew she would want to know one day. Molly nodded as Lilly left and sat still next to her daughter.

After several silent minutes, Molly started speaking in a low, far-away voice. "I hurt so badly when your brother was born. The doctors didn't know at first, but I knew right away that I would never be able to have another child. I don't know how, I just felt it, but that confused me so much, because I always knew I would have a daughter. I used to dream—such vivid, clear dreams of a baby girl with my green eyes and a single dimple.

They never went away, even after the doctors told me Sam was it.

"I love your brother, and I was so excited to finally be a mother, but every time I closed my eyes, there was this baby girl I'd been told could never be. It made me so sad that I finally had to make the dreams stop—I had to wake myself up each time one started.

"When Lilly told me that she was pregnant, my heart started to sing before she'd even asked me. Jenny, you're my baby girl, and you always have been. I've been dreaming about you for longer than you could possibly understand—those green eyes, that dimple."

Jenny looked up, adjusting her head so that she could look Molly in the eye. "If you were so positive you were my mother, why were you too afraid to tell me that Lilly was my birth mother—that she was right here the entire time?"

"Oh sweetheart, I have never worried that you would love me any less. You've got my big green eyes and my big sloppy heart. I've never met anyone who understands better how infinite love is. I know I should have told you, Jenny, but it was so hard to remember a time that I felt you were anyone's daughter but mine."

Feeling the warmth radiating from her mother, Jenny's dimpled smile peeked out from underneath her messy hair.

"Did you know I was the first person you ever saw?"

"You were in the delivery room?" Jenny said, surprised.

"Are you kidding me? Do you think I would have waited a single second longer than necessary to meet you?" Molly laughed. "You should have seen me, feeding Lilly while she was pregnant. I wanted to make sure you knew all my favorite foods as soon as you could. Actually, Lilly only had one real craving the entire time—Lebanon bologna and crunchy peanut butter with a tall glass of pulpy orange juice."

Jenny laughed. "But she looks like she's going to puke whenever she sees me eating the bologna rolls!" She made a face. "I think I'd puke if I had it with orange juice, though."

"I know—she *hates* peanut butter *and* orange juice, passionately!" Molly laughed, thinking back. "I'll never forget the first time she asked for those bologna rolls—I thought it was the grossest thing I'd ever heard of. When I tried it, though, I couldn't believe how much I loved it—that was the first present you ever gave me, out of so, so, so many."

Jenny and Molly smiled at each other.

"Jenny, I know I should never have let you find out by accident. I'm so sorry you felt alone. I do mess up sometimes—more often than you know. I don't think I'm perfect or Wonder Woman, but I love you ferociously, and I'm going to do whatever it takes to make sure that any secrets I've kept, intentionally or accidentally, don't hurt you again."

"I love you too, Mom," Jenny said somberly.

Should I ask about Dad—Steve-dad? The conversation I overheard the other night? Do I even want to know? Can she handle anything else today? Can I?

Would she even tell me the truth?

Jenny hesitated, but eventually finished her thought with, "But I still don't know exactly what I feel about all of this."

"I understand that, sweetheart. It will take time to work through all the feelings you are experiencing, but we are all here for you." Molly stood up, wordlessly offering both arms to help Jenny up. "You matter more to me than anything."

Jenny shook her head at her mother's offer of help. "I'm going to stay here for a while and think, alone."

"Okay, sweetheart. When you're ready to talk again, you tell me. I'm sorry. I love you."

Jenny watched Molly walk away for a few seconds, then laid on her back to watch the clouds and think about everything she'd just learned—and the things she still needed to figure out.

 # Taking the Reins

The landline in the office started to ring nearly the moment Lilly and Molly departed. Charlie walked over to check the caller ID.

"Fire department," she read aloud to no one in particular. "Anything currently actually literally on fire that I should know about?"

Kate chuckled. "Nope, all the fires right now seem highly situational."

Charlie, Kate, and Amanda all stood, frozen in their private thoughts for a moment, with only the piercing shriek of the old phone bleating in the corner breaking the silence.

The ringer died, which seemed to break Amanda of her trance first. She started to quietly slink away, which snapped Charlie abruptly out of her own reverie.

Charlie snapped her fingers. It startled both Amanda and Kate, but her gaze was fixed strongly on Amanda.

"You know, when I walked in here, I was pretty sure you'd ruined my day. Maybe even my relationship," Charlie said. "I have to admit, your latest article cut me to the core."

"Ms. Jenkins, please, let me…" Amanda began, but faltered quickly. "I just…I'm sorry."

"I bet you're a great poker player," Charlie said.

Amanda shrugged off the remark. "Not too bad, sure."

"You know, Kate here was a card shark in college," Charlie continued.

"Not the cheating kind," Kate added. "Just the *I'm-going-to-pay-my-tui-tion-by-being-more-skilled-than-you* kind."

Charlie nodded. "And she did. And she was."

Amanda raised an eyebrow. "Ooookayyyy…"

"I always thought it was funny, because she has all these huge tells. Incredibly expressive face, voice, gestures. You should see her at a horse race—well, I imagine you will see her at a horse race. It's like watching a human-coiled spring."

"That's true," Kate said, grinning at her oldest and best friend. "But they didn't matter for poker, not for me at least. I wasn't passionate about the game, I was just very technically proficient."

Amanda could sense that she was trapped, but she couldn't figure out how. She waited, silently, for the point.

"You don't have as many tells. You're pretty guarded, fearless, and focused, at least from what I've seen so far. But you've got one big one," Charlie continued. She turned to Kate. "Have you seen it?"

Kate nodded. "You get tongue-tied…whenever someone is close to catching you being kind."

Amanda's face was a mask, revealing nothing.

"You didn't seem very surprised by Jenny's outburst," Charlie noted.

"Maybe I'm just not that personally invested in the soap opera," Amanda said, sounding bored and looking at her nails.

"Sure, except we both know that would make great copy," Kate replied.

"I don't know how many times I have to tell you this, but I'm here to learn more about turf journalism. Jenny is not a horse, ergo…"

"Maybe that's what you're here to learn about, but that certainly hasn't been the focus of your articles so far," Charlie said. "They've all been human interest pieces."

Kate nodded, putting together more pieces of Charlie's hunch. "Right.

And the articles you gave me for review that were more balanced and biased, like your piece on barn fires, didn't make the cut. You were probably under some serious pressure to get something more salacious in."

"So, I did. Remember? All those nasty things I wrote about racing Storm? Everything going wrong around here?"

"But you already knew about Jenny," Charlie said gently.

Amanda opened her mouth to deny it, but looking at the faces of the two women, she knew she'd been found out. She shut it again and stared at them for a moment before responding, "I couldn't do that to Jenny. She's just a kid. I…I was going to get pulled from the beat if I didn't give them something good, something that would draw in a lot more readers."

"So, you published this nasty piece of work—because you knew we could handle it," Kate said. "When did you find out?"

"A few days ago. I ran into Jenny at the gas station, and she told me everything."

"So…before we hired you on?" Kate laughed. "Keeping you close enough to stop you from digging into this was…a major motivating factor."

Amanda shrugged. "She needed someone to listen, so I did. Just not as a reporter."

"As a friend," Charlie said. She crossed the small room and hugged Amanda. "Thank you. I mean that."

"I stand by my article," Amanda said. "I think you should seriously examine your perceptions of Storm's wellbeing and your decision to race him. I might not know a ton about horses, but there are people who agree with me that do."

Charlie nodded thoughtfully. "I appreciate that, Amanda. I didn't understand it when I first read it, but I think the perspective—and integrity—you bring can be very valuable. I'm certain Storm is ready. As messed up as some things are right now, I truly believe the Shamrock crew have the best interests of each other and of the horses at heart. I would like to prove all of that to you, if you give me a chance."

Kate nodded. "Charlie and I will have to work out the details, but we could use your help more than ever, if you're willing to travel to Belmont with us for the week. I'm on assignment for *BloodHorse*, so I won't be able to give Storm exclusive coverage. It's a good opportunity for you as well— I'll introduce you around, and you can get a real taste for turf writing and meet some of the best in the business."

Amanda stared at both of the women in front of her, amazed at the turn of events the last few days had taken. "Well…of course, YES," Amanda screamed.

Charlie smiled at her enthusiasm. She was just about to start hammering out the details when the office door banged open suddenly.

Ryan stomped into the room, half carrying and half dragging two mud piles, followed by two very muddy, very happy dogs.

"Ryan, what are you doing? Put those outside, Molly's office is going to be—"

The mud piles giggled.

"Hi Mom!" one of them said, tearing herself away from Ryan's clutches and running to hug Charlie.

Ignoring the filth, Charlie scooped Skylar up into a bear hug. "Hi, messy! I missed you."

"Missed you too," Skylar said, hopping into a chair Charlie realized she was probably going to have to replace.

"Where's Jenny?" Ryan said.

"Jenny and Molly and Lilly needed some space to work some things out," Charlie said smoothly.

"What type of things?" Ryan interrupted, suspicious.

"It's not really your business, Ryan. If Jenny would like to share with you later, that's her decision."

Skylar stopped spinning the chair around and got very still and quiet. Amanda, Kate, and Charlie exchanged looks.

"You okay, Sky?" Charlie asked. "Is this…about Jenny?"

Skylar looked up at her mom, bottom lip quivering, and nodded. "I think I messed up, Mom, and I don't know how to fix it. Have you ever made something so wrong that you can't make it right again?"

Charlie leaned down and wrapped her daughter in another hug. "Oh, yes. Everyone has."

Every other person in the room nodded—even Ryan, though he looked very confused.

"But you'd be amazed by the number of things you can make so much better," Kate added.

"She's right," Charlie said. "That's a big part of being a good person. You try to do the right thing, but when you know you haven't, you try to make it better."

Skylar sniffled and nodded. "Okay."

Charlie smiled at her and straightened back up. "Let's talk later, when it's just us, okay? How about you introduce me to your fellow filth monsters?"

"Oh man!" Skylar said, brightening up immediately. "I forgot! Mom, this is Drew—Drew, this is my mom—and Buster, his dog."

Ryan cleared his throat meaningfully.

"Oh, and…Drew and Buster ran away from home. Can they live with us now? We've already started building them a mud hut near the pond," Skylar said very quickly.

Drew nodded. "I saw it done on National Geographic."

Charlie did her best not to laugh, covering it up with a cough. "Well, let's hear more about this."

"It's going to be in a circle, and when the grasses in the field get longer and die out, we'll make the roof out of those," Skylar said, running over to Molly's printer to grab a clean sheet of paper. "Here, I'll draw it out for you."

"How about we start with why Drew and Buster have run away?" Charlie suggested.

"Oh," Drew said. "Well, I got grounded for coming over here without my phone, but Dad decided that part of my punishment was that we were going to clean up my room together, and then he found his watch that he thought was missing, hidden in my stuff, and he got mad, so I decided to leave. And Buster comes everywhere with me."

"It's the fireman, Mom, the one who yelled at you when the barn was on fire. He's really strict. He's gonna end up sending Drew to military school or something, and Drew doesn't want to go," Skylar added.

"Well, no one is going to military school tonight. I think Drew's dad might have tried to call earlier. Let me call him back, and I'll see what I can do," Charlie said. "Ryan, would you mind taking these two up to Doug's house and seeing about some showers?"

Ryan was about to protest, but thought better of it, shrugged his shoulders, and opened the door. Skylar jumped out of the chair, gave her mom one last hug, and ran out behind Drew and the dogs.

At the last moment, Ryan caught the door before it shut behind him. Crossing the room in great strides, he went back and gave Charlie a big hug too.

"We really missed you, Mom. It's so nice to have you back."

Charlie laughed and returned the hug. "It's only been a few days!"

Ryan pulled back and gave her a crinkly smile. "No, it hasn't."

Charlie stared after him thoughtfully as he left again, realizing he was right. She'd been getting better for a while, but this was the first time since Peter had gotten really sick that she'd felt 100% like herself.

I missed me too.

———————————

Charlie settled back against her sleeping bag and traded Drew the telescope he was offering for the popcorn bowl she was holding.

"Okay, tell me more about—that one," Charlie said, peering through the lens and pointing up at a constellation.

"That one is…" Skylar paused as she consulted the constellation app on her phone, "Draco, the dragon. Minerva threw him into the sky during a battle between the gods and the giants, and he froze there forever."

"Aren't there any horse ones?" Charlie asked.

"It doesn't look like it, not until later in the summer," Skylar said.

"How many horse stars do you need, Mom, really?" Ryan piped in from his seat over by the fire pit with Jenny.

They all laughed.

When Charlie left Molly's office that afternoon, she'd firmly shut and locked the door behind her and banned anyone from returning that day (shy of an emergency). She'd prescribed an early bedtime for Amanda, Cappie, Hunter, and Steve, and sent Molly and Lilly off the farm and out to dinner to talk. Travis, who had been called away to work, had reluctantly agreed to allow Drew to spend the night over at Shamrock under Charlie's supervision.

With pizza on the way, she'd laid out sleeping bags and set up camp with Ryan, Skylar, and Drew on Doug's wide back patio. They had spent the first part of the evening planning a bon voyage barbeque, and the second half throwing sticks for the dogs, taking turns choosing songs on Skylar's iPhone to play over the outdoor speaker, looking at the stars, and roasting marshmallows.

Jenny had joined them eventually. She was quiet and thoughtful, but not necessarily unhappy. When Charlie announced that Hershey was confirmed to join them at Belmont later in the week, Skylar offered her first olive branch.

"Jenny, would you please help me prepare his stall at the racetrack and be there to greet him? I don't want him to get overwhelmed after the time he's had at the hospital, so I only want a few people there when he gets off the trailer. But I know how much he likes you, and I'm sure he's missed you," Skylar had said shyly.

Jenny gave Skylar a big and rather wobbly smile. "I would love to, Skylar. Thank you."

Now the fire in the pit was dying down, as was the patter of conversation, and everyone's eyelids were getting heavy. Skylar snuggled up beside Charlie and let out a deep, contented sigh.

Charlie smiled up at the stars and said a quick prayer for herself and everyone she loved. *Thank you, for showing us that we have the capability to overcome the challenges in front of us in our life's journey.*

Bon Voyage

Charlie awoke first, just as the sun peeked over the horizon, pink and hazy. She snuck past the sleeping children to Doug's kitchen and made a pot of coffee. Cup in hand, she decided to continue her loop out the front door to enjoy a moment alone on the front porch, before everyone woke up and everything got busy.

The sun was warm and pleasant on her face, especially after waking up so many mornings in the windowless hospital room. She breathed in the fresh air and enjoyed how the smell of the fresh coffee mingled with the scent of the dew already evaporating off the grass. This was the first moment of true peace she had felt since before the fire. She remembered back to her meditative session in Sarge's stall and marveled at how overwhelmed she'd felt then—right before life had really, truly blown up. She stretched her back up fully, taking a very deep breath, and appreciated just how much she'd packed into the past week and a half and how much she'd changed.

"Hi," Jenny said softly from behind her, carrying her own cup of coffee as she joined her on the porch, Bart trailing behind.

"Well, hi yourself, Jenny. How did you sleep?"

"Really, really well, thank you."

"I'm glad to hear it."

"Can I…" Jenny trailed off before regaining steam. "I'd like to ask you something. If you don't want to answer it, that's okay, but can you promise you'll just tell me that, and not hide the answer from me?"

"Yes, I can promise that," Charlie answered.

"Is Uncle Doug going to be okay, really?"

Charlie thought for a moment, making sure she was answering honestly and truthfully, rather than just blurting out the answer she wanted to be true.

"Yes, Jenny, your Uncle Doug is going to be more than okay. I'm not sure everything you've been told, but all of his injuries are healing. He'll always have a scar on his head from where he needed stitches, though that will be covered by his hair when it grows back, and he'll probably have some burn scars on his hand forever, but those should be the only permanent changes. His leg will take some additional time to heal, but that's nothing new for you," Charlie said kindly, lightly tapping Jenny's own cast.

"And…mentally, is he okay?"

Charlie took another moment, then responded, "Yes. He's going to be fine. In fact, he seems so good, so lucid already, that it's hard to believe most of the time that his brain has just gone through a trauma. We're all going to have to remember that his mind is also trying to mend itself and be patient. I'm afraid I forgot that yesterday, and when he asked for reassurance about something, I responded as though he'd insulted me."

"Are you going to marry him?"

Charlie laughed. "That one, I won't answer. I haven't given him an answer yet, so it wouldn't be fair to start giving it to other people."

Jenny smiled. "Okay, that makes sense. I just want to know…if something were to happen to Shamrock…that he'd still have something, still be happy."

Charlie smiled at the teenager. "I know everything is changing right now, Jenny. And there are no guarantees in life. And I don't have a crystal ball. But your uncle is a good man—smart, loyal, generous, honest, and brave. I think that if Shamrock disappeared from the map tomorrow, he'd build something else incredible, and he'd keep helping other people build incredible things. That's just who he is."

Jenny gave Charlie a hug. "Thank you…Aunt Charlie," she added slyly.

Charlie shook her finger at Jenny, smiling. "Don't get ahead of yourself. We've got enough things to get done and celebrate right now. Starting with this barbeque."

Jenny nodded. "Alright, captain, I'm ready for orders."

"Then that's exactly what we'll start with. You get on the phone and place the order for the ribs and the chicken, and I'll go wake Ryan up so I can send you two to pick up all our supplies."

Jenny walked back into the house and Charlie followed close behind, taking one last look at the beauty of the rising sun shining over Shamrock.

———————————

Travis woke up to an e-vite.

"Belmont Bon Voyage Barbeque," he read aloud to the empty house.

No, I'm not coming to your barbeque today. I'm going to collect my son and get him measured for a humane restraint system, Travis thought, recalling all the times he'd had to track him down after coming home from work.

Travis shook his head, remembering the gentle lead he'd trained Buster with fondly. *If only there was a pre-teen boy version.*

It took Travis a few tries to reach anyone at Shamrock; when someone finally picked up the phone, it was Kate.

"Hi Travis," she'd said smoothly. "Sorry, we're on a buzz around here, lots going on. What time are you planning on arriving for the barbeque?"

"What?" Travis said. "No, I was just calling to see where on the farm Drew was, so I can come pick him up."

"Ah, sorry, now's not great, he's helping with set up. And it doesn't make sense. You'd barely get him home before you'd have to turn right back around for the barbeque."

"I'm not—"

"Oh, shoot, I've got to take this call. I'll see you in a few hours—probably best if you can get here by noon—oh, and bring ice!" Kate said, hanging up the phone before he could respond.

Travis stared at his phone for a moment, trying to figure out how and when he'd agreed to come to the barbeque.

"Nice job," Amanda said approvingly when Kate hung up.

"Stick with me, kid," Kate said. "I've noticed Kevin's already taught you how to motormouth your way through a no—and that fast New Yorker accent certainly helps. Advanced move: end with a favor request."

"With Chief Johnson, I'm usually just pleased to get away without getting my head bitten off. I can't imagine asking for a favor on top of that."

"Ah, but see, when people do you favors, they think they like you more than they do, since they're accustomed to only do favors for people they like. I've heard it called the Franklin effect, something about mental discomfort."

"Well, we must *love* Molly," Amanda sighed, looking around the cluttered office. "Why else would you volunteer us to clean this mess up?"

"Hmm. Okay, I'm going to share something with you, because I need you to help scan these documents as we file them. Something bothered me about your arson article, the unpublished one. I've been poking around ever since, but I can't find the answers I'm looking for. Do you remember your broader coverage of motives?"

"Sure," Amanda replied, "but none of them made any sense that I could uncover in Shamrock's case. I hoped I was on to something with the insurance angle, because I found out they'd increased their coverage a few weeks earlier, but after some additional research, it all seemed to be valid. They needed additional coverage in order to stable a Triple Crown contender."

"Right. I've been paying attention as Molly's dealt with the insurance companies, though, and there's something not quite right."

"She's still waiting for the report to be filed," Amanda said. "I think it's just a bottleneck there."

"Sure—but I'm not as concerned about the insurance coverage for the barn. We get updates on that saga all the time. What I'm curious about is the health insurance. I happened to overhear that Ben hasn't been able to access his, and he's waiting for approval for physical therapy, and I haven't heard Steve or Molly working on that at all," Kate replied. "So, just keep your eyes peeled. I'm not sure what we're looking for, but if something is going on, I want to find it before someone else does."

The two reporters combed through documents for a while in silence, collecting certain papers off to one side as they went. Once everything else was filed and organized, they sat back down with this small stack.

"Okay," Kate said, "I'm not a forensic accountant, but it seems like the farm might have been a little overextended before the fire. Nothing crazy, I don't see any huge IOUs or anything, but there are pieces here. The cameras weren't installed by their usual security company—it looks like they tried to cut costs by having Steve install them himself."

"So, amateur error could explain why they weren't set up to record properly."

"Right. And it looks like the reason Ben's having problems accessing his healthcare is because Shamrock dropped employee coverage," Kate said, shaking her head.

"How could they do that in the middle of the year? How could they do that without notifying their employees?" Amanda asked.

Kate shook her head. "I'm going to have to do more research. It doesn't seem right, but I have no idea whether it's legal."

"Does this mean Doug's hospital bill isn't covered at all?" Amanda asked.

Kate looked stricken. "I hadn't thought about that yet. I don't know—I hope not. That could ruin anyone."

"So, what do we do?" Amanda asked.

"I'm not sure of anything yet," Kate replied. "I don't know what it means, I don't know what it points to, and I don't know how to resolve it."

The women looked out the window as a few cars came in off the road, past the office, and towards the empty broodmare barn where the tables had all been set up.

"We need to get up there. Don't say anything to anyone yet. Remember, we only have a smattering of facts. The picture might look very different once we have them all," Kate warned Amanda as they filed the last few sheets away.

———————————

There was a woman standing by the paddock fence who looked familiar, but Travis couldn't immediately place her. She turned around and gave him a grin.

"Well, hi, Chief Johnson. I'm Charlie Jenkins, Skylar's mom."

"Right, yes, we met the night of the fire."

"Yes," Charlie grinned sheepishly, "sorry about that. It wasn't the coolest I've ever been under pressure."

Despite himself, Travis begrudgingly returned the smile. "I forget sometimes—well, often—that not everyone has been trained in fire safety."

Charlie nodded. "No, that's true, but I'm a lady who can recognize a blind spot. Molly and I haven't had much of an opportunity to speak about it yet, but I know they're eager to work with you to make sure the whole farm has training, a safety plan, the whole nine yards. I can't tell you how grateful we are to you and your men, and I know I personally never want to be a liability in that type of situation again."

Did everyone attend some type of advanced apology class I missed? Travis mused.

"I also want to tell you how grateful I am for everything your son has done for my family over the past few days, Chief. I've been at the hospital with Doug, and Drew has been an amazing friend to Skylar. He's made all the difference, and I'm afraid we've repaid him by helping to create a conflict in your home."

Travis felt himself bristling. "Ms…"

"Charlie," she interrupted.

"Charlie, thanks for your kind words. What I would appreciate—the best way you could repay Drew's generosity—is if you and the rest of your family and friends and farm stayed away from my son and me. I am more than happy to work with you on a professional level, so you don't end up hurting yourself or someone else in a fire one of these days, but frankly, it's hard enough to raise my boy alone. Teaching him a sense of responsibility when he spends the better portion of every day being feral and unaccountable with your daughter is impossible."

Travis nodded at her curtly and made to open the paddock gate. He was amazed by how quickly she moved to block it with her boot.

"Well, Travis—I can call you Travis, right? Because that's what's happening." Charlie's grin was somewhere between a grimace and just straight baring her teeth. "I'm afraid it's your bad luck to be the last person who's going to blow up on me. It's been days' worth of twenty-four-hour, back-to-back emotional explosions, and I'm done getting hit with the shrapnel. So, what you're going to do, right here and now, is tell me why you're so angry."

"Why in the world do you think I need one reason to be angry with you? Hell, I could name ten without taking a breath. You damn near got me killed, your boyfriend could have injured my entire squad, your daughter is dragging my son through burn sites and horse manure—literal horse manure—and…" Travis, whose angry bluster had been going strong, stopped short when he saw Charlie's face.

She looks—bored? he thought.

"Sorry, you know, if you have somewhere to be—"

He started getting himself worked up again, but suddenly completely ran out of steam. Like a balloon that wasn't tied off properly, he deflated, slumping over and sinking his head between his hands on his way down.

The two of them stood by the paddock gates in silence until Travis was able to pick his head up again.

He stared across the paddock at his son. "I haven't seen him laugh much since before his mother left." He had to work down a lump in the back of his throat as he finished the sentence.

"Skylar is having a wonderful time. My motivations aren't selfless," Charlie said. "Wonderful times haven't always been easy to come by for my family over the past few years, and I try not to let them slip away. Skylar is my sunny optimist, but I think always being the bright spot in everyone's dark days is lonely, especially for someone so young. I don't want her to lose the friendship she's built with your son."

"You know, I've always loved my son with every ounce of my body, but I don't think I was ever the 'fun' parent," Travis admitted. "It hasn't gotten any easier since my wife left. Drew's been acting out all year, and I have to work too much to let anything slide. I just keep getting more and more strict, and he just gets more and more headstrong."

Charlie was quiet for a long moment, but finally said softly, "I understand, but I have been doing the opposite. Since Peter died, I think I've gotten less strict. The kids and I were in so much pain after he left us. Life has gotten better again, bit by bit, but it's harder now for me to be a stickler about every single little rule. The details just don't seem as important as teaching my kids how to be happy and how to love themselves and the good people around them freely and fiercely."

Travis screwed his mouth into a crooked wry smile. "I imagine that's an easier path to take when their ideas of a good time don't involve stealing or running off or hunting rabbits with a bow and arrow. I spend half my work days wondering if I'm going to come home and find out he's literally shot himself in the foot."

Charlie laughed. "Well, if that's what is worrying you most, then you should definitely let him spend more time here at Shamrock. Spending time playing in, as you say, horse manure won't necessarily improve his phone manners or keep him from putting his elbows on the dinner table. But if he took to wandering around a working stable with a bow and arrow, every one of us would tackle him to the ground on sight."

"She's not joking," Ryan piped in as he walked up. "Get up to the barbeque and take a look around. Jenny and Ben will never let him mess around with a slingshot again."

Charlie threw her head back and laughed heartily as her son wrapped her up in a strong bear hug.

"I'm serious," Ryan confided to Travis in a stage whisper. "They will take a baseball bat to some kneecaps over so much as a water gun."

Travis smiled, but he had to push the lump in his throat back down as he watched Ryan and Charlie together. *I remember being that age,* he thought, *lumbering around with limbs that were too long, realizing that my mother had just mysteriously shrank into a person I could pick up and spin around.* He wondered if Drew would ever be that close with his own mother.

"Dad!" Drew cried, finally spotting his father and racing across the paddock towards him. "Did you know horses play hide-and-go-seek? Come see!"

Travis looked at Drew's happy, flushed face, and then at Ryan's, and then at Charlie's.

"You really should try it out, it's pretty crazy. I didn't believe it the first time Skylar showed me," Ryan said.

Charlie's eyes twinkled hopefully. "Go ahead, give us a shot," she said. "You can always change your mind tomorrow."

Travis gave her a tight nod before he launched himself over the fence and took off running towards his son.

"Oh," he called back to them, "would you mind taking the bag of ice in my truck up to Kate?"

Ryan looked as his mother quizzically. "Do we need more ice?"

Charlie laughed. "No, but maybe Kate knew Travis needed to bring it."

Charlie looked down the long table and smiled at the sight of all the friends and friendly well-wishers who had come to see them off.

It had been Ryan's idea to invite some of the local Storm Troopers as VIPs, and to stage this as both a celebratory bon voyage and a rehearsal for the much larger celebration to come if and when Storm won the Belmont. He'd sent out thirty invitations, and twenty had enthusiastically RSVP-ed yes, even with such short notice. Their happy faces mingled with the Shamrock crew and added a refreshing level of exuberance. The Troopers reminded them that all their hard work really was contributing to something extraordinary, which lifted their spirits.

Skylar ran up and gave her mom a hug. "Just for being you."

"Thank you, Sky," Charlie said. She nodded over to Travis and Drew, who seemed to be engaged in an enjoyable conversation with Kate. "How's your buddy? Are we going to have to finish the mud hut?"

"Nope! I don't know what you said, Mom, but he's not even grounded anymore!" Skylar replied, loud enough that Drew overheard.

Drew held up his phone like he was pulling Excalibur. "As long as I keep this on me at all times. Dad says he's going to tie it permanently around my hands if I don't."

Charlie smiled at Drew, and then at Travis. "I'm very glad to hear it, Drew."

"Okay, I'm going to finish getting everything together. I need to be up to New York before Lilly and Storm arrive."

"You're not leaving without saying a few words first, Mom," Ryan warned her.

"Probably a good idea," Charlie said.

She stood up and Ryan whistled everyone to attention.

"The race prep team needs to leave for Belmont Park very shortly, so we can set everything up for Storm's arrival tomorrow morning. I just want to thank you all for coming to wish us luck. I wish Storm could have joined us, but I'm sure we'll be doing this again after the race is over—and hopefully he'll be here with several new trophies to show off," Charlie said.

The crowd clapped and hooted enthusiastically.

"I cannot thank the Shamrock team enough for everything they have done. The entire Triple Crown bid has been an adventure that has required an incredible amount of work and effort and selfless devotion from many people, but the efforts over the past two weeks that these people have put in, in the face of unbelievable misfortune, has been truly heroic. Thank you, thank you, thank you. I am so grateful, and so happy you are in our lives," Charlie continued.

Everyone clapped again.

"Okay, Mom, get out of here—you've got stalls to muck!" Ryan said loudly, making everyone laugh.

"He's right—I don't want to say anything more that could jinx us over the next few days, so I'll leave it there. You all are the best, and I hope we will do you proud!"

Charlie waved behind her as she headed back towards the house, half running with anticipation for the big weekend ahead.

PART SIX

First Glance

Kate drove slowly down Hempstead Turnpike. The two women took in their surroundings, marveling as the vast grandstand of Belmont Park rose on their left.

"Wow, just beautiful," Amanda said, awestruck.

"Yeah, one of a kind. I could have turned back a-ways to go directly to the hotel, but I figured you might want to see what all the excitement is about," Kate replied. "I still get a rush of emotion each time I see the grand old place."

"Those stone pillars are amazing," Amanda said, pointing at the entrance to the racetrack.

"Those four stone pillars were placed here at Gate 5 in May 1903, two years before Belmont Park even opened. They were a gift to the group that built the park from the South Carolina Jockey Club, and they'd previously stood at the entrance to Washington Race Course in Charleston, South Carolina since 1792."

Amanda turned in her seat. "You are just such a wealth of knowledge."

Kate grinned. "As a journalist, it is my job to know all the details of what I am reporting on."

Kate turned into the entrance, but stopped at the curb. "Can't go any further until later, but you can get a good view of the clubhouse from here. The grand opening for the original was on May 4, 1905, but in the early '60s, it was deemed structurally unsound. It was fully demolished in 1963, and they spent from '64 to '68 rebuilding it."

"What? What happed to the Belmont Stakes?"

"NYRA, the New York Racing Association, moved the Belmont to Aqueduct Racetrack, its sister track, just eight miles from here," Kate answered.

"Two tracks so close in proximity to each other?" Amanda asked.

Kate felt herself getting tense with all the questions, but forced herself to be patient. "Racing was big business back in the late 1800s and early 1900s. It was a big part of the social scene of the times. It seemed that every town had its own track where women in carriages and men on horseback would arrive to spend their days. Aqueduct actually opened eleven years before Belmont Park, on September 27, 1894. It's known to most of the industry as the Big A and is actually located within New York City, if you can believe that, in Queens. There have been many tracks that closed over the years, and now the New York thoroughbred racing circuit is just made up of Belmont, Aqueduct, and Saratoga, which is upstate."

"Cool," Amanda said.

"The new grandstand, which reopened in 1968 and isn't so new anymore, is the largest of all the grandstands in racing, able to accommodate more than 100,000 people," Kate finished.

The two women sat in the car staring at the ivy-covered building towering in front of them.

"Don't you think it would have been amazing to live in the days when going out meant spending the day at the races? The fashion articles back then must have been amazing, who was wearing what, who arrived with who…kind of like the modern-day Emmy awards, right? I'd much prefer that scene, rather than trying to meet a guy in a bar in the Inner Harbor," Amanda daydreamed.

Kate smiled. "Well, you have several days to check out the 'social scene' here; maybe you will find your Prince Charming." She put the car in gear. "Let's go meet up with Charlie."

————————————

Pulling into the parking lot of their hotel, Kate was surprised to spot Charlie already waiting outside. She was even more surprised to find her in head-to-toe running gear doing cool-down stretches.

She pulled up beside her slowly and put the window down, waiting for her to realize she was being watched. After a few seconds, Charlie looked over at the idling car curiously, then flashed a happy, sweaty smile.

"My favorite intrepid reporters!"

Kate rolled her eyes fondly, but Amanda beamed.

"I wasn't expecting you until…much…later," Charlie said, noting the time on her phone with surprise. "I figured I would see you out at the back-stretch sometime after lunch."

"Made good time," Kate replied.

"She's being modest," Amanda said, leaning towards Kate and the open window. "She broke the sound barrier, but somehow never dropped her Bluetooth connection."

"That's not true," Kate protested.

Charlie laughed. "Now, Kate, I've ridden with you before, many times. I believe every word. Did you even stop for a bathroom break?"

"She certainly did not," Amanda said, taking the opportunity to jump out of the idling car. "That said, I will see you ladies after I check-in."

The two friends watched the younger woman flee towards the hotel entrance for a moment.

"Did you really stay on the phone the entire ride?" Charlie murmured.

"I had a lot of calls to catch up on," Kate replied.

Charlie looked suspiciously at her.

"Okay. She hopped into my car at six this morning with a list of questions that would have taken far longer than the five-hour ride to address. Six. In the morning," Kate said, shaking her head.

"You never have been a morning person. I suppose we should all be grateful you didn't leave her somewhere on the Jersey Turnpike," Charlie laughed.

"No one is that much of a morning person. Not even you," Kate said, eyeing her friend. "Although, from the looks of it, I would guess you haven't slept at all, and this is not your first run of the day."

"You're right about that," Charlie agreed. "But you know me. Insomnia is my body's reaction to excitement...and stress...and pretty much every other emotion."

"Anything new since I last saw you, or just the minor hiccup of being in the world's spotlight for the next week?"

"This and that. Blackston is here."

Kate bristled. "Tell me you punched him in the nose for everything he did to that beautiful horse. Does he have a horse in the race? Why didn't he show up on the list as a trainer?"

"Oh, get this—he's got *two* horses in the race," Charlie said, shaking her head. "Apparently he's the 'assistant' trainer for Sam Mason now, but Mason is nowhere to be found."

"Hmm," Kate said, riffling through her considerable mental horseracing dossier, "I'm surprised he'd make an allegiance like that now."

"I've never heard of him," Charlie said. "Is he usually a straight shooter? I can't imagine harnessing my reputation to that dirtbag."

"No, he's been under the pall of suspicion for years now. The racing commission quietly dismissed the last investigation about a year ago, so I'm surprised he's not treading more lightly. I'll look into it. Is Storm okay, though? Are you and Lilly?"

"That's the craziest part," Charlie replied. "Lilly and I hadn't even gotten Storm out of the trailer and into his stall before we ran into Blackston. Couldn't have avoided him if we tried, but I was hoping he'd put in the effort. Instead, he walked right up to us."

"No!" Kate said, incredulous.

"He was even trying to intimidate Storm—harsh, barking voice, jerky movements—but Storm took no notice of him whatsoever. Blackston was obviously getting frustrated, so right before he left, before Lilly or I could figure out what to do, he balled his fist and wound up his arm as though he was *actually going to hit him.* Storm looked straight through him. You've never seen a cruel man so spooked; he has no control over Storm anymore."

Kate's heart was thumping hard in her chest as she imagined the scene. "What in the world happened? Where was security? Where in the world was Hunter for all this?"

"It was all over so quickly. Blackston tried to laugh it off, said something about how Storm wasn't paying much attention to his surroundings, which wouldn't help him on the track if a rail jumped out of nowhere. It would have been almost threatening if he hadn't seemed so pathetic and small," Charlie shuddered. "Hunter walked up from the stabling office just as Blackston was walking away, so couldn't be much help. Which between you and me, is a good thing. Lilly's got the ice water of a warrior prepping for battle running through her veins right now, and I was knocked too off-kilter, but Hunter has always been the lunge-first-ask-questions-later type. The whole thing wouldn't have ended well, and we don't need any negative publicity right now."

Charlie followed alongside as Kate slowly but smoothly maneuvered into a parking space, and the two women continued to catch up as they made their way into the hotel.

"So, Hunter's been on good behavior?" Kate asked as they waited for the elevator once they'd finished getting Kate's room key at the reservation desk.

Charlie nodded. "He's no substitute for Ben, but I'm grateful he agreed to sub in until Ben can work through his health insurance snafu and join us."

Kate lowered her voice and nodded down the long hallway to the figure coming out of the room down the hall. "Despite myself, I'm a little excited to see parts of the job fresh through her eyes, walk her through her first real introductions into this community."

Charlie grinned. "Heart of gold."

"I'd tell you to keep it a secret, but no one would believe you anyways,"

Kate said, smiling back as they reached her room and Amanda approached from the other direction.

The younger reporter smiled at both of them, finishing up a line in her notebook with a flourish.

"Whatcha got?" Charlie asked, gesturing to the notebook.

"Just trying to finish up some notes and follow-up questions I picked up on the ride. Eavesdropping on Kate's conversations in the car was a real eye-opener—the breadth of her knowledge about horseracing made me realize just how far behind I am. It was thrilling each time she mentioned something I'd already picked up over the past few weeks. Between those flashes of clarity, though, I was able to fill the last part of this notebook with additional questions and terms to research."

Kate, never great at taking compliments, sucked in her breath a little, but Charlie smiled kindly at Amanda.

"You know, I admire that. I think many people are too afraid to ask questions—more concerned with revealing what they don't know than acknowledging that they still have a lot to learn. Horseracing is a large, complicated machine, and each of the cogs can be a little cliquish, so your ability to charge in and figure things out is going to serve you well."

"Well, what I want right now is to get over to the track and dive in. I've already dropped my suitcase in my room. Did you all want to head over to the track together? I was going to leave now, but I can take the shuttle or walk if you have more to get done around here," Amanda replied brightly as Kate opened the door.

Kate looked down at her watch. "I need to go and get my press pass, or I'm not going to be able to access half the spaces I need to in order to make my deadlines."

"I'd like to tag along and see what that process entails, if you don't mind," Amanda asserted politely.

Usually, she would do whatever she could to get a press pass herself, but she realized she wasn't sure what the proper etiquette was.

Things are finally going well with Kate, she thought, *and I don't want to ruin my valuable access to her by asking for too much.*

"Well, sure," Kate said slowly, thinking through what needed to get done over the next several days, "and maybe you should pick up your own press pass. Unless you plan on sitting outside the gates and waiting until race day to buy a ticket."

"You two go on ahead," Charlie said, starting down the hallway to her own room. "I'll jump in the shower and catch up with you at the track later."

Storm and Lilly were already on the track, trotting easily along the outside of the track oval. Buck swallowed hard as he caught himself watching them, wishing he could just enjoy the simple appreciation he'd have for such a pair of athletes if they were anyone else

By the time word got around the stables that Genuine Storm's arrival was imminent, Buck had cooled down and been ready to smooth over the rough words he and Lilly had shared on their last phone call. He'd made his way towards their assigned stable as quickly as he could, eager to see Lilly and check in on Storm.

"Ah, the competition," Hunter had said playfully as he'd entered. "I imagine I'm not the one you came rushing over to see. Don't worry, they shouldn't be too far behind. Keep me company as I get everything settled, give me the track talk."

The two men had lightly gossiped for a few minutes before Hunter had accidentally dropped a bombshell.

"Poor guy," Hunter had said, laughing sympathetically as Buck finished up a story about a trainer they both knew who had gotten himself in an embarrassing scrape. He'd lowered his voice as he'd continued, "By the way, we're all on scout's honor to keep the Jenny thing in the family, as it were. Cappie and I did what we could to keep it contained after the waterworks when Lilly and Molly told her. Figured you and Lilly had your own plans for how and if you wanted that news to go around, and stable gossip probably wasn't it."

Buck's blood had run cold. "Lilly told Jenny?"

Hunter's face had gone pale. "Aw, shoot...I thought they woulda told ya. I'm sorry, man, I just assumed...it was such a big hubbub on the farm that day..."

Buck had excused himself quickly, reeling away from the stall. He felt claustrophobic, startled and upset that Lilly had once again left him out of a decision and kept yet another major secret from him.

He'd managed to avoid Lilly and anyone else from Shamrock through the evening, but he'd known it was a matter of hours, not days, until they'd run into each other. Belmont Park could seem huge to an audience, but for two jockeys prepping for a big race, it was very close quarters.

Buck had nightmares all night about confronting Lilly, telling her off for making yet another unilateral decision about Jenny. Time and again, he'd woken up in a cold sweat from yelling that Lilly could never share a life with him or anyone else, because she hadn't changed—she was still secretive and evasive with people. The change of scenery was almost a relief when he realized Lilly had fallen overboard of the dream boat they'd been on. He'd tried to save her, but she'd refused to just reach out and grab on.

He'd woken up for the final time with the realization that he needed to focus on something else, anything else, before he drove himself crazy. It hurt, walking away from the woman he loved once again, but Lilly had chosen the path they were taking, and she was already running in the opposite direction. He'd used all his heartbreak once before to become one of the best jockeys of his generation; it would be somehow fitting if he used it now to win at Belmont, the one track he'd never beaten.

The warm sunlight shining down on this beautiful place now made him feel guilty as he wondered if Lilly's broken heart over losing the Triple Crown would be collateral damage or, perhaps, his real target. He tried to separate his feelings for her from his newfound determination to win. He tried to imagine a day where Lilly was nothing more to him than a fellow jockey.

Failing, he tore his eyes away from Lilly and Storm and focused on his own incredible athlete, Royal Duke, as the groom led them through the opening in the rail to start their own workout.

"Alright, buddy," Buck murmured to the horse as he urged Duke into a trot, "it's your turn to shine."

 # The Inside Track

Leaving the office, Kate handed Amanda her press badge. "Well, you are officially part of the press corps."

Amanda rubbed her thumb over the glossy badge, gazing admiringly at her name in bold lettering and *Baltimore Herald* underneath. She looped the lanyard around her neck, realizing she just couldn't wipe away the smile affixed to her face.

I've made it, she thought, *back to the bright lights, a half hour outside the place where I first found my love of journalism, the never-ending news cycle of New York City.*

"Come on, city girl, you have a tour of the press box and I have to be on my way to get some interviews done for *BloodHorse* before deadline."

Kate pushed her through the door and up the stairs, not stopping or slowing down before they reached a room at the top of the grandstand.

As they walked in, Amanda took in the long bank of windows and a never-ending row of swivel chairs, each occupied, most by men busily typing on laptops in between monitoring the workouts of the horses down below on the track.

"Hey Jim," Kate called out, reaching her hand out to the first man who greeted them.

Jim wrapped his second hand around Kate's smaller one and shook it warmly. "Great to see you, Kate. Will you be spending some time up here with us this weekend?"

Kate chuckled. "You know how much I would love to Jim, but the backstretch calls. I am doing some behind-the-scenes interview work that will hopefully bring some light to the general public about the people behind the horses that will race on Saturday. Not the owners or jockeys or trainers, but those who really know each of the horses—the grooms, the hot walkers, the exercise riders. I've even got a few cards up my sleeve with a farrier and a horse dentist."

"Well, if anyone can rally the public, you sure can," Jim commented admiringly.

Amanda stood quietly, half-listening as she took in the entire room and all the activity. As Jim and Kate bantered back and forth, she slowly moved over to the window, mesmerized by the view.

"Pretty awesome, right?" Kate said, coming up next to her.

"Yeah," Amanda whispered, lost in the vast beautiful view laid out in front of her.

"Amanda, let me introduce you to Jim McPherson, one of the most respected experts in all things Belmont, from the racetrack to the race itself."

Amanda turned and held out her hand. "Pleased to meet you."

"I am going to leave you two at it while I go meet my deadlines. Amanda, Jim will be able to show you around and give you the lay of the land and answer any of your questions. Jim, can you please find someone to show Amanda back to Storm's barn when you are done? She's not familiar with the grounds, and I would hate to have her get lost and wind up in Baffert's neck of the woods," Kate laughed, winking at Jim.

"Baffert? Who's that?" Amanda asked innocently.

"She still learning who's who?" Jim asked.

"Yep!" Kate said as she waved to both of them and headed out the door.

"We can talk about Baffert later; instead, let us go back in time, over to this wall and this trainer," Jim said, walking towards the back wall of the room with Amanda close behind.

"Woody's Winners?" Amanda asked, looking at the five plaques of jockey silks hanging on the wall.

"One of the greatest trainers of all time, Woody Stevens. Woody's career training thoroughbreds spanned over seven decades. He trained eleven Eclipse Award winners, which are the year-end awards for our industry, and his horses won over a hundred Grade 1 stakes races. One of his most notable horses was Conquistador Cielo, the winner of the 1982 Eclipse Award for Horse of the Year. Woody trained horses that won the Kentucky Oaks five times, plus the Kentucky Derby twice and the Preakness Stakes once, but he is most remembered for winning an unprecedented five straight Belmont Stakes between 1982 and 1986."

Jim ran his hand over each of the plaques in order. "Here you have Conquistador Cielo in 1982. Woody kept him out of the Derby, as he was healing from a leg injury; instead of running in the Preakness, he won the easier Preakness Prep. Cielo's next race was the Metropolitan Handicap, where he set a track record and won against older horses. Then, this wizard of a trainer surprised everyone by turning around and running Cielo in the Belmont Stakes just six days later, where he beat the Kentucky Derby winner Gato de Sol and won by 14 lengths."

"Next, you have Caveat in 1983," Jim continued, drawing Amanda's attention to the maroon and black silks. "His claim to fame is that he is one of eleven Maryland-breds to win a Triple Crown race. Woody ran him in the Derby Prep, then turned around and ran him a week later in the Kentucky Derby, where he placed third. On his way to winning the Belmont, he strained a ligament against a record field of fifteen horses, which eventual led to his retirement."

"Did Mr. Stevens have a history of running his horses in back-to-back races within a week of each other?" Amanda asked. "I thought horses don't race that often, more like every five to six weeks."

"Good question. That is fairly true these days, but back in the gilded age of racing in the 70s and 80s, these horses were war horses, racing several times a month."

Jim shifted her attention to the next plaque, resting his hand on the painted jockey silks. "Swale was one of my personal favorites, winning in 1984. He was the son of Triple Crown winner Seattle Slew, trained by Hall of Famer Stevens, and ridden by Laffit Pincay, Jr., also a Hall of Famer. There were high expectations for this one. He ran in the colors of the great Claiborne Farm. Story has it that as a youngster, the colt liked to take naps. One day they couldn't find him in the field and panic ensued. The colt was found laid out, snoring, in a dip in the paddock, which prompted Ms. Hancock to name him Swale."

Amanda smiled appreciatively.

"His two-year-old campaign was very successful; Swale won four races. He continued his winning ways as he entered his three-year-old year, winning the Kentucky Derby in textbook form by over three lengths. People may have murmured that Woody trained him too hard leading up to the Preakness, where he finished a dismal seventh, but he redeemed himself three weeks later when he won the Belmont by four lengths. Sadly, eight days later, Swale collapsed and died after a routine gallop right here at this very track."

Amanda put her hand over her mouth, mesmerized by Jim's stories.

"Now, this next one, Creme Fraiche, won in 1985—Woody's fourth consecutive win. He was the first gelding to win the Belmont, and wound up racing into his sixth year, earning over four million dollars."

"Last but not least is Danzig Connection in 1986, the fifth in a row for Mr. Stevens and one that has a few ties to a couple of the previous four. He was actually owned by the same gentleman who owned Conquistador Cielo. And he ran third to Crème Fraiche in the last race of his career, the Jockey Club Gold Cup."

"Wow, winning five in a row—that sounds like a big accomplishment," Amanda finally chimed in.

"Probably never to be equaled," Jim replied and then added, smiling, "Well, unless Baffert has his way."

"There you go again, mentioning this mysterious Baffert," Amanda said.

"Do you follow football, Amanda?" Jim asked.

"Sure, doesn't everyone?"

Jim laughed. "I remember when they used to say the same about racing. Anyways, do you know the New England Patriots?"

"Yes, like Tom Brady as quarterback, multiple Super Bowls, gorgeous model wife, sure." Amanda said, her curiosity piqued.

Jim smiled. "Well, the Tom Brady of racing right now is a jockey named Mike Smith. Bob Baffert…Bob is the Bill Belichick, the coach of the Patriots, the mastermind behind all those winning seasons and Super Bowls. Year after year, Baffert keeps winning the big races. No matter the horses he's training, he finds the ones to get it done. It helps that owners keep sending him tons to evaluate, so he can choose the best ones. He has won numerous Derbys, Preaknesses, and Belmonts, many times taking two of the three Classics in any given year. He won back-to-back Derbys and Preaknesses in 1997 and 1998, and then did it again in 2002. If I were a bettin' man, I'd put my money on Baffert to be the one to get the whole Triple Crown one of these years."

"You not a fan of Genuine Storm taking the whole thing this year, Jim?" Amanda asked.

"It's not that, Amanda. I think that horse is the real deal, and I love the fan base that has gotten behind him and the public interest he's raised. God knows we need that right now in horse racing. But, between the fire and all the setbacks, and the fact that the best trainer in the country, with an enormous stable of the finest horses and every resource available to him, hasn't been able to win the Triple Crown, it would take a minor—no, make that a *major*—miracle."

Amanda smiled politely, knowing she didn't have the knowledge to dispute him but hoping with all her heart he was wrong. She wandered back over to the wall of windows.

"Tell me a bit about this track. I have to admit, I'm shocked to see this much open green space so close to the city. It's not unusual for rural Virginia, but I grew up in Manhattan—if any of this space was open in the middle of the city, they'd be pouring foundation for skyscrapers right over it. That infield looks like it could house lots of people."

"Whoa there, young lady. That infield is sacred ground. We don't let all those partiers out there like they do in Kentucky and Maryland. It will look just as pristine, with its ponds and hedges, on Saturday as it does today." Jim pointed over to the panels of the prior Triple Crown winners on the infield to the left side of the grandstand. "Those mark the history of these three great races, the only horses to take all three. From Sir Barton in 1919 to Affirmed in 1978, a span of fifty-nine years, only eleven of 'em could do it. Over there is the gazebo, where the winning jockey silks are painted each year." Jim pointed to the white gazebo in the center of the pond in the infield to the right of them.

"The Belmont track is the biggest one these horses will probably ever race on; the whole circumference is a mile and a half. It's the longest of the Triple Crown races and the longest Grade 1 race on dirt in the entire United States. Did you know it used to be even longer? Until 1926, the race was one and five-eighths of a mile. I think you'll see that the mile and a half is plenty grueling, though, especially on a deep track. Has to be a big surprise for these young horses. Imagine winning at a fast track like Churchill Downs and then facing down this behemoth. No one can predict what will happen in that last quarter of a mile."

"Wait—what's a deep track? I'm guessing horses prefer fast tracks?" Amanda asked. She whipped through her notebook to see if she had jotted down anything about this over the past few weeks, but came up short.

"Oh, what a horse likes varies from horse to horse—and sometimes from day to day. Every track is different, and most horses perform better on one type of track or another," Jim explained. "Belmont isn't just fifty percent longer than Churchill Downs' mile track, it's an entirely different composition. Nothing is standardized."

"The condition of the track is one of the most important safety issues in racing." He pointed down to a tractor with the largest wheels Amanda had ever seen. "Since the big day is rapidly approaching, they're grading the track now. That man following behind is checking the depth of the dirt every two feet."

"That sounds…" Amanda trailed off, searching for a polite thing to say.

"Tedious?" Jim finished. "Oh yes, I wouldn't want the job for anything in the world, but it's one of the most important ones here—and, to be fair, they wouldn't ever offer it to me. Keeping this track in uniform shape is a huge endeavor, and the man in charge is very highly respected. He goes all out, extremely high-tech and scientific—material sampling, grading measurements, ground-penetrating radar, even biomechanical surface testing. When Keeneland, one of the more prestigious racetracks in the U.S., decided to replace its synthetic track with dirt, they turned to our team for advice. As I said, nothing is standardized, but they are part of a tech revolution in the field. Those workers are entering their data straight into a digital system that will help balance and optimize the track against forecasting models and any number of other data points."

"So, what makes it a deep track in comparison with Churchill Downs?" Amanda asked. "And if it's made of dirt, where did it get the nickname 'the Big Sandy'?"

"Well, both tracks are made out of combinations of sand, clay, and silt, but Belmont is considerably sandier than either Churchill Downs or Pimlico," Jim explained. "According to the latest research, as I understand it, the ideal dirt track composition is like one of those cross sections of the earth's crust they put in textbooks. The top few inches need to be fluffy silt and sand, to provide cushioning for the horse. The next few inches need to be slightly more compact, firmer, with a touch of clay, so the horses don't get bogged down and twist their ankles, but not so firm that they're going to strike hard and shatter. Those two sections make up the better part of the first foot of the surface; underneath that should be an even firmer surface, mostly clay, for another foot or so, to give a solid base for the horses to get even footing, and then, underneath that, a deep sandy loam subbase that can go twenty, twenty-five, thirty feet below, so that even the clay has a forgiving give. Since moisture affects all of this and weather is unpredictable, keeping the balance and keeping the track safe is a constant battle. The crew will be monitoring not only the conditions of the track but the forecast as well to make sure they are able to keep the track at the ideal composition."

"Sounds like a lot of work goes into the big day," Amanda said.

"Sure does, and not just for the track staff and the horses. Plenty around here, even above and beyond the race itself, to dazzle the crowds. You see that stage right at the finish line? On the big day, there will be a mini-Broadway show performed there for the crowds. And just prior to the race, members of the West Point parachute team will land right on the turf course on the other side of the finish line."

"That's incredible," Amanda said. "Can you imagine trying to orchestrate all that? You'd think that the mechanics of hosting one of the biggest horse races of the season would be tough enough—but to throw in a Broadway show and people jumping out of airplanes—it must be a huge, well-oiled machine of a day."

"The biggest in New York horseracing. The North American racing year consists of some 69,000 races, of which only eighty-four are Grade 1—meaning they are the very best and should draw the finest runners. On Saturday, Belmont will be hosting two Grade 1 races, one turf and one dirt. I wish more folks would appreciate Belmont for the race and the place as a stand-alone day, and not just come when there is a Triple Crown on the line. We have a lot to offer."

Amanda swallowed, feeling a little guilty as she admitted, "You know, this is my very first time here, despite growing up so close. I'm not sure I'd ever even heard of the track. I'd never even been to a horse race until I moved to Maryland. I was surprised when I started learning more about the Triple Crown and realized there was another track so close to the city. I guess I never realized how big racing was in New York, it was always associated in my mind with the South—Kentucky, specifically."

"Oh, New York has a fascinating history with horse racing. This area has been crucial to the sport from the birth of New York—before there were even such things as Thoroughbreds to race. Newmarket, the first race course constructed in North America, was built just a few miles east of here, where Garden City currently stands, right after the Dutch surrendered the territory to the British," Jim replied. "It's always been a strange love/hate relationship, though. Racing was popular before the American Revolution, but after the war, there was a concerted campaign to label it as immoral in the Northern states. In the early 1800s, New York passed a law banning the sport entirely. In 1820, the restrictions were lifted, but races were only allowed in May and October."

"So, what we're doing here this week would have been illegal?"

"Yes, but racing became more and more popular, and New Yorkers innovated the sport time and again. Union Course, also established here on Long Island, was the first dirt track ever, and the races could draw in crowds of 70,000. Supposedly, when Belmont Park had its grand opening in 1905, the number of carriages and cars trying to make first post caused Long Island's first traffic jam. Even today, far from the gilded age of racing, at least thirty-five of the annual Grade 1 events take place in the state of New York."

"Kate mentioned something about this not being the original grandstand? That they tore it down and rebuilt in the '60s?" Amanda said, looking around her.

"She's right that this is not the original, but it is actually the third incarnation. The first building had to be replaced after a suspicious fire in 1917, but the second one stood from 1920 to 1963, when it was torn down to make space for the building we're standing in now."

"It's a lot of building," she said, letting her eye sweep the expanse of concrete, brick and steel.

"It sure is. It's 1,266 feet long, about as wide as the Empire State Building is tall. The grandstand can handle 90,000 people—less than the 120,000 it was constructed for in its peak."

"Wait," Amanda said, remembering a detail from the history she'd already learned, "1905? Hasn't the Belmont Stakes been run since 1867?"

"That's right; the Belmont Stakes pre-dates Belmont Park. They were both named after the Belmont family. August Belmont, Sr. was a wealthy banker and racing man in the nineteenth century. He was one of the owners of Jerome Park in the Bronx, another defunct course. He started running the Stakes there in 1867. Eventually the track had to be shut down to build a reservoir for the water supply to New York, and the race was relocated to another defunct Bronx track, Morris Park, in 1890. The Preakness was also run at Morris that year. August Belmont, Jr. inherited both the family fortune and his father's love of racing. He was one of the most talented breeders in the history of the sport; Man o' War was born in his stables. He opened two tracks in the area, Sheepshead Bay in Coney Island and Belmont Park, and moved the Belmont Stakes here in 1905."

"And it's been here ever since?" Amanda asked.

"Well, no…horse racing was banned again in New York from 1911 to 1912, so the race wasn't run those two years, and then in the 60s, it was run over at Aqueduct for four years while they renovated Belmont Park," Jim said.

"And racing was still so big back then that Aqueduct was just eight miles down the road. Just imagine the days when there were so many people going to the track for entertainment that they needed two tracks to accommodate them all." Amanda shook her head at the difference from the present-day sport.

"Sure, and that's just a handful of the important Thoroughbred racetracks that have graced the metro NYC area. There were several other historically important ones, including Brighton Beach, Jamaica, and Gravesend. In fact, the Preakness was hosted at Gravesend Race Track for fifteen years," Jim continued.

"With the public interest in racing down so low, I'm surprised that either Belmont or Aqueduct hasn't been closed," Amanda said.

"Oh, there have been efforts, but the tracks really serve very different purposes. Just a few years ago, there were serious discussions about closing

Aqueduct and selling the land to developers. The idea was that, since Aqueduct's total capacity is something like 40,000, all of that business could move to Belmont."

"Did Belmont jump at the chance? It must be tough to compete with a track inside the city limits for customers."

"It would have required millions of dollars in renovations. Belmont was built as a summer track, and to take on the responsibilities of Aqueduct, it would have needed to operate year-round. Even if they had built new stables and heated the stands, Belmont is one of only three racetracks in the U.S. with a north-facing grandstand. It would have cast shadows over the track in the winter months."

Amanda let her eyes wander across the track into the lush green grass, the massive trees, and the ornate ironwork that fenced the perimeters. "It really is a beautiful park."

"August Belmont, Jr.'s goal was to build the first great racetrack in the U.S., one that could compete for prestige with England's Sandown Park or France's Longchamp. It's a monument to a very special time in Thoroughbred racing, a product of a very special set of circumstances that could never be replicated again, so we need to take care of it and make people appreciate it again before it's lost and gone for good."

Amanda took in a long breath and realized she wanted to be out there, getting a feel for the park and exploring, before it was all too busy for her to appreciate the space and the history. "Jim, Kate wasn't lying when she told me you're an incredible historian. I really want to meet the rest of the press and ask more questions about turf writing, but I'm filled to the brim with inspiration for articles I can write to get people excited about all of this. May we catch up on the rest later?"

"Absolutely! If you've got something in mind that will make audiences understand the beauty of the sport and of this space once more, I'm certainly not going to stand in the way of that. Come back any time; I look forward to sharing more with you, and I can introduce you to others that love to talk about our favorite subject."

Awkward Encounters

"Oh!" Steve exclaimed as he came around the sharp corner to the kitchen and nearly collided with Molly. "I wasn't expecting you'd still be here."

Molly flashed him a tight grimace and took a sip from her oversized coffee mug. "I think the Keurig is broken down in the office. I'm leaving again in a second. Ben's asking questions about when he'll be able to get up to Belmont…if you can't come up with an answer for him soon, I'm going to need to think of something."

Steve nodded, forgetting what he had come into the kitchen for, turned around sharply, and escaped through the back door.

Jenny watched the whole interaction closely, tucked quietly away in the breakfast nook.

Pretty sure that's the longest interaction they've had in nearly a week, she thought.

She really couldn't make up her mind whether she was concerned that her family was falling apart or still angry enough at them that she didn't care. Sighing loudly, she ate the last remaining chip from her lunch.

Molly looked surprised, but her expression softened into a smile as she registered her daughter. "Gosh, sweetheart, I didn't even see you there. I completely forgot you'd be home after your Spanish final. You should have said something when I came in, it would have been nice to sit for a quick lunch with you."

Jenny moved across the kitchen to put her plate in the dishwasher. "You seemed to be lost in thought. I was mostly finished anyways."

"Well, how about we go out for dinner tonight? I wouldn't mind splitting a cupcake or two or three from the new bakery downtown," Molly offered hopefully.

"Oh, my friend Sarah brought some to class the other day," Jenny reported. "They taste just as good as they look."

"That settles it, then. They sent out an email about their June special, peaches and cream, and I've been hungry for it ever since. You can fill me in on how the test went," Molly said as she made her way to the door.

"Sure," Jenny said. "What time will you and Dad be free?"

Molly paused before replying, "Oh, he's working late tonight. It'll just be us girls."

"On second thought, I'll pass," Jenny said, stomping out of the kitchen. "All the secrets you guys are keeping give me a stomachache."

"There you are!"

Amanda tore her eyes away from the tractors preparing the track for the afternoon races and quickly shut her notebook before she spun around to see whose voice was booming behind her.

"Just doing research," Amanda said, giving Hunter a big hug. "Oh, no!" She stepped back suddenly. "I'm so sorry, I forgot all about your burn!"

Hunter laughed. "Oh, don't worry about that." He lifted his t-shirt with one arm, exposing the padded bandage across his chiseled torso. "I finally took your advice and got a doctor to look at it. He gave me some antibiotic cream and dressed it properly—we're good to go."

Amanda smiled at him. "I'm so glad. There's so much here to see! When did you find the time to visit the doctor? You all must have been running ragged, trying to get prepped."

"Just comes with the territory, me being with a big star and all," Hunter narrowed his eyes dramatically, then laughed as Amanda softly punched his arm.

"I'll have you know, I'm officially in the in-crowd. Or, at least, I've got this," she said, proudly holding up her glossy press badge for his inspection.

Hunter whistled appreciatively. "Well, I did mean Storm, but looks like you are just as big a star," he teased, "I should laminate my trainer's license and string that up on a lanyard."

Amanda laughed. "Seriously, when did you find the time to get to the doctor? You are always at the farm or the track."

"Oh, there are doctors at every track to take care of the jockeys and backstretch workers. Horses are huge, powerful creatures, and racing is a dangerous sport. You saw what happened to Ben—and it doesn't take a crisis situation to cause injury. A horse just swinging his head around can break a groom's jaw easy—it connects with more force than a baseball bat."

"Oh, wow," Amanda said thoughtfully, "I'd never considered that. There are so many smaller industries wrapped up in horse racing. Does every track have a different doctor, or do they travel in for the races, or go from track to track?"

"Well, as the racing industry changes, so do all the others that rely on it. It used to be that every track had an in-house doctor—and Belmont still does, as well as an operational track clinic. It also used to be that jockeys were even more determined than they are now to ride injured. Racing is dangerous for jockeys—lots of injuries, concussions, torn ligaments and broken bones. Since jockeys are paid per race and a percentage of winnings, a lot of the doctors were there just to make sure that the jockey could get back on the horse, no matter how badly hurt."

"There's a famous true story from the 1930s about a jockey who died on the Bay Meadows track—his horse fell on him, and he was just flat out dead. The in-house doctor rushed him to the track hospital. He was already toe tagged when the doctor gave him a shot of adrenaline straight to the heart, just to see. The jockey jumped off the table, ran back the track, and was racing again the next day."

Amanda's eyes got huge. "That poor man, I can't believe they forced him back on a horse so soon…I would have needed to find another career on the spot."

Hunter laughed. "Forced? Darlin', if he was anything at all like any jockey I've ever known, he was spitting mad that they wouldn't let him race for the rest of the day. I think he rode for almost thirty years after that. They're tough, committed athletes, and they take great pride in how quickly they bounce back from injuries that would lay us mere mortals up for a long time. Luckily, the culture is changing, slow as it might happen, like it has in professional football. For instance, as we learn more about the harm concussions do, some jockeys are finally starting to take their injuries as seriously as they should."

"Well, well," a nasty voice rudely cut in.

Amanda turned in the direction of the voice and quickly registered the source of the interruption: a man who looked as oily and unpleasant as his voice sounded. She'd seen him working roughly with some of the horses and riders earlier in the day, and he'd seemed oddly familiar. Up closer, she was a little more certain she'd seen him before, but she was positive she'd never heard his voice.

The man, however, seemed to only have eyes for Hunter; Amanda noted with interest that Hunter's jovial face twisted into a mask of loathing.

"I'd heard a rumor you were on the grounds," the man continued. "You haven't been avoiding me, by any chance, have you, my boy?"

"Anyone with any sense is always avoiding you, Dale," Hunter snarled.

The man smiled unpleasantly, pretending Hunter had just made a friendly joke. "Ah, yes. Mr. Sensibility, that's what we'll call you."

His reptilian eyes flickered over to Amanda. "You're not taking any handicapping tips off this guy, are you?" His attempt at being charming fell flat.

"She's a member of the press," Hunter replied before she could respond.

"Are you now? Well then, why are you wasting your precious time chatting with this fellow? Nothing he can say about the Belmont could ever possibly go to print," the man said to Amanda, ignoring the venomous looks he was getting from Hunter. "Everyone will be covering Genuine Storm. You should be talking to me, the only man with two horses in the big race."

"I'd love to sit down with you, Mr…" Amanda trailed off, hoping someone would clue her in.

"Don't you know who I am? You are a greenie, aren't you?" he sneered. "I'm the infamous Dale Blackston."

"Infamous alright," Hunter muttered under his breath.

Amanda brightened up, recalling her research on Storm's bio. "Oh! You're the trainer who didn't see the potential in Storm, basically threw him away!"

"Sweetheart, I'm a businessman. I don't bet on fairytale endings, I invest in probable futures. Storm didn't fit my model then, and he doesn't fit it now," Blackston scowled. He whipped a card out of his wallet and handed it to her. "I'm not on vacation, I'm racing a clock. If you want the real story, call that number and we'll set up a time. Otherwise, have fun in Candyland with jokers like this guy."

Blackston finally addressed Hunter directly. "Boy, I don't want to see you become a stranger. We've got too much history together, it would be a shame to let it go sour and stale. But if you're too good for me now, so be it. Give my regards to your mother."

Amanda's eyes widened as Blackston walked past and made his way back to the stabling area. "What was that?"

"I told you, racing is a smaller world than you'd think. I've known Dale most of my life; he bought a few horses off my folks and came to see plenty more." Hunter shook his head at the memories. "Believe it or not, when I was a kid, I thought he was the coolest. My parents were not fond of him, didn't like selling him horses, and eventually they just refused to. They thought he was too flashy, too hungry, too determined to win, whatever the cost to the animal. Dad tried to warn other people, but the jerk got—still gets—enough owners the results they want at the tracks. I wish we all would have listened to them. You never believe your parents when you are young, but as you get older, you realize how right they were."

"So, he's treated other horses the way he treated Storm?" Amanda asked.

"Believe it or not, Storm's lucky he wasn't one of Blackston's chosen favorites. I'm sure he was whipped, maybe even shocked—Dale has been caught doing both in the past—but the fact that Storm didn't run well for him might have saved that horse's life."

"What do you mean?"

"The number of horses—racing, winning, productive horses—that die under Blackston's watch is statistically improbable, to say it nicely. He's been investigated for doping more times than I can count, but nothing ever sticks."

"How is that possible? Don't they drug test these horses, particularly the winners? I read the rules for the Belmont Stakes: Every horse has a blood test prior to the race, they can't run without a clean bill. The winner and another horse chosen by the stewards are then sent back for tests again immediately after the race."

"You're talking about the Belmont Stakes, one of the top races. The quantity and quality of drug testing and investigation is uneven across the country. Investments in security cameras, out-of-competition testing, and coordinating labs and authorities vary widely from track to track. Even under best practices, they can only find what they're looking for. Those drug panels are never exhaustive, and there are plenty of legal medications that no one would even question showing up on a panel. Doping has cast a shadow over racing the same way it has cast a shadow over so many other professional sports, and there are the same types of unscrupulous vets and trainers for horses as there are doctors and trainers for human athletes."

"What drugs are they giving them?"

"Muscle relaxants, sedatives, stimulants—there are a lot of pharmaceuticals that can be used to enhance performance when they're given to horses who have no medical need for them. Thyroxine is a big one. It's legal when administered as a thyroid medication, but can be used off-label to speed up a metabolism. Lasix probably gets the most press, at least within the racing community.

"Men like Blackston might win by abusing these drugs and with other shady or downright illegal methods, but they capture enough public attention that the struggling racing community will turn a blind eye towards what they're doing. But when the public learns more about how they're doing it, they're turned off to the sport forever. A lot of good people have struck a real devil's bargain, staying quiet and propping trainers like him up because we've been told it's the only way to save the sport we love, unable to see that they're destroying it from within until it starts to feel like it's too late."

Amanda was touched by Hunter's raw emotions, and she smiled at him encouragingly. "Hopefully Storm can ring in a new era, capturing the Triple Crown that has eluded these shady trainers all this time by doing things the old-fashioned way—being the best."

"It's a nice thought, Angel," Hunter said, smiling back at her. "Although sometimes it does feel like the good guys are always finishing last."

He plucked Blackston's card out of her hands, crumpled it up, and threw it over his shoulder.

"Hey!" Amanda protested.

"Horseracing doesn't need Blackston, and you don't either," Hunter said.

The reporter folded her arms. "I don't need you to tell me how to do my job, and the people in charge of maintaining these grounds don't need you making more work. Go pick that up and put it in the trash if you feel that strongly."

"Yes ma'am," Hunter said, meekly picking up the card and handing it back to her. "Do I need to pay a fine for littering?"

Amanda nodded seriously. "Fine is lunch, payable immediately."

New Research Methods

Should have listened to Hunter, Amanda thought ruefully the next day, watching as Blackston stepped out to take yet another call. *This man hasn't given me anything I couldn't have gotten straight from the internet, and he clearly has no issues wasting my time.*

Blackston eventually slid back into the room. "Ah, where were we?"

She didn't even try hide her frustration. "Why don't you tell me what it means to be 'ruled off' and how it is currently affecting you?'" Amanda asked, consulting her notes.

Blackston looked taken aback by the question but covered it with a loud guffaw. "In this case, it means that you're either trying to insult me, or you've been listening to sore busybodies' gossip. Getting ruled off is when a person is banned from stepping foot on racetrack grounds because you've pissed off the wrong people. They'll accuse you of something bad—could be stealing a keychain, could be murder—and if they've got the political clout at the track, they can just get rid of you, no trial or nothing. Maybe you did it, maybe you didn't. It's a judgement on high from the court of public opinion. Hell, even horses get ruled off if they piss off the wrong people."

"Speaking of which, I've heard rumors that one of your horses, Manakin, has been…biting…other horses and jockeys…" Amanda looked confused as she tried to make sense of her own notes. "Sorry, I must have written this down wrong."

"Oh, no, Manakin is a nipper alright. He knows he's the man—get it, 'the man,' as in Manakin?" Blackston smirked before bragging, "He's the best there is, and he's not going to let anyone forget it. Any time somebody walks by that he don't like, he'll take a chomp."

"Oh," Amanda replied, taken aback. "That seems like a serious behavioral problem for a horse, especially one in the public eye. I'm surprised it doesn't get him disqualified in some way. I wouldn't have guessed horses were even prone to expressing aggression that way; seems out of character for herbivores."

"Horses will eat meat if they get hungry enough, and some of them develop a taste for it. And their jaws are certainly powerful enough to handle it. A horse can bite the finger clean off of an adult human hand."

Blackston's voice had gotten very ominous and he searched Amanda's face for a sign he'd gotten to her.

Like I'd show you, she thought, giving him a sweet smile. "How interesting!"

"Anyways," he said, visibly disappointed, "I'm ruled off from a track or two here and there, but not the Belmont. There's a small—almost routine—investigation into me still pending, which is why I'm working as the assistant trainer under Mason for the race. Just gives the owners a little space from any whiff of scandal, makes them feel more comfortable with their investments."

"I've spoken now with several trainers and they'd never mentioned routine investigations," Amanda said.

"Making enemies is just the price you pay to be the best. Who even is Storm's trainer? Doug Walker? He's never made it this far in the races before, and I don't see him here now. I'm here year after year after year—you know why? I'm a businessman, not some gentleman trainer." Blackston snorted derisively, then cut Amanda short when he saw her prepare to defend Doug.

"Listen, owners come to me because I have a system that works, not a big pile of feelings and dreams. Like it or lump it, the world revolves around money, and horseracing is no exception. The owners I work with have entire stables full of horses with solid gold DNA, not one long shot, and we don't try to move heaven and earth to bring them all to their fullest potential. Most of them aren't worth it. They're duds, rats—horses who won't ever win back the money it would take to train them, much less earn anything extra. It's numbers and algorithms and predictions based on solid assessments."

"You don't seem to have much affection for horses," Amanda said.

"They aren't pets or children, they're investments. Getting emotionally involved keeps owners like Charlie from seeing the clear picture—something I believe you yourself accused her of in one of your articles," Blackston said with a nasty smirk.

Doesn't seem like he'd be any nicer to children or pets, Amanda thought.

"All I can say is that whoever is footing the bill for Storm better hope he commands a strong stud fee. Between the resources that team has dumped into that horse and how expensive cleaning up their string of post-Preakness bad luck must be, I imagine they're far in the red right now. They probably need to win a Triple Crown just to break even."

Amanda's mind started swimming as Blackston's words brought up old doubts about Shamrock and the unexplained insurance irregularities that Kate had found.

"Well, I'm glad that's over," Lilly said as she ran a brush over Storm's mane. "The whole post-position draw ceremony has to be one of my least favorite parts of this race. Now that we know our starting gate position, we can narrow in on our workouts a little better. I'm happy with six, so glad we're not on the rail."

"Position matters less on a race this long," Cappie replied. "Plenty of time to make up for a less optimal position."

"Yeah, but you know me—I prefer to be able to feel my way through a race. Knowing in advance that I'd need to correct our position risks me overthinking it, making me less flexible to react to the moment."

Charlie walked around the corner of the barn, pocketing her phone as she joined the rest of the team for their daily debrief. "Doug says hi to everyone, and asked you to give him a call this evening if you can," she said, patting Lilly's shoulder lightly and Storm's shoulder more vigorously.

"Sure thing," Lilly replied.

Conversation petered out quickly and everyone seemed a little subdued, which didn't suit Kate at all. To hit all her deadlines for the week, she'd needed to spend most of the day holed up in her hotel room, researching, organizing, and scheduling. She was craving human interaction.

"Earth to Amanda," Kate said, nudging her. "Why are you so quiet? Where are your thousands of questions? C'mon, I'm ready to tackle a tough one."

Amanda shook herself back to attention. "Sorry, I had the craziest interview today with Dale Blackston—you know, Storm's former owner?"

"Unfortunately, we've all had the displeasure," Charlie said, making a face. "You okay?"

"I am, it's just…" Amanda paused, then smiled and decided to tell them the second-most disturbing piece of information he'd dropped: "I think he might have threatened to feed me to a horse."

It took a split second for each of them to process what she'd said before they all started to laugh.

"His intimidation tactics are notorious," Lilly said sympathetically once she could breathe again. "He's made a special point of saying something to me every morning to try and spook me, make me doubt Storm. He's underestimated me—I don't scare easy, and if I was prone to intimidation, I never would have gotten into this sport in the first place, much less made it to where I am today. As for Storm, I can say with a clear conscience that he's never been more at home on a track, more ready to race. Every time I touch his body, it's like I get an electric jolt. He's just…well, a well-oiled spring ready to be released."

Charlie nodded. "I agree with Lilly. I've been watching Storm gallop every day and watching his competition as well. They're all very impressive horses and serious competitors, but this race feels different, somehow, than the Derby or the Preakness. Storm is different—we all are. Somehow, a lot of the fear is just gone. We still want to win, but with every day that goes by, it seems like we're less afraid of not winning. I think that makes us all stronger."

"Well, if a man like Blackston can't get inside your head, aren't you afraid he'll find some other way to sabotage you?" Amanda persisted.

"He's awful," Charlie agreed, "but he's not Godzilla. Security at the park is too tight for him to try anything on Storm."

"I suspect that he'll have an orchestrated plan during the race," Cappie said. "Possibly he's got one of his horses pegged to win, and the other will be used to try to keep Storm from winning. I've been watching tapes of their races, and Manakin nearly always tries to establish an early lead. Imagine That could be used tactically, to block us from challenging Manakin's lead by gatekeeping the paths near the front, weaving in and out before dropping like an anchor, taking out any horses surging up late."

"Oh, that's interesting. Lilly, do you have a plan like that? My editor asked if we can get something directly from you, sort of a perspective riff off Charlie's blog, where you take us step-by-step through your plan for the race. You know, at what point you're planning on pulling ahead, how you've planned to take on each of the competing horses, how fast you're planning on starting—just everything detailed enough for a viewer at home to follow the race as though they are the jockey. He told me to sell it to you as analog virtual reality. He's calling it 'A View from the Saddle.'"

Lilly raised her eyebrows. "You're kidding, right?"

Amanda shrugged.

Lilly sighed. "Well, to start with, if I can give the view from the saddle, I'm losing the race. Once those gates open, my butt doesn't touch the saddle until after we cross the finish line. I've got too much work to do to sit."

"Well, at what point do you and Doug talk and decide on the plan? Since he won't be able to be in the paddock for this race, are you devising your plays tonight? Can you do it via phone?"

Lilly looked at her like she was crazy. "There's not a jockey on earth who could tell you how things are going to progress during the race. Sure, we know our horse and do our research and try to make the best plan possible, but once the gates open, all bets are off if the horses don't break as expected. Remember Storm in the Preakness? Who would have thought he would have broken fast and been on the lead? I had to make adjustments each step of the way.

"Recognizing that this track is so much longer than the past two races, what is the latest marker you're willing to hit before you make Storm start running at full speed?"

"That's not how it works. I don't *command* Storm," Lilly sighed. "This isn't like driving a temperamental car. Storm and I are a team. At a certain point, I ask Storm to give all the energy that he has left—a little with how I move the reins, and how I move my body, and quite a bit with my posture—but I do it all automatically. If you watch any good jockey run a good race, you watch them make decision after decision after decision on the spot. We've collected the knowledge and experience and relationships and muscle memory—and then we've internalized all of it. That way, we're immediately reacting to the field around us rather than trying to make conscious choices."

"Good jockeys research. We also research the track—how loose the dirt is, how the water drains, what times the sun creates glares and where. We research the competition. We read the *Daily Racing Form* to know how they're performing, we watch them train and practice, we review videos of their other races. Practicing on the track and having every marker memorized is particularly important at Belmont Park."

"Why's that?" Amanda asked.

"Well, as I'm sure you've already heard several times, the mere length of the track poses problems for a lot of horses, but also for jockeys who come in green or out of practice with the distance. It's a hard track to ride, and it's stressful to not know whether your horse can cover the distance. What I've been paying very close attention to, however, are the distance markers—really getting a feel for them. They're in different positions from the mile-long tracks. It's easy to mistake the quarter mile poles and think you're further along than you are. A lot of jockeys lose this race because they confuse the three-quarter pole and think it's the half mile one, and ask their horses for the last burst of energy too early."

"I have to imagine that many of the jockeys in a race as prestigious as this one have ridden the track many times before—I know you and Buck have both competed at this park multiple times," Amanda said, watching Lilly's face for a reaction when she said Buck's name.

Charlie and Kate exchanged a look; the fact that Lilly and Buck were avoiding each other had become apparent, but since Lilly hadn't said anything, neither of them had wanted to pry.

Lilly's face stayed completely composed. "Sure. That's where we all start getting tricky. You can use the length to your advantage, speeding yourself up early to force another horse to leave it all on the table too soon, tire him out while there's still a lot of race ahead. It's what I know I'll have to watch out for with Blackston's two horses. Everyone out there will be trying to force my hand, to convince Storm that he should tire himself out. Storm and I are the ones to beat, and we're going to have a bullseye right on us. Everybody else wants to win, but they also want Storm and me, specifically, to lose."

"Really? You think, even Bu—"

Lilly shot Amanda a glance that made it clear she was approaching the edge of her boundaries.

"Er, even Royal Duke?" she finished lamely.

"Sure. It's not personal, just the nature of the competition. For several of them, the hype around Storm winning the Derby and the Preakness just serves as a constant reminder that we trumped 'em. They're not likely to forget that, and they'll try to correct it as best they can," Lilly said.

The jockey started to gather up her things. "I'm going to give Doug a call and turn in for the night. I'm in full training mode, so it's nearly past my bedtime."

Cappie started to make his way out too. "Need to call Molly and check on things at Shamrock and figure out the plan for picking up our favorite pony."

"Thanks, Cappie," Charlie said, smiling gratefully. She was eager to see Hershey, and even more excited to see Hershey and Skylar back together.

"Night, ladies."

"I know I should probably follow their lead," Charlie said to the remaining Kate and Amanda, "but sleep is many, many hours away for me. Kate, any ideas for a moderate amount of trouble we can get into?"

"I can't," Amanda said woefully. "I got an assignment for the Style section I need to knock out now, so I can focus on more serious turf journalism over the next few days."

"Hm," Kate said. "What's the assignment?"

"Just something about Belmont Park that will appeal to a larger crowd than racing folks. Something historical, maybe, but fun. I'm not sure yet; after my tour of the press box, I was thinking about the architecture of the park, but I'll have to do a lot of research."

Kate snapped her fingers. "Ladies, I've got just the thing to solve both of your issues. Follow me."

———

"See, I'm concerned," Amanda said, looking around the Heritage Club Food Court, "because while that man's pastrami burger looks incredible, I'm not going to score any points with my editor by covering this illustrious institution."

"Ah, prepare for an evening of history, intrigue, and..." Kate paused. "Well, I'll think of a third one. Right now, belly up to the bar."

"Full service, even tonight," Charlie commented. "I wonder what the red selection is."

"Sorry, Charlie," Kate said, settling on a stool between Charlie and

Amanda. "You're part of a historical experiment this evening—no wine."

She cleared her throat and started her lecture. "The Kentucky Derby's official drink is the Mint Julep, and the Preakness has the Black-Eyed Susan, and for now, the Belmont has the Belmont Jewel."

"'For now?'" Amanda asked.

"It's changed three times in the past twenty years. Who is to say this one will stick?"

"Why did they change it?"

Kate grinned and summoned the bartender over.

"Howdy! Are you too busy to educate a few thirsty women on the drinks of the Belmont?"

The bartender smiled at the three women. "Oh, I've got some time right now. I'm gearing up for my busiest day of the year, so being put through my paces will be good practice." He shook Kate's hand. "I'm Bill—what can I do for you?"

"Hi Bill, I'm Kate, this is Charlie, and this is Amanda. Neither of them has ever heard of any of the Belmont signature cocktails, so I'd like to line 'em up and have a taste test. May we please have a White Carnation, a Belmont Breeze, and a Belmont Jewel?"

"Coming right up."

The women watched the bartender as he mixed the drinks, enjoying his running commentary. He dropped each one off in front of them as he finished.

"First, we've got the White Carnation, the Belmont drink from the mid '80s until the late '90s. Vodka, peach schnapps, orange juice, club soda, and cream, all mixed up and served in a martini glass."

"Oh!" Amanda's face lit up. "Like a creamy Fuzzy Navel!"

Looking excited, she took a sip. Her expression changed quickly, as she debated whether she could swallow it, and how rude it would be to spit it back into the glass. She mustered her strength and swallowed.

"Noooo thanks," Amanda said. "I don't know how a drink could manage to taste 'chunky,' but that one does."

Bill nodded. "When the cream interacts with the acidic orange juice, it tends to curdle," he explained. "Most customers agreed with you. It was never very popular."

The bartender stayed in motion while he was speaking, mixing together vodka, peach schnapps, and 7-Up, and handed the new drink to Amanda. "This was the variation that sold a lot better—just a plain old 'Carnation.'"

"Mm, that's nicer," Amanda said, sipping appreciatively and handing it over to Charlie. "I can see this being a much more refreshing drink to sit in the sun with, rather than watching the races in the June heat with a belly full of curdled milk."

"Honestly, it tastes more like a brunch drink to me," Charlie said, sipping the White Carnation. "And the Carnation is just a too-sweet vodka soda."

Kate waved away both the drinks as Amanda and Charlie offered them to her. "I'm of the opinion that a race drink should be built on bourbon."

"I'm with you," Bill said, "but alcohol tastes shift pretty dramatically over time. The White Carnation was a distinctly '80s drink, so by the late '90s, it felt very dated. In 1998, the track responded to that, and the Belmont Breeze was created," he continued, placing another glass in front of them. "Bourbon, sherry, lemon juice, simple syrup, orange juice, and cranberry juice."

"It's...nice," Amanda said mildly.

"Nothing special, though," the bartender finished the thought she was too polite to express. "The cosmopolitan, in all of its incarnations, was the most popular drink at the time—think juicy and light twists on the classic whiskey punch. The Breeze wasn't overly popular, but most people liked it well enough."

"This tastes so familiar..." Charlie said, chasing one small sip with another. "Why can't I place it?"

"Well, *The New York Times* called it 'refined trashcan punch.'"

Charlie gasped. "That's it! I haven't tasted anything like this since college!"

Bill laughed. "One of the big problems was that it was too complicated and time-consuming to make for a huge crowd. Between the logistical issues and changing tastes, a new drink was unveiled in 2012—the Belmont Jewel. It's just three ingredients: bourbon, lemonade, and pomegranate juice."

"Mmm, this is more to my liking—I guess it's really a twist on a whiskey sour, my favorite cocktail," Kate said.

Amanda coughed. "A strong whiskey sour."

The bartender smiled. "It's strong and simple, but it tastes a little like what it is—a drink built for mass production. Nothing wrong with that."

"Wait, so—what about earlier drinks? You said the White Carnation was created in the '80s."

"The Stakes didn't have one. Really, only the Kentucky Derby's Mint Julep tradition came about organically—the Preakness' Black-Eyed Susan was introduced in the '70s, and it's been around that long in name only. The ingredients have changed several times."

"Well, that's a little disappointing," Kate said.

"Belmont Park made it through Prohibition and the height of several cocktail golden eras as a true New York institution, so there are a few drinks that were inspired here, but they were not timeless classics. There's the Belmont, which is gin, raspberry simple syrup, and sweet cream…"

Amanda made a face. "No more creamy drinks, thanks."

"There's the Belmont Park—rum, powdered sugar, port wine, and egg."

This time, all three women made faces. Bill laughed.

"Then the Belmont Stakes, which is vodka, rum, strawberry liqueur, lime juice, and grenadine syrup; and the least offensive, the Jockey Club, which is really a take on a Manhattan—bourbon, sweet vermouth, and maraschino liqueur. There is one more—" the bartender looked around, then leaned in conspiratorially, "but I'll only make it if you promise not to order it again this weekend. It's too time intensive, and I'd go mad if I had to make a bunch on the busiest days of my year."

They readily agreed. "Scout's honor," Kate promised.

"As I mentioned, *The New York Times* took issue with the Breeze, and called the White Carnation 'undrinkable.' As an alternative, they created the Tremendous Machine, in honor of Secretariat's famous win. It's bourbon, dry vermouth, Grand Marnier, rosemary, Angostura bitters, and a whiskey-spiked cherry," he explained as he expertly mixed the ingredients.

"Wow," Charlie said, tasting it, "this really ties it all together and takes the best element from each of the drinks. It's as strong as the Jewel, a little citrusy, like the Breeze and both Carnations, and the herbal rosemary taste makes it seem like a hip Julep."

"Well, Bill, you're a master of your craft, and you've gone above and beyond our expectations. It's time for us to settle up," Kate said.

Bill waved her off. "It's on the house. I just have one request," he said, looking at Charlie.

"Got a bet riding on Storm?" she guessed. "Don't worry, we're doing our best to make sure he wins."

"Oh, no," Bill said. "I mean, of course I have a bet riding on Storm. I have no doubts—he's going to take home the Crown. When he does, though, I want you to come back and try a new drink I've been working up. It would be quite an honor to name it after him."

Good Advice

Travis walked into the office and wondered if the power was out. The lights were out, and the air felt stiff and was already uncomfortably warm, considering how nice the afternoon's weather had been. From the far corner, though, he could still hear the faint whir of a computer processor and see the blue glow of the monitor reflected on the wall in front of him. It took him another moment to realize he was not alone. Molly was sitting in front of the computer, staring blankly at the screen.

Travis cleared his throat and Molly's tired, swollen eyes jerked up, registering her surprise.

"Sorry, I…must have been distracted," she said robotically. "Are you here to drop Drew off?"

"No," Travis replied, "I'm here to pick him up. Took the rest of the week off, I think we're going to take a road trip."

Molly nodded, clearly distracted by the information on the screen again. "Have fun."

The door swung open again, and Ben stepped through. "Hey Molly! Looks like everything is square with the insurance, the bill was paid up this morning. I was going to scrub down the trailer and get it all prepped to pick up Hershey on our way to New York. Mind roping everyone else up and settling the plans? It'd be great to leave bright and early tomorrow morning, and I still haven't been able to track Steve down."

Molly gave Ben a tight-lipped smile. "I'll figure it out."

Ben grinned broadly, all his normal energy returned. "Thanks!" He patted Travis' arm in greeting and bounded back out the door as quickly as the boot on his foot would allow.

"Actually, I was hoping to hit Steve up too," Travis admitted. "Went up into the attic to look through our camping stuff and realized it had all gotten torn up by some mice that were happy to make it their home. Steve offered to let us borrow a tent and some sleeping bags, and I'd like to take him up on that."

"Well," Molly said sharply, "when you find him, you tell him the queue for his attention is growing quite long."

She buried her head in her hands.

Oh, I am the wrong guy to deal with a sad lady, Travis thought, looking frantically towards the door.

Molly raised her head up and breathed deeply. Though there were tears in her eyes, Travis was surprised by her expression. She noticed the shock on his face and barked out a laugh.

"Sorry—my tear ducts appear to be broken. I'm so angry that my brain can't figure it out."

Travis smiled sympathetically. "I happen to know exactly what you mean. Found out I was an angry crier when my wife left. Never would have guessed it. I'm angry a lot, but it turns out, at the breaking point, it's all big hot tears."

"When did you know it was over?" Molly asked more quietly.

Travis sighed and took off his baseball cap to scratch his forehead. Realizing he might be there for a while, he walked further into the room and cracked open a window to let in some of the breeze.

"We were polar opposites, which I thought was good at first. Probably was when we were younger. We met in high school—"

"Steve and I did too," Molly interjected.

Travis nodded acknowledgement and continued, "I was born a grumpy old man, but she was fun and energetic and spontaneous. She brought me out of myself, helped me try new things. I brought her stability, calmed her down a little, helped her focus. Over the years, though, it just turned out we didn't agree on any of the big things, and when we disagreed, which got to be constant, we'd both turn into the worst versions of ourselves—I'd dig in my heels, she'd run away."

"It's not like that with Steve and me," Molly said sadly. "We've always worked well together, here at Shamrock, at home, raising two great kids. We've never really disagreed before now. Then I found out one thing he'd hidden from me, which led me to another, which led me to another…and now I have no idea what's happening, and for the first time in over twenty years of marriage, he didn't come home last night. Now there's money missing from an account I never thought he'd touch." She shook her head. "I feel like a fool. And I'm unburdening on a near-stranger when I should be trying to figure out how to get Skylar and Jenny to Belmont with Hershey, since I don't think I can count on Steve. I won't be leaving to come up until early Saturday morning to make sure all is running smoothly here."

"Well, I wish I would have unburdened on a few strangers when Maggie and I were in trouble," Travis said kindly. "I kept everything bottled up, assumed I knew all the answers. You know, I'm still finding out things I'm wrong about. When she left, my grandfather's pocket watch disappeared, and I thought she'd taken it with her. I was so mad about it that I never reached out, never talked to her about setting up a real visitation schedule with Drew, nothing. Just this past week, I found out it was still in the house, which means now I've got to reexamine myself and my actions, and quite frankly, I don't want to. I want to be the only hurt party, the sole victim."

Travis smiled at himself and continued, "So, as a near-stranger, all I can say is I didn't know everything that was going on, and you might not either. Maybe Steve is a bad guy, a thief. Maybe he is gone for good. I work with the public in crisis all the time, and sometimes people aren't who they seem to be, trust me. But if—correction, *when* you get the chance to talk to him, really talk to him. Ask him the questions you have. Listen to the answers. Don't assume you already know."

"Thank you," Molly said somberly.

"You bet," Travis said. "Now, I haven't thought this through at all, but Drew and I are hitting the road, and I bet he'd have more fun meeting Hershey and seeing Storm win the Triple Crown than he would fishing alone with his old man. What do you think about having me get the kids up to Belmont?"

"I think I'd owe you, again, big time," Molly said, relief washing over her like a wave.

"Are you kidding? I get to be the cool dad, full of surprises. We'll be even. Consider it settled, I'll be back through in the morning to pick them up," Travis said, standing up and walking towards the door. "And Molly? I've done a lot of soul searching over the last few years, and listened to a lot of books on tape looking for inspiration and answers. A motivational speaker by the name of Andy Andrews said something that really resonated with me. I don't recall the exact book or comment, but the jist of it was that, along this road called life, you are either coming out of a problem or heading towards a problem. In my own words, it's all peaks and valleys. Enjoy the peaks and meet the valleys head on."

Molly attempted a smile as Travis closed the door behind him. *If that is the case, then I am in the biggest valley of my life,* Molly thought, *and I really need to figure out what's happening with the health insurance.*

After a day of running around, collecting their own stories and taking care of business at the track, Charlie and Amanda met back up with Kate near the press room.

Kate, standing by the door, was already deep in conversation with another reporter when they arrived. She quickly talked Charlie in, despite her lack of press credentials, citing her as a blogger. The room was filling up quickly as the week marched on towards the big day, and several of the other reporters smirked, recognizing Charlie as the owner of the horse so many of them were basing their stories around.

Settling in, Amanda pulled her laptop out of her bag and quickly scanned through her email. "This is my nightmare," she groaned.

"Is everything alright, Amanda?" Kate asked, genuinely concerned.

Amanda sighed. "My boss just assigned me a new scoop to follow up on while I'm here. Very time sensitive, apparently—Belmont fashion."

Kate's concern turned instantly to exasperation. She rolled her eyes and turned her attention back to her own work without uttering another word.

Charlie laughed.

Amanda groaned, "Not exactly the hard-hitting journalism I'd been hoping to do while I was here."

"Fair enough, but I'm sure we can help you out. The race isn't until almost seven on Saturday, and the rest of the crew will be coming in over the next couple of days. I'm sure Jenny would love to walk around in the crowd with you the entire morning and afternoon and treat it like a street fashion exposé."

Amanda smiled at Charlie's kindness. "Thanks, but my editor wants to run the story tomorrow morning, to get hits from people who will be searching online for their own outfits for the race."

"One day you will move past this fashion beat and be a real reporter," Kate quipped.

Amanda laughed and ignored Kate's comment as she pulled up a new document on her laptop. "Okay, ladies, help me out. You've been to the Belmont Stakes before—how did you choose your outfits? What did you see other people wearing?"

Charlie made a face. "Not me. I've not been before either. My expertise resides in watching the whole afternoon on TV. I would clear my schedule and make Peter and the kids watch from start to finish. We would get to know each of the horses from the stories they documented. Skylar would pick who she wanted to win by who had the best name; Ryan would have one eye on his iPhone, but listened close enough that he almost always picked the winner, and Peter…" Charlie hesitated, going through the fond memories of her late husband. "Well, he was just happy spending time as a family."

Amanda sat quietly, at a loss for the right thing to say.

Kate took the reins and quickly changed the subject. Never looking up from her own laptop, she replied, "My outfit has to go from interviews in the jockey's locker room to interviews in the paddocks to out on the track. I'm all over the place on the day of the race, and half those places are muddy and bustling. Not exactly big-hat territories. As for the people watching, all three races pride themselves on being dressy events. This topic has certainly been covered—Belmont is more New York sophistication, more black and white, less Southern florals, pastels, and hats than Preakness and the Derby."

"Yeah, I guess I can just check out what other people have said about it," Amanda said quietly.

Kate looked over at her and felt a wave of empathy. She remembered what it was like when she'd started her career—city council meetings about speed bumps, two-hundred-word travel guides to small New England towns she'd never heard of, much less seen. She decided to take pity and give her more valuable guidance than she had asked for.

"Any topic can be meaningful from some angle," Kate said, pulling up a search page. "The trick is finding that angle. Here, take a look at this."

"The dress code? The track has a dress code?" Amanda read over the page, then corrected herself. "Whoa, it actually has several dress codes. 'Grandstand: Shorts and shoes required…Box Seats, Gentlemen: Collared shirts required, jackets strongly encouraged; Ladies: Suits, dresses, pant suits.'"

"Don't forget this one—hopefully it'll be the most relevant for us," Charlie said, tapping at the screen over Amanda's shoulder. "'Paddock and Winner's Circle: No shorts or abbreviated wear permitted. Gentlemen: Collared shirts required.'"

Amanda looked thoughtful. "So, the more dressed up you are, the more of the track you can access."

Kate nodded. "That's right. So rather than focusing your article on the styles, you could focus it more on what horse owners and insiders wear and why. You've got a great peek into very exclusive parts of the Belmont that most of the reporters assigned these types of stories don't have; you should take advantage of that. Horse people are also known for being pretty superstitious and sentimental. I bet there are some interesting stories behind some of the ties, socks, and hats you'll see. It also gives you the advantage of being able to conduct your own research, right now, since many of the insiders are already around the track, getting ready for the races."

Amanda sighed loudly. "I know you're right, but this feels like the longest possible path to becoming a serious turf writer."

Kate raised an eyebrow. "Oh? How do you think it's done?"

Amanda shrugged and then brightened up. "I guess there's no better time and place to find out than here and now."

She turned towards the reporter closest to her, an older man who was reading the entries for each race scheduled for Saturday and making copious notes. "Excuse me, what are you working on?"

"Handicapping the races," he replied.

"Hmm," Amanda replied, jotting down a note to herself about learning more about handicapping. "What advice would you give for a freshly minted member of the press who wanted to become a full-time, daily print media racing reporter?"

"Find a time machine," an even older gentleman barked gruffly from his position by the window.

A few of the other reporters in the room chuckled appreciatively, and Kate gave Amanda a shrug.

"A reporter who covers nothing but horse racing for a major newspaper? Not likely. There are sportswriters who cover racing as needed, but many of those positions have been eliminated altogether."

The man next to her read her note about learning more about

handicapping and smiled at her earnestness. Tapping on her notebook, he said, "See, that right there is a life's work in itself. A great handicapper in action is something to behold."

Amanda cleared her throat. "I…ah…well, I'm not even very sure what handicapping means. I get that it is related to betting on the races, but I don't have a clear picture of how or why."

"In the simplest terms possible, it's the way bettors predict the finish order of a given race. It gets very technical, and there are many ways and methods of arriving at a handicap, but when you're done, you'll have ranked all the horses who are scheduled for a race in the order you believe they will arrive at the finish line. Some bettors rely exclusively on the past performances of each horse to guess how they will perform in the race, some people only consider the pedigree of a horse, while others watch the horses prior to the race to pick out which ones look the best—a physical handicap. Speaking generally, there are four basic, accepted pillars of handicapping: speed, pace, form, and class, and studying past performance is usually how to get started. As you get better at parsing through all the data and watching the races, you'll develop your own style. You'll decide which categories and information you want to give more predictive weight to, and you'll have your own theories and methods. I'm afraid the truth is, though, that there aren't many jobs left in the daily newspapers for racing writers, even if you were an ace handicapper. Although it would help—I'm sure a lot of newspapers would be eager to give space to the next Russ Harris or Beyer."

"I've learned a little about Andrew Beyer," Amanda said. "I know Beyer Speed Figures fundamentally changed the way we analyze a racehorse's performance, and that he was the full-time horse racing columnist for *The Washington Post* for more than twenty-five years."

"Sure, and he started young—took an interest in handicapping at the races in Suffolk Downs while he was attending Harvard in the 1960s. He became a household name when he published his first book, *Picking Winners*, in 1975, where he outlined the handicapping system he'd developed."

"Who is Harris?" Amanda asked.

"Only one of the best public handicappers of all time! He started hand-icapping under the name Phil Dancer in 1957, and he picked the winners for an entire nine-race card right here at Belmont Park in 1981. He had an uncanny ability—he was eighty-five years old in 2008, when he picked the most winners at the Saratoga meet," the man beside her said, looking back down at his own calculations. "I can't see many daily papers returning to reporting racing unless the betting becomes a lot more popular."

"That's about it," another writer piped in over his laptop. "Daily race reporting in print is all but extinct. Back in the day, the racing results for nearby tracks would be printed each day, similar to how you see baseball or football results reported today. I can't think of more than a handful of dai-lies that even have a full-time racing writer on staff—just the *Courier-Jour-nal* in Louisville comes to mind. Even in racing cities, many papers just print the entries, handicaps, and results. Outside of the Triple Crown, fea-ture stories are few and far between."

"Even the weeklies don't have much coverage anymore. I'm old enough to remember reading Audax Minor's racing column every week in *The New Yorker*. He published it for over fifty years, but when he stopped in the late 1970s, they never replaced him," the man by the window said.

"'Audax Minor'—was that his real name?" Amanda asked.

"No, real name was George Ryall, a pure turf writer. He earned a lifetime achievement from the National Turf Writers Association."

"The press box will be full this year, what with Genuine Storm's Triple Crown bid capturing public attention the way it has, but it's a sad, empty sight to behold most other days. I've been to some where the only other person in the room was the track's own publicist. Sometimes I get nervous when I see another reporter coming through, particularly if they've got cameras with 'em. Seems more often than not, they're there to cover a trag-edy or a scandal, and they don't have any soft spots in their hearts for the sport," another reporter added.

"Now, to be fair, turf writing was never a field with a straightforward, sin-gle career path. You want to be a doctor, you go to medical school. You want to be a turf writer, well, there were several ways in. There were the ones that wrote exclusively about horse racing for the dailies, weeklies, and monthlies— Whitney Tower was the lead turf writer and editor for *Sports Illustrated*, back when they used to cover it. Charles Hatton pushed for the idea of a Triple Crown in his regular column in the *Daily Racing Forum*, based on the three-race series in the British model. There was Joe Hirsch, Raleigh Burroughs, Jay Hovdey, and Marty McGee. Jennie Rees won Eclipse Awards in four consecutive decades as the turf reporter for the daily *Louisville Courier-Journal*. Maryjean Wall was the first woman accepted into the National Turf Writers Association and one of the first to cover thoroughbred racing on a regular basis; she worked for the *Lexington Herald-Leader* for four decades."

"Personally, I started covering horse racing for my local gazette as a passion project after I retired. I was a senior partner at a corporate law firm for longer than I'd care to admit, and I couldn't imagine anything better than spending my summers outdoors, driving from track to track, meeting my heroes—and their riders," the man next to her replied.

Amanda smiled at him, appreciating the genuine affection so many of the people she'd met over the past few weeks had for horses.

"I probably had already written and submitted, unbidden and unsolicited, a dozen or so articles on the ponies before I heard back from an editor. Well, technically, the editor. She's the only full-time staff left at the paper at all. She enjoyed the columns, and although there wasn't any budget to pay me, she offered a stipend for my expenses to travel from race to race. I consider it my betting money."

"If it isn't a career for you, why not just post it up on the web yourself, or submit it to one of the websites dedicated to racing?" Amanda wondered aloud.

He shrugged. "Just how I wanted it. Liked seeing my name printed on the byline, enjoyed figuring out how many of my neighbors really did still read our little gazette. Even though I might have reached a larger audience online, I doubt it would have reached half the people it's managed to enlighten in my own local community."

Amanda nodded. "Yes, I can fully appreciate all of that. Unfortunately, my student loans won't pay themselves off with token stipends."

"Well, I'm not sure many people have been able to make ends meet through nothing but turf reporting, even in the golden ages of racing. Some of the best recognized turf writers spent much of their time writing and reporting on other things. Barney Nagler split his column time between horse racing and boxing. William Nack won six Eclipse Awards for his turf writing at *Sports Illustrated*, but he was an investigative reporter there—he was covering political scandals and environmental issues at the very same time," the man near the window said.

"And lots of the greats, men and women who have won major awards for their turf writing and reporting, were on their second or third careers. Donna Barton Brothers was one of the leading female jockeys of all time when she retired in 1998 and began a new career covering racing and other equestrian sports on live television," one of the other writers added.

"Bill Mooney was one of the most important turf writers of all time. He was an incredible historian and a man who could drum up interest in any story he was sent to cover. He once said that he'd written on location from ninety-three Thoroughbred tracks, which is even more impressive when you realize he only got into the business after he quit his job as an English and journalism professor."

"Actually, there's a story about Bill that reminds me a little of you, Amanda," Kate said. "Sometime in the early 1990s, he was working at a track that had a major fire, and he lost everything—files, research materials, camera and film, computer and typewriter, everything. When the grocery store nearby opened at 5:30 the next morning, he was there to buy a legal pad and two Bics, and he headed straight back down to the track to start interviewing racing people about the fire."

The man Amanda had initially questioned nodded. "All in all, if I were to give a reporter starting out fresh who really wanted to make a difference in the world of horse racing some advice, it would be to follow Bill's example. He was a stickler for accuracy and context. He did original research and really gave every topic he hit thorough coverage. He'd uncover details no one knew about, and he'd tell the story well, really connect with readers."

"One of the local papers down near Shamrock Hill Farm has been actually doing a great job with this type of coverage surrounding Storm," the gruff man near the window added. "My daughter, who has always told me she heard enough about racing in her childhood to last her a lifetime, follows all their articles. She's really riveted by the cast of characters they've introduced, the peeks we've been given into behind-the-scenes action. Obviously, there is quite a bit happening there above and beyond normal racing stuff, but without this coverage, I'm not sure how many members of the general public would have even connected the fire with the horse. There's a real cohesive narration that we're rarely privy to in this sport. I think my daughter is dreading the end of the Triple Crown, whether Storm wins or loses, because the coverage will stop."

Kate nudged Amanda, who was beaming at the recognition for her work, and gave her a covert thumbs up. As the rest of the reporters in the press room went back to their own work and conversations, Charlie leaned towards Kate and Amanda.

"Well, the public has spoken," she whispered.

"They sure have," Amanda said, still beaming. "And if I'm going to have to forge my own path into this industry, I'm sure glad I'm riding on Storm's strong shoulders."

 # Official Business

As each of the contenders arrived at Belmont in the days leading up to the race, they'd been greeted coming off their trailers by an ever-growing group of reporters and photographers. The trailer pulling in now was marked with the Shamrock Hill Farm logo. It naturally drew in a huge crowd and many questions—namely, who was inside? Everyone buzzed, as they knew that Genuine Storm had been at the track for days. Many people tried to look in as it passed, but they were unable to see the occupant.

Before the ramp could be put down or the door opened, two young children raced around the side of the truck. One held her arms up, garnering the attention of the clustered press.

"Ladies and gentlemen," the young girl announced, "I will be pleased to introduce you to my pony, the handsome and brave Hershey. But I must ask that you back up and give him space to come down from the trailer and be careful with him. He has just gotten out of the hospital, and he is still in recovery. Please pass all treats to my associate," she said, pointing to the young boy beside her, "for inspection."

Several of the members of the press corps smiled and prepared to walk away from the scene, until one of the savvier members yelled out, "Is this Hershey, Genuine Storm's support animal?"

Skylar nodded. "They are best friends, and it will be important to Storm's race to see that this transition happens smoothly."

Photographers scrambled to position themselves in different spots, eager to capture whatever shots they could of the pony, who was, suddenly, a much bigger news story, and scheming how to get the perfect picture of Storm and Hershey's initial greeting. Reporters called out additional questions to Skylar, who held up a hand to officially back them away as the doors to the trailer opened.

The little dark pony who stuck his head out had a bandage still covering some of the burns on his head, but it only served to make him more endearing.

As Ben unloaded Hershey, the reporters turned back to Skylar and peppered her with questions. She handled it like an old pro, running the scene like a press conference.

"Well, I guess I'm not the first to the scoop here," Amanda said as she walked up to Jenny.

Jenny grinned at the reporter. "No, I would say we're both going to have to talk to Skylar—and Hershey—through their own press agents very soon."

They both watched for a few moments as Skylar and Hershey amused and delighted the crowd.

Travis joined them. "I feel like a third… or eleventh…wheel up there."

"I think they've got it all under control," Amanda agreed. "But while they have the crowds distracted, I think I'm going to go search out the trophy room—I hear everything has just been set up, and I'd like to get a good look."

"I'll come along," Jenny said. "Ryan has been talking to me about the trophies for so long that it feels like we already have them."

"Good, I'm sure I can use a guide," Amanda said. "Everything here seems to have hidden depths, you can walk me through."

"Well, could you use someone completely clueless?" Travis asked.

"Always," Amanda said, laughing. "You'll be there to make me look good."

———————

"Is this the trophy for the Belmont Stakes?" Amanda asked, pointing to the large, ornately decorated covered bowl in the glass display case and whistling. "Sometimes awards seem so dinky in person, they get built up so much in my mind. This one, though, doesn't have that problem at all."

"Yup, the August Belmont Memorial Cup. It was cast in solid silver in 1896 by Tiffany & Co., commissioned by the Belmont family in memory of August Belmont. It honored their family horse, Fenian, who won the third Belmont Stakes. The family kept it until 1926, then presented it as the permanent trophy for the race," Jenny said, reciting facts she'd memorized from Ryan's repeated narratives.

"Are all four horses on here Fenian?" Amanda peered closely at the details of the trophy. "They can't be, they all look different."

"Good eye. Fenian is represented by the horse on the top of the cover. These guys," Jenny pointed to the three figures at the base, supporting the cup, "are Herod, Eclipse, and Matchem."

Amanda shook her head, indicating the information was meaningless to her.

"In the 1700s, three Oriental stallions, known for their speed and agility, were brought to England from the Middle East and Africa and bred to sturdy English mares, creating Thoroughbreds. In order to be registered as a true Thoroughbred with the Jockey Club, a horse's tail-male lineage must be traced to either the Byerly Turk, the Godolphin Barb, or the Darley Arabian," Jenny told her.

"Tail male?"

"Their father's father's father's side, all the way back—if you keep following the sire, you have to end up back at one of the three foundational sires. But they weren't Thoroughbreds themselves, obviously." Jenny pointed back towards the Belmont Cup and continued, "In each of the bloodlines, there was an early generation in which only one male sired another male to continue the line-tail connection. Eclipse was the great-great-grandson of the Darley Arabian, Herod was the great-great-grandson of the Byerly Turk, and Matchem was the grandson of the Godolphin Barb—so every Thoroughbreds can also trace their lineage back to one of those three horses."

"Which one is Storm tail-line descended from?" Travis asked.

"The Darley Arabian, via Eclipse. Actually, something like ninety-five percent of modern Thoroughbreds come from that sire line. The majority of well-known horses from the last fifty years have been his tail-line descendants—including Storm, Ruffian, and the great Secretariat."

"Sorry, I couldn't help but overhear part of your conversation," a tidy-looking man interjected politely. "Are you here with Genuine Storm?"

"We are, yes—more as an entourage than in any official capacity," Jenny replied, smiling.

"That's exciting. I'm Dean Nobert, representing Churchill Downs. I flew in last night with the Triple Crown Trophy, and I certainly hope we get to award it this year. They've sent me here with the trophy for several Triple Crown hopefuls, but none of them won the Belmont, so I've never met any of the horse's teams."

The group introduced themselves and began trading questions and answers with Dean about past Triple Crown close calls and current Triple Crown dreams.

"Do you realize that the trophy has only been presented three times? There had already been eight winners by the time it was created in 1950, so we sent them small personal trophies retroactively. Then we had to wait twenty-three years to present it, and that was well before my time," Dean sighed.

"What does it look like? How big is it? What is it worth? Why isn't it on display next to the Belmont Cup? Are there just too many security concerns?" Amanda fired off, rapidly and intently.

Dean looked surprised, but he attempted to answer her questions in order. "I find it very elegant and streamlined. It's a silver vase created by Cartier in 1950, triangular so that each race of the Triple Crown could be represented by an equal plate. It's about fifteen inches tall and fifteen inches wide and weighs about ten pounds."

"I don't know how in the world to go about appraising it—I'm sure most people would tell you it is priceless, but I'm also sure there is a number listed on the insurance policy. I'm not sure exactly why we don't display it. Maybe there's just too much going on here at the track over the long weekend. When it is not traveling to each of the three races, it is on display at the Kentucky Derby Museum in Louisville.

"I do think its exclusivity might be part of the appeal. It doesn't get a lot of photo ops, very few people have one, very few people have even seen one of the smaller ones, much less the permanent trophy. There are some minor security precautions taken, but nothing like you'd see with the Stanley Cup or Super Bowl rings. I think the Triple Crown might be the most rarely earned trophy in sports, but there's actually not a bunch of pomp and ceremony surrounding it."

"That's kind of refreshing, how people don't make it a huge deal—there's more focus on the accomplishment than the trophy, even when it is being presented," Travis said.

"I wear white gloves when I handle it and we get a personal escort through airport security, but I fly with it alone," Dean said.

Amanda seemed suspicious. "Alone like on a private plane?"

Dean laughed heartily. "No, not at all. We flew Delta this time—coach. It did get its own seat, since the flight was pretty empty. I took a cab to my hotel, and it rode in the trunk. It'll stay in my hotel until Saturday morning, when we'll bring it over and put it in the Belmont safe."

"Which hotel?"

"Amanda!" Travis exclaimed, laughing hard. "Are you planning to mug him for the trophy? You're going to scare him off with all these questions!"

"Well, I won't," she sighed playfully, "but I'd sure love to see it before the big day."

"No can do," Dean said, shaking his head. "You want to see it, you're going to have to talk Storm into winning it."

 # Paying Respect

Where did the day go? Charlie wondered to herself.

The flurry of interviews, introductions, and race day planning had stolen the morning and afternoon, and she felt a little guilty as she scanned her mental to-do list and realized she hadn't posted up a single message for the Storm Troopers in days.

Scanning the green beauty of the picnic grounds, she grabbed her bag and quickly found a quiet spot, a bench nestled next to a well-manicured thicket of trees and flowers.

She pulled her iPad out of her bag and opened the blog page, trying to decide what she'd share today. Several false starts later, she turned to the Facebook and Twitter pages for Storm's fan club, crossing her fingers that there weren't hundreds and hundreds of questions and requests she should have gotten to days ago. Kate had been busy with her real job with *Blood-Horse* once she'd gotten on site, so Charlie couldn't blame her for ignoring the social media accounts.

As she'd suspected, the pages were buzzing hubs of activity, but she was very pleasantly surprised to find everything under control. Ryan had kept on top of it all—answering questions, drumming up support, sending out trivia and updates and polls. He'd installed a countdown clock on the Facebook page and made an animated e-card of Storm racing to the finish line. It was all fun and smart at the same time, and people obviously loved it.

Charlie laughed as she read through some of the exchanges he'd gotten into on Twitter, admiring how quickly and cleverly he was able to respond to whatever the Internet volleyed their way.

An iMessage popped up on her screen. "Whatever you're paying me, it's not enough."

Charlie smiled and messaged her son back, "I was just thinking the same thing. Thank you, this is all wonderful."

"It's been fun," Ryan responded, "and I'm glad there was something I could do from here."

"Finals all finished?" Charlie asked.

"Yep. Heading up with Molly tomorrow. Make sure Storm wins, though, okay? I have some ideas for his summer social media that kinda rely on it."

"Well, for you, okay," Charlie said.

Another message popped up on her screen, this one from Skylar: "Where are you?"

"Out in the picnic area, should I come find you?" Charlie replied.

"No, stay there," Skylar texted back.

Charlie and Ryan caught up on pieces of business. Ryan asked her a few questions for his social media campaign, and she marveled to herself about how insightful his tact was.

Seeing Skylar approaching, Charlie said her virtual goodbyes. "Miss you, love you, looking forward to seeing you tomorrow."

"Love you too, Mom."

Skylar skipped over and bear hugged Charlie.

"You found me fast," Charlie said.

Without extricating herself from the hug, Skylar held up her phone. The screen was still lit up with the phone tracking app humming along, showing their two faces right on top of each other.

"Aren't you a smarty," Charlie said.

Skylar didn't say anything and she didn't release Charlie from the hug. Charlie held her close for another few moments, appreciating the quiet and her affectionate daughter.

"Okay, Sky, what's up?" Charlie asked gently, tipping Skylar's face towards her so she could read her response. "Is everything okay? How's Hershey settling in?"

"He's good," Skylar said, smiling at the thought of her pony. "He's gotten lots of treats, and Storm has been very gentle with him."

"I'm sure he missed his friend," Charlie replied.

Skylar hesitated before asking, "Mom…Storm's going to be okay tomorrow, right? He's not going to get hurt or anything, right?"

"Oh, honey, why are you worried about that?" Charlie said. She thought about Amanda's sabotage concerns, and she took a guess: "Did you hear something about someone trying to hurt Storm?"

Skylar shook her head no. "I had dreams about Sarge last night, so when I woke up, I started searching horses that got hurt racing."

A lump had risen in Charlie's throat when she'd heard Sarge's name, but she fought it down and eventually nodded thoughtfully. "And I'm sure you found some who did."

Skylar returned the nod.

"Did you know," Charlie said after a long pause, "that there are two race-horses buried by this track?"

"Really?" Skylar asked, curious.

"Sure are," Charlie replied. "I learned a lot about them because I was going to post an article in their honor on the blog. I decided to push it out, at least for a while, but I wanted to pay my respects to them while I was here. Would you like to come with me?"

"Okay," Skylar said, grabbing Charlie's hand and letting her steer her towards the finish line.

"Are there a lot of horses buried at race tracks?" Skylar asked.

"No. Ruffian and Timely Writer are the only ones here. It is a very special honor for a horse to be buried at a race track, especially a track as famous as

Belmont. Churchill Downs has only bestowed the honor once, to Barbaro."

Charlie stopped at a small plaque and pointed it out to Skylar. "Ruffian, buried here, had the additional honor of being one of the very few racehorses buried intact."

"What does that mean?"

"Well, traditionally, the body of a celebrated racehorse is cremated, with the exception of the hooves, heart, and head. They symbolize the speed, spirit, and intelligence, the essence of a great horse, so they are saved and buried. Many people think Ruffian was the greatest female thoroughbred in history, and they buried her without any cremation," Charlie explained.

"How did she die?" Skylar asked.

"Well, over the years, there have been several attempts to create a filly-exclusive version of the Triple Crown. In 1975, the official Triple Tiara consisted of three New York races—the Acorn Stakes and the Mother Goose Stakes at Aqueduct, and the Coaching Club American Oaks, here at Belmont. Ruffian had just won them all, setting stakes records."

"Three weeks later, she was back at Belmont for a match race—the infamous 'Boy vs. Girl' race against the winner of the 1975 Kentucky Derby, Foolish Pleasure. It had been widely anticipated—there were more than 50,000 people in the stands that day, and over 20 million people across the nation tuned in to watch it on live TV."

"They all saw Ruffian's leg snap as she pulled ahead of Foolish Pleasure. She was so competitive that her jockey had a hard time stopping her, which caused further damage. It was obvious on the field that she was hurt very badly; most horses would have been euthanized on the spot. Because of who she was, though, she was rushed to the hospital. A team of surgeons repaired her leg in an operation that lasted three hours. When the anesthesia wore off, though, Ruffian thrashed around, despite everyone's best efforts to keep her still. She hurt herself and did even more damage to the initial injury. They reluctantly decided that euthanizing her was the only humane course of action, given how badly she was hurt and how painful and unlikely a recovery would be."

"Like Sarge?" Skylar asked softly.

"Like Sarge," Charlie replied, but continued, "Eighty-two official match races were run in North America between 1900 and 1975. After Ruffian's death, though, there have been very, very few, and none with famous horses. There was never a ban set—the tragedy just affected people deeply," Charlie finished.

Charlie searched Skylar's face to see if she was upsetting her. Although she was somber, she still seemed interested.

"Even in her unfair and untimely death, Ruffian actually left a great legacy. Based on the lessons learned during her surgery, a recovery pool was developed. Now horses coming out from anesthesia wake up in a pool of water, so if they thrash around, they cannot hurt themselves as badly. Her contribution to the field is reflected in the Cornell Ruffian Equine Specialists building, just on the other side of the track from here."

"Who was Timely Writer?" Skylar asked.

"Well, much like Storm, Timely Writer was underestimated when he was younger, and he was always a little bit of an outsider to the racing establishment. His bloodlines were good, but his parents had been injured and never raced. Two brothers, butchers from Boston, purchased him for less than fifteen thousand dollars at auction. He won race after race, nine of the thirteen he started, but in between, he kept having to go through all these hard things. He got colic, he survived a surgery with fifty percent odds, he was scratched for doping because he'd accidentally been given an antihistamine. All sorts of things that which would have driven many horses off the track for good. But he kept coming back, and he kept winning. Boston loved him, the grandstands loved him. He was the little guy who had beaten the odds, the people's horse."

"Did he win the Triple Crown?" Skylar asked, her brow furrowed. She'd gone over the list of winners on her mom's blog several times, but she didn't remember ever seeing his name.

"No. He was the favorite for it, but he never competed in a single one of the three races. He missed most of his three-year-old season, recovering from the surgery. He came back in the fall, but it was more to say goodbye to his fans. His stud fee had already been paid, and the 1982 Jockey Club Gold Cup, here at Belmont, was his last scheduled race before retirement."

"Coming around the far-left turn, his front leg broke. He fell, and three horses around him fell over him. The injuries were so bad that Timely and one other horse had to be euthanized on the track. They buried him one furlong from the finish line."

"Skylar, you're a brave girl, and I don't want to lie to you. I won't tell you that nothing bad will happen to Storm, because even though I hope that's true tomorrow and every other day, I can't promise it, for him or anyone else," Charlie said.

"We've had so many tragic things happen, Mom," Skylar said in a very small voice. "I miss Sarge. And I miss Dad."

"I know, sweetheart," Charlie said, "and I think about Sarge and your dad all the time. But the reason we all loved them both so much—the reason people loved these horses so much—is because of how they lived their lives, the incredible ways they showed their love, the ways they blessed us by sharing their talents with the world. They were brave, and thinking about them now makes me braver, not scared. Life is risky, no matter what we choose to do, so when we have the chance to reach our dreams, we should take it."

Skylar thought for a long moment and laughed. "I think most moms would just tell me everything will be alright."

Charlie squeezed her tight by her side. "Maybe. But I can't guarantee alright, so I think we should probably shoot for 'as good as we can make it.' What do you think?"

"That sounds like a better plan," Skylar said, squeezing her mom back. She snuck a sideways look at her before saying, "You know, I think it would be pretty…good, no, great…to live at Shamrock all the time."

"Oh Sky, why didn't you tell me earlier? I'm sure if I ask Doug, he'll give us an extra stall for you and everything," Charlie teased.

"Ha, ha, ha, Mom. Soooo funny," Skylar said, rolling her eyes. "I just wanted to say that I love being there, and if you ever wanted to move there, I'd be okay with that. I think Ryan would be okay with it too. We love you, and we missed seeing you smile."

"Thank you, Skylar. I know what you're saying, and that means a lot to me," Charlie said. "For the next twenty-four hours, though, I need all your good thoughts and wishes going straight towards Storm, okay?"

PART SEVEN

 # A Quiet Moment

In typical fashion, Charlie couldn't sleep. She lay staring at the ceiling of the hotel, knowing that the upcoming day would be long and she really needed to get some rest. She knew she wouldn't have a second to herself, between all the cameras that would be following them, the interviews, and the people. It was thrilling that Storm might become the first horse to win the Triple Crown in thirty-seven years, but for just one minute, she wished she was able to experience it without all the hoopla.

Charlie got out of bed and pulled on her sneakers and sweatshirt. She was starting to work herself into a tizzy and she knew that she needed to keep the panic attacks at bay; hopefully a quick jog in the quiet, cooler night air would help ease her mind. After ensuring that Skylar and Ryan were sleeping, she snuck out, quietly closing the hotel door behind her, and walked towards the elevators.

In the course of making travel arrangements, Charlie had learned that many of the owners and big names in racing left Long Island and stayed in New York City at the posh hotels, like the Four Seasons or the Ritz Carlton. She'd had no desire to subject herself to the unpredictable traffic of the Belt

Parkway, and she couldn't imagine being that far from Storm, especially with everything he'd gone through. Even the Garden City Hotel, the luxury hotel most closely affiliated with Belmont Park and the site where winners historically conducted their post-race celebrations, had seemed much too far. Charlie had eventually booked everyone at the Bellerose Inn, a more modest hotel less than two miles from the track.

The location was convenient and quiet, but there was another unforeseen perk. As word had spread across the hotel staff that she was Genuine Storm's owner, she found that several of the clerks were a little starstruck. Her insomnia had been bad every night, so over the past week, she'd gotten to know every member of the night shift as she wandered through and they struck up conversations.

"Hi, Ms. Jenkins," the front desk clerk called to her as she approached. "What can I help you with?"

"Hi, Michael. I'm fine, thanks. Just can't sleep, so I am going to take a little jog to clear my head," Charlie replied.

"Ma'am, but it's three in the morning," Michael commented.

"I know, but with everything going on and the day ahead, I need to run out all the tension I am feeling," Charlie said.

"Um, well, I wouldn't recommend going by yourself at this time of night," Michael noted, getting a bit anxious himself. He knew the owner of the most well-known racehorse running in this year's Belmont should not be wandering the streets of New York by herself just hours before the race.

"Thank you for your concern, Michael, but I will be perfectly fine. I used to jog in college in the middle of the night when I needed a break from studying for my exams," Charlie smiled. "Plus, I am just going over to the track to check on Storm; it shouldn't take me more than twenty minutes to jog over there. I've got my phone." She showed him her iPhone.

"Still...Ms. Jenkins," Michael looked around the empty lobby, unsure of how to resolve this, then asked, "Will you wait one minute?"

Charlie raised her eyebrows. "Sure."

Michael left through a door marked 'Employees Only.' A few minutes later, he returned with a windbreaker draped over his arm and another desk clerk behind him, who was wiping his eyes like he had been just woken from a deep sleep.

"Kyle will watch the desk for me while we are gone."

"We?" Charlie asked.

"Yes, ma'am. My boss would never forgive me if you went missing on the morning of the biggest race of the year." Michael smiled at her.

Charlie hesitated, then smiled. *So much for alone time.*

"Well, I hope you can keep up in those dress shoes."

"Don't worry, Ms. Jenkins, I ran track in high school." Michael, smiling, followed her out into the dark night.

———————————

Eighteen minutes later, they jogged passed the gate house, with Charlie flashing her owner's badge. Charlie led the way, with Michael a few strides behind her. She was thankful he had respected her need to be alone and not chatted her ear off. Charlie slowed to a walk as they approached the barn where Storm was stabled.

He didn't even break a sweat, she noticed as Michael drew even with her. She made a note to ask him what brand his dress shoes were; if they were comfortable enough to run two miles in and keep smiling, every man on her Christmas list was getting a pair.

"You ever been back here?" Charlie whispered.

"No, ma'am," Michael replied quietly.

"Well, I hadn't either before this week."

"What are you doing here at this hour?" a stern, measured voice asked.

Charlie shot a smile at the man, who was leaning back in his chair in front of an open stall door just ahead of them.

"Couldn't sleep, Cappie. You know that about me by now," Charlie said. "How is he doing?"

"Which one?" Cappie responded.

"Well, let's go with the little one first," Charlie said.

"Hershey's resting quietly...you should see for yourself." Cappie gestured behind his back with his thumb.

Charlie peeked inside, but didn't see anything.

"Not that stall, the next one," Cappie said, pointing over to her left.

Charlie looked at him inquisitively, but moved down the aisle and peered into Storm's stall. She had to put her hand to her mouth to keep from gasping. It was the most touching scene she had ever witnessed. Storm laid, still and awake, with his head and neck cradling the sleeping Hershey laying in front of him. He didn't move, but his eyes met hers as she stood at his door.

Tears sprung to Charlie's eyes as she took in the pink fleshy areas of Hershey's back where the fire had taken his hair. Storm's neck hovered above the pony's body, as if he knew he couldn't touch those sensitive areas. Charlie backed away quietly, not wanting to wake Hershey and disturb the peaceful pair.

"Storm couldn't sleep either and was causing quite a raucous after everyone left. I was even questioning if bringing Hershey here was the best choice. We knew there was going to be a lot of questions and press, but I don't think we took into account the impact it was going to make on Storm, having him here. So, after about an hour of him pacing and calling, knowing he needed a good night sleep before today's race, I moved Hershey into his stall," Cappie explained.

"It seems to have done the trick," Charlie replied.

"Yeah," Cappie smirked, "I still have some old dog tricks in me."

"You're not an old dog," Charlie said, smiling as she noticed Michael hovering in the shadows just outside the shed row. "Hey, Cappie, let me introduce you to my escort on this early morning visit. This is Michael, you know, from the hotel?"

Michael stepped forward to shake Cappie's hand. "Sir."

Cappie shook his hand. "Thanks for looking out for this young lady. She likes to make her own decisions. Sometimes not the smartest ones."

"I was pretty smart when I claimed Storm," Charlie retorted.

"If I recall correctly, there had been wine involved—quite a bit of it," Cappie smirked.

"Yes, well, here we are anyway. Do you mind entertaining Michael here? I'd like to just get a few minutes by myself before the day gets away from all of us."

"Sure thing, but don't you leave the park," Cappie instructed.

"No, sir," Charlie replied over her shoulder as she walked towards the dark grandstand that loomed in front of them.

Charlie walked towards the grandstand, but then veered and walked down the ramp that would take her through a tunnel under the Gate 5 Road, which brought the VIPs to the grandstand on race day.

She moved slowly, tracing the same steps she would be taking with her horse later this afternoon—down the ramp, through the tunnel, and up the ramp on the other side, which delivered her to the paddock area. The full moon reflected off the statue of Secretariat in full flight that graced the center of the paddock.

She walked slowly around the sandy ring, taking in the saddling stalls to her left. She stopped briefly in front of Stall Number 6, the one Storm would occupy. She turned and walked towards the huge pine tree to her right. Sitting on the white picnic bench beneath one of its long branches, Charlie stared at the statue in front of her.

"Any advice for me?" she asked one of the greatest racehorses to ever run.

The statue was silent, as if knowing greatness could not be summed up in just a few words.

Charlie sat for a long time, breathing deeply with her eyes half closed.

I must have drifted off to sleep, she realized, startled awake by the activity around the statue of Secretariat.

The darkest time of night had turned into the haze of early morning light. She glanced at her watch: five in the morning.

She looked back over at the statue. Two men were unpacking a large box, lifting out what appeared to be a cloud. She rubbed her eyes and squinted, trying to make out the true nature of the fluffy white shape.

One of the men looked over and noticed that she was staring. "Sorry, ma'am, we didn't want to wake you."

Charlie got up from the bench and walked towards them. "What is that?" she asked.

"Secretariat's carnations, of course," the other man replied, looking at her as if she was daft.

The friendlier man glared at his partner. "No need to be rude, Harry." He turned back to Charlie and said, "They are the traditional flower of the Belmont Stakes. Each year, we make him a garland of white carnations, similar to the one that is draped over the race winner, to honor him."

Charlie watched as they placed a beautiful floral blanket at the base of Secretariat's feet.

"The winner's garland is made up of more than 700 white carnations, flown in from Columbia to our boss. We have to soak the stems for two days before we remove them and glue each flower to seven yards of green velvet. It weighs over forty pounds once it is completed. He's hard at work right now finishing it up, as it takes five hours and needs to be done as soon as possible. You know what today is, right?" he asked Charlie.

Charlie smiled. "Yes, yes, I do. I was just trying to absorb some good vibes from this great one."

"Will never be another one like him," Harry mumbled.

"You are probably right," Charlie said.

"Hey, you know you were sittin' under a 190-year-old tree?" the friendly man continued, ignoring his less gracious partner.

Charlie looked over at the pine tree she had fallen asleep under.

"Yep, older than the track itself. Pretty cool they use it as their logo."

The men finished closing up the empty cardboard box.

"Been nice chattin', but we gotta go, or our boss will think we're not coming back to help with the big one. You have a favorite in today's race?"

"I do," Charlie said.

"Well, good luck to you, then. My money's on that big grey. I see a Storm cloud a-comin' down the stretch," the man laughed.

"I hope so," Charlie said to their retreating backs.

She stole one last look at the statue of the great Secretariat and started to walk away. Suddenly, she stopped, and retraced her steps.

Placing a hand on his nose, Charlie whispered, "May your big heart be with us today."

She dropped her hand and turned to walk back into the tunnel and the day ahead of her.

Whirlwind

One...two...three...four...five...exhale. One...two...

Molly consciously paced her breathing, trying to calm her jangling nerves. Her whole mind felt like a raw open wound. She just wanted to scream, or possibly cry, and definitely sleep, but now wasn't the time.

It's supposed to be an exciting day, she thought, as she tuned back into Ryan's happy chatter. She glanced over at him in the passenger seat, wondering if he could feel the anger vibrating off her. She guessed not, as he continued to read encouraging tweets from the Storm Troopers off his phone to her.

They pulled into the hospital parking garage and quickly found a spot.

"I'm just going to duck in and say a quick goodbye to Doug before we leave town," Molly said. She was taken aback by her own voice, still cool, calm, and competent, despite her mangled emotional state. "Did you want to just wait in the car?"

"No, I'll join you," Ryan said, patting the pocket of his blue oxford. "I promised Skylar I'd personally deliver a race-day message to Doug."

They moved briskly through the garage and into the hospital. As they turned the corner of the hallway to Doug's room, Molly braced herself. She had been avoiding a series of serious conversations she needed to have with her brother, and she knew he was very much out of the loop. She hadn't told him that Steve was gone, or that money was missing, or that the accounts for the farm were a tangled mess. She hated lying, but she refused to steal the thunder away from Storm today.

Ryan swung ahead, barreling excitedly into Doug's small room. "Oh, hey Steve!"

Molly and Steve locked eyes, but she couldn't read his expression. She looked away first, and immediately registered the wheelchair he stood behind. Doug, dressed in his suit and tie, looked all settled in for a ride.

"What…do you think…you are doing?" Molly scowled hesitantly.

Doug smiled at her, ignoring the tension in the room. "Going to see my best gal and her best horse, I suppose. I heard somewhere it was a pretty big day for them."

"The doctors cleared you for this?" Ryan asked.

"I wouldn't say they're the biggest fans of the plan, but we've come to an agreement," Doug said.

Molly zeroed back in on Steve, but he refused to meet her eyes. Without looking back at him, she addressed her brother. "Doug, if you're determined to go, I will take you. Ryan, please go pull my car around to the front."

She bustled around the room, gathering Doug's belongings, ignoring the uncomfortable looks the men were exchanging with each other.

"Molly, I—" Steve stammered.

Molly held up a hand to silence him. "Not now."

"Molly, please listen to what he has to say," Doug said softly.

"Doug, I love you, but please don't get involved in my marriage," Molly said kindly but firmly.

"You know I usually wouldn't, but I'm afraid I'm already wedged in," Doug replied.

"Whatever he's told you, I assure you there's more, and a good portion of it is just between him and me," Molly said. "Either way, today is about Storm and Lilly and Charlie. Everything else can just wait."

"No, Molly, I'm sorry, I don't accept that. I love you both, and you love each other. Storm is the star today, whatever the outcome of this race, but it took all of us, as a team, to make it happen. He deserves to have a full team behind him," Doug said firmly.

"Steve isn't on the team, Doug!" Molly cried out, exasperated. "He stole money from Shamrock, then tried to hide it by cancelling the insurance plans. When cornered, he drained Jenny's college account to replace the insurance. I have no idea who he is or what he's capable of, he won't even tell me where the money is. For all I know, he lit the barn fire himself."

Ryan's eyes grew wide as Molly unloaded, while Steve stood silently looking down at the floor. Only Doug seemed unfazed, maintaining his clear expression and steady gaze.

"Molly, I understand why you're upset, but you've got it wrong. Steve didn't steal the money. No one stole the money," Doug said. "I overleveraged Shamrock to support Storm's Triple Crown bid. The entry fees for each of the races, coupled with the needs of the farm, along with some of the broodmare purchases and syndications that I got into last year, overextended us, and was more than I had budgeted for. I should have spoken to you, told you what I was doing, but I couldn't bear to see Charlie's dreams dashed. When the new insurance bill came in, I intercepted it and panicked. I went through the books to privately move the money around. I cancelled the insurance plans, and it was a mistake. I was planning on taking out a loan to immediately reinstate them before anyone could notice, but then the fire happened. Steve figured out what was going on, and he tried to cover for me, so no one thought badly of me."

Molly shook her head in disbelief. "So you two solved the problem by stealing the money from my daughter's future?"

"Honey, I love you and Jenny more than I can tell you, and I'm ashamed that I touched that account. It was a temporary solution to an impossible situation. I never should have done it, but I felt stuck," Steve said quietly.

"As a team, we're capable of amazing things—which is what we're celebrating today with Storm. We're lousy when we try to act alone, to save each other from pain by being secretive and sneaky. We're not good when we're not being a team," Doug continued. "Molly, I'm sorry. If Storm wins today, our portion of the prize money will make Shamrock whole again. I don't know what I can do or say to make us all whole again too."

"What happens to Shamrock if Storm loses?" Ryan piped in, looking pale and concerned.

Doug shrugged. "Then we will decide—as a team—what direction we want to go in next. We can tighten our belts or sell some land. Maybe we spin off Hunter's team to another owner. Maybe we start teaching lessons. I don't know. All I know is I almost died. I've got another shot, and I care more about who I'm spending it with than what I'm doing. Please tell me that we can be a team again, Molly. Tell me that we can all do better."

Molly stared at the floor for a moment; when she looked up, she stared directly into Steve's eyes. "I want to be so much more angry with you both than I can muster right now. What you did was wrong, and the sneaking and hiding…but you're right. All of us have made serious blunders over the past few weeks. All of us have to work to make our mistakes right, to ask for forgiveness. But the fire has been a wake-up call. It's shown us all our weak spots. We can either walk away or improve them."

"We will work on them, all of them," Steve said hopefully.

Molly pursed her lips thoughtfully and nodded.

"This is the exact wrong timing, guys, and I'm sorry about that," Ryan said uncomfortably, "but if we're going to be at Belmont by race time, we need to hit the road."

"Go grab the car," Molly instructed him.

"I'll drive," Steve volunteered.

"Not a chance," Molly retorted. "You and Doug are going to sit in the back and think quietly about how you're going to make up for this."

Steve and Doug shot each other a look, knowing they had just bypassed what could have been a very long, uncomfortable car ride, but also let out a sigh of relief that everything was out in the open.

Hunter was laughing so hard that he had trouble catching his breath. "Man, I haven't had this much fun at a race since I was a kid. It's great to do the rounds with you guys—it all feels so new and exciting!"

Amanda grinned as she watched Skylar and Drew chase each other around one of the tents, narrowly avoiding direct collisions with strangers at every turn. "It's incredible! This place is crazy, I love it!"

"It's like this all day—a giant festival, bands and games, face painters, pony rides, lots and lots of food and drinks. Oh, and plenty of undercard races. There's even another Grade 1 race today, a few hours before the main event—the one mile Just A Game Stakes, for fillies and mares," Jenny said happily.

"I swear I've heard more snippets of 'Theme from New York, New York' than I could ever imagine, but I still haven't heard the whole song from beginning to end," Travis said.

"Well, you're guaranteed to hear it later; it's been the post-parade song before the Stakes since 1997," Amanda said, reaching into her Belmont research memories.

"Not quite," Hunter corrected. "In 2010, they made it Jay-Z's 'Empire State of Mind,' but it went back to 'Ol' Blue Eyes' the next year."

Trailing Skylar and Drew as they raced ahead, they peeked in as many of the tents as they could. One of the large white tents they passed by had a small stage, on which several women, all dressed to the nines, were parading.

"Fashion show?" Amanda guessed. She craned her head around, trying to find the signage through a large crowd of people in front of them.

"That's the Longines Most Elegant Woman Competition," Jenny responded.

"The watch company?"

"Yup. They're a big sponsor around here—the official timekeeper for the Belmont. They've got their hands in nearly every activity, from this competition to the fillies' race. They declare an official Belmont watch each year, and they present the owner, trainer, and jockey of the winning horse with a new watch during the awards ceremony."

"Wonder if Lilly will ever wear hers," Amanda thought aloud, trying to imagine the jockey in anything but stable gear.

"Let's grab a snack and make a plan before Drew and Skylar run off for good," Travis suggested as he steered them towards one of the many food stands.

"Yum," Amanda said, holding a Coney Island hot dog in one hand and a black and white cookie in the other, "now I'm home."

They all sat together on the grass and enjoyed their snacks, chatting about the things they'd seen so far and what they wanted to do.

Hunter flashed a wad of cash. "Where should we start?"

"Is it even safe to carry that much cash around? This place is packed, why take the chance?" Travis asked.

Hunter rolled his eyes. "The real betting lines are cash only, and I don't go for those new vending machines that dispense cash cards. It's certainly quicker to pay the vendors in cash than waiting to see if their Wi-Fi connected iPhones work with those credit card attachments. There are ATMs inside, but their fees are ridiculous, and they've always got long lines of fools like you, who don't plan accordingly."

Amanda's phone chirruped with an incoming text notification. She pulled it out and stared at her screen, confused.

"What's it say?" Jenny asked.

"It's from Kate, but it makes no sense—'Come see tongues tied.' Must be a strange autocorrect," Amanda said.

"No, she's inviting you to the stables to watch the grooms tie the tongues of the horses in the next race," Hunter said.

"Wait—horses actually get their tongues tied?" Drew asked. Curious, he stretched out his own tongue as far as it could go and imagined trying to make it a knot.

Skylar laughed. "No, their tongues aren't tied into a knot. The grooms tie them down with this rubber band thing. It goes around the horse's tongue and then under their jaw."

"That seems mean," Drew retorted.

"It doesn't seem to bother them," Hunter said. "Most horses don't even react when you do it. With the rubber band, at least they can move their tongues back and forth a little bit. When I was a boy, they used to do it with a piece of cloth, and that seemed to bug 'em."

"But why do it at all?" Amanda wondered.

"Well, lots of reasons. When they get amped up, they'll get to moving their tongues around, and it's a distraction when racing. A horse can flip his tongue over his bit, which makes it hard for the jockey to maintain control. And I know this sounds crazy, but it could happen that the tongue gets sucked back into their throat and chokes them." Hunter stood up and brushed himself off. "If you're going to work, I'm going to place a few bets, see if I can't come up with a jackpot that could entice me to stop working."

"You should go meet up with Kate, I am sure you could do a great blog about tongue-tying and fashion…" Jenny trailed off teasingly.

"Alright, thank you, I'll text you soon," Amanda said, calling over her shoulder as she rushed off.

Travis peered at his own phone anxiously. "Actually, ah, I was hoping Drew and I could step away from the group for a few minutes too so we can go meet up with…someone."

"Who?" Drew demanded.

"I…well, I invited your mom to come spend the day hanging out with us. Because she's close. And it's been awhile since you've seen her. And I owed her an apology for the pocket watch," Travis said, uncharacteristically nervous.

"Sure," Jenny said, feeling for the father and son. "I wouldn't mind swinging by to check up on Hershey. Skylar, come with me. Then Drew can just give you a call when it's time for us to join back up."

Travis smiled gratefully as she took charge of the plan. "Sounds good, thanks."

They all got up, prepared to move off in different directions, but Jenny's cast put her a few seconds behind. Looking over their spot one more time, she laughed and called out to Drew.

"Hey, it's going to be hard to give us a call if you don't have your phone!"

The boy and his father were too far ahead and the crowd was too loud for her voice to carry through. Looking at the logjam growing between them, she shrugged, picked the phone up off the ground, and put it in her bag.

"They'll figure out how to get ahold of us," Jenny said, taking Skylar's hand. "Let's go see our favorite pony."

 # Clear as a Bell

"Do you think Storm knows the importance of this race?" the reporter from *The Daily Form* asked, stepping between Charlie and Ben to thrust the microphone at Charlie.

Ben just smiled and continued hobbling around in his walking boot. He grabbed a brush and stepped into Storm's stall.

Charlie had tried to convince Ben to let another groom work with Storm prior to the race, but he would have none of it. Charlie was secretly relieved, knowing that their relationship, stretching all the way back to when Storm was born, was something special, and was especially import- ant to Storm here and now, given the presence of Blackston. Ben had been able to keep Storm as calm as possible in the days leading up to the Bel- mont, and he would be right there on the track mere moments before and after the race.

Although, Storm's demeanor seems a lot more reserved since he returned from Pennsylvania—like he's done some maturing over the last two weeks since the fire, Charlie thought, smiling. *Haven't we all…*

Charlie returned her attention to the reporter. "Yes, I believe Storm is well-aware that he is the center of attention."

Storm turned his head at Charlie saying his name and pricked his ears just as the cameras clicked away.

"Now, if you don't mind, we need to get this big celebrity out to walk to the paddock in a few minutes. I can answer more of your questions on the walk over..."

Charlie's sentence trailed off as she got distracted at the scene playing out on the far end of the barn.

"What in the world are you doing here?" she shouted down the row.

Doug shrugged happily and motioned to Steve, who was standing behind his wheelchair, to move him closer. Molly held his hand as she walked beside him.

As they got closer, Doug called out, "Well, we're a motley crew. But I think we all cleaned up pretty well."

Charlie smiled, but reprimanded him. "I thought you had clear instructions from your doctors that you were to be nowhere near the race today, especially not back here, in the barns, with all the dirt that could get your burns infected."

"It's amazing what a small donation can do for you these days," Doug replied, looking up at her innocently.

"We tried to stop him, Charlie," Molly interjected, "but he'd already had the nurses dress him by the time we got to the hospital. I didn't have the heart to refuse him."

Charlie leaned down to give Doug a kiss as the cameras clicked around them.

"Thank you," she whispered, knowing she would need his strength to get through the next few hours. "But I'm banishing you to the owner's box, as you won't be able to steer this wheelchair around in the paddock, and I won't have anyone claiming we spooked their horses on purpose to give Storm an unfair advantage. When we beat 'em, I want them to stay beat."

"Yes, ma'am," Doug replied. "Off to our seats."

"He is so bossy." Molly smiled, giving Charlie a deep hug. "Good luck, may the Storm be with us," she said quietly into Charlie's ear.

Charlie squeezed her back.

One of the reporters spoke up: "How are you feeling, Mr. Walker? From what we've heard, Storm might not be racing today if it hadn't been for you."

"My entire team pulled together the night of the fire. I am just thankful that we didn't lose any horses or people. You can replace barns, but you can't replace the heart and souls of my farm," Doug replied, motioning to Ben, who was keeping busy in Storm's stall. "If you want to talk to Storm's true rescuer, though, this is the man."

The reporters swarmed poor, shy, mortified-looking Ben, and Doug used the opportunity to talk privately to the people he loved. He looked over at Ryan.

"Ryan, I can't thank you enough for the way you jumped in to save the reputation of my farm. Don't let those reporters get the best of your mother out in the paddock."

"Will do," Ryan said, smiling.

"And you," Doug held out his hand to Skylar, "you are growing up to be just as brave as your mom."

Skylar beamed.

"I won't be able to pick you up this race, but you're welcome to stand on my wheelchair to watch this big guy win it all," Doug said confidently.

Skylar held Doug's unburnt hand in both her own. "Thank you for saving Hershey, Mr. Doug," was all she could muster, as tears rolled down her cheeks.

This was the first time she had been able to thank Doug in person for saving her pony, though the cards she'd sent him every day he'd been in the hospital had tugged strongly on his heartstrings.

Doug cleared his throat. "Hey, he saved me, using his strong back to carry me to safety. We are now connected for life, with matching scars."

And as if Hershey knew they were talking about him, a soft whinny came from the stall behind them. Storm's big grey head nodded, impatient to get the show on the road.

"Now, no more talk of the past. We can't change what happened, but we can enjoy this beautiful day, with great friends and family, surrounded by beautiful horses, and appreciate the journey."

The reporters who hadn't taken the Ben-bait stood in silence around them, not wanting to impose on the sensitive moment shared by this team that had been through so much.

"I know why we're over here," Amanda murmured to Jenny, including Kate with a gesture, "but you really belong on that side of the line."

Jenny looked lost in thought as she stared at the group of reporters flocked around Charlie, Ryan, Skylar, and her family. Finally, she gave a small shrug.

"I don't think the space is hurting us."

Just then, Ryan broke through the media line and rushed over. She allowed herself to get wrapped up in a pretty great hug.

"Man, I've missed you!" Ryan said.

Jenny smiled. "You'll always have Twitter."

He shook his head. "Yeah, it might be time to set some boundaries between me and technology. I dream in 140 characters. There's lots we should talk about, but it'll have to wait until after the race. I just wanted to say hello."

Ryan started to walk back to his mother and sister, then spun back around. "Actually, would you mind holding my phone for me while we do the walk into the paddock? I'm so amped up about the race that I'm afraid I'd reach to check my notifications out of instinct and completely ruin the photo op."

Jenny held out her hand for his phone and he silently turned it over, followed with a kiss on the cheek that made them both blush a little. He hurried back to his family while Jenny fumbled with the top of her backpack.

"Oh shoot," Jenny said as she got it open and peered inside. "I'd forgotten I'd picked up Drew's phone earlier. Remind me to give it back to him."

Amanda looked at it. "Oh, I recognize that. It's not Drew's, it's Hunter's."

"Where is he?" Jenny asked, looking around the stable.

"He's actually packing up the car right now. I think he was going to watch the race from the sidelines and then sneak out as quickly as he could to avoid traffic. He's got to get back to Laurel to race again tomorrow." Amanda checked her watch and held out her hand. "Actually, I've got enough time to run it over to him before the race starts, so he's not on the road without."

"Enough time for me to hop along? I'm getting pretty fast on these things," Jenny said, thumping her crutches on the ground.

Amanda glanced at her watch again and nodded. "Yup, just enough time, let's scoot."

"Wait!" Skylar cried out, cutting through the reporters to catch up to the two women as they moved off in the opposite direction. "I need Lilly's water bottle."

Jenny nodded and flipped the top of her bag open once more, grabbing the light blue reusable bottle with the Shamrock logo from the very top and handing it to the girl before she disappeared again.

"You keep everything in that backpack?" Amanda teased as they stepped away from the crowds heading towards the paddock and hurried towards the back of the stabling area, where Amanda knew Hunter kept his truck parked.

———————————

"I hope everything is okay," Jenny said, looking concernedly at the vibrating phone as they walked briskly. "This is like the third time this number has called and let it ring straight through before calling back."

Amanda laughed. "Well, if I've got Hunter pegged right, it's either a woman or a creditor."

They paused as the number started ringing through again.

"Maybe he's calling from someone else's phone to find his," Jenny suggested.

"The number does look familiar," Amanda said. She gestured for Jenny to hand her the phone and flipped it on speaker.

"Hello, Hunter's phone," she answered brightly.

"Is this some kind of joke?" A man's voice growled over loud background noises. "Put him on."

"I'll have to have him call you back," Amanda said, trying and failing to place the voice. "May I ask who is calling?"

"Very funny. You tell him that if everything isn't taken care of, he doesn't need to call me back. Two of my stronger associates will find him—and bury him—the moment another horse crosses that finish line."

The line went dead, and Jenny and Amanda stared at each other.

"What's going on?" Jenny croaked.

"I'm…not sure," Amanda replied, her heart racing in her chest. "But we need to find Hunter, now."

She flipped through his contacts, searching for Cappie or anyone else who might be near him, but it was a short search. There was only one number saved—the one she'd just spoken to—and all incoming and outgoing calls were to the same.

"This isn't possible," she murmured. "I know we've spoken on the phone before."

Jenny pulled out her own phone and found Hunter in her contacts. He picked up on the first ring.

"Hey Jenny, what's up?"

Jenny looked like a deer in the headlights, and Amanda snatched the phone away. "Hey Hunter, where are you right now?"

"Out in the back lot—is everything okay?"

"Of course," Amanda forced herself to lie. "Just stick around a few more minutes, I've got something for you."

She hung up and took off across the lot, running as fast as her high heels would allow.

Poison

Jenny was close enough behind that she had to stop short to keep from running into the reporter when she came to a screeching halt beside a familiar truck. Hunter was beside it, rooting around in a duffel bag. He came up with a simple gray t-shirt and a big, calm smile.

"Well, hello there, ladies," he said, pulling off the shockingly yellow t-shirt Amanda had come to associate with him. His bandaged burn was only exposed for a moment as he fluidly put on the new gray shirt. "Just getting changed before the race so I can hit the road right after. Hate driving in sweaty clothes."

"Sure thing, Hunter. We just wanted to return your phone," Amanda said, smiling brightly.

Hunter looked surprised, hesitating just a moment before he accepted it. "Thanks, Angel. I keep telling you, I'd lose myself without you." He turned back to his bag, reorganizing everything. "You two should hurry back in and grab your seats, I'll be right behind."

Amanda leaned in and grabbed the keys dangling from the open truck door. "Hunter, why do you have two phones?"

He laughed. "Okay, Angel, no reason at all for you to get jealous. It's obvious you'd like to have a talk, but I need to get back to Laurel. I'm racing tomorrow, and with the boss out of the hospital, I know he'll want a full report. Heck, I'm more than half expecting him to drop in to check on us at the track tomorrow on his way home. I'll be back at Shamrock tomorrow night, and I can explain everything."

Hunter moved in closer for a kiss, but was caught off-guard when Amanda shoved him away.

"You're not going to Laurel. You're not going to Shamrock. You can't, and we both know it. The moment you get in that truck, you disappear," Amanda said bitterly.

"Disappear?" Hunter drawled in a calm, amused voice. "You moving away from journalism and into detective fiction? The phone isn't a big deal, Amanda. Shamrock pays for my phone, and I've got a little betting hobby on the side that I feel guilty using a company line for."

"Hunter, we picked up a call. We saw your logs. Your betting business is pretty exclusive, isn't it?" Amanda grabbed her own phone out of her back pocket and flipped through her own past calls. "I thought it looked familiar: Blackston."

"Okay, so what? You knew we knew each other. I placed a rather large bet with him on the outcome of this race. I didn't want to advertise it. End of story."

"See, I don't think it is," Amanda said thoughtfully. "Jenny, call Travis. Or…maybe just call the police."

"Wait, what?" Jenny asked.

Hunter looked pale and truly scared for the first time. In a fluid motion, he grabbed the keys from Amanda's hands and opened the door hurriedly. Jenny pushed it shut again with her crutch before he could jump in.

"If you call the cops, I promise you, you'll rip any chance Storm and Lilly have at the Triple Crown away from them," Hunter said nastily.

"Well, why would that bother you? Thinking back, you've tried to dissuade and block their path whenever you could—influencing my articles, voting against Storm going to the whisperer…" Amanda trailed off, lost in thought. "Maybe you've even done more than that. Why don't you tell me about the fire?"

"Why?" Hunter demanded.

"That burn across your chest—you got it while lighting the fire, not trying to help, didn't you?" Amanda said, the wheels in her head visibly spinning. She smacked her forehead. "I can't believe I didn't put it together before."

Hunter barked out a derisive laugh. "You're crazy."

"No, I don't think I am. I think you just need a bigger wardrobe. When I met you at the scene, you were wearing that obnoxiously yellow shirt. The shirt is still intact, which, given the placement of your burn, would have been nearly impossible if you had been wearing it when you were injured."

Amanda paused, waiting for Hunter to mount a defense or offer an explanation. He was silent.

Amanda shrugged and continued, "Of course, there are reasonable excuses—you could have taken it off to cover your mouth at some point, you could have left the scene to change sometime in the middle of firefighting. But I don't think you did."

Jenny, stunned, stared into Hunter's face, but his expression was blank.

"Then there's the phone," Amanda said. "I bet there are calls between you and Blackston reaching back farther than you could explain away with a wager on this race. I bet there are calls from the night of the fire."

"That wouldn't prove anything," Hunter croaked.

"Probably not," Amanda replied, "but he didn't sound pleased when he called. Almost like he asked someone to take care of a horse-sized problem, and it still hasn't been done. How would you react, I wonder, if I just called him now and asked him to come meet us and clear it all up?"

Hunter scanned the lot, visibly frantic at the idea of running into Blackston.

"I know I can't prove anything that I suspect, but I'll be damned if I walk away from here without some plot holes plugged up. And I think you'd like to get out of here before someone worse than Jenny or me comes looking for you. So, if you help me..."

Hunter looked at her, and a sly expression crossed his face. "Your...fictional...plot holes?"

Amanda looked over at Jenny for confirmation. Sighing, she shrugged her consent. Amanda nodded.

"Well, I don't think your villain is really a bad guy. He's messed up before, but who hasn't?" Hunter started, quickly building up his bravado.

He flashed a flirtatious grin at Amanda; she and Jenny both grimaced in disgust, and he seemed to realize his charm had worn very thin.

He straightened up and continued, "Let's say that he's had a string of bad luck bets that landed him in debt to some very serious, violent men—men like Dale Blackston. Maybe these men offered him a clean slate if he eliminated Storm from the race.

"Usually, your villain would have just packed up and moved on, let everything cool down, but this time he liked what he had going on. He liked his job, he liked his whole situation, and he wanted to keep it. He'd done some bad things in the past—what was one more bad thing when it meant he could live a good life afterwards?"

Amanda's blood boiled at Hunter's rationalization, but she tried to keep her face neutral. "So...he decided to burn down the barn with Storm inside?"

"Not at first, no. He wanted to wait until the races were closer—actually, knocking the jockey off balance somehow was the original plan. That way the villain could place a large bet of his own on the horse that would win, and his slate wouldn't just be clean—he'd have some good money.

"The real bad men, though, wanted Storm out of the way sooner, and threatened the hero—I mean, villain," Hunter said, obviously feeling quite clever.

"They threatened him...via a burner much like this one?" Jenny asked, holding up the flip phone.

"Right. So, you know...fire." Hunter shrugged. "I mean, you figure, well, it's kind of sporting."

"Excuse me?" Amanda yelped.

"Well, I…er, the villain…"

Jenny bristled. "Drop the cute stuff, Hunter. We've already made our deal."

"Fine. I had nothing against Storm, or Doug, or Charlie, or Shamrock. None of this was their fault, it just was what it was. A fire still gave Storm fighting odds. Sure, worst case, he would have died…but he could have just gotten hurt or suffered from smoke inhalation. As it turned out, he got the best case—he was just too freaked out to run. He got it too good, in fact, since that horse whisperer fixed him up and he didn't get scratched." Hunter shook his head. "Poor Doug and that pony got hurt for no reason."

Jenny rolled her eyes. "You're a master of the passive voice, Hunter."

Amanda held out a hand to silence her. "How did you start an untraceable fire?"

"Well, I had a little experience when I was younger." Hunter squirmed around, unsure how much to reveal, but his desire to brag and show off quickly overtook his hesitation. "I was down in Florida when the economy crashed in '05, and lots of people were stuck with SUVs they couldn't even afford to fill up. I helped them out and made a few dollars by torching their cars for the insurance payout. I always did it the same way—lighting a bag of chips on fire. Cheetos, actually. The fat and oil burn hot and fast—think of a kitchen grease fire—and the evidence disappears quickly."

"And you disconnected the WiFi so the cameras wouldn't record."

Hunter nodded.

"What about the burn on your chest?" Amanda asked.

"I was concerned that the fire wasn't going to take hold, so I swept up some hay to feed it before I left. I must have put my bag too close to the fire, because the nylon strap had turned into molten lava by the time I threw it on. Burned straight through my shirt, so I had to change."

"The threats and rumors online? Oh, God…my article." Amanda buried her face in her hands.

"Listen, Angel, I really do like you. I was just trying to scare and shame them off racing Storm."

Amanda wanted to scream at him, at the callousness with which he just blew through everyone's life without regard. "Why just Storm, though? Imagine That isn't a sure bet, even with Storm out of the way—there's always going to be Duke."

"So, yeah. I was actually supposed to take Duke out too—sponging, here at the track. I realized that no bookie was going to give me the odds I wanted on the long shot, not with Blackston blackballing me. But I could place a sizable bet on Duke at similar odds. I knew Blackston would be mad, but if this plays out, I'm going to be set."

"But if it doesn't, you're just doubly screwed? You'll still owe Blackston serious money…and more to the bookie behind your Duke bet?" Jenny realized.

"Yeah. So if it's all the same to you two, I'm going to get going before I bump into anyone I don't want to bump into."

"You're crazy if you think we're just going to let you walk away from this mess," Jenny said firmly.

Hunter scratched his head. "See, you need to. Because I don't think the police are a real threat against me, but they are for you. You're the one that dosed Lilly."

"What?" Amanda yelped, looking over at Jenny.

Jenny looked puzzled for a moment, then horrified. "The water bottle."

Hunter gave a slight nod, but Amanda still looked confused.

"Right before we met up with the rest of you in the stables, Hunter gave Skylar and me Lilly's water bottle and asked us to deliver it to her. He said he had things to do and didn't want to be another body in the way…and I just handed it to Skylar before we left," Jenny explained, looking both panicked and miserable.

"Hunter, you need to tell me what's in it—is it poisoned?" Amanda grabbed her phone and quickly started to dial 9-1-1, but Hunter grabbed it from her hands.

"It's not poisoned. All that's going to happen if you call it in right now is you'll ruin the race. Even if you demand a drug test, it would eventually come back clean, unless she's been doping herself."

Amanda stared at the ground, thinking hard, recalling the details of the drugging conversation she'd had with Hunter just a few days ago. "Ketamine. It doesn't show on standard drug test panels. If anything, they would usually pick up on whatever was used to adulterate it—but since it's primarily used in veterinary practices, the pure stuff would certainly be easy enough for you to come by, right? What was your vet friend's name again?"

Hunter shrugged. "Maybe. It's a good guess. Ketamine works fast on horses and humans alike—five, ten minutes. No one saw me anywhere near her or the stables before post time." He checked his watch. "If you're right, she'd be through the worst of it in like half an hour. I've known plenty of horse people who take ketamine just for the high; she'd be fine. There's always a chance she didn't even get enough in her to bumble the race."

Amanda shook her head, trying to clear her mind and run through all the options.

Jenny looked worried. "Amanda, what if he's bluffing? If we tell Charlie and Doug and Lilly, they'll report it to the racing commission. Jockeys get scratched for doping."

Amanda looked bewildered. "I really have no idea what we should do. If he did dose her, and she got enough in her system to affect her, she should be through the worst of the side effects very soon. Ketamine takes effect quickly, but only lasts an hour or so. There's no antidote; any medical attention we could get her would just be to ease symptoms that might never surface. Like, there's a good possibility that she won't ever realize she was drugged if we don't tell her. If we do tell her, the Triple Crown slips through everyone's fingers."

Both of the women were quiet for a moment.

"Well, I'm going to leave you two with that moral dilemma and hit the road. You send the cops after me, the decision will be made for you—I'll report Lilly for doping and tell them exactly what panels they need to run," Hunter said lazily.

"How many days does it take to clear her system?" Amanda asked, her eyes hard.

"I figure I have about a twenty-four-hour head start," Hunter replied, sliding on his sunglasses as he got into the truck and started the engine. "I'll see you around, Angel."

Amanda and Jenny watched the truck as it pulled away. "I wish I had something on me I could throw at it," Amanda sighed.

"What are we going to do?" Jenny half-whispered. "Amanda, I don't think we can try to hide this."

"Okay. Then let's try to get to her before she drinks that water bottle."

The Last Minute

Charlie waited until Doug was out of sight, heading towards the grandstand, before turning to Ben.

"Alright, Ben, bring him out."

The sun shined off of Storm's dapples as he was released from the confines of his stall. Skylar held Hershey's halter to keep him safely out of the way and softly closed the half-stall door.

"You stay here and wait to congratulate Storm when he comes back," she said, nuzzling his face affectionately.

Charlie started the walk towards the tunnel that would take them to the paddock with Ryan on one side and Skylar holding her hand on the other. She thought it was a fitting end to their adventure that it was just the three of them making this walk and standing in the paddock together. They were the survivors who had dreamed so much to make this moment a reality, but there were the others, without whom she wouldn't be here today. She briefly closed her eyes, allowing herself to think of Peter and of Sarge, and she took a moment to honor them.

"Charlie, how do you think Storm is going to handle the post position today? He will be right in the middle of the gate with half the field to his left and half to his right," one of the reporters asked.

"Oh, I think he will handle whatever comes his way. It is a long way around the track, so he will have time to figure it out, no matter if he is in the front, or towards the back," Charlie said calmly.

"But Lilly has a plan to do one or the other, right?" the reporter persisted.

"As you saw in the Derby and the Preakness, Storm has won from both coming from behind and on the lead. We just hope for a safe break from the gate," Charlie said.

"What do you think of Blackston sending both Manakin and Imagine That up against Storm? He is using Manakin as the rabbit and he's planning to come out fast and be the speed in the race. Are you planning on going after him?" the reporter continued his questions.

"I can't predict what any other trainer is planning on doing. Lilly and Storm will run their own race." Charlie was done answering questions, so she added, "Thank you," making her message clear.

"Nice job, Mom," Ryan said as they walked through the tunnel.

They continued up the ramp into the paddock area, which had been overseen by the Belmont Oak for over a hundred years. The crowd was thick and all calling for Storm, the first potential Triple Crown winner in thirty-seven years.

Ben led Storm over to stall number 6 as Lilly and her valet approached with her saddle.

Lilly hugged each of them in turn. "Ready?"

"As ready as we ever will be," Charlie smiled.

"He will do great. He has grown so much mentally over the last week. Even if we don't come home with a win, we have all won with what we have been through the last two weeks. Heck, the last two months! I have to be honest, I am looking forward to it all being over," Lilly confided.

"Me, too," Charlie laughed.

"Here, Lilly!" Skylar said, thrusting the water bottle up towards her.

"Thanks, Sky," Lilly said, smiling down at her. It was too close to the race for her to drink much at all, she didn't want a belly full of water sloshing around inside her on the track, but she took a small gulp to show her appreciation for Skylar's thoughtfulness.

She immediately made a face, but masked it quickly. "Oh, orange juice! That's a surprise."

Charlie smiled and shrugged sympathetically, taking the water bottle back from her. "I'll go ahead and save the rest of this for after the race."

"Oh, please dump that," Lilly said quietly.

Charlie nodded. "We'll have some fresh water ready."

Lilly's valet went about putting the saddle on Storm, as he surveyed his surroundings. Head held high, nostrils flared, Storm let out a long whinny. The crowd cheered.

"He's letting his presence known to the challengers," Lilly patted Charlie's arm.

"Just so long as he stays away from Blackston's beasts. I don't trust any of them," Charlie said.

"I know the plan. Blackston will take Manakin to the front to try and burn some speed. He can have it. Storm will be fine in the back, especially given the mile and a half race. None of these horses have run that far, so we are better off conserving energy for the long stretch run. That's when Blackston will send Imagine That at us, hoping we have tired. But we have already talked all about the strategy, you know that. Bottom line, hopefully it will all go as planned, otherwise, I will need to improvise," Lilly said, smiling.

"No matter what, everyone comes home in one piece," Charlie said seriously and gave Lilly a quick hug.

"Riders up!" came the call.

As Ben walked Storm past their small group, Ryan reached out. Lilly put her knee in his hand and leaped into the saddle. The horses finished their walk around the paddock and made their way towards the tunnel under the grandstand that would lead them to the track.

As Storm walked into the tunnel, Lilly looked up at the sign: "Belmont Park, Where Champions are Made."

"You are already a champion. Now, let's go prove it to the world," she whispered to Storm, patting his neck.

———————

As they stepped onto the track, Cappie greeted them on his side pony.

"Who do you have today?" Lilly asked.

"Liberty," Cappie said. "I had to wrestle him away from his regular rider, but it was an easy sell once he knew he would be chaperoning Storm."

The two of them walked together as "Theme from New York, New York" played from beginning to end, as promised.

"Did you know the first post parade wasn't held until the fourteenth Belmont, in 1880?" Cappie said to Lilly, trying to calm both their nerves.

"Why, aren't you just a wealth of knowledge," Lilly said, posting to Storm's trot as the announcers called out each horse's name and listed their connections.

"Just nuggets of information to keep you on your toes," Cappie replied.

Lilly laughed. "I appreciate that."

Cappie loosened the leather strap looped through Storm's bridle and released him. Lilly pushed him into a gallop to warm him up.

"See you at the gate," she called behind them.

———————

Jenny and Amanda raced into the stables, but Charlie and Storm and Skylar were already gone.

"There, through the tunnel," Jenny said.

They raced over, but were promptly held back by security.

"No, we're with Storm!" Jenny protested.

"I'm sorry, ladies, but the post parade has started. You'll have to find your seats."

Amanda opened her mouth, but quickly realized any explanation she could give wouldn't work. She pulled Jenny to the side.

"We're too late," Jenny moaned.

They heard the announcer's voice crackle over the loudspeaker.

"It's in Storm's hands now," Amanda said, as they hurried towards their seats.

Tough Ride

Lilly eased Storm as they approached the starting gate. The large, expansive grandstand filled with thousands of fans stood to their right.

"One loop around the Big Sandy, big guy," Lilly said to Storm, watching him as he took in all the sensations around them with his ears, eyes, and nose.

"Pretty cool that the starting gate sits in the exact spot as the finish line, right?" she continued, grabbing the reins a bit to keep his mind on the task ahead. "This mile and a half will test us all, but I have faith in you."

The gate handler approached to lead Storm into the starting gate. "Ready to go?"

"A beautiful day for a race," Lilly replied.

Storm was the sixth of eleven to enter the starting gate. There were ten challengers to his quest for the Triple Crown. Only Duke and Buster Brown had been consistent competition in the previous two races; today, there were eight fresh contenders. Shooting Star and Blackston's Imagine That had raced in the Derby, so they were on what could be considered typical five weeks rest. That left six unknowns.

Lilly ran through them quickly as she waited for the others to enter the starting gate. Blackston's Manakin, the expected speed horse; Potomac

Eagle, a closer; Kickstart, she knew he excelled on a muddy track, which wouldn't be a factor, given today's sunny skies and fast track; Rising Star, an international wonder who hadn't taking well to the dirt tracks since his arrival; Iron Stark, another one she would need to worry about in the stretch; and Blue Bird Day, truly an unknown, as this was only his second race. Lilly figured she would have to keep a close eye on him due to his inexperience; given his lack of track record, he could wind up being a dark horse. His 60-1 odds were deceiving as Lilly had made it a point to watch him work in the mornings this past week; Blue Bird Day was not to be discounted. Hadn't Sarava proven that in the 2002 Belmont Stakes? He toppled War Emblem's bid for the Triple Crown at 70-1, the longest shot to win the Belmont and what is largely considered one of horse racing's biggest upsets.

Lilly could feel Storm's heart beat through her body, rushing up to 200 beats per minute, ten times its resting rate, as he too anxiously awaited the entrance of the other horses.

Lilly took a deep breath to settle her mind as the last horse to her right entered the gate. Buck was a few slots down, perched tight up on Duke's neck; she couldn't reflect on their relationship right at this moment and pushed the thoughts aside.

Storm looked through the gate ahead of him as he pawed the ground waiting for the other horses to be settled. The gate handler held his head straight in anticipation of the bell that would spring open the gates holding him back. Rising Star in the end stall reared up, unseating his jockey.

"Hey, hey, not yet, not yet," he yelled.

The handler tried to straighten Rising Star out, but he kicked out at the gates behind him, forcing the handlers to open them up and back him out.

Lilly sat tight in her saddle, murmuring to Storm, watching his ears flick back and forth. The longer-than-anticipated wait in the gate was causing all the horses to fidget. Lilly tightened and released the reins in her hands, which had developed a slight but growing tingle. She felt them slide a little on the braids of her reins as she broke out into a clammy sweat. Lilly grabbed a fistful of Storm's mane to ground herself. She sensed when they finally got the horse straightened out and re-entered the gate.

"Whoa, not yet!" yelled a jockey to her left as the number one horse half reared due to all the waiting.

The starter used the exact moment that his hooves hit the ground to hit the starting button. The gates opened, releasing over 12,000 pounds of horse flesh.

Lilly sat quietly as Storm found his racing rhythm. Manakin raced to the front, as anticipated. Given the length of the race, Lilly had no desire to rush Storm along. They sat three wide as they raced for the first turn, with two running ahead of them. The rest of the horses were bunched up behind.

Storm's hooves dug into the firm track as he raced along. Lilly glanced to her left and was surprised to see Buck coming up between horses, which set them four wide heading down the backstretch.

Why is he making a move so early in the race? Lilly wondered.

Lilly didn't mind the number of horses to her left, as it meant that Storm was further away from the white inside rail that he hated so much. But she also knew being four wide meant that Storm had a longer way to travel around the track, and that would take its toll in the last quarter mile.

As Lilly pondered what her next move should be, her peripheral vision blurred slightly. She shook her head, trying to clear the distraction. The tingling in her hands got worse and she could feel the reins slipping, giving Storm too much head. He jumped into his unexpected freedom, but Lilly quickly corrected, grabbing up the slack.

Not yet, Storm. What is happening? Her vision tunneled again, and she could only clearly make out the track directly in front of her. She blinked several times.

Buck was racing close to her left. When Storm had jumped a bit ahead, he'd brought Duke along with him. Buck knew he couldn't allow Storm to get too far ahead. He glanced over at Lilly just as she swayed a bit and grabbed at Storm's mane to steady herself. *What's wrong?*

"Lilly!" he yelled across to her.

She turned her head slightly towards him, and he could see the fear in her eyes as she struggled to maintain her balance. In an instant, Buck grabbed his reins in one hand and reached out to steady Lilly in her saddle.

Lilly's adrenaline kicked into overdrive to fight off whatever was trying to overtake her body. She tightened her legs and entwined her arms into Storm's mane and willed herself to keep her wits about her.

Buck kept Duke racing alongside Storm, just in case Lilly needed his help again, but he was relieved to see her eyes come back into focus and her body get tight in the saddle.

It happened in an instant; instinct took over.

The horses behind Duke and Storm overtook them and raced on as they came out of the first turn and into the backstretch. Lilly sat still as she continued to fight off the blurred vision and numbness that had overtaken her hands. She was losing strength, but she had to hold on to help Storm do his job. He was running on the tight rein she had needed when she'd wrapped her hands in his mane, but he was starting to get frustrated now, with the other horses overtaking him. She didn't know how much longer she'd have the strength to keep fighting him, but it was too soon to make a move to the front.

At most racetracks, the move to the front begins when you enter the far turn, about 770 yards from the finish line; however, Belmont's track was an entire mile and a half oval, a half mile longer than Churchill Downs, Pimlico, and most of the other tracks these horses had raced on leading up to the Triple Crown events. Horses had a lot further to run than they normally would coming out of the far turn and into the homestretch of Big Sandy, so any moves to the front were best made as they started coming out of the turn. Otherwise, horses tended to run out of gas a quarter mile before the finish line.

Storm didn't know the difference between this track and the others he had raced on, though. He would be fully ready to run at the end of the backstretch, as he entered the far turn, and Lilly didn't know if she could hold him.

———————————

"What is wrong with Lilly?" Ryan whispered to his mom.

They had both seen Buck reach out to steady her.

"I don't know. She seemed fine in the paddock, but right now, she looks like she is holding on to Storm for dear life," Charlie replied, handing Ryan the binoculars. "Look at her hands. They are woven into Storm's mane, and she is crouched lower than she normally would be at this point in a race."

"Storm doesn't like the tight hold. Do you see him tossing his head a bit?" Ryan pointed out.

Charlie leaned down and spoke into Doug's ear, as the noise around them was getting loud as the horses raced down the backstretch. "Doug, have you ever seen Lilly unsteady during a race? Maybe all this has taken a toll on her. Do you think she is having an anxiety attack?"

"No. She has always been in top shape when it came to riding, whether it was a race or just morning exercise," Doug replied.

Molly had overheard their conversation and decided to pitch her opinion. "Maybe it's the emotional toll of this past week, between Storm's healing and Jenny finding out who her parents really are and whatever has gone wrong between her and Buck. She handled Jenny's anger so well, but maybe it's all caught up with her."

"In the middle of the most important race of her life?" Charlie asked.

"You know anxiety better than anyone, Charlie; it can rear its ugly head at any time. Maybe Blackston's jockey said something to her in the post parade that set her off and got her distracted," Doug said. "You know he would do anything to prevent Storm from winning."

They all kept their eyes glued on Lilly and Storm as they entered the far turn.

"I can't watch," Jenny whispered, though she kept her eyes trained on the horse.

Amanda clenched her jaw and looked around the group of people they'd managed to slide in beside when they raced into the grandstand right before the gates opened, wondering what the team from Shamrock was making of this from their seats.

Buck kept Duke close to Storm, about a half length behind on the inside. He was prepared to help Lilly in an instant, but he was also prepared to win this race. Lilly seemed to be more secure in her saddle as they went into the far turn. Several of the other horses had passed them shortly after Lilly had wavered and when they'd each taken a hold of their own horses.

Storm was getting frustrated with the tight hold she kept on him, and Buck could sense he was getting ready to explode from all his pent-up energy. For everyone's sakes, Buck wished Lilly would just let Storm go.

Lilly regained her focus and forced the worry from her brain. She needed to get this done, and time and track were running out on her. Storm was now towards the back of the pack; he needed to make up seven lengths to overtake the leaders as they headed into the far turn.

Her vision was still slight blurry at the edges, so she turned her head slightly to the left and could see Duke's head off her hip. She knew Buck would make his move along with her.

She looked right, taking in the other two horses racing closely next to Storm. She evaluated easing Storm out from behind the horses racing in from of them, but knew she would have to do it without fouling and impeding these horses. *God knows we already had to live through that unfortunate event in the Preakness.* Swinging Storm would also cause him to be running four horses wide around the turn, a longer route that would use up crucial energy needed in the final surge for the finish line.

Lilly sat tight as they moved through the turn.

It just isn't time yet to make my move, she thought.

She could feel Storm tense and knew he wanted to be released from her tight hold.

"Not yet, Storm," she said, while trying to communicate the need to be patient through her hands and legs.

All eleven horses, tightly bunched, began to race out of the turn and into the homestretch.

The crowd was wild with the anticipation of having a potential Triple Crown winner. Over 90,000 people moved as one big wave, urging Storm forward, concerned that he was towards the back, rather than leading the way into the homestretch.

Charlie squeezed Doug's hand, while Skylar jumped up and down next to her.

"Come on, Storm! Come on!" Skylar pleaded.

No one else said anything, their emotions held in check by their own personal prayers for Storm to get to the front.

With all the noise around her, Charlie felt enveloped in a cone of silence. She could feel the screams and noise around her, but all her senses were trained on her big grey horse. Her mind flashed back to the lazy days of the previous fall, watching Storm play in the paddock with Sarge, watching Skylar play hide-and-seek with him, the late night chats at his stall door when she couldn't sleep. Charlie couldn't stop the tears from streaming down her face as she watched her big, beautiful, grey horse, who had helped give her life back when things had been at their darkest.

Storm had had enough. He knew he should have made his move already, so when Lilly made a move to adjust her reins, he violently tossed his head, and the reins slipped through Lilly's sweaty hands. She just couldn't contain the grey thundercloud anymore.

With the unanticipated freedom, Storm released a burst of speed that took Buck by surprise. He had been pondering his own situation, considering dropping Duke behind Storm and coming around on the outside, since they had the whole width of the track at their disposal. However, when Storm jumped ahead, it created an opening to his immediate right, which he took full advantage of, moving Duke out a bit from the rail. Then, the horse in front of Storm tired and drifted out from the rail. Buck held his breath as he considered going inside to get to the front. To his surprise, another horse beat him to the hole.

Lilly saw the opening at the same time Buck did. She knew she couldn't control the beast beneath her, but she hoped she could still steer him.

The horses to the outside of Storm had made their moves the same time Storm had been released of his hold, so Lilly knew he couldn't force his way around the horses running in front of them.

"Come on, Storm, it's now or never," Lilly called to him.

Lilly guided Storm towards the inside rail, hoping all the work the horse whisperer had done with him had included overcoming this fear. Storm hesitated, but Lilly continued to encourage him. They were running out of track and heading into the final quarter mile, the no-man's-land for all these horses who had never attempted racing this distance.

Inhaling deeply and overcoming his fear, Storm thrust himself forward through the space left by the tiring horse on the inside rail and started bearing down on the leaders in front of him. Lilly sat quietly over his neck, feeling Storm reach into his reserves to race to the wire.

The crowd to their right was in a frenzy as Storm raced the last furlough with the leader two lengths ahead. Lilly could already hear them echoing in her brain; then, suddenly, the noise reached a new crescendo as she made out another horse coming up the middle of the track to her right. Buck had Duke in full flight. This race was just going to come down to which horse had the most endurance for the test of champions.

Lilly felt like the three horses—Iron Stark to her left, Storm in the middle, and Duke on her right—were moving in slow motion over the last fifty yards.

She could feel Storm reach to the ground and level himself lower as his heart willed his body to go faster. Inch by inch, Storm fought back the challengers on both sides.

He would not be denied.

As they crossed the finish line, Storm lowered his head and pushed his nose in front to win the Belmont Stakes and take his place in history.

 # Good Deals

Lilly let Storm gallop himself out, knowing the effort he'd made in that last 100 yards had taken a lot out of him. Her arms still felt like lead weights, but she managed to ease him to a trot as Donna Brothers approached with her microphone.

"What an effort, Lilly! Did you think he had it in him, coming down the homestretch?"

"I was just the passenger, Donna, Storm did all the work." Lilly's tongue felt a little too big for her mouth, like it had been shot with Novocain. She concentrated on the rest of Donna's question, and continued, "You know he has a reputation of not running on the rail, and he overcame that today to get the win."

"He certainly did. You seemed to overcome a struggle of your own on the track today. I think time stood still for every spectator when Buck Wheeler on Royal Duke reached out to help you steady yourself. Is everything alright?" Donna thrust the microphone in Lilly's direction again.

"Yes, I was feeling faint and my vision was blurry. Maybe it's food poisoning or something, I still feel a bit woozy. For a second, I felt like I was sliding out of the saddle. Buck was very kind to reach over to steady me.

Thankfully, my adrenaline and instinct took over, and Storm took care of me in the end. I'm grateful everyone came home safely."

"Well, it was an amazing race, and Storm showed a lot of courage in the last 100 yards. Congrats on being the first Triple Crown winner in over thirty-seven years!" Donna said.

"Thanks," Lilly replied.

The two mounted riders made their way back towards the grandstand and the winner's circle. Ben approached to grab Storm's bridle.

"What a race, Lilly!"

"It was all Storm," she replied.

Lilly felt like she was floating above the hubbub as people approached to splash Storm down with water, shake her hand, and congratulate them both. Charlie ran up with the racing commissioner close behind, carrying Storm's blanket of carnations draped across his arms. Lilly leaned down to grab Charlie's hand.

"He did it," Lilly said.

"Yes, he did! You both were great!"

The commissioner laid the carnations on Storm's shoulders and shook Lilly's hand. Ben, Charlie, the commissioner, and a small army of track staff led Storm in a few victory laps in front of the photographers' line to thunderous applause. They all walked into the winners' circle to meet up with the rest of the Shamrock crew. Lilly dismounted, and everyone gathered around Storm to get his saddle off, wrap him in a white horse blanket, and spread the carnations across his broad back.

"Storm is certainly getting used to all these flowers," Skylar said.

"Look—he's getting his colors painted at all the tracks," Ryan said, pointing over to the gazebo, where the green and pink of Storm's jockey silks were replacing last year's winning colors on the cast-iron jockey. "When the race is won next year, Storm's jockey will permanently join those of the other Triple Crown winners in the center of the track."

"Just think—his name will be on a wooden sign right next to Affirmed's in the infield forever. No one will ever forget Genuine Storm," Ben added, as Storm rubbed his sweaty face up and down the front of his shirt.

Cappie and Ben led Storm back to the stables for water, treats, and a well-earned quiet moment. The rest of the group stayed in the winners' circle, chatting excitedly as the green trophy table was brought out. They formed a horseshoe around the table as the trophies were put on display.

Travis leaned over to Kate and whispered, "Are those trophies multiplying? How many races, exactly, did Storm just win?"

Kate laughed. "Actually, there are a few that won't even be brought out for this ceremony. Both the Belmont Cup and the Triple Crown Trophy are perpetual trophies—so, although Charlie, as Storm's owner, will be presented with them, they aren't hers to keep. She'll have the option of taking the Belmont Cup for the year, until another three-year-old wins it next year, but the Triple Crown Trophy will go back to the Kentucky Derby Museum right after the ceremony. They get to keep the smaller replicas."

"Shhhh!" Drew said, nudging his dad in the ribs. "They've started the ceremony."

They hushed themselves and listened as the racing commissioner made his speech congratulating Charlie, as the owner, on Storm's historic win. The cheers from the audience were still audible in the background—the grandstands were full of people talking about how they would remember this race for the rest of their lives.

Charlie thanked him and accepted the trophies and the microphone. "I cannot express what an honor and what a team effort this has been. From the moment I met him, I knew Storm was an incredible horse, and I wanted him to be a part of our family. He not only proved me right, he blew me out of the water. I could have never guessed about his genius on the track, or how many more family members he would bring into our lives. We have been through an incredible ordeal together, and this feels like the fairy tale ending. I could not be more proud of Genuine Storm, of Lilly, or of Doug Walker—Storm's trainer and my future husband."

The Shamrock team gasped and Doug's explosive smile grew, somehow, even larger.

The commissioner threw his hand out to Doug in congratulations. "Well, Mr. Walker, this certainly has been a huge day for you."

"Oh, Charlie and Storm are both full of surprises, in the best way possible. It's a remarkable family, all of them—and I'm so proud they're willing to add me to the fold."

"Lilly looks like she's made of lead," Kate whispered to Amanda, watching the jockey sway slightly in place as far from the microphone as she could manage.

Amanda raised an eyebrow to Jenny, and the three women shuffled towards Lilly discreetly.

"Hey Lilly," Jenny said gently. "You were incredible out there."

"It...it feels like a dream," Lilly said softly. "I need to sit down, I feel so oddly heavy."

Amanda caught her by the arm and steered her discreetly to a chair. Kate, taking cues from Jenny, protectively blocked them from sight of the cameras. Amanda's heart sank as she watched Lilly's bright blue eyes move from side to side.

"You two need to tell me what's going on," Kate said.

Amanda and Jenny gave each other a long look, both knowing that if anyone would know the right thing to do, it was Kate. They spilled the entire story and waited anxiously for her response.

"Wonder what Travis would say if we told him the barn fire was Cheeto-based." Kate looked shell-shocked.

"Oh, the insurance companies would love that. Poor Mom would lose her mind," Jenny replied.

"And we don't have anything to pin Blackston with, do we?" Kate said.

Amanda shook her head. "Nothing. We could report our suspicions to the racing commission, but from what I've heard, he's made of Teflon."

"So..."

"So..."

They stood in silence for another minute before Kate snapped to attention.

"So, today is a screwy day, but it's also historic and incredible. We saw the first Triple Crown win in thirty-seven years, the twelfth win ever. Lilly was the second female jockey to ever win any Triple Crown race, and the first to win the trifecta. I think Charlie is the third woman to ever own a Triple Crown champion, and Storm is probably the first claiming race horse. Everyone at Shamrock has risked their necks—sometimes literally—to make today possible. Lilly certainly didn't gain an unfair advantage—quite the opposite. I vote that today, we celebrate how amazing this is. If we feel like it, we can always throw this new bag of wrenches in tomorrow."

"Kate, the truth usually comes out," Amanda said, "and I'm an awful liar."

"Well, Amanda, I suggest you get better at it. I promise you, the only reason you think the truth usually comes out is because you only hear about it when it does. I've been in the newspaper business too long to be under the same delusions," Kate said authoritatively.

"Jenny, I need you to listen to me. You need to glue yourself to Lilly. People will try to get pictures and interviews—send them away firmly. Tell them they're interrupting an important conversation. Don't let her out of your sight for a moment—not even to go to the bathroom. You need to get very close to her—if her breathing slows down or she loses consciousness, scream for immediate medical attention, and tell the responders you believe she's been poisoned."

Jenny nodded calmly and settled quickly into her post next to Lilly, taking up as much space around them as she could with her crutches.

"We're just going to leave them here?" Amanda asked.

Kate pulled out her phone and sent a quick text. "Not for long—their ride will be here shortly. You and I need to go head off people at the pass and start telling the story of Storm's victory the way it needs to be told."

"Are you sure this is the right call?" Amanda asked.

"Sometimes there just isn't one," Kate responded.

———————————

Lilly woke up in a soft bed in a strange hotel room two hours later, a little groggy, with a mild headache and intense cottonmouth. The shower was running in the background.

Kidnapped? She wondered. She considered screaming, but she felt oddly at peace.

"Hey Lilly," Jenny said softly from a chair on the other side of the bed.

"Oh hey—am...I okay? Did something happen? Where are we?"

Just then, the shower stopped, but moments later, the faucet came back on, full blast.

"Yes, you're fine. You seemed a little under the weather after the race, so we brought you back to lie down for a few minutes."

"Nerves, I guess," Lilly said, puzzled. Nerves had never affected her this way before—but then again, she'd never won the Triple Crown before. She grinned widely, her memories of the finish line looming back. "But where are we? Who is in the shower?"

The bathroom door opened as if on cue, and Buck stepped out, his wet hair still dripping down his clean shirt and jeans.

"Sorry, Lil, I needed to get the track dust off me. I'm drawing up a bubble bath for you now." He walked over to the mini-fridge and handed her a bottle of water. "Are you feeling better?"

"I think so," Lilly responded. She wasn't sure how to react or where they stood.

Jenny sensed the tension and cleared her throat. "Okay, if you two have this covered, I think I'm going to take an Uber to Garden City. Kate's telling me there's an impromptu party for Storm at one of the fancy hotels, if you want to join up with us later."

Lilly laughed, glancing at the clock next to the bed. "It's nine at night, Jenny, and I don't think I've had a great night's sleep since..."

Buck smiled, realizing he'd also not had a good night's sleep since before the fire. "I think I'm done for the night, Jenny. I'll get Lilly back to her hotel, you go on ahead."

"Great job today, both of you," Jenny said, waving as she left the room.

"Buck, I'm not sure what happened out there today, but thank yo—"

Buck shook his head, cutting Lilly off. "Lilly, you won all on your own, fair and square. I tried to lend a hand when I realized you weren't feeling well, but you did it on your own, as usual."

"Not this again," Lilly groaned.

"No, you're right, not this again. Lilly, it was my gut reaction to come try to save you, but I'm so glad you didn't let me. I watched you do it on your own, whatever you needed to do, with the focus of a champion despite the fact that you were barely conscious. You're the most incredible rider I have ever met, and I'm glad the history books won't have some footnote about how another rider helped you, even if that rider was me."

"Well," Lilly said carefully, surprised by his change of heart, "thank you."

"Lilly, we started a conversation the night of the fire, and I want to finish it now. Marry me."

"What will the papers say?"

"Oh, they're going to talk either way. If you and Storm had lost, they would have said I was marrying you out of pity, or that I picked you up and dusted you off, or got you at a bargain, or something equally absurd. You won, so it'll probably be something all about how we got caught up in the thrill of the moment, or that I'm some type of Crown-digger…"

Lilly grinned. "Trying to become a kept horseman?"

"Exactly. I'm not going to be bothered by what the press says; they don't dictate our future. We can build one together that is right for both of us," Buck said. "It's not going to be perfect, but it will be wonderful. It'll take me awhile to stop trying to fix everything for you, but I'm willing to give it a shot. Every day for the rest of my life, if you'll let me," Buck said.

"Maybe sometimes you'll be allowed to help out," Lilly said, smiling. "I have to admit, it's nicer to wake up in a bed than where I would have passed out on the track."

"Is that a yes?"

"Yes, of course. Wait—did Doug and Charlie get engaged at the trophy ceremony?" Lilly asked, mining her foggy memory.

"They did—you have to see the look on Doug's face," Buck said. "Go get into your bath before it overflows, and I'll bring in the tablet. The video has to be online already."

That look was still plastered on Doug's face as he sat around a table, hand in hand with Charlie in the large hotel ballroom.

"So, what's next?" Ryan said, smiling at how happy his mother looked. "Elope tomorrow and catch the beginning of British racing season later in the week?"

Charlie's eyes got wide. "You weren't kidding when you said you had some summer plans for Storm. Wonder if they'd let him ride in the cabin with Lilly as her emotional support animal."

Everyone around the table laughed at the thought.

"I think it's about time for us to get back to Shamrock and make everything right again," Charlie said.

"What makes you think you're invited to come live with me?" Doug teased.

"You're the one getting a great deal. I'm bringing a Triple Crown dowry with me, and I have some thoughts about the future I'd like to share with you all," Charlie said. "You can't tell me that housing our winning horse hasn't taken a financial toll on the farm."

Molly and Steve looked like twin portraits of relief, and Skylar said, very seriously, "We're going to have to make Hershey his own special stall, with a raised floor and everything, so he can always see his friend Storm."

"Do you hear that, Mom?" Drew shouted. "I'm going to be living right next to the Triple Crown winner!"

Missy, whose day at the races had been a great salve for her son and her family, hugged Drew. "Oh man, I'm jealous of that! You'll have to send lots of pictures."

Travis smiled at his ex-wife, glad to be friends again. "You should come visit this summer," he generously offered.

"What about you, Amanda?" Charlie asked. "Tell me you're not going to abandon us now."

"Kate got me an interview with *BloodHorse!*" Amanda said proudly.

"Sure did. She'll be traveling around with me for the season, learning the ropes, strengthening her turf portfolio," Kate replied.

"Sounds like a busy summer for everyone," Charlie said. "We'll have to plan carefully so everyone can make it to the wedding."

"Make that a double wedding," Jenny said breathlessly as she joined the table. "I just eavesdropped for a few minutes at the door, and Buck asked Lilly to marry him too!"

Molly looked shocked. "Jenny! That wasn't your secret to share!"

Jenny blushed, ashamed for a moment, before Steve touched his wife and daughter both lightly on their shoulders. "Maybe we can just call a truce on secrets in the family."

Molly looked skeptical for a moment.

"You're definitely getting a good deal out of this one," Jenny said.

The three of them smiled at each other and nodded, sealing the deal.

"Well, there's one more surprise for tonight," Kate said, getting up from her chair. "Sit tight, I'll be right back."

They watched as she hurried towards the bar and came back with Bill, the bartender from Belmont Park and several trays of drinks.

"Bill! You won your bet!" Charlie said.

"And you won the whole Triple Crown!" Bill replied happily, passing around the drinks. "As promised, I whipped up a new cocktail just for our champion—including a mocktail version—that will be served at Belmont for as long as I'm working there. It's going on the menu tomorrow, but tonight, please be the first to try the Genuine Stormy!"

Kate took a sip and smiled. "Bourbon based, just the way it should be."

"Right you are—bourbon, spicy ginger-ale made from fresh ginger, just a little lime juice, and a lightly sugared lemon peel. The mocktail replaces the bourbon with pineapple juice," Bill replied.

Everyone appreciated another sip of their drinks before Charlie came to her senses. "We have to toast!"

They all raised their glasses and waited while Charlie composed her thoughts.

"To Storm, who blew into our lives and changed them all for the better. To my incredible children, Skylar and Ryan, for chasing this incredible dream with me. To Doug, for being the one at the rail when a tipsy woman decided she needed to claim a racehorse, and to the entire Shamrock crew, for being the best support group along the way. To Travis and Drew, for helping us through the last two weeks, from fighting the fire to finding Storm in the woods. To us all, for riding out the storms in our own lives, and to Lilly, bless her, for her courageous ride in all three races. We are, as my future husband noted this evening, a motley crew. What we have in common is that we all know the immense amount of work behind every fairy tale. While everyone in the world will always know what we accomplished today, tonight I would like to thank you for every day before, when you believed in what we could do together, no matter the obstacles in our way. I love you all."

The group cheered and clinked their glasses, knowing they could overcome the challenges any storm cloud on the horizon could bring.

Epilogue

Charlie could tell it was going to be a beautiful day for a barbeque before she even opened her eyes. She was looking forward to seeing everyone, but right now, she needed a little horse therapy.

Doug continued to snore lightly on the other side of the bed, so she slipped on her sneakers and closed the bedroom door softly as she left. Her insomnia had gone away, but she still enjoyed getting up with the sun and getting a head start to her days.

"Come on, Bart, let's go see him," she said to the dog blocking her way out the door. *Like you would have let me go without you,* she thought fondly.

They made their way down the hill in front of the house she still caught herself referring to as Doug's house, moving towards the barn. They walked past the statue that had been installed in the center of the rectangle that had been the main barn, the perennials surrounding it in full bloom.

They'd decided not to rebuild the main barn in the same location as the one that had burnt to the ground—too many memories that no one wanted to relive every time they walked into a similar structure. Instead, they'd erected a brand-new barn off to the right, behind the office, complete with safety improvements and an elevated stall to house one of its most celebrated inhabitants.

As she walked with Bart, Charlie pondered all the wonderful paths that her family and friends had taken.

Ryan, the guest of honor for the afternoon's barbeque, was graduating from UVA with a business degree and a minor in communications. Everyone was coming to celebrate, including, of course, Kate. She had been lobbying him hard, trying to entice him to come to work at *BloodHorse*. Charlie knew it was going to be hard for Ryan to turn it down, but it wasn't what he wanted to do. Last week, he'd privately confided to her that he had applied to law school. He wanted to follow in his father's footsteps.

Skylar had just been accepted to Virginia Tech, where she was set on becoming an equine vet. Charlie sighed, knowing that path would bring more heartache to her daughter than she'd faced just living through their own equine tragedies. At the same time, she knew Skylar was stronger for it, and had the smarts and the heart to help other horses in need. She smiled, knowing that Skylar still couldn't decide between specializing in the racehorse industry, trying to reduce the number of breakdowns on the track, or becoming a broodmare vet.

Travis was on call, so he wasn't sure he would be able to come, but Charlie knew he'd make his best effort. He had taken the permanent fire chief position, and his help designing the new barn had been invaluable. Either way, Amanda would be coming with the baby and Drew. Charlie chuckled, thinking back about what a surprise that turn of events had been for them all—particularly for Travis and Amanda themselves. As much as Amanda had wanted to live the high, fast-paced life of a journalist, traveling the country with Kate hadn't lasted very long. Coming back to the area on a break, Amanda and Travis had realized that the strong working relationship they had built over her time covering Storm had turned into love. They'd gotten married just over a year ago. Charlie loved that they were so close, and having a new baby around was a much-needed new beginning, with all the teenagers moving on.

Drew would also be heading out of town at the end of the summer, although a bit further away. He'd been accepted to NYU. He was ready for a change of pace from farm life and wanted a taste of the big city. His time at the Belmont had made him realize how much he liked to be around lots of people. Drew's relationship with his mother had flourished over the last few years and he wanted to be closer to her; she had a small farm in Connecticut, just outside the city, where she kept her show horses.

Lilly, Buck, and Jenny were flying in later in the morning from a much needed mini-vacation in Sedona. Jenny had just broken her apprentice bug, and they'd snuck out of town to celebrate, as well as to rehab their minds and bodies from the rigors of riding racehorses every day. Of course, being the offspring of two talented race riders, Jenny was destined to follow in their footsteps. She had quickly risen through the ranks of apprentice riders and was vying for top apprentice jockey of the year. Lilly and Buck, on the other hand, were slowly easing out of the everyday riding. Buck had taken on some horses to train and was toying with the idea of becoming a full-time trainer. Lilly wasn't interested in continuing to try and win races and hit milestones. She wanted to go back to helping the horses themselves overcome their fears. Cappie had once told her that every horse wanted a job and to feel important, but that sometimes the jobs that people wanted for a horse just didn't fit. Lilly wanted to help find them jobs that fit them best, whether as racehorses, jumpers, or trail horses. Lilly had taken it upon herself to spend time in Pennsylvania with Doc, learning more of his ways working with the minds and bodies of horses. She had recently talked about entering the Retired Racehorse Makeover contest with one of Doug's recently retired racehorses.

Charlie slid the big barn door, and she and Bart squeezed through the opening. A soft rumble came from the stall a few down on her left.

"Looking for your peppermint, old man?" Charlie called out. A high-pitched whinny came from the stall further down.

"Yes, I have one for you too, little one."

Charlie reached into her pocket as she walked down the aisle, unwrapping mints as she opened the latch on the stall door.

"Still liking your new job?" she asked as the soft grey nose reached for the candy. "All those ladies coming to visit you every day?"

Storm sniffed her pockets for the additional mints he knew were there. Managing a stallion and the mares that were booked to him had been new to all of them. At first, Charlie had bemoaned Hunter's disappearing act after the Belmont Stakes, as he had extensive experience that she thought would have been helpful, and had even considered hiring someone to find him. Jenny, Kate, and Amanda shared some suspicious looks when the idea came up, but she never got them to divulge whatever secret they shared. She was finally dissuaded by more than one person sharing a story of how Hunter had gone out of his way to make life at the stables difficult.

Thankfully, Cappie and Ben, along with Molly and Steve, had jumped in, wholly supporting Shamrock's new breeding division. Part of the new barn configuration included the detached breeding shed, and it had breathed new life into the farm. Now they had all aspects of the industry: their own stallion, their own broodmare band, and their own racehorses.

Maybe one day, history will look back at us as one of the great racing dynasties, Charlie thought, *like the great days of Calumet.*

An impatient whinny called from the other side of the bars, taking Charlie to task for being slow with the mints.

"Makin' lots of babies sure is hard work," she laughed at Storm as she unwrapped another mint.

"And of course, Hershey," she said slipping another mint into a different set of lips reaching through the barrier, though at exactly the same height.

Charlie smiled at Hershey; it always seemed funny that such a small pony was the same height as a racehorse. They all knew the unspoken reasoning behind his elevated stall floor, though: no one wanted to forget he was in the stall ever again. His white-haired scars, plainly visible along his bay back from where his burns had fully healed, were a constant reminder.

"I hear congratulations are in order, Daddy Storm—Minnie is in foal," Charlie said aloud, thinking of the pretty mare—one of Doug's best, who had won a lot of races many years ago. "Yep, that's one we will keep a close eye on. Hopefully, he or she will be grey just like you, though."

Storm shook his head up and down, tossing his forelock across his eyes.

"You certainly have filled out to be quite the stallion, Storm. Hopefully, you pass all your passion to run and your desire to win on to all those babies that will be born next year. They will be in hot demand, but don't worry, not one of them will take your place in my heart."

Charlie slid down the wall of the stall, closing her eyes, at peace with her horse, knowing there would never be another like him.

Author's Note

The timeline of this book had already been written when American Pharoah won the Triple Crown in 2015. I published the first book of my trilogy, *The Calm Before the Storm*, in March 2015, then watched in awe as the first horse in thirty-seven years to win the Kentucky Derby, the Preakness Stakes, and the Belmont was crowned. In 2017, *The Eye of the Storm* was published, and a year later, to everyone's surprise, Justify came roaring home to capture all three races again. After a drought of thirty-seven years, our generation has been able to watch two great racehorses in the span of three years. Who knows when it will happen again, but we have been able to relive the glory days of the 1970s, when the Triple Crown was won three times in a span five years with Secretariat in 1973, Seattle Slew in 1977, and Affirmed in 1978.

As this is a work of fiction, much of my research entails the details of the intervening years between Triple Crown winners Affirmed and American Pharoah, so I hope that you indulged me in reading my story as written and appreciate what it takes for a horse and its team to win all three races and take home the Triple Crown.